Irish author **Abby Green** ended ~~a~~ career in film and TV—which ~~i~~ lot of standing in the rain outsi~~de~~ pursue her love of romance. After she'd bombarded Mills & Boon with manuscripts they kindly accepted one, and an author was born. She lives in Dublin, Ireland, and loves any excuse for distraction. Visit abby-green.com or email abbygreenauthor@gmail.com.

Emmy Grayson wrote her first book at the age of seven, about a spooky ghost. Her passion for romance novels began a few years later, with the discovery of a worn copy of Kathleen E Woodiwiss's *A Rose in Winter* buried on her mother's bookshelf. She lives in the US Midwest countryside with her husband—who's also her ex-husband!—their baby boy, and enough animals to start their own zoo.

HEIR FOR HIS EMPIRE

ABBY GREEN

PRINCE'S FORGOTTEN DIAMOND

EMMY GRAYSON

MILLS & BOON

First published in Great Britain 2024
by Mills & Boon, an imprint of HarperCollins*Publishers* Ltd,
1 London Bridge Street, London, SE1 9GF

www.harpercollins.co.uk

HarperCollins*Publishers*, Macken House, 39/40 Mayor Street Upper,
Dublin 1, D01 C9W8, Ireland

Heir for His Empire © 2024 Abby Green

Prince's Forgotten Diamond © 2024 Emmy Grayson

ISBN: 978-0-263-32006-0

05/24

This book contains FSC™ certified paper
and other controlled sources to ensure responsible forest management.

For more information visit www.harpercollins.co.uk/green.

Printed and Bound in the UK using 100% Renewable Electricity
at CPI Group (UK) Ltd, Croydon, CR0 4YY

HEIR FOR
HIS EMPIRE

ABBY GREEN

MILLS & BOON

PROLOGUE

THE SEXUAL TENSION between Erin Murphy and the man in the elevator was thick enough to cut with a knife. A million and one sensations fizzed through her blood and body. Triumph. The satisfaction of a job well done. But more than all that was desire.

But even the word *desire* was too polite. It was sheer, raw lust. And danger. Illicitness.

Because the man was no mere man. He was her boss. Not even her boss. He was her boss's, boss's boss. With probably a couple more bosses in between.

It had been building for the last few weeks, while they'd been locked in rooms with the most intense negotiations taking place.

Obviously she'd been aware of how gorgeous he was. How sexy. The whole world knew it, and it had hit her right between the eyes the day she'd been hired on to his legal team as an attorney, proving she was no different from the masses. But she'd buried it down deep—because she knew it was *so* inappropriate to fancy him, and because she was eager to make a good impression. This was her first job since completing a master's degree in corporate law, and she'd been hired specifically because of that additional expertise.

She'd thought she'd had her crush under control. Until these last few weeks of being in the professional equivalent of a pressure cooker.

Ajax Nikolau was a Greek god. Or, as near to a god as a mortal could be. Beautiful, with mesmeric deep-set green-blue eyes that popped from a chiseled face, and a mouth that called to mind sin and sex. Thick wavy dark hair. Tall, powerful build. Athletic. He wore suits, but the way they moulded to his sculpted form was downright provocative.

Together with a mind as sharp as a rapier, it was a potent combination.

He was also, arguably, one of the wealthiest men in the world—since approximately an hour ago, when the last contract had been signed. He now had full control of his family logistics business. He'd been rich before—astronomically—but now he was on a par with fabled Indian steel magnates and media titans.

But Erin didn't care about any of that. Because it didn't mean anything to her beyond the fact that she'd done her job. All she could see was *him*. The man. Flesh and blood. Sinew and bone. Hard muscle. Eyes blazing with a heat that connected directly to her core in a way that had never happened to her before.

They'd had champagne to celebrate with the rest of the team after the signing, and the sparkling wine still lingered in her veins like bubbling electricity. She couldn't believe that this was happening. Even though nothing had actually been articulated. It was in the air. Potent.

Just moments ago they'd been in the foyer of Ajax Nikolau's office building in downtown Manhattan, and as Erin had been about to leave, along with the rest of the legal team, he'd called her name.

She'd turned around, fixing a polite smile to her face. 'Yes?'

'I have some papers in my home office. I think it's best if you take them for safekeeping. Is that okay?'

Erin had frowned briefly. The last thing Ajax Nikolau had to worry about was the security of anything. The man was more well-guarded than a head of state. Along with his offices, he had properties strewn from one end of the globe to the other. So it had been an odd request.

But then she'd looked into his eyes and she'd seen the veneer of civility stripped away.

He wants me.

It had hit her like a thunderbolt right in the gut. She'd suspected, but whenever she'd caught him watching her over the previous weeks she'd looked away, telling herself she was being ridiculous. Mortified to have been caught looking at him.

Why on earth would a man like Ajax Nikolau be remotely interested in a woman like her? She didn't incite men to paroxsyms of desire. Especially not men like him. She was reasonably fit. Her features were symmetrical enough. But there was nothing about her that drew attention, and that was how she liked it.

Except now she was in this elevator, with *him*, and she had to face the unbelievable fact that somehow she'd drawn the eye of one of the most exciting men in the world. There wasn't enough oxygen going to her brain for her to try and figure out why.

This was, without a doubt, the most spontaneous, out-of-character thing she'd ever done in her life.

Meanwhile the elevator kept ascending to the penthouse. And suddenly Erin went cold with a flash of panic. What if she'd read the signals wrong? What if the triumph of the deal, the champagne, had all gone to her head and here she was, mentally climbing the man like a monkey, when he literally meant to just give her some papers and send her on her way?

But then, as if reading her mind, he put out a hand, pressed a button, and the elevator came to an incongruously smooth stop between floors.

Nikolau's voice was a little rough. 'Just so we're clear: I want you, Erin. But you're under no obligation to do any-thing except take the papers and leave.'

Erin gulped. *Had* he read her mind? Had she spoken out loud?

He does want me. I'm not hallucinating.

A mixture of relief and dizzying excitement made her tremble. She said faintly, 'There are actually papers?'

He nodded. 'But I won't lie. I used them as a pretext to get you alone. For weeks now you've been driving me crazy. I know this is crossing a million boundaries—and, believe me, if I felt I could resist… I would.'

His jaw clenched at that, as if he was irritated with him-self, with his own lack of control.

The mere thought of pushing this man to the edge of his control was beyond heady.

Something ridiculous ocurred to her. 'What do I call you?' She'd always referred to him as 'Mr Nikolau', even though he had said to them all that they should call him Ajax.

'My name is Ajax.'

She tried it out. 'Ajax…' It felt strange. Illicit.

He touched her jaw. 'I like the way it sounds when you say it.'

Erin might have rolled her eyes if she'd been less in awe and not still reeling.

What he'd just said—that he couldn't resist her—was just so beyond her comprehension of who she was—essentially boring—that she almost felt like giggling a little hysteri-cally. But then the look on his face stopped her. It was stark. Hungry.

For her.

Plain, academic, serious Erin Murphy.

She'd led an academically driven existence for as long as she could remember. As the only child of a professor, it was all she'd really known. Her life had rarely, if ever, been given over to moments of spontaneity or just…fun. Not that this moment could be described as 'fun', exactly, when Ajax was looking at her with such an intense expression that she realised she'd never really seen him smile.

She knew there were reasons for that—he'd tragically lost his wife and child in an accident some years ago—and suddenly, as if galvanised by that reminder, and the sense of her own somewhat staid life, instead of doing the sane thing, the *safe* thing—stepping back out of this moment of madness—Erin moved towards him. Towards the madness.

She touched her mouth to his, trembling all over. For a second he didn't move, and Erin became acutely aware that she was pressed up against a wall of steel. She went cold again. Maybe she'd overstepped the mark? Even though he'd told her he wanted her, maybe he was the kind of guy who didn't appreciate women making the first move?

But before she could overthink it he took her elbows in his hands, holding her to him, and his mouth moved over hers. Any suspicion that she'd done the wrong thing because she'd initiated contact was gone. Melted. Turned to ash.

She couldn't feel her legs. His mouth was hard and soft, demanding but asking, all at once. It was like no kiss she'd ever experienced. Erin had to pull back for a second, dragging in a breath. Her vision was blurred. Kissing Ajax was like being pulled into a vortex, going faster and faster.

As if he sensed she was overwhelmed, he stopped and cupped her jaw. She felt her hair being freed from its tidy chignon, falling around her shoulders. His eyes followed the movement, and then his fingers were in her hair.

'It's like burnt gold.'

She couldn't find a breath. He was making her hair sound…extraordinary. But really it was nothing special. It wasn't blonde, or red…it was somewhere in between.

Her mother's hair. But her mother was the last person Erin wanted to think about at that moment, because thinking of her inevitably brought painful memories of abandonment, so she reached for his tie and loosened it, opening his top button of his shirt.

The hollow at the bottom of his throat was exposed, and it felt ridiculously intimate even though they were both still fully clothed.

As if reading Erin's mind again, Ajax pushed her jacket off her shoulders and it fell to the ground. Long fingers efficiently undid the silk bow at her neck and then moved down to her buttons. She imagined them slipping free of the silk, eager to please him.

She almost felt like giggling again, but sobered up when he pushed her open shirt aside and looked at her for a long moment. At her breasts, encased in silk. Erin felt a blush rise into her face. She'd always had a slightly embarrassing preference for expensive materials close to her skin. A taste for luxury that didn't exist anywhere else in her life.

He dislodged her shirt so that it fell off one shoulder. He slipped his fingers under the strap of her bra, dropping it onto her arm, and the cup immediately fell down over the curve of her breast.

She shivered.

Erin had no idea what to expect…she hadn't gone as far as audaciously fantasising about what it would be like with a man like this. But she knew she never would have imagined this…this exquisite slow-burn torture.

He cupped her breast and her nipple pinched tight. Her breath became more shallow. And then he lowered his head and his mouth closed over the straining tip.

It was like an electric shock to the system, the laving of his tongue and the sucking of his mouth…all that hot moisture. Her hands tangled in his hair. She couldn't even remember putting her hands there. She wanted to do the same to him—take off his clothes, bare him—but he was kissing her again and palming her breast, fingers trapping that nipple and pinching.

She gasped into his mouth.

His tongue was hot, demanding, and she had no choice but to submit with an eagerness that might have mortified her if she'd been capable of rational thought.

Erin could feel his erection pressing against her and she moved against him instinctively, seeking more contact. He pulled her skirt up, bunching it over her hips, and then his fingers were spreading over her thigh, lifting it to hook her leg around his waist, bringing her into even deeper contact with his body.

She broke the kiss. His hardness was *right there*. At the apex of her legs. Where every nerve-ending was throbbing. Erin wanted to free him and push her underwear aside, so there would be no barrier to a more intimate connection. The need was so intense she could hardly breathe.

She tried to communicate it with her eyes. She'd never wanted anything so badly. So urgently. *Here. Now.*

Time stood still, and for an infinitesimal moment she could see that he was as hungry as her. But then something flickered across his face. So fast she couldn't decipher it. Yet it looked like shock.

He pulled back, and Erin almost whimpered. Mortifyingly.

He put her leg back down and said roughly, 'Not here… like this. I'm sorry. I don't know what came over me.'

Erin's brain was too heated to fully understand until he pushed the elevator button and it softly jolted into movement again. Upwards. She breathed out when she realised he wasn't taking them back down to the ground level.

They ascended so high her ears popped. Then the elevator stopped again and the doors opened, straight into what had to be Ajax's apartment. She'd never been there. His offices were a few levels down.

The apartment was sleek and minimalistic. Huge ceiling-to-floor glass windows. Modern art on the walls. Sofas and chairs that looked inviting but which Erin had a feeling had never really been sat in. She knew Ajax tended to entertain in venues. Not at home.

Even though she'd been working for him for weeks, she still wasn't used to the level of opulence in his world. But she wasn't given a chance to linger or look around. He took her hand and led her silently through the dimly lit space, down a corridor and into a room at the other end of the apartment.

His bedroom. There were huge walls of glass again, giving what had to be a breathtaking view of lower Manhattan at night, a glittering skyline of lights. The blinking lights of a helicopter flew across the night sky.

But then it was all eclipsed. Because Ajax turned her around to face him and she swallowed. Suddenly intimidated to be here, in his private space.

'Are you sure you want to do this, Erin? You can stop… walk away at any time.'

Something inside her eased. She'd known he was a man of integrity after watching him do business, but to have him really care about her consent was something she hadn't even realised she needed.

She nodded. 'I want this.' *You.*

She'd never considered herself a very sexual person. She'd had one boyfriend in college, here in Manhattan, and they'd both decided to amicably split up when they'd graduated and he'd moved to Los Angeles. There had been no major grief. She'd had no intention of leaving New York, where she'd been born and had grown up. And the sex… Her boyfriend was the only person she'd had sex with, and at no point had she ever felt for him what she was feeling now.

Desperate. Hungry.

It was exhilarating and terrifying all at once. As if she wasn't as in control of her own reactions as she'd always thought she was. Erin was a cerebral person, and she'd never been so aware of her body.

Ajax started to take off his clothes. Jacket shucked off and thrown to the floor. Tie pulled off. Shirt opened, revealing a broad, muscled chest with a dusting of hair across his pectorals.

Erin had hardly caught her breath when his hands were on his trousers and he was undoing them, pushing them down over lean hips. Stepping out of them. Shoes and socks gone.

Now he stood before her fully naked, and she was…in shock. She didn't know where to look and she wanted to look everywhere. Her gaze travelled over inches of dark golden flesh, the evidence of his lineage from Greece. Down further. Flat stomach, slim hips and…his erection. She gulped. He was big. The sheer evidence of his virility was daunting.

'I'm feeling a little underdressed here, Erin.'

She looked up and could see his mouth twitching. That beautfiul sexy mouth.

Her heart hitched. *Oh, my.*

She realised her own state of undress. Shirt and bra half on, half off. Jacket gone. Still in the elevator? Skirt still ruched up over one thigh. Hair tumbling over her shoulders. Too long. She hadn't had time to get it cut.

Before she could figure out where to start, Ajax stepped close and pushed her shirt down over her arms and off. It fell to the floor. He reached around behind her to undo her bra. It too fell away.

For some inexplicable reason Erin didn't feel self-conscious. Maybe it was because Ajax had already bared himself. He reached for the fastening at the side of her skirt and opened it, easing it down over her hips.

Now all she wore was the matching underwear. Silk and lace. Decadent.

Ajax looked down. 'I like your choice in underwear.'

'Thank you.'

Literally words she'd never have expected to be exchanged between them, when up to this evening any dialogue had been focused solely on the dense legalese of delicate contract negotiations.

'May I?'

She wasn't sure what he was asking until he was at her feet, looking up. Another revelation. Ajax Nikolau at her feet. She nodded dumbly.

He tugged the sides of her panties down over her hips and thighs until they were at her feet. She stepped out of them.

But Ajax didn't stand up. He said, 'Sit on the edge of the bed.'

Erin realised it was right behind her. She fell more than sat on the edge. Ajax put his hands on her knees, pushing them apart. Her heart was thumping so hard she thought it must be audible, but his gaze was fixed on her body, giving her an awareness of sensuality she'd never experienced before.

He stroked the back of his hand over her belly. Her muscles quivered.

'Your skin is so pale...'

Erin felt breathless. 'My parents were...are Irish... Or at least...you know...second or third generation.'

Ajax looked at her, a glint in his eye. 'With a name like Murphy I never would have guessed.'

Her mouth almost fell open. He was joking with her! But now he was looking at her body again, moving between her legs, forcing them further apart. Cupping her breasts.

'I used to fantasise about this during all those boring moments in the negotiations. You became a distraction.'

Erin struggled to get the words out, 'You fantasised about…this…?'

He nodded. His thumbs were moving back and forth over her nipples and it was hard to focus on what he was saying—which was annoying, because what he was saying was… unbelievable.

'I fantasised about what was under your prim suits. The silk shirts, the tight skirts… Do you have any idea how delectable your ass looked in those skirts?'

She shook her head. And then a memory flashed back. She'd been helping herself to some coffee during a break recently, and had bent down to pick up a fallen spoon. When she'd turned around she'd almost dropped her coffee cup. Ajax had been staring at her so broodingly she'd thought she'd done something wrong.

He leant forward now and placed his mouth over one nipple, sucking and then biting gently. Every cell in Erin's body seemed to spasm at once with pleasure. Ajax put his hands around her back, holding her to him as he administered the same torture to the other breast, until they were throbbing peaks of exquisite pain/pleasure.

And then he pulled away. 'Lie back.'

She did, almost relieved at the respite. But there was to be no respite.

He pushed her thighs apart and she felt his eyes on her. Then his breath feathered on her inner thigh, his lips glancing across her skin as he came closer and closer to where all her nerve-endings were tingling… His breath was hot, but not as hot as his mouth when he pressed his lips and tongue to the core of her body.

Erin had to bite down on her hand to stop screaming, even though she was pretty sure there was no one to hear them. The man was remorseless, exploring her with a thoroughness that made her whole body clench, as if she could possibly stave off the inevitable.

She couldn't. It broke over her in an unstoppable wave. She had nowhere to hide. She'd never been so exposed, and yet she'd never felt more liberated. With her boyfriend, sex had felt self-conscious and a little laborious. Her orgasms hadn't had the power to break her apart. Sex had never felt this earthy or raw.

She was barely aware of Ajax moving, doing something, before he moved her up the bed as effortlessly as if she was a boneless, pliant lump of flesh.

He was on his knees between her spread legs and she looked up to see him rolling protection onto his body. His very hard body... Erin's inner muscles clenched in response.

He looked at her. 'Are you okay?'

Was she? There wasn't a word invented for what she was right now. All she could do was nod. Stupidly.

He put his hands on her thighs and lifted her up towards him so that his erection was nudging the slick folds of her body.

But then he stopped and looked at her. 'You're not...innocent?'

Erin shook her head quickly, a little mortified by how desperate she was to feel him inside her. Her voice was rough, breathy. 'No...but it's been a while.'

'We'll take it slow.'

Erin silently begged for mercy, because she knew this was going to be— *Ohhhh!* He thrust into her in one fluid, cataclysmic movement, watching her reaction. Her back arched. He was so big... She felt stretched, just on the border of being uncomfortable, but then he went deeper and she let out a shaky breath.

She'd never felt so...full.

Ajax adjusted his body so that he was almost completely

over her. He slowly withdrew and she could feel her muscles massaging his length. His jaw was gritted. Sweat sheened his brow. Erin's own skin was slick with perspiration.

He moved back in again, and she gasped at the sensation as little flutters of pleasure emanated from the centre of her body. He moved rhythmically, in and out, and her tension wound higher with each move of his body.

Desperation pooled low inside her... An urgency. A need for *more.* She wasn't even aware she'd spoken out loud until Ajax was moving faster, going deeper.

Harder.

Had she said that? But soon he was moving with more force and her head tipped back. There was a force building inside her and she wanted to plead or beg, but she couldn't articulate what she needed.

Ajax threaded his fingers through hers and held her hands above her head. She felt like growling at him. She bit his shoulder. She heard a low huff of a chuckle.

I made him laugh.

But before that could register, he was releasing her hand and cupping her breast, feeding it to his mouth, teeth nipping at her sensitised flesh. Suddenly everything went very still—and then she was falling, tripping, end over end, down into a whirlpool of pleasure so intense that this time she couldn't stop herself from crying out.

She was only barely aware of Ajax's guttural shout as he followed her, his big, powerful body slumping over hers. She put her arms around him without even realising what she was doing.

A month later

Ajax stood at the window. Fully dressed. As if his clothes were some kind of armour.

Against what? asked a snide voice.

Against the naked woman behind him on the bed.

She was still asleep. He could see her reflection in the window. The pale skin, the graceful curves. The soft swells of breasts and buttocks and the flare of hips.

The long red-gold hair spread over the pillow. The same hair that trailed across his chest and down as she explored his body with her mouth, before wrapping a hand around him and—

Skata! Enough.

She was just a woman. Like any other.

So why had he vowed not to touch her again after that first night?

Because he'd known, even then, that what they'd shared had been…unprecedented, and that it should not be indulged again because he was not looking for encounters that went beyond being casual.

He'd woken the following morning—late. Unheard of for Ajax, who hadn't slept past dawn for years. He'd felt hungover. As if he'd been drinking. But it hadn't been a hangover from drink—again, not usual for him. It had been a sex hangover.

He'd had his share of sexual experiences—he wasn't a monk—but he'd never had sex like that. He'd had to have her. It had been building for weeks. She'd been distracting him from work. Unheard of.

In the aftermath of that night he'd put their chemistry down to the intense circumstances leading up to the negotiations that had finally put him in full control of Nikolau Industries.

Ajax and his legal team had been all but sequestered for weeks, in order to prevent any leaks. So it was no wonder he'd started to notice Erin Murphy, the newest member of his legal team. Who, he'd been assured upon her appointment, was brilliant.

She hadn't said much at first. Just watched. And listened. She'd been quiet. But something about her had kept drawing his eye. Something about her poise. Her quiet confidence. While others jockeyed for attention or kudos, she didn't.

Then one day, when tensions were high, there'd been a dispute about the wording of part of the contract. In the heated tense silence between arguments she'd posited a totally novel way to word it that had instantly defused the situation.

Ajax had seen in that moment that she'd made a couple of enemies among the more ambitious of the group, but she'd seemed oblivious.

She'd intrigued him in a way that no one else ever had. He'd found himself looking for her every day. Checking she was there. One day she hadn't been there, and her boss had informed Ajax that she was working on another project.

Ajax had told him to bring her back, as he didn't want the contract team broken up before they'd reached agreement. Which hadn't been entirely untrue. But his main motivation had been purely selfish.

The following day she'd been back in the room and their eyes had met. That was the other thing that had intrigued Ajax. She hadn't looked away. Not for a long moment. She hadn't been fazed by his regard. She hadn't sensed his interest and then exploited it, as most women would.

The sense of intrigue had grown into full-blown lust. Until it had been hard to focus or think straight. She wore practically the same thing every day. Pencil skirts. Silk blouses. Jackets. Court shoes. Muted colours. Minimal make-up and jewellery.

But she was provocative. Ajax hadn't been able to put his finger on why and that had irritated the hell out of him.

He'd become transfixed by wondering what she would look like if her hair was down. And what was underneath those suits? Was she pale all over?

Her hair was a unique shade of dark strawberry blonde. He'd found himself wondering if she had hair the same colour *there*, guarding her sex, and that had resulted in a raging erection. In the middle of a meeting. Humiliating.

By the time the deal had been done and they'd celebrated there'd been no way he wasn't going to explore his fascination. He hadn't even been sure if she wanted him too—but as soon as he'd asked her to wait and she'd looked at him with those huge hazel-brown eyes, colour scoring her cheeks a tantalising blush, he'd known that she did want him.

They'd barely lasted a few seconds in the elevator. It had been the hottest, most erotic experience of his life.

But the following morning, when Ajax had woken late, she'd been gone. Long gone. He'd never experienced that before. Most of his lovers were all too keen to cultivate intimacy the next day—which was why he never hosted lovers in his own home. Something he'd apparently forgotten that night.

She hadn't even left a note. And when Ajax had seen her in the office a few days later, she'd looked at him as if nothing had happened. On one level he'd known he should be welcoming her lack of clinginess, but on another level he'd been incensed.

Had she not enjoyed the night? It had blown his mind… That suspicion alone—that she hadn't experienced it the way he had—had made him feel exposed and uncomfortable.

Eventually he'd managed to get her alone and he'd asked her what was going on.

'What do you mean?' she'd asked.

'We slept together, Erin.'

'Yes, I know.'

'You left the following morning.'

She'd gone a little pink at that reminder. 'I didn't think you'd appreciate waking up to find me making breakfast.'

The fact that she was right hadn't comforted Ajax. Perversely. And then he'd realised what was going on. He'd cursed himself.

'This is a play, isn't it?'

She'd frowned. 'What do you mean?'

'You're playing coy because you know it'll engage my interest and curiosity.'

She'd looked angry—the first time he'd seen any extreme of emotion on her face. And the fact that he'd noticed had made him feel more prickly.

She'd said tersely, 'I don't play those kinds of games. I thought I was doing us both a favour…that neither of us wanted a post-mortem. It was just a one-night thing.'

Ajax had been a little speechless. He'd realised he believed her. And that she was speaking sense. Women didn't usually captivate him to the point where he had to discuss anything.

Feeling exposed, he'd said, 'You're right.'

And so he'd walked away. And brooded for almost a month. But every time he'd seen her she'd seemed utterly serene—as if their night wasn't lingering in her blood and body the way it was in his, no matter how much he tried to deny it. Like a decadent aftertaste of something that you just want one more bite of.

Just a one-night thing…

But what about one more night?

It became an obsession. If he had one more night with her surely it would burn out—whatever this fascination was?

And so he'd said it. Yesterday. After a meeting he'd asked her to stay behind and he'd asked her bluntly, 'Do you want one more night?'

She'd looked at him, cheeks going pink. Suddenly the veneer of serenity was slipping and Ajax had felt something victorious move through him.

She still wanted him.

'I...' She'd hesitated. 'I'm not sure if it's a good idea.'

'I think it's the only way we can move on.'

It was definitely the only way he could move on.

'You think one night is all it'll take?' she'd asked.

No. But he ignored the assertion. That was the lust talking. No woman had ever held his interest for longer than one or two nights.

He'd nodded. 'Absolutely.'

There had been a long moment, as if she was battling some inner demon, but then she'd said, 'Okay. When and where?'

Ajax liked that about her. Straight up. As she'd said, she didn't play games. And so she'd come up to his apartment last night.

Ajax had planned on them having dinner, but as soon as the elevator doors had closed behind her any attempt to be civilised had disintegrated. They'd been naked in seconds.

They hadn't eaten dinner until midnight—a surprisingly companionable interlude, with Erin dressed in one of his shirts, sitting on opposite sides of the kitchen island, picking at chicken salad and drinking wine.

It had been so unlike anything he'd ever indulged in with a woman he'd found it disconcerting. It had reminded him uncomfortably of the past, and how different it had been with his wife—a woman he'd committed to in the most permanent sense, in spite of the fact that he'd had no feelings for her.

Yet suddenly Ajax had found himself comparing the two experiences and wondering what it might be like to actually like a woman enough to want to spend more time with her...have a relationship.

A sound came from behind Ajax on the bed. He tensed

against the inevitable surge of blood. Of awareness. So much for hoping one more night would douse the fire… He feared it had only made it worse. Even more reason, though, to do what he had to now. To say what he had to.

Because one thing was certain after last night: this woman was a danger to him. To everything he believed and had built up.

He wasn't in the market for a relationship and never had been. It wasn't in his DNA and never would be. Not after what had happened. If there ever had been a moment when he might have been persuaded, it had died a long time ago.

He steeled himself and turned around. Erin was up on one elbow, looking deliciously sleepy and well-loved. She had pulled the sheet up to her chest. Ajax lamented it while at the same time welcoming it. He didn't need the distraction. She'd distracted him enough.

'Morning,' she said, and her voice was husky enough to almost make him change his mind. *Almost*.

But he was stronger than that. He had to be. He had a duty to his business and he had to transcend personal temptations.

Ajax had had his chance to make a personal life work and it had ended in tragedy. There would be no more *personal* for him, and it had been a mistake to allow Erin Murphy under his guard again.

If anything, last night just proved that he should have listened to his gut the first time round. The fact that the woman was making him even think of personal temptations and reminding him of what he'd lost was all the proof he needed. She was exposing his weakness and he could not afford to be weak.

Ajax said, 'We need to talk.'

CHAPTER ONE

Twenty-one months later, Manhattan

ERIN STOOD BY the cot, watching her one-year-old daughter finally—mercifully—fall into sleep, legs and arms splayed as if fighting to the very end. The small room was bathed in dim undulating lights that threw various shapes of unicorns, dogs, rabbits and birds across the ceiling, chasing each other on a loop.

Erin smiled as she looked at her. She was a sturdy, feisty little thing and she didn't resemble Erin at all. She was all her father. Dark skin...dark curly hair. The only thing she'd taken from Erin were her hazel eyes.

Erin had almost grown used to the ache near her heart whenever she looked at her and was reminded of Ajax Nikolau—which was far too often for comfort. The ache was fast turning into a kind of heartburn.

Her conscience pricked. *Hard.* Her father had been minding Ashling today and he'd said it to her again.

'You can't keep putting it off. He needs to know. She's almost walking.'

Erin knew he was right. She'd made attempts to let Ajax know—she'd even written him a letter—but there had been no response and she'd not pushed it, partly because it had been a reminder of his rejection, but also because of unwelcome memories from far closer to home, within her own family.

She'd told herself she had more important things to get on with. Namely becoming a single parent to her daughter and searching for a new job.

In fairness, Ajax had pointed out that she wasn't under any pressure to leave, and that if she'd requested a transfer to a different office or department they wouldn't have to see each other again. She could stay working for the law firm his company used—it was vast.

She'd been tempted. It would have made things easier. But even without having to see him she knew that she would have been aware of him. And people talked. He was a dynamic, enigmatic man. Single. Available. She would have heard gossip about who he was with. And, as much as Erin would have liked to deny it to herself, and pretend that what had happened between them was just physical, he'd crept under her skin and got to her on an emotional level.

Which she knew was ridiculous. They'd had one conversation outside of the bedroom, that second night, and needless to say that hadn't strayed into anything personal.

Erin had known she was way out of Ajax Nikolau's league—that what had happened between them had been as out of character for him as it had been for her. That was why he'd dumped her so unceremoniously after that second night.

Erin's break-up with her college sweetheart hadn't sliced as deep as that rejection by Ajax. Even before the unanswered letter, it had called to mind the deep and abiding pain of her mother's rejection and abandonment, and its effect on her father, when Erin had been just a toddler. A pain that she had successfully managed to avoid all her life by not allowing anyone to get too close.

But Ajax had got too close. And that had terrified her. So she'd accepted his ending of their brief affair.

When she'd been head-hunted by a rival firm not long afterwards, she'd used the opportunity to leave. They'd been good to her, considering her pregnancy, and she'd been working part-time for them since returning from maternity leave recently.

So, to say things had changed drastically since her short-lived affair with Ajax Nikolau was putting it mildly.

Erin grimaced and moved silently out of the baby's room, half closing the door behind her.

Frankly, she was too exhausted to think about any of that now. She finally had a moment to heat up her dinner and—

The buzzing of her doorbell broke through Erin's thoughts. She assumed it was a mistaken delivery—drivers often pressed the wrong apartment number—but when she lifted the receiver and the camera came on she went cold all over.

It wasn't a delivery driver. It was a man. Too tall for his face to be visible on screen. All she could see were wide shoulders and a suit, but even through the grainy image she could appreciate the cut of the suit and the distinctive breadth of the chest and shoulders.

And then a face came into vision—devastatingly gorgeous, instantly recognisable. *Ajax Nikolau.* The fact that he was here, just a few floors down, as if manifested straight out of her guilty imagination, was unbelievable. So unbelievable that Erin found herself pushing the button to admit him before she'd even made the decision to let him in.

She heard the big door open and he said, 'Apartment six, yes?'

Somehow Erin must have said something in return, because he disappeared from view and she heard the heavy clang of the door far below. He would be coming up in the elevator now—which immediately made Erin think of another elevator, vastly more luxurious, when they'd almost—

She heard the distinctive *ping* of the elevator's arrival and the doors opening.

He was literally outside her door now, probably wondering why she hadn't opened it yet.

There was a light knock. 'Erin?'

Erin felt slightly disembodied. Her brain had seized, as if protecting itself from thinking about the reality of what was happening.

She opened the door and had to adjust her gaze up. She'd forgotten how tall he was. And she was in bare feet, having kicked off her high heels as soon as she'd stepped through the door earlier. His impact hit her like a physical jolt through her body. Electricity crackled.

He frowned at her. 'Your hair is short.'

Erin lifted a hand and touched her head self-consciously. She'd had it cut a few months ago, because the baby had kept grabbing it.

She went cold all over. *The baby.*

Her hand dropped. 'Mr Nikolau…what are you doing here?'

He looked at her. '*Mr Nikolau?*'

Erin's hand gripped the door handle tight. She was beginning to recover some very necessary cognitive function. She realised she'd never actually referred to this man by his first name outside of the bedroom, because they'd gone straight from the boardroom to the bedroom with very little interaction in between.

She tried again. 'How can I help you?'

She would have asked him how he knew where she lived, but for a man like Ajax Nikolau nothing was a barrier to information.

Erin Murphy looked different with short hair, but no less attractive. The minute she'd opened the door and Ajax had seen her his entire body had clenched with recognition and need. Hunger.

He still wanted her. He'd never stopped thinking about her.

Even after almost two years. As each week had gone by, and then months, he'd been sure she would fade in his memory. She hadn't. But neither had that sense of panic he'd felt that she'd got under his skin on an emotional level. It had been strong enough to stop him from giving in to the temptation to seek her out again.

Until now.

Much to his irritation, no woman had managed to come close to making him feel the way she had. The two nights they'd spent together were engraved on his brain like a brand he would never be able to remove. He'd had many a sleepless night enduring X-rated dreams, waking hard and aching.

He'd resisted the memories and dreams for as long as he could. And life had helped in that respect. He'd never been busier. In the aftermath of the business deal of the century, Ajax's time had been monopolised by consolidating his position, in case anyone had any doubts he could pull his family's business together.

In the past year and more he'd silenced any critics or doubters. So much so that in the past couple of months he'd finally had time to take a breath and take his foot off the accelerator, and he'd realised that in spite of the many challenges he faced day to day, and the vast responsibility he had as CEO of Nikolau Industries, he was a little…bored. Jaded.

And, as if it had just been waiting in the wings for the right moment, the tantalising possibility of seeing this woman again had filled his mind. He'd told himself that the impression he'd had of her getting too close had been brought on by their amazing chemistry, nothing more.

She'd lost weight. He didn't remember her looking so

delicate. Her shorter hair drew attention to the fine bone structure of her face. Her huge eyes. The long slim neck. Elegant collarbones visible under the neck of her silk shirt.

His body tightened. 'Can I come in?'

She didn't move. 'What are you doing here?'

Ajax, a man used to people allowing him access to wherever he wanted to go, realised that this wasn't proceeding as he'd envisaged. His arrogance mocked him.

'I'm here to see you.'

'Why?'

The blunt question reminded him of how she'd been able to cut through a lot of waffle and point people towards what was important. She'd been good at her job. He missed that.

Before he could speak, voices became audible in the corridor behind him and Erin seemed to make a split-second decision.

She stood back. 'You'd better come in.'

The offer was ungracious, but Ajax wouldn't object. She was flushed in the face, and that made him think of how she'd looked under him as he'd joined their bodies.

He looked away from her and around the apartment, to try and regain some control. It was airy and bright. Homely. Books on shelves. Throws on a well-loved couch. Something about it caught at him, in his chest, creating a kind of yearning. Disconcerting...

'Mr Nikolau—'

He looked back at Erin, a little more in control of his faculties. 'Really? You're going to stand on ceremony?'

Her mouth tightened. 'It was almost two years ago, and a very brief...thing.'

Thing. That was one way of describing it. It had been a conflagration that had moved Ajax to cut it off, starve it of oxygen, for fear that it would run rampant. But if he'd let it do that then maybe he wouldn't be here now.

'I think the time for ceremony has come and gone. Please call me Ajax.'

Erin's jaw gritted momentarily. Then she said tightly, 'Very well, Ajax. What can I do for you?'

'I understand why you might have felt the need to resign from the law firm, but you didn't have to.'

Erin went pale. 'You…want me to work for you again?'

Ajax's conscience pricked. His motive for coming here was far more ulterior and earthier. 'I hear you're doing well at your new firm. Certainly your old boss misses you.'

'You've come all the way here to tell me I was a valued employee?'

Now his skin prickled with a sense of exposure. He wasn't used to people questioning his motives. He wasn't used to questioning his own motives. But he'd made this journey without really thinking it through—not like him. He was behaving like some sort of homing pigeon, guided by forces beyond its comprehension or control.

Erin was looking at him, waiting for a response, once again reminding him of how forthright she was. Her eyes were beautiful, brown and green, ringed with long dark lashes.

It struck him then that he was here because he was looking for some sort of connection—something he hadn't felt since he'd been with this woman.

Erin still couldn't believe Ajax Nikolau was standing in her small one-and-a-half-bedroom apartment talking to her. Saying…nonsense. She needed him to be gone. This situation was too dangerous. She wasn't ready to let him know he was a father right now. She had intended to go to him and be cool and collected. Calm. Not in her stockinged feet with her baby—*their baby!*—just feet away.

Before she could think of something appropriate to get

him to leave, he asked, 'Why did you leave the law firm? Because of what happened between us?'

Erin swallowed. She wasn't about to explain her emotional vulnerabilities to the man who had been responsible for them.

She managed to force out, 'Don't be ridiculous. I took my new job because it offered better prospects.'

Then he said, 'I haven't had a lover since you.'

He sounded almost accusing. He was looking at her intensely, the same way he had in that elevator. Blood rushed to her skin, making it tingle. Between her legs she pulsed with awareness and it shocked her. She hadn't felt so much as a blip of desire since the baby.

Since Ajax.

She was confused. She was afraid to think too much about what it meant that he hadn't had a lover since her. Or how that made her feel. Slightly giddy...

Erin tried to ground this rapidly evolving situation in some reality again. 'Why are you here?' She was confused. Did he want her to work for him?

Ajax shook his head slightly, as if clearing it. 'I think I came here because I haven't forgotten what it was like... Have you?'

As if to help her, a memory flashed back of how it had felt to have Ajax's body moving in and out of hers, skin slick with sweat, hearts pounding, straining to reach the building pinnacle of—

'Yes,' Erin lied desperately. 'I've had other things to think about.'

Like his daughter.

Her guts churned as memories of finding out about the pregnancy flooded her brain.

She'd thrown herself so completely into her new job, to try and put what had happened between her and Ajax Nikolau behind her, that three months had almost gone by before she'd acknowledged the bouts of morning sickness that had lasted for about a month, and noticed that her already irregular periods had actually stopped.

And that the bloating wasn't going away. In fact, it was getting worse. She could barely fit into some of her clothes any more.

And when yet another male client's gaze had gone to her bigger than usual chest she'd had to face the fact that she ought to take a moment out of her schedule to get her symptoms checked.

Until the doctor had said those fateful words—*'You're pregnant, almost thirteen weeks along'*—she'd literally not even contemplated that possibility. Or maybe she'd been too scared to let the possibility exist.

She had a mild form of endometriosis, so whenever she was irregular or there were strange symptoms she put it down to that. And stress had always had a big effect on her periods, too, so to say finishing an affair—even short-lived—and starting a new job was stressful was an understatement.

The doctor had looked at her incredulously. 'You really had no clue?'

Erin had shaken her head, feeling stupid.

Pregnant.

She'd been in a daze for days.

Ajax's voice cut through the memories as he said, 'You're not married or engaged?'

Erin covered her hand. 'That doesn't mean anything. I could be in a relationship.'

'Are you?'

She'd forgotten how blunt he was. *'Just so we're clear, I want you, Erin.'*

She shook her head. 'No...but are you really suggesting that there's still something between us?'

He didn't have to answer that. It sizzled between them, as much as Erin would like to deny it.

Desperately she tried to pretend it wasn't happening. 'Do I need to remind you that you were the one who cut things off?'

'Maybe I was a little too…hasty.'

The memory of how close she'd allowed him to get made Erin say tartly, 'It's been almost two years—the opposite of hasty, I would say.'

His gaze met hers, and the intensity of his unusually light eyes made Erin quiver inwardly.

He said, 'I've been a little busy.'

'Well, so have I.'

Birthing his daughter.

Tell him.

But her mouth wouldn't form the words. Guilt was like acid in her stomach.

Ajax took a step closer to Erin. She knew she should step back, but her limbs were like lead.

He said, 'How can you deny it when it's running like electricity between us right now?'

His scent washed over her and she breathed it in—distinctive and achingly, instantly familiar, musky and woody with something spicy underneath. It hurtled her back in time and all Erin could see was Ajax. She was engulfed in memories and, treacherously, lust. The stresses and strains of the past months dissolved. She was just a woman again, standing in front of the man who had seared himself onto her psyche in more ways than one.

She'd really felt as if she'd been reconfigured after those two nights in his bed. Her cells realigned. Even though she hadn't been an innocent, she'd felt as if he'd transformed her into a woman. A sexual woman. With a sense of her own sensual power. He'd given something to her—something she couldn't even name—but it had felt precious.

She'd forgotten about it until now. Or maybe she'd blocked it out. But here, under his avid gaze, she was feeling all those things again. Sensual. Powerful. Desired.

He reached out and touched her hair lightly. 'It suits you.'

Erin felt self-conscious. 'I… Thank you.'

Ajax kept his hand lifted, said, 'May I?'

Erin wasn't sure what he was asking, but everything in her body had her nodding her head.

His fingertips traced the line of her jaw, down to her chin. He lifted it slightly, looked at her mouth. 'I've dreamed of you…'

Erin had been too exhausted to dream much, but there had been nights when she'd known she'd had torrid dreams. She'd just been relieved not to remember much about them. She'd felt them lingering in her body, though, because she'd woken aching, feeling unsatisfied.

Ajax moved closer. Erin didn't step away, even though she knew she should. Right now she couldn't quite remember why. She was caught up in the intensity of Ajax's proximity and the way he was looking at her, and so when his head lowered towards her and his mouth touched hers she felt nothing but a wild surge of desire.

Yes, please.

Had he asked if he could kiss her? She didn't care. She'd given her assent just by accepting it. His mouth moved over hers, more insistent. Asking a question. Erin answered without hesitation, her mouth opening under his, allowing him to deepen the contact.

He moved closer, wound an arm around her back and pulled her into him, so she could feel the hard thrust of his desire for her. It sent arrows of need right to her core, where she was melting, and—

Ajax pulled his head back abruptly. 'What's that sound?'

It took a second for Erin to register the cry of her baby. She reacted instantly, pushing free of Ajax's arms, and ran to the bedroom.

Ashling had pulled herself up and was standing in her cot, crying. She stopped as soon as Erin appeared, giving a gummy smile with glimpses of her newly formed teeth—undoubtedly the cause of her distress.

Erin went in and picked her up. Her cheeks were hot—a classic sign of teething pain. She'd almost forgotten about Ajax, so she was startled when she turned around and he was in the doorway.

Ashling saw him and went still in Erin's arms.

He was looking at the baby, his face like stone. Then he stepped back from the doorway so Erin could come out. She had no choice. She went into the sitting room.

Ajax looked at Ashling again. And then, after a long moment, at Erin. 'You said you weren't with anyone.'

'I'm not.' She clutched Ashling to her like a shield.

He looked at the baby again. 'Who...? What?'

Reaction was starting to set into Erin's body. She felt herself trembling. 'Her name is Ashling.'

Ajax was transfixed. The resemblance between father and daughter was almost laughable as they studied one another. Olive skin...dark hair.

He dragged his gaze away from the baby to look at Erin. He said, 'She's mine.'

It was emphatic. But even though Erin knew this was her opportunity to admit that he was right, she heard herself blurting out, 'How can you be so sure?'

Ajax was grim. 'Because she's the image of my son.'

CHAPTER TWO

AJAX WAS HOLDING on to the edge of the kitchen island as if that could help anchor him in the midst of the storm surging around him. Belatedly he saw baby paraphernalia that he hadn't noticed the first time around. A bottle steriliser, teething rings, toys. A high chair. They mocked him now. Erin had taken the baby back into the bedroom to try and put her down again.

A baby. His baby.

He knew she was his as he knew his own name. She was the image of Theo at that age. Theo, his deceased son.

Ajax had spent so many of the recent years trying to block out the past, but now it was hurtling back with all the devastation of a bomb going off inside his brain.

His ill-fated marriage had been to a woman who had never been meant for him because she'd been promised in marriage to his older brother. It had been an arranged, strategic marriage, between two of Greece's most notable families, so when his brother had died tragically Ajax had taken his brother's place.

Sofia, his wife, had already been pregnant on the wedding day, and for appearances' sake Ajax had agreed that the baby would be named as his.

In fact he'd been his nephew. But Ajax had loved that boy as if he was his own son, and Theo had known only Ajax as his father. A small, sturdy boy, with a mop of dark curly hair and bright mischievous eyes, he would grab Ajax's hand with his own little pudgy one, 'Papa, come see!' and he'd drag Ajax off to look at a snail or a frog in a pond, or the latest toy he was obsessed with.

The devastation of Theo's loss was suddenly acute all over again, making a lie of the cliché that time healed all wounds. Time would never heal that wound.

Ajax had grieved for his wife too, even though there'd been little love lost between them. Her death, and Theo's, had thrown into sharp focus how they'd been treated like commodities by their families. Coming from one of Greece's oldest and dynastic families, marrying a woman purely for duty's sake had always been Ajax's destiny—he'd never been under any illusions that love existed after witnessing his parents' loveless marriage and lack of loving parenting—but the reality of the cold and hollow experience of his marriage had only confirmed his cynical world view, and that he wanted no part of such a charade again.

Hence his all-out conquest of the family business, so that he would be the one calling the shots.

Ajax heard a noise from behind him and steeled himself. This visit to indulge his curiosity and his lingering lust for Erin Murphy had morphed into something else entirely. Something unwelcome and life changing. He had a child. A daughter. When he'd vowed after Theo's death never even to contemplate having another child. Yet it had happened. And Ajax couldn't process the full magnitude of that right now.

He turned around. Erin was gently closing the door to the small bedroom.

Even now, in spite of this bombshell, he couldn't stop his gaze from roving over her body, or stop his response. It made his blood volcanic, a mix of shock, anger and desire.

He looked at her. 'Why didn't you tell me about my daughter?'

* * *

Ajax's stark question landed in Erin's gut like a cold, heavy stone. It had been a shock to hear him mention his son. It was no secret, the awful car accident that had taken his wife and son's lives some years ago, but he never spoke of them publicly and he and Erin had certainly never delved into such personal territory during their brief affair.

She couldn't speak for a moment, but then she said weakly, 'I did try…a few times…'

She was still reeling at the reality that Ajax was here, that he now knew about his daughter, and that their kiss had proved he still held a power over her that she couldn't fathom or control.

He frowned. 'When?'

Erin forced her sluggish brain to work. 'When she was about five months old, I called your office—they said you were in Greece. I didn't have a personal number for you. Obviously I couldn't leave a message with that information.'

In spite of their intimacies.

That drove home even more to Erin how inconsequential she'd been in his life.

Ajax's face was like stone. 'You said you tried a few times. That's once.'

'I wrote you a letter.'

Ajax looked as if he wanted to laugh. 'A *letter*?'

She nodded. 'I figured that would be as good a way as any to get the message to you.'

'Everything is electronic now. Letters are all but obsolete.'

Erin felt defensive. 'Yes, I'm aware of that. But as I no longer had a company email address, I knew that any email I sent would most likely end up in spam. Or it would be opened and vetted by an assistant. I thought a letter would be safer and more private.'

His expression changed for a second, and then he said a

little stiffly, 'Actually, that wouldn't have made much difference, they open all correspondence even if it's marked private. I have nothing to hide, and I have a policy of my staff immediately destroying any such correspondence. A woman making a claim that I'm the father of their child is unfortunately seen as an easy way to get some kind of engagement with men in my position. It works more effectively when the man in question is more promiscuous than I am.'

His words came back to her. *I haven't had a lover since you.*

Erin folded her arms, shutting out that reminder. So one of her messages could have got through, only to be thrown out before he'd even seen it. 'Well, in this instance it was a genuine claim—isn't that ironic?'

Ajax's jaw clenched. 'Did you try again?'

Erin nodded. 'I went to your offices one day, to try and see you—shortly before the birth. But before I could even give them my name I started to feel pains... I was going into labour.'

The colour left Ajax's face. 'You went into labour with my child in my building and I had no idea?'

Erin nodded, swallowing. He looked... She couldn't even decipher the expression on his face.

But then his expression blanked and he said, 'I'm sorry I wasn't aware. How did my staff not notice?'

Weakly she had to concede, 'That wasn't their fault. I was wearing a big coat—it wasn't necessarily obvious that I was pregnant. But...as you might appreciate... I was occupied with a newborn after that, so telling you wasn't high on my list of priorities.' She finished, 'Those were all the attempts I made.'

'So were you going to try again...? When, exactly? In another year, maybe?' Ajax's tone was ascerbic.

Erin squirmed inwardly. She knew she deserved this. 'No, I knew it had to be soon.'

About three months ago she'd prepared to make another attempt to contact Ajax, but then she'd seen him in the paper, in the society pages, pictured at an event with a beautiful woman. The urge to contact him had dissolved—she didn't like to admit that she'd been jealous. And yet if she believed what he'd said here today, he hadn't taken another lover. So he hadn't slept with that woman...

His voice cut through her circling thoughts. 'Well, wasn't this timing serendipitous?'

'That's one way of looking at it.'

He emitted a frustrated sound, and then, 'I'm not royalty, Erin. I'm not that hard to contact. It wasn't as if you would have been a stranger trying to contact me.'

'True. But you made it very clear after our last...meeting that no further contact would be welcome.'

The sting of that rejection was as painful and vivid now as if it had just happened. He'd said, *'This was a mistake. It won't happen again.'*

Erin pushed down the old pain. She couldn't afford to let him see that vulnerability now.

'That was before I knew you were pregnant,' he pointed out.

She countered, 'I didn't know you hadn't received the letter. I assumed you had, and that you weren't interested in your daughter.' *Or me*, she didn't say.

'Of course I would have wanted to know. I'm not made of stone.'

A flash of heat went through Erin's body. She knew very well that he wasn't made of stone.

She brutally slammed down on that reminder.

'Look,' she said, 'I'm sorry again that I didn't get to let you know before now. I could have tried harder. But the truth is...it wasn't just because you were hard to contact.'

Ajax frowned. 'What are you talking about?'

Erin swallowed before divulging, 'My mother left me and my father when I was still a toddler. Just walked out. I've only seen her since then sporadically. When I believed you'd got my letter and had ignored it I thought you were rejecting Ashling. It made me less inclined to pursue telling you. Obviously I would have... But I didn't want her to be rejected the way I'd been. And then,' she said, 'there's what happened to your family.'

There was instant tension in the air. Ajax said, 'What are you talking about?'

'Your wife and son who died. I thought maybe that was the reason why you mightn't want anything to do with another child.'

Ajax looked incredulous. 'I had a right to know, in spite of what happened in the past. There's a difference between choosing to have a family again and an unplanned pregnancy.'

Oof. That landed in Erin's gut like a punch. And it shouldn't. Their passion had burned bright and hot for a very brief moment. That was all it had been. A moment. An aberration. A man like this would never have chosen a woman like her to have his child. He came from a Greek dynasty. She came from second-generation immigrants. Her father and mother had been the first in both their families to go to university.

Erin lifted her chin. 'Yes, you did have a right to know, and I've explained my side of it. You might remember what it's like with a newborn? I'm sorry to mention it but—'

Ajax put up a hand, every line in his body tense. 'Then don't.'

Erin closed her mouth. She'd been right about his son, but it was no comfort.

Ajax was still rigid with reaction at the mention of his son. Her words *'You might remember what it's like with a new-*

born' had precipitated a slew of images and memories of holding the soft weight of Theo in his arms as he'd walked him up and down, getting him back to sleep. The wonder of that small form and the immensity of awe he'd felt. Like nothing he'd ever experienced.

He shook his head, as if that might dislodge the painful images. He had to focus on the present moment. *His daughter.* And how it had happened and what they were going to do next.

'We used protection.' He couldn't help but sound accusing.

'I know...it obviously failed. I hadn't expected this either—believe me.'

'Who takes care of her while you work?'

Erin's eyes flashed, as if she resented being asked the question. *Well, tough.*

She said, 'My father sometimes—he had her today. Or I leave her in a creche that is right across the street from where I work.'

'How old is your father?'

'Sixty-eight.'

At Ajax's obviously sceptical look, Erin said defensively, 'He's physically and mentally very sprightly.'

'It's not ideal.'

'No, it's not. But it's all I can afford right now, as I'm only working part-time.'

Ajax's mouth was tight. 'I could have been supporting you.'

She lifted her chin. 'You once accused me of playing games to get your attention. I support myself and I can support my child.'

'Who is also *my* child,' Ajax pointed out.

Erin suddenly blanched, as if she was fully realising that Ajax was now here and knew that he had a daughter. He might have almost felt sorry for her if he hadn't still been reeling with the full extent of this news himself.

The sudden blast of a siren outside reminded him of something. He glanced at his watch and cursed silently. He looked at Erin. 'I have to go—I have a business dinner this evening. But we're not done talking about this.'

Erin said, 'I can meet you when it's convenient.'

Ajax held out a hand. 'Give me your phone.'

She retrieved it wordlessly from her bag on a chair, unlocked it and handed it over. Ajax gave it back after a few seconds.

'You have my number now. Text me so I have yours. I'll be in touch.'

Within seconds Ajax was gone, seemingly taking all the air in the room with him. Erin went to the window and opened it, sucking in a deep breath. She saw Ajax emerge onto the street below and cross the road, and how the driver hopped out to open the back door of a his car. Ajax slid in and the gleaming silver SUV moved away into the Manhattan traffic.

Erin let out a shuddery breath. So now he knew.

He still wants you.

She shook her head to negate that assertion. He might have come looking for her on a whim, but there was no doubt that the discovery of a daughter he'd known nothing about had doused any desire he still felt.

Erin turned from the window and sent a simple text to Ajax.

Erin.

She got one back almost immediately—a terse acknowledgement.

I'll be in touch.

She had no idea what to expect next. She didn't really know Ajax Nikolau at all. In spite of their intimacies. In spite of watching him at work over those intense few weeks. He was as good as a stranger. A stranger who was one of the most powerful men in the world.

And the father of her child.

She was bound to him irrevocably, for life, no matter what happened. But she was determined not to let Ajax upend their lives to suit him. Whatever was coming, she would be prepared.

'Mr Nikolau is ready to see you now.'

Erin took a deep breath and stood up. It was strange to be back in the building where she'd worked with Nikolau's legal team. And where, a few floors above them, she and he had—

No, not going there now.

She straightened her suit jacket and flicked an invisible speck of dirt off the silk shirt that was tucked into slim-fitting pencil trousers. She couldn't look more professional— even if she was quivering inwardly. The briefcase she carried felt as if it weighed a ton, even though it only held paper.

Ajax's assistant opened the door to his office, standing back to let Erin through. The woman had barely acknowledged Erin, apart from saying the minimum required to greet her and ask her to wait for a few minutes.

Erin stepped over the threshold and it took her a minute to orientate herself. She'd forgotten how big his office was. He was standing at the very far end, near a massive desk, in front of windows that took in a truly intimidating view of downtown Manhattan.

He was wearing a shirt tucked into dark trousers. No tie. Sleeves rolled up. It was one of the things that had appealed to her about him from the start—he was a man who was happy to get stuck into things. It had surprised her, because men at his level usually left it to their minions to do the work, but he'd wanted to be over every little nut and bolt of the negotiations.

And now that memory struck a shard of fear into her. Would he be the same when it came to his daughter? It had been a week since she'd last seen him. He'd sent a curt text the day before yesterday, telling her to give him a couple of options of times for meetings, and now here she was.

The sun was setting over Manhattan behind him, bathing the iconic city in a golden light. But all Erin could see was him. Tall and formidable.

'Come in.'

What had seemed like a great distance between them now felt minuscule as Erin crossed the luxuriously carpeted floor. She stopped at the other side of the desk. He couldn't have looked more stern and remote. A million miles from the charming man who had come to her apartment to seduce her again. Now his light eyes were like two chips of ice. She felt it in her blood. Making her cold.

A moment stretched between them, taut with tension. But Erin wasn't going to say anything until he spoke.

Eventually he asked, 'Who is minding the baby?'

The baby.

Her hackles rose. 'Her name is Ashling and she's with my father—her grandfather.'

'A name that until a week ago I'd never even heard before.'

Guilt struck Erin again, like a little piercing needle. 'It's Irish...it means dream.'

He didn't seem particularly impressed by this. And then, as if remembering his manners, he offered, 'Would you like something? Water? Coffee?'

Erin's throat suddenly felt as dry as sandpaper. 'Maybe just a little water, please.'

She watched as he came around from behind the desk and

walked with loose-limbed grace to the drinks cabinet. He poured her a glass of water and brought it back. She plucked it from his fingers as quickly as she could, afraid that her skin would touch his.

As it was, she was battling flashbacks to that second night, when they'd had an impromptu midnight feast in his kitchen. She'd laughed when it had become apparent that he didn't know where basic things were in his own kitchen.

They were a long way from that moment now.

She took a sip of water. Ajax went back behind his desk. He put out a hand, 'Please, sit down.'

Erin shook her head. 'I'm fine standing.' Then, before her nerves could consume her, she blurted out, 'What are your plans?'

He'd had a week to absorb the news and think it all over... consult with lawyers. Erin was acutely aware of that.

A muscle in Ajax's jaw pulsed. 'My plans are to discuss how we proceed from here.'

Erin swallowed. He sounded terse. Angry. He had every right to be.

'For what it's worth, I'm sorry again that you had to find out the way you did. That I couldn't get a message to you sooner.'

He said, 'There's no point going back and forth over a past we can't change, we need to think about the future.'

Erin's gut clenched. Ajax was in no mood to be conciliatory and she couldn't blame him. She was in this situation and had to deal with it as best she knew how.

She said, 'I agree, to that end, I've drawn up a legal document, if you'd like to see it?'

Ajax focused on the woman in front of him, who was taking a sheaf of papers out of her briefcase, head bent. He was momentarily glad not to be looking into those far too mesmerising eyes. One second brown, the next green, and then gold. They were too distracting. Too perceptive. They made him forget what was happening here. The huge betrayal of her not telling him about his daughter.

He wasn't sure what he'd expected today, but Erin taking legal documents from her case, as if this was a business meeting, was definitely not a scenario that had come into his head over the past week.

She was looking at him now and holding a sheaf of papers over the desk towards him. He took it, bemused. Glanced at it. It was entitled: *Custodial and Visitation Agreement between Ajax Nikolau and Erin Murphy.*

She said, 'First of all a DNA test needs to be done to establish paternity.'

Ajax put the contract down. There was a needling sensation at the back of his neck. Normally he was the one who took others by surprise.

'I know she's mine.'

'I appreciate that, but it's for your benefit. Without legal confirmation that she is yours, you don't have any rights to claim paternity or custody.'

She shouldn't have had to remind him of that.

The needling sensation got stronger.

He said, 'And presumably you wouldn't have the right to demand paternal support?'

Erin's face flushed. 'There are no *demands*. She will be entitled to support from her father the same as any child. I can support us quite well, in any event—'

'On a part-time attorney's salary?'

She flushed even darker now.

Ajax found it beyond satisfying to see this evidence of emotion. Satisfying and arousing. He cursed his weakness.

'I have other means,' she divulged, a little hesitantly.

Ajax arched a brow.

With obvious reluctance she elaborated. 'My mother sent me a monthly allowance until I was eighteen. I put every cent into savings. I never intended to use them unless absolutely necessary, but they're there. I own my apartment outright. I'm not here to look for anything outside of fair maintenance, and to establish some ground rules for custody and visitation.'

Ajax heard the pride in her voice and thought of the fact that her mother had left her. Against his better intentions he felt a tug of empathy. His parents might have been more physically present than her absentee mother, but they might as well have been absent for all the actual parenting they'd done.

This woman had intrigued him from the very first moment he'd seen her. She still intrigued him. The fact that he couldn't say in any moment what she would do was…refreshing, when he was used to people contorting themselves into pretzels to do what they thought he wanted.

What was *not* refreshing, though, was how she affected him. He was used to being surrounded by the most beautiful women in the world, and yet it was this one—uniquely—who seemed to have infiltrated his body and mind in such a compelling, comprehensive way that he only wanted her. Even now, after the bombshell discovery of the daughter she'd kept from him.

He said, 'Obviously I'll have to go through this with my legal team.'

'Of course. I'd expect nothing less. But I think you'll find it very reasonable.'

Curious now, he said, 'Give it to me in broad strokes… what you've set out.'

'Once your paternity is confirmed, I've proposed a child maintenance payment system until Ashling is an adult, depending on whether or not she goes to university, until such time as she's graduated.'

That prospect made Ajax feel slightly winded for a moment. He had an image of a tall, slim, dark-haired woman, smiling, with a mortarboard cap on her head. He hadn't even imagined that for Theo.

'Go on,' he bit out, regretting having asked the question now.

'Her life will be here, with me, and I will be her primary carer. But you will be permitted access regularly. Holidays can be negotiated too. I recognise that she will have family in Greece. I want her to have a relationship with you, and the other side of her family. Both my parents were only children. I don't have aunts, uncles or cousins.'

Ajax turned and walked to the window, taking in the vast view of downtown Manhattan without really seeing it. He had legions of cousins and aunts and uncles, but they might as well have been inanimate statues for all the warmth or affection he and his brother had ever received from any of them. Cousins had been pitted against one another in annual get-togethers that had had more resembled *The Hunger Games* than a fun family occasion. Rivalries had been fostered, not friendships.

He knew from what Erin was saying that that wasn't what she envisaged at all. She had no idea what his family were like. He'd told her he wasn't royalty, but in many aspects, when it came to marriages and bloodlines, his family behaved as if they were.

She said from behind him, 'One thing is non-negotiable. If you don't intend to foster a relationship with her—a *real* relationship, with regular meaningful meetings—then I must ask that you simply provide financial support and step back. I will not allow inconsistency—it's not fair. You're either in, or out.'

Meaningful meetings.

Like his relationship with Theo.

As someone who had never really known love, and certainly not unconditional love, having a child had taken Ajax unawares, and before he'd had time to protect himself it had been too late. He'd fallen in love with his son. Who hadn't even been his son. Loving Theo had broken Ajax wide open, leaving him exposed and vulnerable.

If that was what love was, he had a better understanding now of why generations of his family had had arranged marriages and kept their distance from their children. Because the pain of losing Theo had destroyed him.

It had killed something fragile and nascent inside him. It had mocked him for believing he was deserving of love... that he might experience something so pure.

The toxicity of generations of calcified emotions was what he knew. Not something as unbridled and outrageous as actual real emotion. He'd learnt that lesson the hardest way possible.

And yet here he was, being offered another chance to destroy himself all over again. His daughter might not suffer a tragic accident—Ajax knew instinctively that Erin was a conscientious mother, unlike his deceased wife—and that she would do her utmost to protect her child. *Their* child. But no power on earth could promise that no harm would come to her.

The thought of embarking on a relationship with his daughter and living with the terror of losing her every day almost made Ajax's legs buckle. He broke out in a sweat. His heart started to thump irregularly. Panic filled his veins.

He couldn't do it. Couldn't put himself back in that place of losing himself to a greater force only to have it snatched away from him like a punishment. He'd seen the child. She would be impossible *not* to love. Cherish. Protect.

She would do far better without him. Without this terrifying strangulating fear in his veins. After Theo, Ajax knew he couldn't endure such pain again. Loving or losing. That was why he'd vowed to himself that he would never try to have another family.

'Ajax?'

He forced down the panic. The fear. He said, to his own reflection in the window, 'I had a child and I lost him. I won't go through that again.'

'But—'

Ajax turned around. Steeled himself. 'Non-negotiable.'

Erin closed her mouth. She obviously sensed that this was not a moment to push it. She'd clearly seen something on his face.

Eventually she bent down and pulled something else out of the briefcase. A small padded envelope. She put it on his desk.

'This is the DNA self-test kit. You need to take a swab from inside your mouth and package it up, then send it over to my doctor. All the information is there. He has Ashling's DNA sample already. Once they're matched, you're her legal parent.'

Ajax walked back towards the desk. He felt a heavy weight in his chest.

Erin said, 'So, are you saying...you don't want to be involved?'

He forced himself to look at her and said, very clearly, 'That's exactly what I'm saying.'

CHAPTER THREE

'BA-BA-BA-BA-BA...'

Erin smiled at Ashling, who was cooing and babbling to herself in the bath as Erin washed her. Ashling loved water.

A small plastic duck went flying. Erin caught it and handed it back so she could throw it again. But her mind kept looping around and around Ajax's final devastating pronouncement after their meeting the other day.

He didn't want anything to do with his daughter.

Erin felt guilty. Had she pushed him into a corner where he'd felt he had no choice except to push his daughter away?

Obviously losing his son had had a huge effect on him. More than Erin had appreciated. She got it. The thought of anything happening to Ashling made her feel dizzy with fear. But to let that inhibit any future relationship with a child...? Erin couldn't understand that.

Maybe it wasn't just grief for his son. Maybe Ajax had realised that he really didn't want children. After all, it wasn't as if Ashling had been planned—as he'd pointed out.

Erin deftly plucked her out of the bath and dried her, dressing her in her nightclothes before giving her her evening milk. Ashling was tired. They'd been in the park for the afternoon with Erin's father. She went down with only the smallest objection, falling asleep in spite of herself.

Erin traced her daughter's plump cheek and then let herself out of the room. Evenings like this were rare, and she was grateful after the turbulence of the last week.

Erin hadn't yet had the heart to tell her father that Ajax had rejected his daughter at the first opportunity. He was just happy that Ajax now knew.

Even though Erin was desperately disappointed with Ajax's reaction, on some deep level it didn't surprise her. After all, she knew well the capacity of a parent to leave their child.

When Erin's mother had left her, she'd also walked away from her husband—Erin's father. He'd confided in Erin that he'd wanted a family and that her mother had not. But when she'd fallen pregnant with Erin, her father had hoped for the best—only to watch in despair as his highly intelligent and academic wife had become more and more suffocated by the domesticity of having a child.

Eventually she'd left, choosing herself and her academic career over being a mother and a wife, scoring a deep wound inside Erin.

It was only since she'd had Ashling that Erin had felt that wound start to heal. But along with that had come more pain. Because now that she knew what it was to be a mother, and to feel that ever-expanding humbling love, she understood even less how her mother could have abandoned her the way she had.

How cruel was it that she'd unconsciously chosen a man who had the same ability to walk away from a child as her own mother? She smiled at herself humourlessly. No doubt a psychotherapist would tell her she was still playing out her childhood trauma, and looking for someone to heal that wound. Well, she'd failed at the first hurdle.

The DNA test results had been delivered to Erin by courier that morning, confirming what she already knew. Ajax Nikolau was Ashling's father. He would have received the results by now too, and it obviously hadn't precipitated a change of heart as she'd heard nothing from him.

Her daughter was destined to grow up—as Erin had—without the love and presence of one of her parents. It would be up to Erin and her father to shower Ashling with all the love and confidence-building support they could.

Erin woke the next morning not to her daughter's unintelligible babble, but to her phone ringing on her nightstand. She looked at the clock. It was early. She saw the name *Ajax* and came instantly awake, sitting up in the bed.

'Hello?' Her voice was rough with sleep.

Ajax was terse and to the point. 'Something has happened. We need to talk. Can you arrange for the baby to be looked after? I'll send a car for you in an hour.'

Erin struggled to take in what he was saying. Luckily her father lived only around the corner, and he was always up early.

She responded, 'I... Yes, I guess so. I'll let you know if there's—'

But Ajax had terminated the call. Erin looked at her phone in astonishment.

How rude.

An hour later her father was pushing Ashling out through the main door of the building in her pram. Erin said a hurried goodbye and went to the blacked-out SUV waiting for her by the kerb. The driver was holding open the back door, and as she approached he said, 'Good morning, Miss Murphy. I'm to take you straight to Mr Nikolau.'

The streets of Manhattan at this hour were still relatively quiet. Erin wondered what on earth was going on to make Ajax behave in such an urgent manner.

She wouldn't have to wait long to find out.

The car pulled up outside his building and she got out. An

assistant led her into the elevator. The same elevator where she and he had combusted. Her cheeks started to burn, but luckily the serious assistant wasn't looking at her.

The elevator opened straight into Ajax's apartment, as it had done both times she'd been there. Morning light flooded the luxurious space. It still looked unlived-in. She couldn't imagine letting Ashling crawl around on these undoubtedly priceless carpets, leaving sticky handprints everywhere.

And then suddenly he was there. In dark trousers and a light shirt. Top button open. Hair a little messy, as if he'd been running a hand through it. Jaw dark with stubble. He hadn't shaved yet.

It made Erin think of that last morning, when she'd woken to find him dressed and looking at her with a grim expression. Shaved jaw. Making her feel very disheveled.

'I'm sorry I couldn't come to you. I've been tied up here with calls and I had to speak to you as soon as possible to get ahead of everything.'

Erin's brain still felt a little sluggish. 'Ahead of…what?'

'Come with me,' Ajax said as he turned around again, and then he asked, 'Do you want coffee? Anything to eat?'

'Coffee would be great.'

It might help her wake up and not feel as if she was dreaming. Another assistant said she'd bring it through, and Erin barely had time to say how she liked it before Ajax was disappearing down a corridor.

She hurried after him, deliberately ignoring the door that she knew led into his bedroom.

She found herself following him into a large corner room that turned out to be a home office. There were books on shelves, multiple computers, screens showing various images and information. A TV built into the wooden panelling was showing a news channel on mute.

The assistant materialised with Erin's coffee. She took it gratefully and noticed that she closed the door behind her.

Ajax's scent had caught at her as soon as she'd seen him. Woody and earthy, with something that was deeper...spicy. Uniquely him. Very male. Every nerve-ending in her body was humming with awareness, in spite of her best efforts to remain immune.

Erin took a quick gulp of coffee in a bid to be more alert. Even though she knew any desire he'd had for her had died, she wasn't sure she could trust that she wouldn't betray herself, alone in a room with him. Their history in that regard hadn't exactly been without incident.

She took a moment to acknowledge that she felt very underdressed. Ajax and his assistants looked as if they'd been up for hours. She'd just thrown on a pair of sweatpants and a matching top after a quick shower before she'd woken Ashling. She'd let her hair dry naturally, and could imagine it was sticking out all over the place.

Ajax was looking at a screen, and then he stood up straight. 'You need to see this,' he said.

Erin felt a clench of trepidation at the expression on his face. She put her cup down on the table and went around the other side of the desk to stand beside him.

It took her a moment to take in what she was seeing. A slew of lurid headlines and...

She bent to look closer and put her hand up to her mouth. There was a picture of her, with Ashling in her buggy, and it looked as if it had been taken yesterday, when they'd been coming back from the park. There was even a picture of her kissing her father goodbye.

The headlines were all a variation on *Who is Nikolau's mystery baby-mama? Baby joy for tragic Nikolau! Second chance for happiness! Will Nikolau put a ring on it?*

Erin stood up straight again. For a moment she felt dizzy. 'What...what is this?'

'This,' said Ajax, sounding as grim as he looked, 'is the result of someone on my team leaking news for personal gain.'

Erin backed away until she came up against a hard surface. She went around the desk again, wanting to get away from the pictures and the headlines. For someone who'd never merited so much as a blip of a mention anywhere outside of academic notices, and who had no social media, this evidence of invasion into her privacy felt like a physical violation.

She could almost feel the colour leaching from her face.

Ajax looked at her and came around the desk to take her arm. 'Sit down.'

She did. Her legs were wobbly. He handed her some water. She took a sip. Put the glass down. Tried to get her head to function. Ajax was pacing.

She said, 'I hadn't even thought that far ahead...to the public knowing about you and the baby...but obviously it would have happened at some point.'

Or maybe not, she rebuked herself.

Hadn't he said he wanted nothing to do with her? Maybe he would have denied being her father. It was the way it sometimes happened in celebrity circles, and then there was always a very public spat to force acknowledgement...

'Erin?'

Ajax was looking at her. She said, 'What did you say?'

'That I'm sorry. I never intended it to come out like this. I was planning on announcing it far more discreetly and ensuring that you would both be well protected from the inevitable ensuing interest.'

The relief that he had intended to acknowledge his daughter, even if he still couldn't seem to bring himself to use her name, was almost as destabilising as seeing those headlines.

He continued, 'But now it's out, and any attempt to control it will be like trying to put out a raging wildfire. By now there will be people in every newsroom tasked with finding out who you are and your entire life history.'

That didn't bother Erin too much.

She shrugged. 'They won't find anything of interest.'

Her most outrageous behaviour had been in an elevator with this man. Her cheeks started to burn again. She took another quick sip of water.

As if she hadn't spoken, Ajax was saying, 'You'll be hounded. You'll have to leave your apartment and go somewhere else.'

Erin *did* mind that. 'We can't just leave. Everything we need is there. And my father is just around the corner.'

Ajax looked at her. 'Your father won't escape their scrutiny either.'

'He's a professor of advanced mathematics,' Erin offered dryly. 'I'm sure they'll lose interest quickly. Surely if we hole up for a day or two they'll lose interest?'

And then, even as she said that, she thought of the intense interest Ajax attracted whenever he appeared in public. The constant speculation if he was pictured with anyone. She'd been one of those people poring over his image recently, wondering who his date was, if it was serious.

He shook his head. 'It'll take longer than a couple of days. The photographers who took those pictures yesterday won't be so discreet from now on. They're probably gathering outside your building right now.'

Erin shivered at the thought of being at the centre of such scrutiny.

'And it's not just you. It's the baby.'

Something cold went down Erin's spine. 'What do you mean?'

'Now that it's out who she is, she's a target.'

'Why?'

But even as she asked, Erin knew. She was the secret daughter of one of the richest men in the world.

Ajax was pacing again, saying almost to himself, 'If I'd had time I would have made sure you were protected, but now...' He turned around. 'I'm due to go to Greece today for a month. A mixture of work and social events.'

Erin frowned. 'Why are you telling me this?'

'Because there's only one solution, to contain this story and make sure you're both safe. You and the baby are coming to Greece with me.'

CHAPTER FOUR

ERIN COULD SEE the heat shimmering over the brown landscape as they descended onto an island bathed in the golden light of the rising sun. It was one of the Cyclades chain, strung like jewels across the Aegean Sea.

There were darker patches of green, and bright splashes of blue and turquoise lakes emerging from the volcanic earth. Villages appeared in clusters on hills and closer to the coast, distinctive with their white and blue paint. And it was all surrounded by the sea in varying shades of green and blue.

Ashling was sleeping…a heavy weight in Erin's arms. Her first time on a plane and she'd been amazing. Erin could hear the low rumble of Ajax's voice behind her, talking on the phone or with his assistants, who'd accompanied him for this leg of the trip. Apparently the staff would be travelling on to Athens after this flight, while Erin and Ajax went to the Nikolau villa.

She'd tried to resist this dash across the planet to escape a brewing media storm, but when she'd seen the throng of media outside her apartment building she'd had to concede that Ajax had a point. And what had really swayed her was the thought that Ashling would become a target for media interest and, worse, the potential danger of kidnap.

She'd managed to get a weekend call with her boss and had explained that there was a family emergency and she wasn't sure how long she'd be away. If she was gone for longer than two weeks her pay would be docked, but as she was only part-time her absence shouldn't cause too much of a ripple.

Her father had helped her to pack and get Ashling ready for the journey, and then they'd been collected by Ajax's driver from the back of the apartment building, giving the media the slip. They'd been on a plane within hours of Ajax's dawn wake-up call.

Erin was glad she'd at least had a chance to change into something other than sweatpants. Now she was wearing soft faded jeans and a loose linen shirt. Slip-on sneakers. She'd no idea what she'd packed—she'd been more concerned with making sure she had all Ashling's things.

The flight attendant came down the aisle to prepare them for landing. Erin buckled Ashling in without waking her. She'd been fed and she was in her night clothes—hopefully she would sleep again once they'd got to the villa, as it was still their night-time.

Ajax had assured her that his team would have prepared their rooms before arrival and ensured she had all the necessary requirements for Ashling. Erin didn't doubt it. In Ajax's world, things materialised and happened as if by magic. She wouldn't be surprised to see an exact replica of the nursery from her own apartment recreated in his villa.

But, apart from making sure they were comfortable at the start of the flight, Ajax hadn't come near them. Erin was beginning to see how his 'hands-off' approach might work, and it was as disconcerting as it was effective.

She hated to admit that she was still so aware of him.

The plane landed and Ashling woke with the *thud*. Predictably, after being so amenable, she was now cranky and tearful. It had been a long day.

Ajax appeared when the seatbelt sign went off. He was

wearing his suit jacket again, and looked annoyingly fresh, as if he'd slept in the vast bedroom at the back of the plane. But Erin knew he hadn't. He'd worked the whole time.

She felt a little sorry for his team. But then, she'd once been one of them.

Not going there now.

She stood up, holding Ashling, who curled into her.

Ajax said, 'Okay? How is she?'

Erin noticed that he barely glanced at Ashling.

'She's been great, but she's still tired and I can sense a storm brewing. How long will it take to get to the villa?'

'Only about fifteen minutes. Think she can last that long?'

'She'll be fine.'

The heat hit Erin as soon as they stepped out of the plane, like a wall, even at this early hour. Ashling's head came up and she stopped whinging, as if she was sensing she was back in the land of her ancestors.

Erin could only imagine what it would be like later in the day. Insects were loud in the grass on the other side of the runway.

She was vaguely aware of officials greeting Ajax and documents being checked. The perks of travelling with a billionaire.

An assistant led her over to a sleek silver SUV and opened the back door. There was a car seat for Ashling. Erin secured her in the seat and gave her a teething toy to chew. Then she got in on the other side and sat beside the baby seat.

It was only when no driver appeared, and she saw Ajax peel away from the assistants and officials to stride towards the car, that she realised he was driving them himself. He shucked off his jacket before he got in, and Erin couldn't help her gaze moving over his broad shoulders.

She was sitting behind him, to his right, so she could see his eyes in the rear-view mirror.

Suddenly feeling a little light-headed at the speed with which they'd traversed the globe, she asked, 'Is this villa your family home?'

Ajax shook his head, taking a road heading away from the airfield and small airport. 'No, I bought it years ago—for myself.'

'Where did you grow up?'

'Athens, mainly, when I wasn't at boarding school in England and then Switzerland.'

'How old were you when you were sent to boarding school?'

'Eight.'

Erin gasped. 'So young...' She couldn't imagine packing Ashling off at the age of eight to go anywhere.

Ajax shrugged lightly. 'My older brother was there already.'

'Were you close?'

Erin saw Ajax's eyes in the mirror, his gaze narrowed on the road in front of him. 'Yes and no. Our parents encouraged us to compete more than collaborate.'

Erin absorbed that. 'Your parents are still alive?'

'Yes.' Terse. And then, as if conscious of Erin's silence, Ajax added, 'They're in Athens. We also own some islands, and they pick and choose where to go for holidays or family events. Or they travel to their other homes around the world.'

'Family events...? Are there many of those?'

'There's one in a couple of weeks.'

He was avoiding meeting her eye in the mirror. Erin didn't have to ask him if his family knew about Ashling—it must have hit the papers here too by now. She wondered how the news had gone down. She was beginning to suspect a certain level of conservatism and snobbishness...

'Ab-gab-bab-dada...'

Erin smiled at Ashling who was looking out the window and pointing to the sky.

A sensation on the back of Erin's neck made her look up to find Ajax looking at her through the mirror at last. Instantly she was warm and tingling. The hairs on her skin were standing up. She couldn't look away, and eventually he did.

He was a good driver—fast, but safe. Not showy. Erin was acutely aware of his hands on the wheel. Big and strong. Masculine. She remembered how they'd felt on her. Not soft. Firm. Possessive. A pulse throbbed between her legs. She cursed herself.

She could see they were approaching a village, with houses strung along the road. Bright red and pink bougan-villea spilled over walls and roofs. It was quiet at this hour of the morning. Fairy lights were strung over doors and be-tween buildings. Erin could imagine them lit up at night. It was unbelievably pretty.

But Ajax kept going a short distance out through the other side of the village, until he turned abruptly down a narrow track which then opened out again revealing iron gates and a wall on either side.

A man emerged from a security hut.

'Kalimera,' Ajax greeted the man, and they conversed for a moment before the gates opened and they drove up along a wide drive bordered by flowering plants on both sides.

Erin could see pristine green lawns. And then her breath was taken completely when they drove around a bend and the driveway opened out into a huge courtyard with a fountain centrepiece, and a two-storey villa appeared before them.

The rising sun bathed the building in a bright glow, the pale and weathered stones of the villa making it almost fade into the background. It looked majestic, but also warm and rustic. Erin wasn't sure what she'd been expecting, but it had definitely been something more modern—perhaps stark white with sharp edges.

This was warm and inviting and beautiful, and it made something in her chest tighten. As if she'd had a dream of this image but hadn't realised it till now.

Ajax opened the car door and for a moment Erin felt almost superstitiously that once she stepped on this land her life would change for ever. *She* would change. But she was being ridiculous. She got out, avoiding Ajax's eye, not wanting him to see how this place was affecting her already.

There was a small breeze, bringing scents of the sea and wild herbs and plants.

Ashling emitted a cry from the car, a demand for attention, and Erin hurried around to take her out of the seat and hold her in her arms. A woman appeared in the massive front doorway, beaming. She was dressed in black, wiping her hands on an apron.

She greeted Ajax in rapid-fire Greek. He was smiling at her. The tightness in Erin's chest intensified. She hadn't seen him smile since their last night together. And she hated it that it mattered to her.

He looked at Erin. 'This is Agatha, my housekeeper. She lives on the property with her husband, who is the caretaker.'

Erin nodded at her shyly, and to her surprise the older woman came over and immediately held her arms out for Ashling, who went quite willingly into them, as if she knew this woman.

'We will have some milk, yes? And maybe a change of nappy?'

Erin was surprised to hear her speak English. She started to say, 'I think she's okay, actually—' but the woman was already disappearing into the villa with the baby.

Erin felt a bit stunned. 'She still needs the right milk—'

'I ordered ahead for all your requirements. You gave my assistant a list.'

Erin looked at Ajax. 'That was only on the plane.'

'She called ahead. Agatha has had six children. She'll be fine.'

Erin felt impotent all of a sudden.

Ajax said, 'Let me show you around.'

She felt that if she protested she'd be overreacting, so she followed Ajax around the side of the villa and up some steps to a terrace with a wall that overlooked a vast lawn. There was a swimming pool in the distance, just visible behind a wall of bushes, and just as she was thinking it was a potential hazard for a very curious baby who could crawl at the speed of light, Ajax pointed to the gate acting as a barrier between the terrace and the lawn.

'She'll be quite safe...don't worry.'

The fact that he'd thought the same thing at the same time was some comfort.

French doors were open into a sumptuously decorated reception room which led into a formal living room and a dining room. The kitchen was on the level below, huge and gleaming. There was a home gym down here too.

Back upstairs, Ajax showed Erin another informal living room, complete with a massive screen for watching TV or movies and a sound system. Books on shelves... The latest magazines...

Then they went upstairs to the bedrooms. Ajax indicated to where the guestrooms were located—too many for Erin to count—and then moved down another corridor. He stopped outside a door and then pointed to the end of the corridor. 'That's my room, down there. This is you and the baby.'

Erin was about to remind him of the baby's name, but he was opening the door and Erin stepped into the most beautiful room she'd ever seen with the softest carpet underfoot.

A warm off-white on the walls with a gold trim. Simple but elegant furniture. A huge four-poster bed, muslin drapes held back by silk ties. White linen that looked so inviting it just reminded her how sticky and tired she was.

And hungry, she realised, just as Agatha appeared in the doorway with Ashling in her arms, who saw Erin and immediately leaned towards her mother, cribbing a little.

Erin took her and cuddled her close. She smelt fresh. 'Thank you, Agatha, you didn't have to change her.'

'No problem. Come and see the nursery—you let me know if you need anything.'

Erin followed her to an adjoining door. The nursery was a plain room, with one of those circular cots that Erin had always coveted but hadn't been able to afford.

Agatha was saying, 'We didn't have time to decorate, but it'll be done by the end of the week.'

Erin noticed lots of things in boxes, but there was a changing table, and supplies of nappies and creams and wipes. A nappy bin. A chest of drawers stuffed full of more clothes than Ashling would ever be able to wear.

The suitcase Erin had packed with Ashling's things looked very shabby in this pristine space.

Agatha pointed to a monitor on the chest of drawers. 'Yours is in the bedroom, beside the bed. Its range will cover the whole property, so you'll hear if she makes a squeak.'

Erin hadn't needed baby monitors up to now, as her apartment was so small.

Agatha said something to Ajax in Greek, and he nodded and said, *'Efharisto.'*

Agatha left and Ajax turned to Erin.

'Please, make yourselves at home. Agatha has prepared some breakfast on the terrace downstairs for you, and then you'll probably need to sleep for a few hours. I noticed you didn't get much rest on the plane.'

He'd noticed? But at the mention of food, her stomach rumbled. Classy. She blushed.

'Okay, that sounds good.'

'I have some work to catch up on. I'll come for you before dinner this evening, after you've had a rest.'

Even though he'd worked all the way through the flight clearly Ajax wasn't at the mercy of such human failings as needing to rest.

He was still looking at her, and she said quickly, 'Yes, of course, that's fine. You don't need to entertain us.'

'It's no problem. I'll see you later.'

Ajax left and Erin let out a long breath. She looked around. The French doors were open onto a small balcony. She walked out and took in the view of lush rolling gardens. The sky was lighter now, losing the golden touch of dawn. The heat was rising too. She could hear the faint splash of waves in the distance. The air was scented with a mix of flowers and sea and grass.

It was paradise.

Ashling's head was tucked into Erin's neck. She was exhausted. Erin made her way downstairs to the terrace and put Ashling in a highchair, feeding her bits of fruit and pastries while she helped herself to the same.

Once she and Ashling had eaten, she thanked Agatha and made her way back upstairs, where Ashling went down with minimal fuss. A sign of her exhaustion.

Once the baby was fast asleep, Erin left the door to the nursery ajar and turned on the baby monitor, then checked the other one was on. It was so sensitive she could hear Ashling's breaths.

She explored further, to find a dressing room with all her things already unpacked. Were there other staff here apart from Agatha? Invisible? She wouldn't be surprised. It seemed all too magical.

Then there was the bathroom, with its footprint about the same size as her entire apartment. There were two sinks, a bath the size of a small pool, and a huge shower. Honey-coloured tiles... Exclusive beauty products and a large fluffy robe...

Erin couldn't resist washing the stickiness of the journey off her body and she stripped off on the spot, before stepping under the steaming spray of the shower. It was bliss.

After drying herself, she kept the towel wrapped around her and lay down on the soft bed. She fell into a dreamless sleep.

That evening, even though she was expecting it, Erin still jumped when there was a light knock on the bedroom door. *Ajax.* Her heart thumped at the thought of seeing him again. *Pathetic.*

Luckily she *had* packed appropriately, and she was wearing a plain shirt-dress, teaming it with a leather belt and flat sandals.

At the last moment she'd resisted reaching for any makeup apart from some tinted moisturiser. She'd left her hair to dry naturally. Dinner with Ajax wasn't a date.

She checked quickly that Ashling was still asleep and that both monitors were on, before taking hers with her. She took a breath and opened the door—and nearly melted on the spot.

Ajax was wearing faded jeans and a dark polo shirt. Short sleeves. All she could see was how his biceps bulged under the material. His skin was bronzed and gleaming. He made her feel very pale and washed out. She cursed herself for not making more of an effort. He must be wondering what he'd ever seen in her.

'Ready?'

Erin nodded. She left the door open and fell into step beside Ajax.

He said, 'She's asleep?'

Erin nodded. 'It took a while—her body clock is all over the place. We slept for a few hours this morning, and then I kept her occupied for the afternoon in the garden. Hopefully she'll sleep through to dawn. I'm lucky—she's a good sleeper.'

Erin felt as if she was babbling.

She slid Ajax a glance as they went down the stairs. 'Did your wife and son spend much time here?'

He shook his head, and when they reached the ground floor he put out a hand to indicate which way to go. 'No, they were never here.'

Erin had a vague memory that the accident had happened in Athens.

They were walking out onto the terrace now. Night had fallen and candles were burning, imbuing the pretty space with a soft golden glow. A wrought-iron table was set with a white tablecloth, gold-trimmed crockery and silverware, sparkling crystal glasses.

Ajax pulled out a chair. Erin sat down. Ajax took his own seat. It suddenly felt very intimate.

A young girl Erin hadn't seen before appeared, smiling shyly as she filled their water glasses before disappearing again.

Ajax said, 'This island isn't owned by my family, so it's a better place to stay off the radar.'

Erin tried not to gape. 'You mentioned that your family do own islands?'

'A few.'

She'd bet that that was an understatement. She said, 'This is a beautiful place. It's a pity your wife and son didn't spend any time here.'

Ajax's expression was hard to read. 'My wife preferred life in Athens and on islands like Santorini or Mykonos,' he said. 'This would have been too quiet for her.'

Erin couldn't understand that. Who wouldn't want to come and relax in this idyll, away from the chaos of everyday life?

Before she could persuade him to talk more about his previous existence, the young girl appeared again, with two plates of simple Greek salad, crisp and delicious. The feta cheese was fresh and salty and creamy, the tomatoes ripe and juicy from the sun.

Ajax held up a bottle of chilled white wine and looked at her. She nodded her assent. He poured her a glass and she took a sip, letting it slip down her throat, zesty and perfectly dry.

She could feel it hitting her veins almost immediately, making her feel even more as if she must be hallucinating. She'd wake up soon, back in her apartment, with the sounds of Ashling waking up and the non-stop sirens outside.

She blinked.

Still here.

'You enjoy your food?'

Erin looked at her clean plate, and then back up to Ajax. She arched a brow. 'Not used to women clearing their plates?'

Totally unfazed by her jibe, he took a sip of wine, unhurried. *Sexy...* Erin pressed her thighs together. The delicate wine glass should have looked ridiculous in his hand, but it only made him look even more masculine.

The young girl took their plates and then returned a couple of minutes later with the main course. The smell was mouthwatering.

Ajax said, 'Moussaka made with beef—one of our most traditional dishes.'

Erin took a few mouthfuls. She hadn't realised how hungry she was, but she hadn't eaten much since breakfast, when they'd arrived.

The moussaka was perfect and light, in spite of the rich tomato sauce.

'Delicious,' she said to Agatha, when the woman came out to clear their plates.

The housekeeper smiled. 'My grandmother's recipe. How is the little one?'

Erin nodded towards the monitor, with its light spiking intermittently when Ashling made a move or a snuffling sound. 'She's fast asleep, thank you.'

When she'd left with their plates, Ajax leaned forward with the wine bottle, but Erin put her hand over her glass.

'Not for me, thanks.'

Apart from wanting to keep her wits around this man, she also needed to have a clear head for Ashling, who might wake during the night.

He poured himself another half-glass. Erin found herself blurting out, 'How long ago was it...? Your wife and son?'

Ajax put the bottle back down. His jaw was tight. Erin knew she was straying into territory he didn't welcome talking about, but she had a right to know. After all, Ashling was his son's half-sister.

'Five years ago.'

'I'm sorry. I can't imagine how devastating it was.'

He looked at her, and she almost gasped out loud at the pain in his eyes.

'It was the worst.'

Erin's chest tightened and something dark prickled in her gut—something that spoke of jealousy, because he'd obviously loved his wife so much and he hadn't rejected his first-born child.

Sensing he wouldn't welcome any further platitudes, she said, 'So what happens now?'

'I'll work from here for the next couple of days, to make sure that you and the baby—'

'Her name is Ashling,' Erin interjected. She was feeling prickly. This whole scene was too seductive, and she was so acutely aware of him, but they weren't here for a romantic interlude.

She was here under sufferance, because the press had found out about Ashling, and if that hadn't happened Erin had no doubt that Ajax would be in Athens, probably wining and dining another woman, not even thinking of her.

Here he was being civil. Yet not civil enough to refer to his own child by her name.

Ajax's expression was unreadable. A little stiffly, he said, 'I hadn't ever planned on this again.'

Erin hesitated a second, then said, 'But you planned it… before?'

Ajax looked at her. And then he took his wine glass and stood up. He went over to the stone wall, turned his back to her. Erin couldn't help her gaze moving over the width of his shoulders and then down to his narrow hips. Firm buttocks, lovingly outlined by the faded denim.

She looked away hurriedly, afraid he'd turn and catch her ogling him. But he didn't turn around. He said, 'Actually, no, I didn't plan it.'

'So…how…?' Erin trailed off, confused.

He turned around and rested his backside against the wall, looking at Erin. 'My older brother was due to get married and start a family. He and Sofia were the ones who were engaged. But a few weeks before the wedding he was on board one of our ships and a storm blew up. He was trying to help the crew when he slipped and hit his head. He never recovered and he died a few days later.'

'I'm sorry,' Erin said. To have the death of his brother and then his wife and son…it had to have been almost impossible to get over. But then she frowned, 'You said your brother was engaged to Sofia?'

Ajax nodded.

'How did *you* end up marrying her?'

'It was a strategic marriage, designed to forge a strong union between my family and hers. When my brother died she was already pregnant with Theo. It was agreed that I would marry her—to protect the agreement between the families and to minimise the gossip about Theo. But it's a relatively open secret that he was actually my nephew.'

This was huge. Too much for Erin to take in all at once.

'So you and she...?' Erin trailed off again.

Ajax arched a brow. 'She and I...what?'

Erin felt foolish for asking, but some part of her needed to know. 'You didn't marry for love?'

Ajax looked at her for a moment, and then to her shock he emitted a sharp laugh.

'Love? No. She wasn't marrying my brother for love either—although they were better suited. Physically, at least.' He continued, 'Sofia and my brother and I come from families where anything as frivolous as love was weeded out generations ago. Marriages are as strategic as business deals.'

So Theo hadn't been his son. His marriage hadn't been based on a love match, as Erin had assumed. For someone who considered herself to be healthily cynical, she felt exposed—and very gauche.

Of course men like Ajax Nikolau moved in very different circles. There was too much money and power at stake to merely fall in love. And yet she knew that losing Sofia and Theo had been devastating. Or at least losing Theo...

As if reading her mind, Ajax said, 'I don't—' He stopped and amended his words. 'I *didn't* consider Theo a nephew. He was my son. I was there for his birth. I had no idea what to expect, but when he was handed to me...'

'You fell in love?' Erin said quietly.

He looked at her, and she could see even now the slightly bewildered expression on his face. 'Yes, I did.'

No wonder he'd decided never to risk it again. Loving and losing… She could understand it now, even if it didn't make it any easier to accept.

She wasn't so different herself. The thought of loving someone enough to be hurt by them was terrifying to her. Witnessing her father's devastation had been almost worse than her abandonment by her mother.

After her one relationship at university she'd realised that focusing on her career brought her more satisfaction, and no man had come along to distract her from that or persuade her otherwise. Until Ajax. It wasn't that she wanted to emulate her mother's obsession with work above all else, but more that she didn't want to risk the devastation she'd witnessed growing up with a heartbroken and lonely father.

She forced her mind away from such concerns. There was no danger of that here.

Erin said, 'Her name is Ashling and she exists—no matter how much you want to distance yourself from that fact.'

Ajax's mouth tilted on one side in a rueful half-smile. 'I think that horse has bolted by now.'

It was something, and Erin clung to it. 'Thank you for telling me what happened. So, what is the plan?'

Ajax said, 'Like I said, I'll stay here for a couple of days, to make sure you and the—'

He stopped and Erin held her breath.

He continued, 'To make sure you and Ashling settle in okay.'

Hearing him say his daughter's name was seismic. Erin wanted to thank him, but that would be weird.

She thought of what he'd said and then shook her head.

'You don't need to stay—we'll be fine. We can walk down to the village if we need anything.'

'*No.*'

Ajax's voice was sharp, and he'd straightened up. Erin could see his knuckles white around the glass. He seemed to notice his own tension and relaxed a little.

'Sorry, but there's no need to leave the villa. I'll make sure you have everything you need.'

Erin frowned. 'We're not allowed to leave?'

Ajax looked irritated now. 'If you need anything you can ask Agatha to get it for you—or her husband.'

Erin stood up and said slowly, 'I know you don't mean to keep us here as prisoners. And, while it is beautiful here at the villa, I like to go for walks. And Ashling will need stimulation. When we drove through the village I thought it would be a nice place to go for morning coffee, or lunch.'

His face was like stone.

Erin tried to push down a lurch of panic. After all she was half a world away from home, with a man who she really didn't know that well at all.

'Ajax, what is it? Surely we're allowed to move around freely? We're not in danger here?'

His expression softened. 'No, of course not. It's just…' He swept a hand through his hair, clearly agitated. 'Sofia and Theo died because she insisted on driving into Athens. She wouldn't let a driver take her in spite of my requests.'

Her panic subsided. Ajax didn't strike her as a control freak, so perhaps there had been more to it. And his son—*nephew*—had died in that crash, so perhaps he had a right to feel a little paranoid. It clearly meant that he felt protective over Ashling, whether he wanted to admit it or not.

Carefully, Erin said, 'Okay… Well, I can't drive. I never learned because it wasn't necessary. I grew up in one of the busiest cities in the world, so I think I can handle a sleepy Greek village, but if it makes you happier someone can drive us in and out and I will keep you informed as to our whereabouts.'

Ajax said, 'That's...fair.' And then, 'I didn't know you couldn't drive?'

Erin made a small face, 'Well, actually, I can. But I just never got around to doing my test. A car is a burden in Manhattan.'

The night was soft and fragrant around them. Warm. No sounds from inside. Had Agatha and the young girl gone to bed?

A wave of weariness washed over Erin. She picked up the baby monitor. 'I think I'll go to bed now. It's been a long day.'

As she was turning to go, Ajax said, 'Thank you for trusting me enough to come with me.'

Erin stopped. She hadn't even considered that she'd trusted him enough to let him derail their lives within hours. Yet she had. More or less without question. She felt exposed now, even though she knew that all his reasons for leaving New York were very valid and compelling.

She faced Ajax. 'How long do you think we'll have to stay here?'

'A few weeks at least.'

Even though she'd cleared the absence with her boss, and she was still only part-time, she hoped for a more permanent position as Ashling got older. She didn't want to push the firm's generosity.

'If it's any longer than that I'll have to clear it with work.'

'I'm sure something else will have materialised in the news by then, and the vultures will have moved on. By the time you return to New York they'll no longer be interested.'

Erin was about to turn away again when Ajax spoke again.

'But I think there is something that we can do to nip any further speculation in the bud for good.'

'What's that?' she asked.

Erin already knew she wasn't going to like his answer.

'Appear together.'

'As in...where? How?'

'In public. As if we're a couple.'

CHAPTER FIVE

AJAX KNEW HE should be feeling mildly insulted at the look of abject horror on Erin's face, but then he was becoming used to her reactions around him being the opposite of what he might have expected with other women.

She looked tired. His conscience struck. He remembered what it was like with a baby. He'd done a lot of the waking at night when Theo was small. Those had been some of his favourite moments, just him and Theo in the dark, walking up and down while the world slept. Those huge eyes on him, as if he held all the secrets of the universe. And yet he hadn't been able to keep him safe...

Suddenly he felt as if Erin could see all the way down inside him, to where his guts hadn't stopped churning ever since he'd found out about the baby. *Ashling.* His daughter. The thought of holding her and looking into her eyes made him feel clammy with something he didn't want to name.

He said, 'You know what? Let's leave it till the morning. It has been a long day and I'm keeping you up.'

'I'd prefer to know what you mean now.'

Ajax cursed himself. He should have kept his mouth shut. He'd been trying not to notice Erin too much all evening, but it was impossible.

She couldn't be dressed any more plainly—a shirt-dress and bare legs, sandals... Patently little make-up. Her hair slightly messy and rough from drying naturally. And yet she couldn't have been more alluring. Her eyes were huge. Golden-brown. Serious. But when she smiled…her whole face lit up.

Not that he'd given her much cause to smile since they'd met again.

Since he'd discovered his secret daughter.

A spark of anger helped him to focus on what he had to say and not on her. For a moment, at least. Although what he was about to propose was going to throw him all the way into the fire unless he exerted every ounce of control.

He said, 'I had a meeting with my PR team on the way over here. They pointed out that if we're photographed together to coincide with this news of a baby, then it'll take some of the heat out of the press interest. But if we're not seen together they'll dig and dig until they know everything there is to know about you.'

'What about you?'

Ajax shrugged. 'They already know everything about me. You're the unknown quantity. Being seen with me will protect you to a degree. There's little for them to get excited about if it looks like we're together after having a baby. We can spin it that we managed to keep it a secret.'

Erin looked suspicious. 'Can't we just hide away here and then go home in a few weeks, when it's all died down?'

The fact that she didn't want to be seen with him shouldn't be pricking Ajax's ego the way it was. She was right to want to protect herself from scrutiny. He'd been used to it all his life. From the moment he and his brother had been born they'd been watched and judged.

'I know what I'm asking—for you to put yourself under the spotlight—and it might seem contradictory, but by doing that just for a short time I do believe it'll have the desired effect of taking the heat out of speculation and rumour. Then we can release a statement saying we're no longer together.

Although I will obviously always ensure that you and Ashling are protected.'

Erin sounded suspicious, 'When you say "a short time"… what does that mean?'

'While we're here in Greece. If you agree, we'll attend a few events.'

'What's "a few"?'

'Two or three in public…one with my family…'

Ajax was very aware of not letting his gaze drop to her bare shapely legs. He had a vivid flashback to pushing those legs apart—

No! The woman in front of him was the one woman on the planet he could not touch again. Things were already complicated enough. She was the mother of his child and he had no intention of playing happy families again. Under no circumstances.

He would take the heat out of the press's interest in Erin and Ashling and then they would get back to their own lives. He wouldn't abandon his daughter; she would be provided for as long as she needed it. And, as he'd told Erin, he would make sure they were protected. But he would not pretend that he could be a hands-on father again.

'Is it okay if I let you know in the morning?'

Ajax looked at Erin, his head still full of unwelcome thoughts. He nodded quickly. 'Of course—it's your decision.'

'Night, then.'

'Goodnight, Erin.'

He watched her leave, with the understated elegance that had caught his eye the moment he'd seen her. Then he cursed and turned around, placing his wine glass down on the wall. It was a wonder he hadn't snapped the delicate stem, he was so tense.

Bringing her and the baby here to this villa had been a bad idea. It was too full of memories of what he'd once wished for. Something that had been snatched from his grasp. The chance of a family—even with a wife who had been in name only.

Ajax hadn't ever expected anything more with Sofia. But he'd wanted to create a family with Theo. Do it differently. Be a proper father. Not treat his child as a pawn, to be moved around for the benefit of the family name and business.

The thought of actually fostering a relationship with his son had been audacious, because it was so alien to what he'd grown up with. No affection, no tactility. Tight, cold expressions. No love. The almost unbearable weight of a legacy so embedded in Greek society and lore that Ajax and his brother's lives had been mapped out before birth.

Clearly by buying this villa and making his dreams for a different existence concrete he'd angered the gods.

Ajax smiled mirthlessly.

He didn't believe in the gods, even if some people joked that his family line was so old they were descended from them. But he did believe in not being foolish enough to think that he could try again. Erin, and Ashling would be better off with him at a distance. The sooner the news interest died down and they could get back back to their lives in New York, under the radar, the better.

Ashling was already down for her mid-morning nap by the time Erin saw Ajax again. She was having a coffee on the terrace, with the baby monitor beside her. She'd been up with Ashling since dawn and she was tired because she hadn't slept well.

She'd taken in a lot of information the previous evening. All that stuff about the reality of Ajax's marriage and the fact that his son was really his nephew.

She'd also Googled herself and Ajax and what she'd seen had made her blood run cold. Lots of speculation as to who she was and how they had eluded the press before now. Questions asking were they together, and if not, why not?

She'd had to grudgingly admit that Ajax and his PR team were probably right. Give the media a little of what they wanted to see and the heat would die down.

A sound made her look up. *Ajax.* The object of far too many of her thoughts. He was dressed formally, in dark trousers and a white shirt...top button open. He looked fresh and vital, and not as if he'd spent a sleepless night. She wanted to scowl, but she forced a smile and ignored her pulse tripping.

'Morning.'

He looked at his watch. 'Almost afternoon.' Then he looked back at her. He noted the baby monitor. 'Napping?'

Erin nodded. 'She woke at dawn, so we had breakfast and explored the gardens a little.' Erin hesitated for a moment and then said, 'She's almost walking. Any day now.'

Ajax's expression didn't change, but it was as if he was consciously not allowing any titbit about his daughter to impinge upon him. 'That's good. There's lots of space for her to experiment here and not get hurt.'

'Yes, it's a big change from our apartment and the small park two blocks away. We could get used to this.' Erin had only been joking, but the minute the words came out she wanted to swallow them back. She said, 'I didn't mean that the way it sounded.'

Ajax waved a hand and came over to sit down, helping himself to a cup of coffee. A little dryly he said, 'I think you've proved that you're not bent on fleecing me of my fortune.'

'I wouldn't know where to start,' Erin admitted. She shrugged. 'I wasn't brought up to value money like that. We had enough to get by. I got a good education, went to university...that was enough.'

'You and your father?'

Erin nodded. 'As I said, my mother left when I was small.'

'You said you were a toddler?'

Surprised he'd remembered, she said, 'Pretty much, I'd just turned three.'

'But she supported you?'

'She sent an allowance that I put into a savings account. I wasn't going to touch it…but then when I got pregnant…'

'Your father is a professor?'

'Yes, of mathematics. His head is always in the clouds obsessing over formulas and problems to be solved.' Erin was smiling at the thought of her absent-minded father.

'You have a good relationship?'

She nodded. 'I adore him. It was just us. He was a good father, in his own scatty way. I was probably responsible ahead of my time, but I knew I was loved.'

Ajax shook his head. 'That's something rare in my world. Rarer than rare. A myth.'

Erin tried not to show how curious she was. 'Your parents…they weren't loving?'

Ajax let out a curt laugh. 'Loving? No. I don't think they even know the meaning of the word. Their marriage was arranged, and my parents have never pretended it was anything more. They've conducted discreet affairs on the side for as long as I can remember. My brother and I were brought up by nannies until we went to school—first in the UK and then in Switzerland as I mentioned. We hardly saw them, and yet our lives were beholden to their wish for us to follow the same path they had. A path of loyalty and dedication to a legacy that has become a massive global industry.'

'Didn't you ever want to do something else?'

'That was never really an option—and especially not after Demetriou died.'

'It doesn't sound like you're all that happy about it.'

Ajax's jaw clenched. 'I don't have the luxury of choice.

Thousands depend on me for their livelihoods now. The company—as you know—has been restructured to give me more control.'

'Surely that's the opposite of what you really want?'

'It means my life is my own now. No one can put pressure on me to marry, or have heirs, or run the business by committee.'

'You have an heir. Ashling,' Erin pointed out, struck again by how adamant he was about not having another family. Or remarrying.

For a second Erin felt a jolt, thinking of him changing his mind some day and marrying someone else. She pushed it down. It shouldn't concern her. Their connection had been purely physical. At one point she'd felt as if her emotions were involved, but she'd convinced herself otherwise by now.

Ajax shook his head. 'I wouldn't let her get within a hundred miles of this business.'

'She might be interested.'

'If there's one thing I can do for her, it'll be to allow her to live her life under no pressure from me or this family. She'll have choices I never had.'

'Is that what you'd planned for Theo?'

Abruptly Ajax looked at his watch and said, 'Sorry to be rude, but I have to take a call. Did you think about what we spoke of last night?'

She'd touched a nerve, mentioning Theo, obviously. But she could understand why. She said, 'Yes, I did, and I think you're right. If we're seen together it'll cause some interest, but once they know how essentially boring I am it'll die down.'

Ajax frowned. 'You're not boring—far from it.'

Erin felt hot, and it wasn't from the sun. 'I don't usually behave in such a spontaneous manner...jumping into bed with people I hardly know.'

Not to mention making love in elevators.

'Neither do I.'

For a second, the air was charged. Erin was trapped in that blue-green gaze, and couldn't look away. He looked down, and her breath caught. Her breasts felt heavy, her nipples tightening under her thin top. A very plain thin top that suddenly felt invisible.

He looked back up again and Erin sucked in air. She felt as if he'd touched her. Just with his eyes. And yet she must have imagined the whole moment, mortifyingly, because he was looking at her with no discernible expression.

She tried to recall what they'd been talking about. Appearing with him in public…

'So…yes. Okay, I'll do what you suggested. Go out with you.' Heat climbed into her face. She sounded like a teenager.

'Okay. Good.' Ajax was brisk, further making Erin feel as if she'd conjured up that hot little moment. 'You'll come to Athens with me at the end of the week. We'll attend an event on Friday.'

'What about Ashling?'

'She'll come too.'

'But who'll look after her? It's only ever been me or my father or the crèche.'

'We'll hire a nanny.'

'Like the ones you had?' Erin knew that wasn't fair, but suddenly she had visions of a woman in uniform looking at Ashling disapprovingly.

A shadow crossed Ajax's face. 'No. Not like that. Agatha has family in Athens. I can ask her if she knows someone.'

Erin's fears subsided. She liked the woman—she was normal. Maternal. 'Okay, that sounds good. I trust her.'

'You only just met her.' He looked at her curiously.

Erin looked back at him. 'I'm a pretty good judge of character and she's kind.'

Before Erin could consider the fact that she was more or less telling Ajax that she'd judged his character and liked it enough to jump into bed with him—twice—she thought of something else.

'Is the event going to be very fancy?'

'It'll be black-tie.'

'I don't have anything formal with me.'

Ajax waved a hand. 'Don't worry about that. I'll have a stylist put together some choices.'

'I… Okay.'

Erin could hardly protest. And it wasn't as if she was going with him for romantic reasons. It was practically a job. Maybe if she looked at it like that it wouldn't feel so loaded?

At that moment there was a squawk from the baby monitor. Ashling was waking up. Erin stood up, glad her legs stayed steady. 'I should go. She'll be hungry for lunch.'

Ajax didn't say anything, but Erin felt his eyes on her back and wished she was wearing something more exciting than her thin top and linen trousers. She usually prided herself on feeling pretty well put-together, but under Ajax's gaze she felt dishevelled. Unkempt.

The prospect of him seeing her in something other than casual or work clothes made her heart beat far too fast. She had to remember that these public appearances were purely a means to an end. An end where their lives parted again so he could carry on not engaging with fatherhood and she could continue being a single parent.

A few days later, being driven through the streets of Athens after the relative idyllic peace of the island was a little jarring, but Ashling was fascinated, staring out through the windows in the back of the car as if she'd never seen buildings before.

Erin felt a pang of regret that she hadn't made more of an effort to tell Ajax about his daughter before.

The man in question turned to her from where he sat in the front passenger seat. 'Not long now.'

Erin forced a smile, but her gut was churning at the thought of what was ahead. She'd always been on the periphery of worlds like this—in the background, doing the paperwork for titans of industry. Not front and centre under the spotlight.

They were headed to Ajax's villa, in the hills overlooking the ancient city. The Acropolis came into view, high on its own hill in the distance. It humbled her. Yet another reminder of Ashling's ancestry.

Athens was teeming with people—tourists and locals. They'd passed through majestic Syntagma Square, and Erin had caught glimpses of the narrow, cobbled streets of the Plaka area. It was a beguiling city even as it baked under the sun.

But soon they were climbing up out of the city and into the hills. It became greener. The car stopped outside ornate gates that had appeared as if from nowhere, and a security guard in uniform opened up to let them in.

The driveway was long and winding, uphill, bordered by lush bushes until it opened out into a large courtyard area, revealing a sleek and modern split-level house. Sunlight glinted off the massive windows. It was in stark contrast to the more traditional villa on the island, but Erin liked it.

An attractive woman with glossy brown hair tied back into a ponytail, dressed in black trousers and a short-sleeved shirt, met them at the door. Ajax introduced her as his house manager, Marta. The woman was friendly, but serious…

efficient. Clearly here in Athens things ran on a different schedule.

Then a younger woman appeared, pretty and shy, but smiling. She looked familiar, and it became clear why when Ajax said, 'This is Damia—Agatha's great-niece. She's going to help us with Ashling. She's studying English at college, and has plenty of experience in looking after babies as she has four younger brothers and sisters.'

Erin smiled at her and the girl immediately connected with Ashling, who smiled too, showing her emerging teeth. Erin felt a sharp pain near her heart to see how Ajax resolutely kept his gaze off his daughter.

Damia offered to take Ashling at once, so that Ajax could show Erin around. The little girl went happily, and Erin was simultaneously proud of how content she was and also piqued that she wasn't more clingy. But she knew to take advantage of these moments.

The villa was as sleek and modern on the inside as outside, but Erin was heartened to see that baby-proofing had already been undertaken, with the sharp corners of tables softened with pads. And the open-plan nature meant that Ashling would be able to roam pretty freely.

The living space, decorated with comfortable couches and chairs and coffee tables covered in glossy hardbacks, flowed into a formal dining space. Huge glass doors opened out directly onto a patio, which led to a pristine lawn sloping gently downwards to a row of trees behind which, Ajax told Erin, was a swimming pool and changing rooms.

The air was scented by the abundant flowers blooming on the edges of the garden. Erin wistfully thought of her father, who would immediately lose himself in identifying these exotic plants—a hobby of his.

Around to one side of the patio Erin gasped at the view of Athens laid out before them. The Acropolis looked like a toy replica in the distance. It was almost possible to make out the hundreds of people clambering over it like tiny ants. There were no skyscrapers or modern structures to ruin the view from this angle. It was truly impressive.

Back in the villa, she saw a baby gate had been installed on the stairs, ruining the architectural lines somewhat, but very necessary for a curious baby on the cusp of walking, who would soon be able to tackle stairs quicker than a flash of lightning.

As Ajax led her up to the second level Erin gestured to the temporary addition and said, 'Thank you for this.'

Ajax commented, 'I remember how it is.'

Erin followed him silently. He might not want to engage with his daughter, but he was already proving that he wasn't completely oblivious by taking such care over her safety.

Upstairs was elegant, with plush carpets and elegant minimal furnishings. Doors led off a long corridor and Ajax opened one for Erin. She walked in and could hardly take in the scale of the room, it was so huge.

The bedroom, with a bed big enough for a football team, had two doors leading into an adjoining walk-in dressing room and then a bathroom that more resembled a spa. There was even a massage bed.

Yet another door Ajax had just opened led into a smaller anteroom which had been turned into a nursery, decorated with whimsical murals on the walls of dogs and bunnies and birds. Something struck her. Maybe…

She looked at him, but he seemed to read her mind and shook his head.

His voice was clipped. 'No, this wasn't Theo's. His and Sofia's rooms were elsewhere.'

One of the other doors they'd passed? She forced her mind away from speculating and took in the bright decor and the doors leading out to the wide balcony that ran outside the main bedroom too.

There was a cot and a changing table. A chest of drawers full of clothes from an exclusive French children's label.

She looked at Ajax. 'You didn't have to do this. She'll have outgrown most of these within a few weeks.'

'I wanted to make sure you have all you need.' He pointed to a door on the other side of the room. 'That leads into Damia's room, so she'll be right beside Ashling when we're out.'

When we're out.

As if they were a couple. But of course they were nothing like a couple. Couldn't be further from a couple. And that made her feel bereft—which was something she never would have expected.

Having a baby had changed her. She now knew that deep down she hungered for companionship, and that she'd never put her career over that. Erin wasn't like her mother.

What about love? whispered a voice.

No, not love. Love had the potential to betray and destroy. Erin was realistic enough to hope for something that didn't have the power to wreck a life…a family. Since Ashling's birth she'd realised that some day maybe a family would be nice, with a partner she could like and respect. Trust. Companionship. Not the loneliness of her father's existence. She'd always longed for brothers and sisters—she'd like that for Ashling.

But that dream was shattering before it had even fully taken root. And it wasn't even Ajax's fault. He'd never promised anything. He'd never led her on. They'd had two hot nights when they'd connected with maximum physicality and minimum emotionality.

And yet here they were now, connected for a lifetime and having to navigate emotional territory that he obviously didn't welcome.

The sooner they got through these social events and defused the press interest, the sooner she and Ashling could get on with their lives. But a sobering realisation made her go cold. Their lives would never be their own again, no matter what happened. Ashling was the daughter of a billionaire and the whole world knew it. Ajax had even alluded to the fact that they may need security.

Feeling unsettled, she said to Ajax, 'Speaking of going out…the first event is tomorrow?'

Ajax nodded. 'Yes, in the evening.'

Erin's belly lurched. Being in this billionaire's world was suddenly all too real. She tried to hide her trepidation.

Ajax said, 'I've arranged for a stylist to come today, with a selection of outfits for you to choose from.'

Her belly was churning now. 'I know how to dress for work events—not high society. What if I wear the wrong type of dress?'

'Georgiana is very experienced. She'll know exactly what you need to wear.'

Erin couldn't help wondering if this *Georgiana* had dressed other women for Ajax. His wife? Even if he hadn't loved her, they'd have had to feel some affection for each other? Shared a bed at least?

'I…' What could she say? She'd agreed to this. 'Okay.'

'A statement will be put out by my PR team in advance of the event. That will hopefully nip most of the speculation in the bud.'

'I'd like to see it beforehand.'

Ajax arched a brow. 'To make sure it's legally acceptable?'

'Of course.' Erin couldn't stop her professional instincts from kicking in, even though she was fairly certain Ajax's team would be going out of their way to ensure the statement held no hint of a more permanent relationship in the near future.

'I'll have my assistant send you the draft copy.'

'Thank you.' Erin felt stiff and formal. The space was suddenly too small around her, as if all the air was being sucked out of the room. Ajax seemed huge. A solid wall of muscle.

'I should go and check on Ashling...she'll be getting hungry.'

Ajax looked at his watch. 'I have to go into my offices for a few hours. Go ahead and eat later without me. I'll find Damia for you and send her up.'

He left.

Erin went straight to the French doors and opened them, sucking in a lungful of air. Had she made a huge mistake in agreeing to go along with Ajax's plan for them to be seen out together? That last exchange had been as chaste and civil as any conversation between two colleagues. He hadn't even touched her. And yet her skin was prickling all over, tight and sensitised.

It was so humiliating to still be attracted to the guy when he'd moved on so long ago...

'Miss Murphy?'

Erin whirled around to see Damia in the doorway, holding Ashling, who immediately put her arms out for her mother. She pushed all thoughts of Ajax and the future and how he made her feel out of her head and focused on her baby.

She smiled at the young woman. 'Please, call me Erin.'

CHAPTER SIX

THE FOLLOWING EVENING, Ajax stood at the bedroom door, where it was open just a crack. He felt like a voyeur, but he couldn't move a muscle. He was frozen at the vision of Erin, standing in front of the mirror, looking as stunned as he felt.

He'd always known she possessed an understated kind of beauty—the kind that mocked you for not noticing it at first. But now there was nothing understated about her... she was breathtaking.

She wore a strapless floor-length dress. Black. Its structured bodice-style design pushed her breasts up and cinched in her waist, and then the dress fell in soft silken folds to the floor.

Her skin looked very pale. She wore no jewellery apart from an elaborate diamond necklace and a matching cocktail ring. Luxuriant long black lashes framed smoky eyes. Blusher highlighted cheekbones so high and defined they could cut glass, and a nude gloss on her lips made them seem plump and provocative.

As if she was asking to be kissed.

Ajax was finding it hard to remember why that would be a bad idea.

Georgiana was talking to her. 'Your short hair really sets the look off. What made you decide to cut it?'

Erin replied, 'The baby...she kept tugging on it.'

Ajax tried not to let that image get to him, but it was

hard. He remembered Theo pulling on Sofia's hair, and himself lifting him out of her arms when she got irritated. He couldn't imagine Erin getting irritated…

Georgiana said, 'Most women wouldn't get away with it but with your bone structure…'

Ajax could see that Erin was self-conscious, embarrassed by the praise. Again, not like Sofia, nor any of the women he was used to. They were born confident, expecting compliments, reveling in them. Erin looked as if she wanted the ground to swallow her whole.

Erin smiled at the stylist. 'Thank you for your help. I wouldn't have had a clue where to start.'

Georgiana winked. 'That's what I get paid the big bucks for.'

Ajax was about to knock on the door to announce his presence when Erin asked, 'Did you…er…work with Mr Nikolau's wife?'

'Sofia?'

Erin nodded. Georgiana shook her head, 'No, Sofia had her own ideas about style. She favoured a more modern aesthetic.'

That was a diplomatic understatement, thought Ajax. The two women couldn't have been more different. Sofia could have danced naked in front of him and he'd have felt nothing. Erin, on the other hand…

He slammed a lid on the surge of fire in his blood.

He knocked on the door and opened it, still not prepared when Erin turned around and his gaze met hers, gold and tawny. He was wearing a classic black tuxedo and he saw how her gaze swept down and up again, how a little flare of colour came into her cheeks.

He gritted his jaw.

Ajax forced himself to look at the stylist. 'Thank you, Georgiana.'

'My pleasure, Ajax. I'll be back when you need me again.'

Georgiana handed Erin a sleek black clutch bag and said, 'Good luck this evening—not that you'll need it. You're going to knock everyone out.'

Ajax was soon standing in front of Erin. She looked nervous.

'Is it…? Am I okay?'

He might not have believed it if he hadn't known better. He wanted to turn her around and put her in front of the mirror again. Say, *How can you not see how beautiful you are?* But he was genuinely afraid he might not be able to stop himself from tearing down that zip and undoing the exquisite picture she made.

Instead, he just said, 'You look…beautiful.'

'I feel strange. This isn't really me.'

'It is…for now.'

Until they were done with this charade and living separate lives again.

He said, 'My driver is waiting…we should go.'

As they walked downstairs, Erin tried to steady herself after seeing Ajax in his tuxedo. He oozed sophistication, but with an edge of sexy, brooding darkness that made her a little weak.

She wondered what he'd meant when he'd said *for now.* Did he mean just for this period of time, while they were acting out this charade of togetherness? And then, like Cinderella, she'd go back to her much less glamorous reality? She felt that was what he'd meant.

But Cinderella got her prince in the end.

Erin shook her head mentally. She'd never believed in fairy tales and she wasn't about to start.

In the hall, he asked, 'Do you need to see Ashling?'

Erin shook her head. 'Damia is feeding her, and then she'll

bath her and put her down. It's probably best for me to go without drawing attention to the fact.'

'If we need to return at all we can, so don't worry about that.'

The little clutch of anxiety in Erin's chest eased. 'I think she'll be fine, but thank you.'

Ajax let her precede him out through the front door and Erin still felt wobbly in the delicate high heels. Her bare upper back prickled, as if she could feel Ajax's gaze on her.

The driver was holding the car door open. She got in, feeling awkward in the dress and shoes.

Ajax got in on the other side. The car moved down the hill and into the streets of Athens. It was early evening and the sun was starting to set, bathing everything in a golden glow. Tourists strolled easily, choosing somewhere to eat among the tables spilling onto the streets from cafés and restaurants. There was a youthful, vibrant atmosphere, a contrast against the ancient backdrop.

The car wound through the streets and then back up into the hills again. They joined a queue of cars entering gates like Ajax's villa's gates. Erin wondered if they'd gone in a big circle...

Ajax said, 'This is the Parnassus villa. Leo and Angel Parnassus are hosting their annual event to raise funds for charity.'

Erin had vaguely heard of Angel Parnassus. 'Isn't she a jewellery designer?'

Ajax nodded. 'Yes—very successful.'

'And Leo is...?'

'Like me, a Greek, who grew up mainly in America. We go back a long way. He returned here permanently some years ago, to take over the family business.'

'You lived in Greece while you were married?'

Ajax nodded, 'Yes, but America is my home now.'

He didn't elaborate. Erin speculated that perhaps the long distance from here made it easier for him to deal with the loss of his son.

They were at the top of the drive now, and the villa opened out before them. It was of a more traditional design than Ajax's. Vast, impressive.

They got out at the bottom of the steps leading up to the front door. Ajax took her by the elbow and Erin resisted the urge to pull away for fear he'd see how he affected her.

The sounds of soft jazz could be heard, and as they entered the hall behind other guests, a tall man broke away from a group of people and came over, a broad smile on his handsome face.

'Ajax! Please tell me you've decided to stop pretending you prefer Manhattan to Athens and are coming home.'

The men hugged each other warmly.

Ajax said, 'No chance.'

The man looked at her and Erin felt self-conscious.

Ajax said, 'Leo, this is Erin Murphy.'

Leo put out a hand. 'Erin, welcome to my home. And congratulations on your daughter. Our youngest is three, but maybe they'll play together some day.'

Erin couldn't help but smile at his effusive greeting. 'Thank you. I'm sure she'd love that. She's not walking yet, but any day now, I think.'

Leo made a face. 'Once they're on their feet you need eyes in the back and both sides of your head.'

Erin laughed. 'She's already crawling at the speed of light, so I know what you mean.'

She glanced at Ajax and saw he was looking at her with a transfixed expression on his face. Erin blushed.

A woman—stunningly pretty, in a white strapless column of a dress, with her dark hair pulled up into a classic chignon—came and joined them, sliding her arm through

Leo's. She must be Angel. Her husband looked down at her, and his look was so full of hunger and love and tenderness that Erin felt like a voyeur. She'd never seen a man look at a woman like that…

After greeting Ajax with a kiss, the woman put out her hand to Erin. 'I'm Angel…so nice that you could come.'

Erin shook it. She noticed Angel's jewellery—a necklace of tiny diamonds strung on several interlocking delicate silver chains. She asked shyly, 'Is that one of your designs?'

Angel touched it and looked pleased. 'Yes, a new one I'm trying out. Do you like it?'

'It's lovely.'

Angel transferred her arm from her husband's to Erin's and led her away, saying, 'Then you must come with me, because these two wouldn't know how to appreciate art and design if it jumped up and—'

Leo protested. 'Hey, I've improved a lot.'

Erin let herself be led away by her hostess, charmed by her easy warmth and friendliness. They went into a huge room—a ballroom with gilt mirrors set into panelled walls and chandeliers hanging from an ornately decorated ceiling. Candles flickered from tall tables, imbuing everything and everyone with a glow.

Angel handed her a glass of champagne and said, 'A word of warning: be on your guard. I'm afraid that high society in Athens can be a little…cut-throat, and you've arrived on the scene with the biggest ace up your sleeve.'

Erin looked at her. 'What do you mean?'

'Ajax's baby. A baby no one expected him to have after… Well, you know.' Angel took Erin's hand and squeezed it gently. 'But I'm glad. He deserves to be happy. Theo showed him it was possible, but then it got snatched away.'

Someone approached Angel from the other side of the room and spoke into her ear.

She grimaced at Erin. 'Look, I have to run—but please, make yourself at home.'

She walked away, leaving Erin in the middle of the room alone. She looked around for Ajax, but couldn't see him straight away. As she turned she saw people stopping and looking at her. Whispering. Making little effort to hide their interest. She could see some of it was benign. But most of it was suspicious. Hostile. What had Angel said? *Cut-throat.*

Her hand gripped the glass of wine she held and suddenly she felt too hot. She walked towards the open doors that led out to a wide patio, where she could see more people milling around.

As she walked through the room she heard the whispers.

'She's some sort of ambulance-chaser lawyer...'

'She's not related to anyone...'

'She did it on purpose to trap him...'

'He's not going to marry her...'

Erin all but stumbled out through the open doors, and for a moment she was tipping forward perilously in thin air. Then a hand wrapped around her arm, steadying her. She recognised the familiar sizzle in her blood and looked up.

'Perfect timing,' she said. 'I'm sure they would have loved to see me go splat on my face.'

Ajax led her towards a low stone wall, beyond which stretched stunning gardens and a panoramic view of Athens laid out before them.

He asked, 'What do you mean?'

Erin took a sip of wine and nodded her head towards the room full of people. 'Well, according to some I'm an ambulance-chaser, and I'm not related to anyone important, and—oh, you'll probably like this one—they don't think you'll marry me, so you're definitely off the hook there.'

Erin raised her glass in a mocking salute.

'I'm sorry. I didn't mean for you to be left alone.'

'It's fine. I was with Angel, but she was called away.'

Ajax's jaw clenched. 'This is why I don't like to live here full-time.'

'I guess Athens is a small enough city when it comes to this kind of thing.'

'Exactly.' He turned to her. 'By the way, the statement has dropped.'

Erin looked at him. 'The statement?'

'About us. To the press.'

The man addled her brain when he was close. No wonder these people thought she was just an ambulance-chaser.

She'd looked over the statement earlier and approved it.

Ajax Nikolau and Erin Murphy would like to announce that they have a daughter and are together. They ask for their privacy to be respected.

It couldn't have been more succint.

Erin nodded. 'The statement... Yes.'

She looked up at Ajax again and her eyes widened. Had he moved closer, or had she? Even though they were outside, it felt as if she couldn't draw in enough oxygen.

'Considering the fact that almost everyone here is now looking at us,' he said, 'it might be a good moment to reinforce that statement with a display.'

'A display...?'

But Erin's words dissolved in her mouth as Ajax's fingers tipped her chin up a little, and then his head was lowering and his mouth covered hers in a light kiss. A light kiss that burned her all the way through to her core.

She wanted to lean into him, absorb his strength and heat, feel that heat surrounding her and his big hands moving over her. For a moment she was sure he wanted to deepen the kiss. His other hand was on her waist and she felt him tighten it, but then he pulled back abruptly and Erin opened her eyes to see him watching her.

A wave of mortification washed through her body. She was exposing herself spectacularly, but he seemed completely unmoved.

He took her hand and led her down the patio towards another door. They were going back inside to the ballroom.

Erin took her hand from his when they were among the throng again. He glanced at her, but she pretended not to notice.

'What is it, Erin?'

That sense of exposure was still prickling over her skin. 'I'd like it if you warned me in advance of any…touching or kissing.' She knew she sounded unbearably priggish, but the way she'd wanted to cleave to him at the first touch of his mouth to hers was terrifying.

'Can you consider it a warning if I say now that we may have to indulge in spontaneous shows of affection if I deem it an opportune moment? I may not have time to ask the question.'

Now Erin was sorry she'd said anything. Next he'd be asking if she wanted to draw up a contract, laying out the terms and conditions for these public displays of affection.

She still wouldn't look at him. 'It's fine. Forget I said anything. I just wasn't expecting it…'

'Erin, look at me. Please.'

Reluctantly she did so, vaguely aware that a charity auction was starting. She resolutely didn't look at Ajax's mouth.

'You're right. I shouldn't have just assumed it would be okay to kiss you like that. Please know that I would never want to do anything to make you uncomfortable, so if you'd prefer we didn't touch at all—'

That suggestion sent a shard of panic down to Erin's gut. 'No… Look, I'm overreacting. Forget I said anything. It's fine.' In a bid to defuse the tension she'd created, she asked, 'What's the charity in aid of?'

'It fights against domestic abuse. It's a cause very personal to Leo and Angel.'

Erin looked at him and he said, 'I don't know the details—I don't think anyone does—but I believe that Angel's father was...violent.'

Erin went cold at the thought. 'That's awful.'

Leo and Angel were up on a dais, urging the crowd on to make bigger bids for different lots. There was a lot of raucous cheering and laughter as people vied with each other.

The next lot flashed up on the screen behind Angel and Leo: a romantic dinner for two at one of Athens' most exclusive rooftop restaurants.

To Erin's shock, Ajax put his hand up, and a friendly bidding war broke out between him and a couple of others.

It was soon whittled down to just two, and the price rose and rose beyond anything that might be considered acceptable for a dinner for two. Erin kept waiting for Ajax to bow out—it was getting ridiculous—but he seemed determined. Finally, when the price was eye-wateringly high, the other bidder faded away and Leo Parnassus brought the gavel down on Ajax's bid.

Ajax turned to Erin and took her hand. He lifted it up, gave her a subtle look, as if in question, and she nodded barely perceptibly. Her heart was racing. He pressed a kiss to the back of her hand, causing a flurry of whispers and sighs. More whispers than sighs.

Erin's face burned. Because even though she knew it was all for show, and entirely cynical, the imprint of Ajax's mouth on her hand was like a brand, and she knew that somewhere deep down she wished that this was a real romantic gesture.

So sure your emotions aren't involved? asked a little voice.

That incendiary thought made her pull her hand free. She didn't look at Ajax—she didn't want to see his expression.

The auction had ended and the crowd were milling around again.

Erin thought of something. 'I got the signed contract back.'

Ajax looked at her. 'I have signed over full custody to you.'

'I saw that.'

Erin felt only a flat kind of acceptance. It would have been strange if he'd had a sudden change of heart, and the last thing she or Ashling needed was someone not being consistent. But still... It was confirmation of his intention to have very little to do with his daughter.

Erin reminded herself that it was absolutely necessary to set out these boundaries. Her own mother had used to just appear at random times and stay for a day or two, making Erin hope and wish that she was coming back for good, only to disappear again. As she'd grown older she'd refused to see her mother on those visits, needing to protect herself from the inevitable disappointment and her resentment at being squeezed into the space between two conferences when she happened to be in town.

Erin said now, 'It can be renegotiated at a later stage if you want to make any changes. Maybe when she's older you'll feel differently.'

Someone jostled Erin from behind and she fell forward into Ajax's chest. He caught her to him with his hands on her bare arms. They were pressed together, chest to chest. She could feel his heart. Or was it hers, pounding too hard?

He looked down at her, and for a moment she thought he was going to kiss her again, but he said, 'I won't want to make any changes.'

The haze of desire in Erin's head cleared. She pulled back, steadied herself, and for the rest of the evening kept a rictus smile on her face. Thankfully Ajax kept their physical contact to a minimum from then on, just hand-holding or lightly touching her back.

She had to nip this seed of hope in the bud. The seed of hope that somehow he'd change and realise that of *course* he wanted a meaningful relationship with his daughter. She'd learnt a harsh lesson from her mother, and she couldn't afford to forget it now.

A few days later, Ajax was looking out through the window of his home office. Laid out before him was the back garden, with Athens in the distance. But he could only see the little tableau unfolding on the lawn.

Erin, Damia and Ashling and much excitement. Ashling had just taken her first steps. Erin appeared to be crying and video calling someone—Ajax guessed it had to be her father—and Damia was holding Ashling. She let her go and the little girl wobbled on two sturdy legs towards her mother as Erin filmed her. Then Erin threw the phone down and caught Ashling to her, standing up and twirling her high in the air.

Ajax could hear their shrieks of delight from here. But it was as if there was a block of ice in his chest. Numbing him. Keeping him safe. At a remove. Memories of Theo's first steps threatened to surface, but Ajax pushed them ruthlessly down.

The pane of glass between him and them was more than a physical thing. Every self-preserving instinct inside him told him to stay far away from this moment, even as another part of him ached to see it.

He could feel his skin getting clammy and his heart starting to pound erratically. Nausea climbed up from his gut. He turned away and walked blindly out of his office and out of the villa, his heart rate only returning to normal as he got further and further away.

* * *

It was early evening, and Erin was standing in front of the mirror again, with Georgiana behind her. She felt completely intimidated by what she was wearing.

'Isn't this a little…too much?'

Georgiana stood back and looked at Erin, almost comically insulted. 'Do you have *any* idea where you are going for dinner? Do you know how impossible it is to get a booking? You have to book years in advance!'

Erin said, 'I feel naked.'

'You look *amazing.*'

Erin found it hard to believe. She was wearing a jumpsuit—dark brown-silk, long harem-style trousers. So far, so respectable. But the top was merely two pieces of fabric, slashed almost to the navel, held up by a clasp behind her neck, leaving her back bare.

Her hair was slicked back. Her eyes looked even bigger than usual, shimmering with gold. A gold bangle encircling one upper arm and chunky gold earrings were the only adornments. She wore gold high-heel sandals.

Georgiana said, 'It's daring, chic and elegant. Every man within a ten-mile radius will want you.'

Erin smiled weakly. One thing was sure: she was making up for all those times she'd stayed in studying when her college mates had been out partying.

There was a knock on the door and Erin's heart nearly jumped out of her chest. Surely Ajax would take one look and be horrified? He didn't strike her as the kind of guy who went out with women who were practically naked from the waist up.

She turned around slowly and steeled herself, barely aware of Georgiana slinking away. There was silence. Ominous. Thick with a tension that Erin remembered from before…in that elevator.

She risked a glance at Ajax, and gulped. His eyes were wide and he was looking her up and down. Her skin tingled. She felt sure he had to be horrified.

He was wearing a black shirt and black trousers. Thick hair swept back. She was glad he wasn't in a tuxedo—she couldn't handle that again.

Erin finally blurted out, 'It's too much, isn't it? I'll change... Georgiana tried a dress before this. I can put that on.'

She'd turned, as if to go back to the dressing room, but Ajax said roughly, 'No, it's fine. You're fine.'

Erin turned around again. 'Are you sure?'

A muscle ticked in his jaw. 'Absolutely. We should go.'

In the back of the car as they drove into Athens, to try and defuse the thick tension in the air, Erin said, 'Ashling started walking just the other day.'

'I know. I saw it.'

'You did?' She was surprised.

He nodded. 'From my office.'

'You should have come out. She was so excited.'

Ajax looked straight ahead, as much to avoid looking at Erin in that provocative outfit as to hide his reaction to that image of watching Ashling walk. He felt a familiar tightening in his chest.

'I couldn't. I had to go into the office.'

Erin sat back. He could almost feel her deflation.

'Wow...' she said eventually. 'You really are determined not to get involved at all.'

He looked at her. 'I told you I'm not doing that again.'

She needed to understand, so that she didn't hope he could be more.

Her golden-brown eyes narrowed on him. 'Have you ever

considered that your reaction could be due to some kind of trauma, brought on by the death of Theo? Like PTSD?'

Ajax knew what that was. He had a good friend who'd been a French Legionnaire and he'd suffered with it. His friend had even opened a clinic to help others. But Ajax had never considered that the death of his child could have brought on something similar. And yet Erin's words resonated somewhere inside him. Touched on a raw place.

Luckily the driver was pulling up outside the restaurant now, and he took advantage of the distraction to avoid answering Erin's unwelcome perceptiveness.

He went around the car to help her out, taking her hand, noting the apprehension in her expression as she stepped out and straightened up. It was a novelty to be with a woman who wasn't used to this world under the glare of the cameras…a hundred of which seemed to go off as they rounded the vehicle and approached the door which led to an elevator that would take them to the rooftop.

Erin's hand tightened in Ajax's and he put an arm around her waist, tugging her into his side. She fitted against him so easily. Security men opened the door and they slipped inside, where a concierge called for the elevator.

Ajax noticed that Erin was trembling slightly. He looked down. She was pale. He cursed softly in Greek.

'I'm sorry,' he said. 'I should have warned you. I'm so used to the paparazzi being everywhere that it doesn't occur to me that you're not.'

Erin was mortified that she was so shaken, but the barrage of lights exploding in their faces had felt almost like a physical assault. How did anyone get used to that level of aggressive interest?

She moved out of Ajax's embrace. 'I'm sorry. I'm fine. I just wasn't expecting it. I didn't even see them.'

'Don't be sorry—it's not your fault. You're reacting as any sane and normal person would.'

Erin sneaked a glance up at him. His jaw was hard. She had an almost irresistible urge to touch him there, get him to soften. As a girlfriend or lover might. But she wasn't either. She curled her hand into a fist just as the elevator arrived.

It was dark inside, with walls covered in murals. It took Erin a second to realise that they were all tiny depictions of people in various sexual poses. She blushed and looked away—only to find her own image sent back to her by the mirrors, fragmented and disjointed. The curve of a shoulder...her bare back...the curve of her buttocks under the silk. There was a scent like leather and wood. Decadent...

To her relief, the doors opened again and she saw a man waiting to escort them through an archway of thick foliage into the restaurant. Ajax put his hand on her elbow. Erin noted that they hadn't even checked who Ajax was—they *knew*.

As did everyone in the restaurant, it seemed, as heads swivelled when they walked past and conversations stopped.

The restaurant itself was enough of a conversation-stopper. At the top of one of Athens' highest buildings, it commanded views over the city taking in everything from the Acropolis all the way down to the port of Piraeus, gateway to the islands.

They were led to a table with arguably the best views, secluded from most of the other diners by lush potted plants. Candles flickered on the table laid with white linen and crystal glasses and gold cutlery. The air was warm and balmy.

Erin's phone vibrated in her clutch and she took it out to see a message from Damia and a picture of Ashling asleep.

All well here. Enjoy dinner!

From the other side of the table Ajax asked, 'Everything okay?'

Erin smiled. 'Fine. Just Damia sending me a picture of Ashling sleeping.'

She almost moved to show it to Ajax, but after that terse exchange in the car she put her phone away, ignoring the pang near her heart.

The waiter arrived with two glasses of champagne. 'Compliments of the manager.'

Erin smiled her thanks and took a small sip. She looked out over the view. 'It's beautiful up here.'

Ajax was unfolding his napkin, looking down.

Erin protested. 'You're not even looking.'

His head came up and his eyes met hers. 'I'm looking.'

Heat curled through Erin's blood. She had to be imagining the intensity in Ajax's gaze. It was so dimly lit up here... He looked away and Erin breathed in.

'You're right—there's a lot I don't notice, that I take for granted.'

'I guess that's not hard to understand when you grew up in a such rarefied world.'

'I can't deny that. I was born into privilege.'

Erin leaned forward, putting her chin on her hand. 'And yet you're not spoiled.'

Ajax frowned and took a sip of wine. 'That's a good thing?'

She nodded. 'You're not entitled or rude or lazy. You don't have to work, but you do. You don't live a life of empty sybaritic pleasure like a lot of rich people.'

He put his glass down. 'Careful or I might think you actually like me.'

Erin blinked. 'I don't *not* like you. We were...intimate. That wouldn't have happened if I hadn't liked you.'

She suddenly realised the truth of that. The fact that he'd

impressed her on lots of levels from the moment she'd seen him. His work ethic. The way he treated people.

She shook her head. 'Why aren't you a spoiled playboy, travelling around the Mediterranean on a yacht?'

He made a face. 'I can't say it ever appealed to me. The thing that was paramount in our family was the respect our name held and the family business. We didn't have time to rebel or zone out.'

The waiter came back and took their orders. Ajax recommended certain Greek specialities to Erin and she happily complied, eager to explore the cuisine.

When the waiter was gone, she said, 'You said you and your brother weren't encouraged to be close?'

A shadow passed over his face for a moment before he responded, 'Yes and no. We were pitted against each other. He was always going to be the first to inherit control of the family business, but I was encouraged to compete with him, as if to keep him on his toes.'

'It's a pity that you weren't just allowed to be brothers.'

'Yes, it is. I did love him…but I felt I never really knew him.'

Their starters arrived—a courgette, peach and sea urchin salad. Erin said, a little regretfully, 'It looks almost too good to eat…'

But then she speared some peach and closed her eyes in appreciation.

When she opened them again Ajax was watching her. Not eating. Erin put down her fork and wiped her mouth with the napkin. 'I'm sorry. I'm probably not meant to really eat it, am I?'

Ajax grinned, and it took Erin's breath away. He looked younger…carefree.

He speared some sea urchin and salad and said, 'Here's

to actually eating food!' And he popped the laden fork in his mouth.

Erin felt lightness bubble up inside her as she took some more of the exquisite salad herself.

It was only after the starter was cleared that she had the nerve to ask a question that had been going around in her head for days.

'Were you ever going to marry and have a family? Or was that just expected of your brother?'

CHAPTER SEVEN

AJAX SAT BACK, his fingers on the stem of his wine glass. He seemed relaxed, but Erin felt the sudden tension. Cursing herself inwardly, she said, 'It's a personal question. You don't have to—'

But he put up a hand. 'You first. What were your plans?'

Erin hadn't been expecting that, but it was only fair. 'All I knew was that I didn't want to be like my father…abandoned and sad. I mean, I was abandoned too, but it was different for me. A parent is one thing…but a partner, a lover… That was devastating for him. He never met anyone else. He was a single parent. It was lonely. I always wanted siblings. But I think I put off thinking about it until I had Ashling, and now I have to think about it.'

'You want a family? For Ashling not to be an only child?' Ajax stated this almost as if it was something outrageous.

Erin looked at him. 'I do. I'd like brothers and sisters for her. And I'd like to meet someone I can spend my life with… I don't want Ashling to be lonely, or to see me be lonely.'

'You surely don't believe in love?' He sounded faintly mocking.

Erin avoided his eye. 'I'm not that naive. In some ways I think perhaps there is some merit in arranged marriages… partnerships.'

So why did that feel like a lie even as she said it?

'You're a good mother.'

Erin risked a glance at him. 'Apart from the fact that I took so long to tell you about your daughter?'

Ajax shook his head and sat forward. 'You were right, I'm not that accessible, and I know how consuming pregnancy and a new baby is. Even though Sofia had an army of nannies on standby from before the baby was even born, she wasn't immune to the stress and change it brought into her life.'

'Did she want to be a mother?'

'It was more that she was *expected* to have an heir. I don't think she and my brother had quite factored in the speed with which she got pregnant, though,' Ajax said. 'Women don't *mother* in our world,' he added. 'They delegate to others.'

Erin smiled wanly. 'We aren't all that different, give or take a few hundred million euros and a dynasty spanning generations.'

The main course arrived, and Erin was surprised. She was genuinely enjoying talking to Ajax. Even about prickly things.

The main course was sea bream with sautéed seafood, house special mayonnaise and baby potatoes roasted in herbs. The food almost distracted Erin enough not to pursue her questioning—but not quite.

She took a sip of wine. 'So now it's your turn. Were you ever planning on marrying and having a family?'

When Erin had looked Ajax up online, after they'd had their brief affair, nothing salacious had come up before his marriage to Sofia. There were pictures of him with stunning women, but no one had appeared with him more than once or twice.

Ajax sat back. 'I can't say that I'd given it much thought. My brother was already on his way to creating the next generation. If I was to have had a family it would have been purely strategic—to get ahead in the business. There were several women from prominent families who would have been suitable, but now, in restructuring the family business,

I've ensured that we're no longer dependent on something as archaic as marriage to foster security or longevity.'

Erin recalled that the future of the company would now be made secure through an independent board of management, under Ajax's control, well out of the hands of family.

'Why was it so important for you to change things?' she asked.

'Because my brother and I had been used as pawns all our lives, purely to carry on the Nikolau legacy. When he died, and I was all but forced into marriage with Sofia to avoid a scandal, I realised just how toxic it was. But really it was Theo who made me see things differently. He reminded me of when I was young and used to see other parents and families...they looked happy in a way I couldn't understand. I didn't want him to have the kind of life I had, brought up and moulded into a good servant of the business and family. He was his own person, and I was determined I wasn't going to force him into anything.'

Erin was touched. 'I think he would have appreciated that.'

Ajax shrugged. 'My grand revelation didn't matter in the end.'

'You changed things anyway,' Erin pointed out. 'You could have left it alone. You could even have walked away.'

Their plates were cleared. Erin declined coffee, but she was told she had to try the baklava—a Middle-Eastern staple and speciality of the restaurant. As expected, it was delicious. Creamy and sweet, encased in delicate filo pastry that melted on her tongue.

'Amazing!'

She put her spoon down and looked up to see Ajax watching her. Immediately her heart sped up. She really wished she could be immune, so they could navigate this temporary faux romance and move on to the time when he would stay on the very periphery of their lives. All she could hope for was that maybe in time he would come to realise what a mistake he was making in choosing not to parent his daughter.

'Ready to go?' he asked.

Erin nodded, suddenly aware that a lot of the people around them had left.

Ajax let her precede him, then put a solicitous hand on her lower back—which would have been fine if her back hadn't been bare. She could feel his fingers against her skin and they burned.

The manager bade them goodnight and waited by the open elevator doors. They stepped in. Was it Erin's imagination or had the space got smaller? Darker…more decadent? The images of couples cavorting in X-rated poses, small enough to trick the eye but impossible not to notice once you knew what they were, seemed to mock her.

The doors closed, encasing them in the dark, moody atmosphere. The elevator slowly moved downwards. Ajax stood on the other side, back against the wall, hands in his pockets. Supremely relaxed. And yet he had the air of an animal about to pounce.

Or was Erin losing it completely after champagne and a little wine? Quite possibly…

'I really enjoyed that dinner. It was delicious… A little overpriced, considering what you paid at the auction, but—'

'Erin.'

She stopped babbling. Ajax took his hand out of his pocket and came towards her, reaching behind her to press a button. The elevator came to a stop. She looked up at him, her mouth going dry.

She moistened her lips. 'What are you doing?'

'Do you have any idea what you've been doing to me all evening in that outfit?'

Erin shook her head, mesmerised by the look on Ajax's face.

'Driving me insane.' He looked down at her chest. 'All I

could think about was sliding my hand under your top and touching you. Feeling the weight of your breast…your nipple growing hard.'

As if on command, Erin's nipples tightened against the material of her jumpsuit. Her breathing was shallow. 'I thought… I didn't think you wanted me like that…'

His gaze moved back up. It was like a beam of heat leaving her skin.

'I haven't stopped wanting you since we were together. I told you that.'

Erin swallowed. 'But that was before you knew…'

He shook his head. 'I still want you. I want to touch you right now. Kiss you.'

Erin had an overwhelming sense of déjà vu…back to another elevator on another continent. But that had been then and this was now. And he still wanted her. And she wanted him. And whatever else was going on suddenly seemed inconsequential.

But a small, sane part of her tried to resist. 'There's no one here to see.'

'I don't want anyone to see.'

Ajax's voice was a throaty growl that resonated deep inside Erin. All the way down to the pulse between her legs, hectically throbbing. Her resistance melted like snow on a hot stone.

'I want you too.'

Ajax moved closer and put his hands either side of her head, on the wall behind her. She could see, out of the corner of her eye, their reflections. His tall, muscular body covering hers.

But then her focus narrowed down to Ajax's mouth as his head lowered and came closer. It covered hers so gently that she wondered if she was imagining it. She reached up and twined her arms around his neck. Suddenly he pressed closer, and the gentle touch turned into something much harder and more incendiary.

Her mouth opened under his, inviting him in, stoking the flames. One of his hands went to her head—she could feel her hair being mussed up—and his other hand splayed across her bare back, before moving around, fingers trailing across her skin, until he found the opening at the front of her top. His hand slipped inside and cupped her breast, thumb flicking against her pebbled nipple.

Erin almost lost the use of her legs, and she had to lock her knees. Ajax tore his mouth away. They were both breathing heavily. She could feel his erection against her lower belly. Hard.

Ajax pulled back a little and, leaving his lower body pressed against hers, used both his hands to push aside the flimsy silk covering her breasts. He looked down and Erin's gaze followed his. He cupped her breasts in his hands, the darkness of his skin making her own look even more pale.

Her nipples stood out, tight and pink, as if begging for his touch. He bent his head and encircled one straining tip in exquisite heat, sucking and laving it with his tongue.

Erin's fingers speared his hair, holding his head. She writhed against him, unconsciously seeking more. Seeking for him to fill the aching centre of her body.

A voice broke through the heat haze in her brain. It took her a second to figure out that someone was speaking in Greek through the intercom. Erin tugged Ajax's head back up and almost slid to the floor. His eyes were heavy-lidded, dark blue with desire, his cheeks slashed with colour.

At that moment he registered the voice too and stood upright, pulling Erin's clothes back into place. She was shaking.

Ajax said something rapid in response to the voice. He looked at Erin.

She caught a glimpse of her reflection in one of the mirrors and let out a squeak. Her hair was on end and her top was askew, showing half a breast. She smoothed her hair and adjusted her clothes.

Ajax said in a rough voice, 'Ready?'

Erin nodded. She couldn't trust herself to speak. He took her hand and pushed a button. The elevator resumed its progress downwards. The doors opened and Erin couldn't look the doorman in the eye.

Luckily Ajax's car was right outside and she all but dived into the back seat, face burning with a mixture of shame, embarrassment, and also a very illicit excitement. This man brought out a side of her that had never existed before. Not even at college.

The car journey back to the villa was made in silence, but the air was thick enough to cut with a knife. Ajax was a couple of feet away from her, but she could still feel his heat. The impressions his hands had left on her skin…her breasts. They still throbbed, the peaks sensitised. Between her legs she felt molten.

Was he just going to walk away and say goodnight? That would be the wise thing to do. Not to relive the past. So if he did she wouldn't betray how much she wanted him.

But when the car pulled to a stop outside the main door Ajax came and held out a hand to help her out. He didn't let go. They went inside. Wordlessly, he led her upstairs. They stopped outside Erin's bedroom and he said, 'Do you want to check her?'

The implication was clear. It wasn't over.

Erin nodded. She slipped inside and stood at Ashling's cot. The little girl was in more or less the same position as when she'd left her. The door to Damia's room was ajar. The baby monitor was on. She took her own anyway, just in case.

She kicked off her sandals and left her clutch behind. She went back to the corridor, where Ajax was waiting. He took her hand again and led her down to his room. Closing the door behind them.

Erin put the baby monitor down.

He moved closer and took her arm, removing the bangle. She took off the other jewellery. He led her over to the bed. The room was dimly lit. The French doors were open, allowing a warm breeze to flow through.

Ajax stood in front of her and said, 'I want you, Erin. This isn't over between us.'

She looked at Ajax. 'I'm not sure what "this" is,' she admitted, 'but I want you too.'

He cupped her jaw. 'It'll burn out…we just didn't give it time.'

As if *it* was an entity. Maybe it was. Maybe it would burn out. For him. Erin couldn't ever imagine not wanting him. But then she was less experienced, and so—

Ajax kissed the swirling thoughts out of her head, pulling her to him with his two big hands on her waist. Then he moved them over her back. He opened the clasp at the back of her neck.

The top of the jumpsuit fell away, exposing her breasts. Ajax looked at her, eyes hot. She couldn't wait. She reached for his shirt and undid it, pulling it open, over his shoulders, down and off. She undid his trousers, pulled down his zip, the backs of her fingers brushing against his body and making him suck in a breath.

She stopped, looked up.

He replaced her hands with his and quickly stripped until he was naked. Then he found the clasp at the side of her jumpsuit and opened it, pulling down the zip. The rest of the jumpsuit fell down to the floor and she stepped out of it, wearing nothing but her underwear.

'Get on the bed. I've waited for this for so long.'

That admission landed somewhere that made her feel a

little vulnerable, so she shut it out and focused on the physical. Her skin felt hot and tight. She did as he asked, lying back, looking up at him. He was magnificent. All hard muscle and sinew. A smattering of dark hair across his chest. Narrow waist.

He put on protection and then pushed her legs apart. He said, 'I need this—*you*—now. Okay?'

Erin nodded wordlessly, humbled by the evidence of his attraction to her. How had she not seen it?

He lodged his body in between her legs and took her in one smooth, cataclysmic thrust. She was ready for him, but she still gasped at the sensation of his body joining hers, stealing every last breath and any rational thought. She also—dangerously—felt emotional. She hadn't thought she'd experience this again with him.

He moved, slowly, torturously, in and out, letting their bodies get reacquainted, but it wasn't long before need gripped them both and their movements became more and more urgent, frenzied.

They reached their peak at the same time, both bodies taut, pressed against each other, before spiralling down and down into the never-ending waves of pleasure.

Ajax's body was heavy over Erin's for a long moment. She revelled in it, holding him to her as the breeze whispered over their sweat-slicked skin. And before she could stop it the ebbing waves of pleasure were pulling her down into a deep state of relaxation.

She didn't notice when Ajax pulled free of her body and went to the bathroom, nor, when he came back and got back into the bed beside her, pulling the sheet over them and curling himself around her body.

When Ajax woke he was alone in the bed. Dawn had broken. It was the second time Erin had left the bed before he'd woken, making him feel exposed. Discombobulated. On all counts where this woman was concerned nothing had ever gone to plan.

Like his intention to keep the boundaries between them in spite of his desire. But last night…in that flimsy, silky jumpsuit…the boundaries had been burnt to ash. He'd almost taken her in that elevator. The second time he hadn't been able to control himself in a confined space with her.

Clearly there was unfinished business between them, and he wouldn't feel a sense of control again until whatever this was between them had burnt itself out. If he hadn't let her go when he had, nearly two years ago, maybe he would have known about her pregnancy at the start and things would be very different now.

How, exactly? asked a sly voice.

Ajax ignored it. He got out of bed and showered and dressed.

He heard the sound of the baby's babbling before he saw her. He felt a clutch of his gut, the urge to turn around and go in the opposite direction, but something made him stop. And go towards her.

Erin and Damia and Ashling—in a highchair—were on the terrace, having breakfast. They all looked at him, and Ajax fought down the prickling feeling of panic and exposure.

He met Erin's eyes. As before, when they'd slept together that first time, she looked composed and as if nothing had happened. Her hair was still damp from showering. She looked fresh in a sleeveless top that turned out to be a sundress, he saw, when she stood up momentarily to pick up the spoon Ashling had dropped to the ground.

The housekeeper came out with coffee for Ajax. He sat down. Damia excused herself and left them alone. Ajax willed Erin to look at him, but she was fussing with Ashling, who was looking at him with big eyes—brown and green, like her mother's. Other than that, she'd inherited his colouring. Thick dark hair and dark golden skin.

It was the first time he'd really taken her in, and something about that shamed him now.

As if sensing his focus on her, the baby held out the spoon she'd just dropped. Ajax knew he was on shaky ground, and that if he stayed here, engaged with her, he would be blasting apart the walls that had protected him for the last few years.

He was taking a risk. But he couldn't look away from her. In spite of the fear, he put out a hand. 'For me?'

Ashling smiled. Something turned over in Ajax's chest. He took it. 'Thank you.'

She smiled again, showing glimpses of emerging teeth. When he glanced at Erin she was looking at him warily. But then she schooled her expression and went back to feeding the baby what looked like a mixture of yoghurt and fruit.

'You were up early,' he said.

A little colour washed into her cheeks. 'I didn't want the baby to wake you.'

'Her name is Ashling,' Ajax pointed out, with not a little irony.

Ashling reacted. *'Abba!'*

'I don't think it was a good idea…last night,' Erin said in a low voice, as if he might not know what she meant.

Everything in Ajax rejected that. 'I think it was inevitable.'

She shook her head. 'We shouldn't…again.'

'No one is forcing you into anything, Erin.' He watched more colour flood her cheeks. Good. Maybe she was remembering that she'd been with him every step of the way last night.

She looked at him. 'It's not that I don't want to…it's just not a good idea.'

'Probably not,' agreed Ajax. 'But I think it's obvious that it won't be finished until we've let it run its course.'

She wiped Ashling's mouth and looked at him, 'You make it sound like a virus.'

It *was* a kind of virus—in his blood. A hot and urgent virus. And it was the same for her and they both knew it.

Damia came back out and took Ashling to get washed and changed. The baby looked at Ajax over Damia's shoulder as they went out, her gaze seeming far too old for her age. As if she knew the turmoil she caused inside him.

'We're going into Athens to go sightseeing today,' said Erin. 'It's a bit cooler with the clouds.'

Ajax looked back at her. *'We?'*

'Me and Damia and Ashling.'

'I'll arrange for you to have a driver.'

Erin protested. 'We can get a taxi or use public transport.'

Ajax shook his head. 'Non-negotiable.'

Erin looked as if she wanted to argue, but eventually she said, 'Okay—fine.'

Ajax got up and went over to where Erin sat. He put his hands on the arms of the chair either side of her. He saw how her pupils enlarged and the colour in her cheeks grew more hectic. His blood hummed.

'I enjoyed last night.'

She looked up at him. He could see the resistance in her expression, in her eyes. She wanted to lie. To refute it. But she couldn't.

She seemed to sag a little. 'So did I.'

He stood up and couldn't stop a smile.

She scowled at him. 'Is that it?'

He put out his hands. 'Are you trying to invite me to make love to you here on this terrace, right now?'

He turned and walked away, chuckling, and then felt

something hit him between his shoulder blades. He turned around. It was a small *pain au chocolat*.

Ajax picked it up and backed away, still facing Erin. He took a bite and exclaimed with relish, 'Almost as delicious as—'

She threw another pastry at him and Ajax let out a laugh.

It only occurred to him as he was driving to the office in Athens that he couldn't remember the last time he'd felt so light.

Later that day Erin and Damia were wilting in the heat. They'd stopped to sit outside a café in the shade. Ashling was in her buggy, with a muslin cloth shading her and a fan blowing cool moist air over her sleeping form.

Erin loved how child-and-baby-orientated the Greeks were, fussing over Ashling everywhere they went. It seemed to be so at odds with what Ajax had said about his family— but then they weren't exactly mere mortals.

Erin smiled at Damia. 'Thank you for being tour guide today. You were fantastic and your English is superb.'

The young woman blushed and smiled. '*Efharisto*, Erin. And your Greek is really coming on.'

Erin lifted her glass of chilled water in salute. She was doing her best to pick up some Greek, feeling that it was only respectful to do so.

Damia's gaze went to something behind Erin just as the back of her neck prickled with awareness.

Ajax appeared at her elbow.

She knew it was him before she saw him.

'Good afternoon, ladies, I trust you've had a good time?'

Erin smiled up at him, hating the way her body went into roadrunner mode, her pulse skyrocketing. 'Lovely, thank you. Athens is an amazing city.'

'Well,' he said, 'if it's all right with you, Damia, I'd like to steal Erin away.'

Immediately Erin protested. 'That's not fair. She's been out with me all day—she shouldn't have to work into the evening too.'

Now Damia protested. 'It wasn't work, really, and of course I don't mind. Do you want me to take Ashling home? It's almost time for her supper anyway.'

Erin felt a little redundant. After a year of being a single parent, suddenly she wasn't alone any more.

Reluctantly, she said, 'If you're sure you don't mind?'

Damia shook her head. 'Not at all.'

Ajax said, 'Damia has agreed to come back to the island with us when we go tomorrow. She'll work with us for the duration of your visit.'

Erin looked at the young woman, 'Can you do that?'

'I have the summer off to work and learn English, and working for you ticks both those boxes. Plus, I'll get to visit my great-aunt.'

It was all working out so seamlessly Erin felt suspicious— but she wasn't even sure of what she should be suspicious. This was a world where things appeared as if by magic and there were no obstacles.

Damia stood up and gathered up their things. The driver parked nearby and Erin lifted Ashling out of the buggy. She was a heavy weight, still dead to the world.

She woke up briefly when she was installed in the baby seat at the back of the car, but after a sleepy smile at Erin fell asleep again. Erin gave instructions to Damia, told her to call her if Ashling wasn't settling, and then they drove off.

'She'll be fine with Damia,' Ajax said.

Erin felt prickly and disgruntled, and all for no reason she could put her finger on. It was this man…inserting himself under her skin.

'I'm just not used to this level of support.'

'You'll have this level of support whenever you want it now. Money isn't an object.'

Erin rolled her eyes. But she still found it intimidating, Ajax's level of wealth. 'It's not all about the money. I don't mind caring for my daughter.'

'If you go back to work full-time you'll need a nanny.'

Erin stopped. She hadn't even realised that they were walking away from the café. Ajax must have paid their bill.

She looked at him. *Work...* She hadn't even thought about work. She was in danger of forgetting an outside world existed.

That revelation didn't help her prickliness subside.

She thought of what he'd said about working full-time. 'I never mentioned going back to work full-time. Not explicitly.'

Ajax shrugged. He was wearing sunglasses. Together with chinos and a dark blue short-sleeved polo shirt he looked like a movie star.

'I just assumed. You're good at your job.'

They continued walking. The early-evening air was still balmy. Erin just wore a light top tied around her waist over the sundress, and her cross-body bag. She resembled every other tourist there. The prickliness faded, She realised in that moment that she felt more carefree than she could recall feeling in some time. If ever.

It was an unwelcome revelation when she was with someone who didn't inspire feelings of carelessness or freedom. But since she'd noticed that little moment at breakfast, when Ajax had interacted with Ashling, albeit briefly, it had felt as if there'd been a subtle change in the air. Signifying what, exactly, Erin didn't know—and she wasn't sure if she wanted to know. For some reason she didn't want to dwell on it, sensing some kind of danger.

She diverted her mind back to what Ajax had said. *'You're good at your job.'*

She stopped walking again. 'I am good at my job.'

'You are.'

But something was striking her now. She continued walking and said, 'You know… I just automatically pursued the career that I had the most aptitude for without ever really stopping to think about it. My parents are both academics, and the standards they set were high, but they never put pressure on me. It was all my own pressure.'

'Are you saying you don't really want to be an attorney?'

Erin's stomach lurched at that audacious idea, but she felt something like a fizzing excitement. 'I don't know… I know that I'm not missing my job as much as I thought I might. And I know that working full-time and leaving Ashling with nannies is not something I want.'

'You can do whatever you want, Erin. You're qualified to choose from a myriad of roles.'

She hadn't thought about it like that before. And she certainly wouldn't have had Ajax Nikolau down as a careers advisor. But since he'd told her about the expectations his family had put on him and his brother she was realising that her experience hadn't been that dissimilar.

Ajax came to a stop outside a boutique. In the window mannequins were dressed in jewel-coloured gowns.

Erin quipped, 'Not quite your colours, but I'm sure you'd look great in them.'

'Ha-ha.' Ajax took her elbow in his hand. 'Not for me— for you.'

Erin resisted. 'But Georgiana has brought more clothes than I could wear in a lifetime.'

'Indulge me,' Ajax said. 'There's an event next week, hosted by my family, and it will require something…specific.'

'What kind of event?'

'An annual family gathering.'

Erin could feel her blood drain south. 'Is it a good idea for me to meet them?'

'You're the mother of my child,' Ajax pointed out.

'A child you don't intend having much to do with.'

Ajax's jaw clenched. 'Maybe I'm rethinking that.'

Alarm bells rang. 'What's that supposed to mean?'

He ran a hand through his hair. He obviously really didn't like being questioned. Well, tough. He couldn't flip-flop like this about something as important as his daughter.

'Something you said about Theo's death having a profound impact on me... It made me think. I realised that my motivations in staying out of Ashling's life are based on fear. Blind, irrational fear. And that's not good enough. For me or her. Or you. You both deserve more.'

Erin was speechless. She knew she should be welcoming this development but for some reason she felt unsettled. Maybe because she didn't trust that he meant it? Or thought that he would change his mind? She was only protecting her daughter after all.

Ajax arched a dark brow over his glasses. 'I thought you'd be happy.'

Erin flushed. 'Of course I am. But if you make any connection with her now it will cause upset if you can't continue.'

'I'm aware of that. That's the last thing I want to do.'

Erin knew instinctively that he would be a good father. His devotion to his nephew told her that. So why wasn't she more happy about this change of heart?

'Shall we?' Ajax indicated the boutique.

She'd forgotten about it. Up to now Ajax hadn't wanted to be involved and Erin had resigned herself to getting on with their lives without him. But now she felt as if she was on shifting sands, and suddenly she wasn't sure where they were headed any more.

CHAPTER EIGHT

AJAX HAD GIVEN instructions to the boutique owner and, after taking Erin's measurements, she'd gone to pull out a selection of clothes.

'What's wrong with the clothes Georgiana has brought?'

Ajax made a face. 'Nothing at all—for an Athens crowd. But I just want to make sure you feel comfortable. My family are conservative. And snobs.'

'That sounds ominous.'

'Think of it as a kind of armour.'

'Wow...now I really can't wait to meet them.'

The owner came back and indicated for Erin to come into the changing room. She left Ajax outside.

The clothes that the woman had chosen—far from the classic Chanel-type suits Erin had been envisaging—were relaxed. Elegant and not a million miles from what she would have chosen herself. There were trouser suits with pencil trousers and structured jackets. Dresses in every colour of the rainbow, long and flowy, that swirled around Erin's body. Beautifully cut jeans and soft cashmere tops. Silk shirts...

And then the evening wear.

Erin tried on a dress that she could appreciate might fit a more conservative environment than a restaurant or his friends' charity auction, but to her it seemed even more daring than anything Georgiana had picked out.

It was made of a green silk that made her hair look even redder than usual. It had spaghetti straps and a piece of fabric that covered her breasts, with cut-outs at her waist. The dress then fell in soft, Grecian-style folds to the floor.

Erin said, 'Um… I'm not sure about this one—'

She stopped when a movement caught her eye, and looked up to see that Ajax had pulled aside the curtain to look. She could feel the heat in his gaze from a couple of feet away and quivered inwardly, remembering how it had felt to have his body surge into hers the previous night, stealing her soul piece by piece.

'We'll take it,' said Ajax. 'And the rest.'

Ajax pulled a pair of jeans and a silk top out of the pile of clothes, and a pair of high-heeled sandals.

'Put these on for now.'

Erin knew she should protest, but she was ashamed to admit that having Ajax telling her what to put on, dressing for him, gave her a bit of a thrill. She put on the clothes and the boutique owner told her that everything else would be packed and sent to the villa.

Erin sighed. She'd have to try and remember this wasn't how things worked in the real world.

When she'd changed, they walked outside and found Ajax's car waiting. They got into the back and it moved into the traffic.

'Where are we going?' she asked.

'Just a little taverna I know.'

Just a little taverna turned out to be an exclusive restaurant, tucked away in a picturesque square in the ancient Plaka area. It was full already, with a mix of tourists and glamorous locals. Erin was in awe of the Greek women, blinging with jewellery and stunningly beautiful.

A table was found for them in a discreet corner. When

they'd sat down, Erin said, 'More opportunities for us to be seen out and about?'

Ajax shook his head. 'No, actually. I'm hungry and thought you might be too. There are no paparazzi here.'

Erin's insides dipped. Was this a date?

'So what is this? What are we now? Friends?'

With benefits? She didn't say that.

Ajax's mouth quirked. 'You know, that's one of the things I like most about you—your directness.'

Erin wasn't sure if that was a compliment. She could imagine other women being more coquettish. It just wasn't her style.

'I could say the same of you.'

She shivered a little at the memory of how 'direct' Ajax had been that first night. In the elevator.

'We're lovers,' Ajax said then. 'Lovers for as long as this mutual attraction lasts.'

Erin wanted to ask, *How long?* But a waiter arrived and took their order, brought water and wine.

Erin took a sip of the chilled white wine. 'What if one of us loses interest first?' She knew it wouldn't be her, as humiliating as that was to admit.

Ajax shrugged. 'Let's cross that bridge when we come to it.'

'Our contract will have to be drawn up again, to reflect your desire to have a relationship with Ashling.'

'We're in no rush. I trust you.'

Erin absorbed that. It was huge. She literally had a contract signed by them both, stating that he was giving her full custody. She could go back to the States with Ashling and refuse him access. He'd have to take her to court to re-negotiate.

But of course she wouldn't do that.

As if reading her mind, Ajax said, 'I know you wouldn't use that against me.'

'No,' she admitted, 'because I've worked for you, and all I can say is I'm glad I was on your side.'

Ajax widened his eyes. 'I'm a pussycat.'

Erin snorted. 'You're a shark.'

He smiled, showing his teeth, but all that did for Erin was remind her of how he'd nipped at her bare skin in intimate places. She squirmed on the chair, glad he couldn't see into her mind, which seemed to be stuck on one track: *Ajax*.

After revealing that he wanted to have Ashling in his life, Erin felt newly exposed. As if a layer of protection had been taken away. That was something she couldn't unpick now. Not while Ajax was looking at her.

'So, both your parents are still alive?' she asked.

Ajax nodded. 'My father handed over the reins of the business to my brother, and then to me when Demetriou died. Essentially, he's retired now.'

Erin was curious. 'He wasn't that passionate about the family business, then?'

Ajax's mouth flattened for a moment with distaste. 'The only thing he's passionate about is whoever his current mistress is. All very discreet, of course. She won't be at the family gathering.'

'You don't approve?'

'It's disrespectful. He was the one who had affairs first, and I could see what it did to my mother, even though she'd deny it to her death. It made her vulnerable. Brittle. It pushed her further from us, her sons, because her life became all about competing with my father to try and make sure he knew she wasn't hurt.'

'But it sounds like she *was* hurt,' Erin observed. 'Maybe there were feelings there after all.'

Ajax didn't respond to that.

Erin couldn't help asking, 'Did Sofia have affairs…?'

'Yes. Of course. We didn't share a bed.'

'Oh.' Erin hated how that made her feel lighter. 'But surely you weren't going to live your life celibate?'

'To be honest, I was consumed with Theo. I didn't think too much beyond him for the first couple of years. Sofia and I had already made an agreement that after a respectable amount of time we'd quietly divorce, and I would get full custody of Theo.'

'She was willing to hand him over?' Erin knew she shouldn't be shocked after her own experience.

Ajax shrugged. 'I told you—women in my family don't really do mothering well. They're not expected to.'

'I know not everyone automatically feels that rush of love—for some parents it can be incredibly complicated— but *you* felt it…and you weren't even Theo's biological father.'

Erin was surprised when a waiter appeared to clear their plates—she hadn't even noticed that they'd been served starters and had eaten them. Ajax seemed to have an effect on her that meant she was in some sort of bubble, where the world didn't impinge. Dangerous. Seductive.

She'd had to be responsible for so long, due to her father's scattiness, that she'd never really had the luxury of taking her foot off the pedal. But here in Greece she felt as if she was having the first holiday of her life.

Albeit along with the rollercoaster effect of Ajax on her body, mind and emotions.

No, refuted a voice. *Not emotions.*

It was just physical. As he'd said, it would burn out—even if it felt as if it was burning brighter and hotter now than it had even on that first night.

When they'd returned to the villa, Ajax stopped beside Erin, outside her bedroom door. They looked at each other.

Her heart thumped. The air crackled between them with un-spoken desire. She went inside, checked on Ashling—who was asleep, with Damia's door open nearby—and then went back out to Ajax, who was waiting.

He held out a hand. Erin took it, even as she felt, supersti-tiously, that some line she couldn't see was being crossed.

In Ajax's room they were naked and on his bed in seconds. Ajax's big body was moving over hers with such mastery that Erin could only hope he wouldn't see how he triggered her emotions. She couldn't deny it here...naked. She could only ride the wave and pray that when she was washed up on the shore again she would still be in one piece.

When Ajax woke the following morning it was early. The bed was empty beside him, but he wasn't surprised now—even if he didn't like it.

And since when had he wanted to wake up with a woman? *Since Erin.*

He scowled. His body was heavy with sensual satisfac-tion, and yet he could already feel the edge of hunger form-ing again, just thinking of the previous night and how he'd felt he would die if he didn't sink into Erin's tight, slick em-brace before taking another breath.

It would burn out.

It had to.

And yet even as Ajax automatically formed that thought, a part of him was asking, *what if it doesn't?*

He didn't dwell on that ridiculous notion—because de-sire always burnt out.

He got up and showered and dressed, then left his room, stopping by Erin's bedroom door.

He pushed it open and saw that she was in bed, on her back, in a T-shirt. Even seeing her clothed turned the spark into a flame deep in his belly.

Not burning out yet.

She was fast asleep.

He heard a sound and looked towards the open door leading into the nursery. Even though he felt the urge to turn and walk away, not to engage, he went into the room.

Ashling was standing in the cot, hands on the bar, gabbling to herself, quite content. Then she saw him, and for a second Ajax held his breath, expecting her to cry. After all, he'd barely engaged with her at all.

But she didn't cry. She smiled. And Ajax's chest swelled so much he couldn't breathe. Somehow he found his way to breathing again and his feet took him over to the cot.

Ashling immediately held up her arms. Ajax lifted her and closed his eyes against the wave of déjà vu.

He'd told himself he would never feel this again...the soft, heavy weight of a child. But here he was.

Ashling looked up at him and said something unintelligible. Ajax knew that there was no going back from this moment.

Just then, a sleepy Damia appeared in the doorway, tying a robe around herself. She said, 'I'm so sorry, Mr Nikolau. I didn't hear her.'

He shook his head. 'She wasn't crying. It's fine. I've got this—you go back to bed and get some sleep.'

'Are you sure?'

He nodded and she left, closing the door. A familiar pungent smell hit Ajax's nostrils. He wrinkled his nose and looked at his daughter. 'Ah, yes...the not so pleasant bits of parenting... Let's see if I can remember what to do, hmm?'

Ashling just looked at him with a wisdom beyond her years, as if to say, *I'll indulge you for now, but don't push it*, and Ajax pressed a kiss to her head, silently praying that he could cope with the fear and hope that it didn't consume him.

* * *

When Erin woke she was disorientated. Alone in her bed. Then it came back in a rush. The urgency that had gripped her and Ajax. The aftermath when she'd felt torn apart but also more whole than she'd ever felt.

That was what had spurred her to leave his bed as he'd slept. She'd checked on Ashling, showered, and then crawled into her own bed. And now... She squinted a look out through the windows and sat up in a panic. Now the sun was high.

She jumped out of bed and went straight into the nursery, to find it empty. Damia must have taken Ashling down for breakfast.

Erin quickly washed and changed into denim shorts and a loose shirt. Barefoot, she went downstairs and followed the sounds of Ashling's babbles, a deeper voice, and Damia's laughter.

Not sure what to expect, she walked out onto the terrace to see Ajax with a napkin over his face, playing peekaboo with Ashling, who was in the highchair. The detritus of breakfast, bits of food and a spoon, were all over the ground in the vicinity.

Ashling was squealing with delight every time Ajax's face was revealed. Erin could empathise, she thought, but there was something about the tableau that unsettled her.

Like a coward, she shied away from investigating why this evidence of Ajax playing with his daughter wasn't causing her to feel any sense of happiness. She almost felt... scared. She told herself it was because she feared Ashling would get hurt. Every moment with Ajax like this now had the potential to cause damage when he inevitably got bored or changed his mind.

He's not your mother, whispered a voice.

Ashling spotted her and immediately held out her arms, saying, 'Mama-mama-mama.'

Erin scooped her up, feeling almost guilty to be breaking up her moment with Ajax. Ashling snuggled into her.

Ajax stood up. He was wearing a suit—dark grey—a white shirt and a tie. Erin spotted a blob of something and pointed. 'I think you have some baby food on your jacket.'

Erin waited to see how he'd react, but he was sanguine. He got a napkin and dampened it with water and dabbed at the mark. Another tick in his favour. But consistency would be key.

He looked at Erin and she fought not to blush as she sat down and poured herself a coffee, holding Ashling in one arm.

He said, 'I'm going to the office for a couple of hours. I'll meet you and Damia and Ashling at the airfield. My assistant will come and help you pack, and the driver will bring you to meet me.'

Erin glanced up. 'Okay, we'll be ready.'

When Ajax had walked away, with Ashling looking after him over Erin's shoulder, Erin said to Damia, 'Thanks for getting her up this morning. I didn't hear a thing.'

Damia said brightly, 'Neither did I! It was Mr Nikolau. He changed her and dressed her and brought her down for breakfast.' Damia stood up. 'I'll clear up and then go and get ready. Just shout if you need me for anything.'

The girl walked away, towards the kitchen, and Erin sat there, stupefied. Ajax had got Ashling up and changed her nappy. Not an especially remarkable thing at all—especially for a father. But for a man who just a little more than twenty-four hours ago had been intending on staying out of his daughter's life it was not just stepping over a boundary—it was smashing it aside and setting it on fire.

Erin forced herself to calm down. This was a good thing.

He was obviously familiar with babies after Theo. Changing a nappy wasn't a big deal for him, evidently. He'd confided in her that he'd intended on getting full custody of Theo. He'd obviously been very hands-on.

She assured herself again that this was a good thing. A positive development. So why did she feel so uneasy?

Agatha welcomed them back to the villa with open arms. Damia was clearly delighted to see her great-aunt, and conversed with her in rapid Greek for a few minutes, with Agatha making dramatic exclamations in response.

Erin was surprised and a little disconcerted at how much it felt like coming home.

Agatha and Damia swept into the house, taking Ashling with them before she could even protest. Ajax took Erin's hand and led her straight upstairs to his bedroom, closing the door.

'Ajax, we can't… We just got here… I need to change Ashling and give her something to eat.'

'Agatha and Damia are fighting over her right now.'

Erin's back was to the door. Ajax put his hands by her head, caging her in. She could easily duck down and slip away but, fatally, she didn't want to. She couldn't help revelling in Ajax's hungry gaze. He'd shown her a sensual side of herself she might never have explored with anyone else.

Never would again.

Her heart hitched.

She tipped up her chin. 'Well, then, what do you propose we do?'

'One thing I've wanted to do with you but haven't yet… because each time I wake up you're gone.'

He'd noticed she was gone. And he didn't look all that happy about it. Something flip-flopped inside her.

'What's that?' she asked.

'Take a shower together.'

Erin nearly melted into a puddle at his feet, but she managed to say nonchalantly, 'I do feel a bit...dusty.'

Ajax reached for her hand and led her into the bathroom, 'Well, then, let me help you feel less...dusty...'

Erin followed him on jelly legs, giving up any attempt to rationalise what was going on.

The sun beat against Erin's closed eyelids. She could hear the sound of crashing waves. The air was scented with sea and sand and earth. Her body felt heavy and deliciously replete.

They'd had lunch at the villa not long ago, and afterwards Ajax had taken Erin and Ashling off to explore the island, bringing them to this secluded beach that was totally empty.

Erin was momentarily out of the shade, trying to get her skin to warm up to a shade of golden brown that she'd never attained before. She could hear splashes and squeals of delight, and she came up on one elbow and put her shades on. She couldn't quite believe what she was seeing. Ajax, in snug swim-shorts, in the shallows of the sea, held Ashling in his arms, ducking her down into a wave as it crashed around them.

She was loving it. She'd never been to the sea before. She was covered in factor fifty—as was Erin—and she was wearing an adorable flowery onesie and a sun hat.

Ajax's volte face with his daughter still unsettled Erin. She felt sure that this was just a phase, perhaps brought on by memories of Theo. Once they returned to the States and Manhattan, and the realities of co-parenting sank in, they'd see less and less of Ajax.

Erin bit her lip. She should be protecting Ashling now, from inevitable disappointment, but maybe she was young enough that when Ajax gradually disappeared she might not be devastated.

Erin had little doubt that this was how it would play out, because the alternative was something she couldn't even grasp. The thought of Ajax being part of Ashling's life but not Erin's...of him moving on and marrying...as she might do herself some day. Blended families? He didn't strike her as the kind of guy who would put up with that, so he would just excise Ashling from his life.

But the image in front of her now mocked that assertion. Father and daughter, playing in the surf, Ashling clinging on to Ajax like a monkey.

In the last couple of days he'd become her new favourite person. His ease with her and his tactility was unbelievably impressive, and seductive in a way that impacted on Erin deeply.

He beguiled everyone—even babies. When he looked at you, it was like the sun shining all around you.

It was what would happen when that sunbeam moved elsewhere that Erin needed to be ready for.

As if hearing her thoughts, Ajax turned around with Ashling and looked at her. The sea water was sluicing off his tall, broad body. Ashling put out a pudgy hand and gabbled something that sounded like *'Mama...mama...'*

Erin levered herself up from the sand and walked down the beach towards them, very conscious of the green one-piece swimsuit she'd chosen. It was perfectly conservative, but under his devouring gaze it felt positively indecent.

Something was happening here that Erin hadn't expected. A family was forming, in spite of every instinct screaming at her that it couldn't possibly be real.

And yet as she neared Ajax and Ashling in the sea, and they both reached out for her, she told herself not to trust in the shimmering possibility that this might exist. This was fleeting and temporary. All of it. She couldn't afford to forget that.

* * *

'I feel a little overdressed for the village.'

Ajax slid her a look from the driver's seat. 'You look perfect.'

He was taking her to a local restaurant for dinner. She was wearing a dress that Damia had picked out. A cream silk sleeveless wrap dress that fell to her feet. She tucked a wayward lock of hair behind one ear.

'Your hair is getting longer.' Ajax observed.

Erin made a face, 'I cut it because Ashling kept grabbing it when she was a tiny baby, and because—'

She stopped suddenly. She hadn't been intending on elaborating.

But of course Ajax had noticed.

'And because…?'

Reluctantly she divulged, 'Because it reminded me of my mother. Her hair was long…and I used to be fascinated by it. One of my earliest memories is of lying in bed and wrapping it around my hand. Maybe even then I knew she was going to leave.'

'So you cut it for practicality, but also maybe to send a message that you weren't going anywhere?'

Erin looked at him. She wanted to scowl. Ajax was far too perceptive sometimes. 'I hadn't thought about it like that.'

Ajax parked the car on a quiet street and they got out. The evening air was warm and balmy. The sun had set, leaving the sky pink and rusty and golden.

They walked down a cobbled street towards the water. The houses were white and blue, with colourful flowers blooming from pots and planters. Children were running in and out of houses, squealing with excitement.

Erin couldn't help smiling at their effervescence. It made her yearn a little for Ashling to have this kind of experience… But the reality was that Erin probably wouldn't be here to witness it. Ashling would be coming to spend time with her father on her own. Perhaps with half-siblings. Erin couldn't help but think that Ajax might now be more open to children, marrying again...

She was lost in that train of thought when Ajax, beside her, said, 'Look up.'

Erin lifted her head and gasped. They were at a small marina, with the sea lapping against the wall just in front of them. Boats bobbed gently on the water. Restaurants were spread out on each side, buzzing with locals and tourists. Candles and fairy-lights added to the atmosphere. Soft music came from the tavernas. Handsome waiters lured prospective diners into their establishments.

Ajax led her to the left-hand side, to a taverna at the very end. The owner welcomed Ajax like an old friend and gave them a table right by the water's edge.

'This is...stunning,' said Erin. 'I've never been anywhere like it.'

'You haven't been to Europe before?'

Erin wrinkled her nose. 'Only the main attractions like London and Paris on school or university tours. I was too busy studying and then working. During my summers I'd work to make money.'

'Even though your mother was giving you an allowance?'

Erin could appreciate now how she'd shut off a vital part of her youth in a bid to show her independence. Her work ethic.

She looked at Ajax. 'It's a bit pathetic and boring, isn't it?'

He shook his head. 'I never did the travelling thing either. I've just travelled a lot with work. I think I'd prefer to come somewhere like this for the first time at the age of twenty-eight and really appreciate it, rather than see it on a whistle-stop tour at eighteen and forget it.'

Erin looked out at the sea. There were fishing boats in

the distance with their lights on. The moon was rising. She said, 'You could never forget this.'

The waiter came, with Greek wine and food. It was rustic and delicious. Fish so fresh Erin could taste the sea.

She sat back when their plates were cleared, refusing dessert. 'I couldn't eat another bite. That was…amazing.'

Ajax couldn't take his eyes off Erin. She eclipsed the view. She wore practically no make-up, but her eyes were huge and her mouth an enticement to kiss her until she was breathless, arching her body into him in a way that blew his mind.

Her skin was turning a very delicate shade of golden. Freckles had appeared on her shoulders and nose. Traces of her Celtic heritage. Her hair *was* getting longer, softening around her face. His gaze drifted down, taking advantage of her looking out to sea. Her arms were slim, but strong. Hands elegant…short nails, no varnish. No frills, no fuss. Straightforward. And yet he sensed hidden things…depths that he didn't yet know.

Usually at this point with a lover Ajax veered instinctively away from wanting to delve into anything personal. But this woman… She still intrigued him, and he wanted to know more.

He looked back up and saw there was a small smile playing around her mouth. Ridiculously he felt piqued.

'What's so amusing?' he asked.

She looked at him and he felt the impact of that golden and green gaze in his solar plexus. And lower. He shifted in the seat, cursing his lack of control.

She lifted her hand, put her forefinger and thumb about an inch apart, and whispered, 'I think I'm a little bit drunk.'

Ajax grinned. She'd had a little more wine than usual, and he'd had less as he was driving. She seemed looser…

less vigilant. She looked altogether too seductive to resist—
and he had no intention of doing so.

He stood up and put out his hand. 'Come on, let's go
home.'

To his surprise a shadow crossed her face, and she suddenly looked a lot less loose. But then, as if he'd imagined
it, she put her hand in his and let him pull her up.

They walked back up to the car and he couldn't help asking, 'What was that back there?'

'What?'

'Your reaction to what I said...*let's go home.*'

There was something there. Ajax could sense it.

But Erin shook her head. 'Nothing at all.'

She wouldn't meet his eye, though, and for the first time
since he'd known her he suspected she was lying.

When they got back to the villa, Erin moved down
through the garden towards the pool.

Ajax stopped. 'Where are you going?'

She turned around, but kept walking backwards. 'For a
swim.'

Ajax shook his head and followed her through the gap in
the bushes. The pool was visible under the moonlight, but
Ajax went and turned on the low pool lights.

Erin pointed. 'This is the deep end, right?'

'Yes...' Ajax said, wondering what she was thinking.

But before he could wonder for too long she'd kicked off
her sandals, stepped up to the side and executed a graceful
dive into the water, fully clothed.

She swam underwater the entire length of the pool, a
shimmering elongated shape, before emerging at the other
end. She stood up and pushed back her hair with both hands.

Ajax nearly lost control of his legs and had to lock his
knees. The water had made her dress completely translucent.
He could see the curves of her breasts and the pebbling of

her nipples. And down between her legs he could see the darker shadow of the hair that covered her sex, where he imagined her slick and ready.

He dragged his gaze back up. She was just looking at him.

For some reason he felt it was important to resist the almost overwhelming urge to join her. 'Why do I have the feeling that you're trying to distract me?' he asked.

She arched a brow. 'Because you have a suspicious mind?'

That was it.

Ajax's control dissolved in a rush of lust.

He pulled and tore off as many clothes as he could and dived into the water, barely making a ripple. He swam to Erin's legs, under the water, and put his hands around her calves, tugging her under.

They looked at one another under the water, the world blocked out. Ajax had the impression that she was a siren, a mermaid, and that he would never really know her.

He put his mouth over hers and she wrapped her arms around him. There was something fierce about the urgency that gripped them as he surged up out of the water with her. They gasped for air.

He pulled her dress apart and it came away from her body. He threw it to the side. Her bra was transparent. He didn't even bother taking it off. He cupped a breast and covered the pouting flesh with his mouth, sucking and nipping at her, making the nipple harder.

He was barely aware of her breathless entreaties and moans. He reached under the water and pulled her underwear down. And his own. He lifted her and instructed her roughly to wrap her legs around his waist.

She did. She lay back against the side of the pool, the water lapping around her.

Ajax's body was so hard it hurt, but he delayed the gratification, spreading his hand up over her belly to her breasts, exploring the plump flesh, and then moving up higher, tracing the elegant line of her neck and jaw.

Her eyes were huge, bright with desire. 'Please, Ajax…'

He looked at her. In this moment everything was stripped away. He still didn't know her secrets—but he would.

He hitched her a little higher and then with one movement entered her slick body. She threw her head back, the sinews in her neck standing out.

He moved in and out slowly, and then gathered pace, driving into her body harder, faster. She lifted her head. She was biting her lip and Ajax covered her mouth with his, just as the storm gripped her and her inner muscles clamped down so hard on his body that he couldn't breathe for a second.

He exploded deep inside her, felt her muscles gripping him and milking him of everything. Every last piece of strength.

In the aftermath, as the world returned around them and the laboured sounds of their breathing diminished, Ajax was aware of something niggling at the edge of his mind. Something urgent. But he couldn't focus on it.

He pulled free of Erin's body and levered himself out of the pool with effort. He reached down and helped her out, trying not to let her body enflame him again.

He took her hand and led her over to the changing area, fetching a couple of robes. He helped her put one on. Her eyes were half closed and she looked flushed and languorous. He belted the robe tightly around her waist, as if that might help him maintain control.

He put on his own robe and, after gathering up their discarded clothes, took Erin's hand again to lead her up to the villa.

Halfway across the lawn, though, she stopped and took her hand away from his. He looked at her and saw she was pale. She looked back at him and said, 'Protection. We didn't use anything.'

Immediately the niggling sensation stopped. That was what it had been. And for a man who would usually have been zealous about protection, he found to his surprise that the thought wasn't causing him a sense of panic.

Erin's expression *was* reflecting panic, though. But then it cleared a little and she said, 'Actually, I think it's okay. I'm at a safe place in my cycle.'

Ajax didn't want to decipher why he wasn't feeling more relieved. 'That's good… I'm sorry, that was my fault. I should've stopped.'

CHAPTER NINE

Erin's heart was still pounding after what had just happened, and also with the gut-churning panic of realising they'd made love without protection. But she was pretty sure it would be okay…

Ajax's face was hard to read in the moonlight, but Erin had the distinct impression that he wasn't overly perturbed about the fact that they'd just had unprotected sex.

She winced inwardly. Not that having protected sex had been all that effective twenty-one months ago.

Her body was still tingling all over. She couldn't quite believe she'd had the audacity to jump into the pool with her clothes on, and then what had ensued…

But he'd been right—she had been trying to distract him. From how it had made her feel to hear him say so casually *'let's go home'* after dinner.

Let's go home.

As if they were a regular couple on a date night. Enjoying some alone time away from their baby and then returning to their home.

Their home.

When it wasn't remotely her home. It was Ajax's home. And yet in that unguarded moment she'd desperately wanted it to be her home too. *Their home.* The kind of place where there were two parents and one of them didn't just get up and walk out one day, leaving a trail of destruction in their wake.

The fact that he'd exposed that deep-seated desire had made her feel very vulnerable. Vulnerable to the possibility that she might even be hoping for something more than she'd ever dreamed of.

So she'd acted on instinct. And diving into the pool had almost been as much about waking herself up out of that dream as anything else. But then Ajax had joined her...and madness had taken over, scrambling her mind and making her forget that she needed to stay vigilant and not be dreaming of impossible things.

Erin took a step backwards now. 'I should go and check on Ashling...go to bed... Goodnight, Ajax.'

She turned to walk away and reassured herself that any day now the heat in Ajax's gaze would fade, this insane interlude would end, and they'd go back to New York and—

'Would it really be so bad?'

Erin stopped. She didn't turn around. She was afraid she was having some sort of aural hallucination—that Ajax had probably said goodnight, but she'd heard something else. Something ridiculous.

She turned around. Ajax's face was still in shadow. Not helping.

She said, 'What did you say?'

He stepped forward and into the soft light coming from the villa. He should have looked ridiculous in the short towelling robe, but he didn't. He looked sexy.

He said, 'Would it be so bad if you were pregnant?'

It took a moment for that to really compute in Erin's brain. For her to try and interpret the dozens of threads that question contained, all leading in directions that had alarm bells screaming.

'Of course it would—what are you talking about?'

Ajax took another step forward, closing the distance between them. There was an intent look on his face. Erin's sense of extreme vulnerability came back.

He said, 'Think about it. We already have a child. We have amazing chemistry. We like each other. You and Ashling are making me think about family again, even though I swore I wouldn't.'

We like each other.

A tepid emotion, at best. Not the kind of emotion that could sustain a long life, build a family.

You need love for that.

Erin clamped down on that rogue thought. She didn't want love. But she wanted more than just 'like'.

She shook her head. 'You said yourself this chemistry won't last. Only days ago you were still determined not to have anything much to do with your daughter. And have you forgotten that you dumped me?'

Ajax's face tightened. 'I never forgot you.'

'I had no idea you were still thinking about me.'

'I came back for you.'

Erin all but rolled her eyes, the memory of him dumping her and the hurt and humiliation still vivid. 'It sounds like you expected me to be waiting for you, frozen in time from the last moment we'd seen each other.'

A muscle ticked in his jaw. 'I admit I handled it badly. I wanted you too much. You got too close, It freaked me out. I shouldn't have let you go.'

'And yet you did.'

But the sense of betrayal suddenly felt less. Ajax's admission that he'd made a mistake settled deep inside her, where she didn't want his words to land. They were too easy.

Too seductive.

She waved a hand. 'Look, the past is the past. We are where we are. We have a child, and what we're doing is protecting her future. The fact that you want to be involved is very welcome, but I don't want a family with you, Ajax.'

'You want a family with someone else?' He said this flatly. 'You'd prefer that our daughter would be brought up by someone who isn't her father? For her to have half-siblings?'

'There's nothing wrong with that. Many families—'

'I know.' Ajax cut her off. 'I'm not saying there's anything wrong with it—if that's how it happens organically. But I think we have something we can build on. Some marriages are made on a lot less than that—you said so yourself.'

Had she? This was different, though. She felt confused. Her priority was to protect Ashling from harm. From being rejected or abandoned by her father. Yet now Ajax was asking her to consider having more children—which, as far as Erin could see, would only multiply that threat.

She imagined a scenario where she *was* pregnant again and what if Ajax changed his mind? Or maybe realised that the trauma of losing Theo was too big to surpass and he retreated back out of their lives again?

His change of heart was still too recent, too sudden to trust. That's what she told herself now.

Erin shook her head. 'No, I don't think it's a good idea.'

'I'm offering marriage, Erin.'

'Is this a proposal?'

That muscle moved in his jaw again. 'Not the most romantic, maybe, but yes.'

At this evidence that he would actually be willing to marry her for every reason except for love, or romance, Erin had a seismic realisation. The realisation that she *did* want love, even though it scared the life out of her. She knew now that it was the only thing that would sustain a happy life. And maybe she'd find it someday with someone, but not with Ajax.

She said, 'This isn't about romance or love, I know that. But if my parents had had love—mutual love—then maybe my mother wouldn't have left. Because she would have loved my dad enough to stay. Loved me enough at least to try.'

For a second—a heart-stopping moment—she wasn't sure how Ajax would respond, and the sense of being on the edge of a cliff about to step into the void was dizzying.

Then he said, 'I can't offer you love, but I can promise to be faithful and supportive. To respect you.'

Erin's dizziness faded. Of course he didn't love her. And she didn't love him. She didn't want him to love her.

She shrugged. 'Then I think I'll be a better parent to Ashling living authentically, rather than turning our fake relationship into a fake marriage and bringing more children into the mix. That's not the antidote to how I grew up—it's just another form of dysfunction.' Before he could say anything else, and confuse her, Erin went on, 'You can't admit that your parents' example of an arranged marriage was any better? We'd be somewhere halfway between that and what I had. And,' she said, 'I don't think we should do this again.'

'Do what again?' Ajax asked, civilly enough, but she could hear the steel in his voice.

'This…' Heat came into her face. 'Sex.'

The air seemed to throb with the tension between them.

Eventually Ajax said 'So what, you're saying you want more now? A real relationship? Love?'

'Maybe…would that be so bad?'

'I've told you I can't offer that.'

'I know.' Erin felt hollow.

At Ajax's stony expression she said, 'Maybe we should just go back to New York?'

But he shook his head, 'What about the event with my family? They should meet Ashling, at least.'

She wondered why, after everything she'd just said, she was feeling a sense of relief that he wasn't agreeing to put her on the next plane out of Greece.

He said, 'The event is this weekend. We'll be travelling to another island not far from here for a couple of nights. In the meantime I'll have my PR team assess the situation in New York—and, yes, I think you should be able to go back to New York after that.'

Erin looked at him. 'I think that would be for the best. And then we can establish a routine that suits Ashling.'

Everything in Ajax was rejecting Erin's, oh, so cool reaction to his proposal. He—Ajax Nikolau—had just *proposed*! But he realised in that moment how arrogant he had been to assume Erin would be impressed enough to collapse at his feet in a heap of acquiescence.

This was Erin. Had he learnt nothing?

But as for her assertion that they wouldn't have sex again…

The thought made him feel feral. Dangerously unmoored.

How could she stand there and say that when the flush of their lovemaking was still on her skin? After that…conflagration? This woman uniquely had the ability to turn him from civility to primal instinctiveness within seconds.

She'd talked about love. Of course he didn't love her. Theo's death had almost destroyed him. He knew that if anything happened to Ashling it would destroy him all over again, but all he could do now was put blind faith in the universe not to be so cruel for a second time.

But as for Erin… The thought of allowing himself to feel for her what had almost destroyed him…

No. His blood went cold at the thought.

Erin was looking at him, waiting for a response. He could deal with everything else she'd said in time, but as for *no sex*…

He walked closer to her. Close enough to touch. He saw how her eyes widened and flared. The way the pulse beat hectically at her throat.

He said, as coolly as her, 'I know this proposal has come as a bit of a surprise, and I wasn't expecting to talk about this here...now... But I would just ask that you think it all over before making a final decision.'

Her jaw was tight. 'Okay. Fine.'

Quickly, before she left, he said, 'As for the other thing... not making love again... I've never forced a woman in my life and I'm not about to start. But if you think this is over between us, then you will have to prove you have the control to resist it.'

She went red in the face. Ajax imagined that if steam could come out of her ears it would. With that, he sauntered away and into the villa, leaving her standing there.

But it was a pyrrhic victory, because he was very much afraid that she would prove to have far more control than him.

A few days later, Erin was still stewing over Ajax's parting bombshell after that cataclysmic moment in the pool. He'd all but dared her...told her that she couldn't possibly hold out against him.

Luckily, she hadn't been tested. Since that night he'd spent most of his time in his office, working, and had appeared only briefly for meals, or to play with Ashling—who was now his biggest fan.

Seeing her bonding with her father made Erin both delighted and terrified at once. Because with every day that their bond deepened and became stronger the stakes were rising. And if he ever walked away from Ashling...

And the proposal. Had that really happened? Or had she dreamed it? In any case, it hadn't been a proposal—not in any romantic sense. It had been a proposition: *We get on, we have a kid, we should get married.*

The thought of agreeing to marry Ajax and living a life

where the desire between them gradually fizzled out to be replaced with companionship... if they would even have that...sent shudders through Erin. She'd been fooling herself to think she could live with a scenario like that and it was beyond ironic that Ajax was the one who had made her realise she wanted more.

Ashling squealed from somewhere behind her on the small plane that was taking them to Ajax's family event on another island. An island owned by the family.

She looked behind her, and against every instinct she melted inside. Ashling was on Ajax's lap. He was trying to read some paperwork, and she kept trying to grab it. He put it down and lifted Ashling to face him. She put her hands on his face.

Erin felt a very inappropriate twinge of envy.

She got up and walked down the plane. Ajax looked up. Erin felt the effect in her blood.

She put out her arms. 'I'll take her—you're working.'

Ajax lifted her towards Erin and for a second their hands met as she took Ashling. Erin had to grit her jaw against the spark. *No.*

Ajax said, 'We'll be landing shortly anyway.'

Erin sat down on a nearby seat, suddenly trepidatious. 'So, who is going to be there?'

'My parents. Aunts, uncles, cousins. Some of Sofia's family.' Ajax's mouth thinned. 'After all, that's why my brother was going to marry her. Her family are also one of the oldest and most prominent in Greece.'

'It must be hard for them...losing her and Theo.'

Ajax made a rude sound. 'Not that you'd know it. Our marriage united the families and that's all they care about.'

'They sound truly...inhuman.'

Ajax shrugged. 'It's just a different world for them. It's how they've been brought up.'

Erin hugged Ashling a little closer.

Ajax saw the movement and said, 'It's exactly what I don't want.'

He looked at her then. Explicitly. The offer was still there.

Before he could see how he affected her, Erin fled back to her seat and occupied herself with Ashling for the rest of the flight.

It was a small, pretty island, with a bustling harbour town, iconic white and blue houses all along the sea front. They were driving up over the hill behind the harbour, towards a massive villa in the distance, surrounded by lush greenery.

Erin had noticed at least a dozen private jets parked up at the island's airport. Nerves churned in her belly. She was definitely out of her comfort zone now. She recalled what those people in Athens had said about her: *ambulance chaser*. She smiled a little grimly at herself. They'd also said Ajax would never want to marry her, but they'd been wrong about that.

If she wanted it…but she didn't.

She'd asked Georgiana for advice over a video call, and the stylist had helped her pick out some clothes. She was wearing a relaxed light blue suit—culottes and a matching jacket—with a cream sleeveless silk top underneath. Wedge sandals. A little more make-up than usual to feel fortified. Minimal jewellery.

She'd dressed Ashling in a cute romper suit with a matching sun hat that she kept trying to pull off.

Erin suddenly felt a surge of protectiveness for her daughter, at the thought of bringing her into this lions' den. She wanted to ask Ajax to turn the car around and take them home.

Home.

She had to stop thinking of here as home. New York was home. Where she had her life with Ashling.

They were at the villa now, and pulling into a huge courtyard. Uniformed staff hurried out to greet them. Damia was
in the car behind, and Erin was grateful not only for the help
but to have a friendly face.

Erin got out of the car and lifted Ashling out of her seat.
The little girl was tired. She hadn't had her morning nap on
the plane, too excited by everything, and Erin could sense
a cranky storm brewing. She hoped she could put her down
soon.

Ajax put a hand lightly on her lower back, but it burned
even through two layers of clothes. He said, 'Might as well
get the initial introductions over with.'

He led Erin into the villa—a vast space. Her first impression was that it was cold—which should have been welcome,
considering the heat outside. But it was cold in a way that
signified little human emotion.

Lots of white pristine surfaces. Expensive art. Furniture
that looked as if it had never been touched…

And then a slim, older woman appeared, walking towards
them, tall and impossibly elegant, with a cap of silver-grey
hair and light eyes. Beautiful but remote. Erin realised this
had to be Ajax's mother.

They greeted each other with air-kisses and Ajax said,
'Mother, how nice to see you.'

Erin just watched, wide-eyed at this dry exchange. Even
Ashling seemed to have been struck dumb.

The woman turned her gaze to Erin and Ashling. Ajax
moved closer, and despite everything Erin was glad of the
sense of protection.

He said, 'Mother, I'd like you to meet Erin Murphy and
your granddaughter Ashling.'

'Erin, this is my mother Andromeda.'

A fittingly intimidating name. Erin tried to imagine her

smiling and saying, *Call me Andi*, and almost wanted to giggle, but she knew it was just a little hysteria.

The woman held out her hand. 'Lovely to meet you, Erin.'

Erin shook her hand. 'You too.'

The woman's light blue gaze went to Ashling. She said, 'So this is the child?'

Ajax's tone was dry. 'Yes, Mother. Your granddaughter.'

'Ashling. Yes, I know. An Irish name. I looked it up.'

Erin tried to hide her surprise.

'She's a pretty thing,' Andromeda said. 'Very like—' But she stopped there abruptly.

She'd obviously been about to say *Theo*. To Erin's further surprise, she thought she saw a flicker of something on Andromeda's face—a flash of emotion. But then it was gone.

She stepped back. 'Your father is out on the terrace.'

They went out there, with Erin letting out a shaky breath. The tension in the air was almost unbearable.

Ajax's father was tall and handsome. Dark eyes. He showed no great interest in Erin or Ashling.

Erin felt Ashling starting to squirm and took the opportunity to excuse herself, fearing a meltdown.

Ajax led them away. As one of the staff showed them up to their rooms he said, 'Well? What do you think?'

Erin had to say, honestly, 'They're pretty much as you described them.'

Except she couldn't forget that little flicker of something on Andromeda's face when she'd almost mentioned Theo. Surely the woman had some humanity in her somewhere?

Erin was shown into a vast bedroom with an en suite bathroom and dressing room. It also led into a room that had been decorated as a pretty nursery.

'Did your parents do this especially?'

Ajax said from behind her, 'No, this was Theo's room.'

She turned around, immediately concerned. 'Is this all right?'

But to her surprise, Ajax looked…okay. Sad, but okay. Erin's heart clenched.

He said, 'I haven't actually been back here since he died. All his things are gone—they did that at least.'

'Ashling can stay in the main room with me. We don't have to use this.'

Ajax shook his head. 'No, it's fine. It's good that it'll be used again.'

He knocked on yet another door and Damia opened it after a few seconds, revealing that she too was just next door.

Ashling clapped her hands and Damia reached for her, saying, 'I'll change her and put her down for a nap.'

'Are you sure?' asked Erin.

Damia nodded. 'Absolutely. That's why I'm here, remember?'

Erin smiled wryly. She still wasn't completely used to having assistance on tap. 'Okay, thanks. But shout if you need me.'

Ajax said, 'I'll show you around and then we'll get a coffee.'

As Erin followed Ajax around the impressive property she had an appreciation of just how vast the Nikolau wealth was. He wore it lightly, so it was easy to forget just how rarefied his world was.

There were numerous gardeners tending to gardens as far as the eye could see. There were several guesthouses. A private stairway led down to a private beach and a jetty where a small yacht was moored.

They stood on the bluff above, with spectacular views out over the sea. The horizon was dotted with other islands.

'Most of the family have their own villas on the island. We'll be hosting some relations and close family friends in the guesthouses, but you probably won't even notice them.'

Erin wrinkled her nose. 'Your family have friends?'

Ajax chuckled. 'In their own dysfunctional way, yes.'

Erin felt warmth spreading through her. It was so easy to be with Ajax like this. Even in the midst of such grandeur and obvious tension. Too easy. Too seductive. She wanted to slip her hand into his and curl closer. Touch him. Use their desire to try and negate his family's chilliness.

But that wasn't her role. And she wasn't going to give him the satisfaction of giving in.

She took a step back. 'Where is the event taking place this evening?'

Ajax looked at her. 'At a rented villa.'

'This one wasn't up to scratch?' Erin quipped.

Ajax shook his head, the corner of his mouth lifting slightly. It made Erin's heart thump. She'd once wondered what it would be like to see this man smile or laugh.

He said, 'Oh, no, this isn't sufficient at all for showcasing the Nikolau dominance.'

Erin loved it that he was able to see his family for what they were. And on that note she took another step back. The word *love* was creeping into her head far too frequently for her liking. It was as if now that she'd given herself permission to desire more for herself, a floodgate had opened. It was just dangerous to conflate *love* and *Ajax* together.

'I think I'll go and get a bite to eat and then give Damia a couple of hours off. She'll be babysitting tonight.'

'I'll come for you when we're leaving...around five.'

Erin nodded. 'I'll be ready.'

Or as ready as she could be. Meeting Ajax's parents hadn't done much to quell her nerves.

CHAPTER TEN

IF ERIN HAD been impressed by his parents' villa, this one was on another level entirely. Apparently it was owned by another Greek billionaire, who was currently renting it out rather than living in it.

It was a soaring, white modern edifice on about three levels. It had been taken over by an events team and decorated with lanterns and fairy-lights. Uniformed staff in black and white moved through the guests—of which Erin counted about two hundred—with trays of sparkling wine and canapés that looked too good to eat. So she didn't. Anyway, she was terrified of getting anything on her evening dress.

She'd thought it was over the top, but Georgiana had convinced her and she was glad she'd listened now because she did blend in. The dress was cream silk with a halter-neck design, leaving her back bare, and slashed from her throat to navel where a jewel detail pulled the slinky fabric together before it fell in folds to the ground. She'd teamed it with high-heeled silver sandals.

Damia had helped her with her hair and make-up while Ashling had played with all the new toys that they'd found in the nursery—a nice touch, Erin had thought.

She'd nearly fainted when Ajax had told them they were taking a helicopter to the other island. Her adrenaline was still pumping and Ajax's hand was on her bare back, which wasn't helping. She would have asked him to remove it, but she remembered that they were supposed to be together.

Maybe she could convince him that now would be an appropriately public time to have a spat. But he was steering her towards people, and she soon got used to nodding and smiling inanely as he introduced her to distant relatives and acquaintances.

Everyone was perfectly civil, but there was a distinct lack of warmth, or fun. And since when had Erin been into *fun*?

Since you started making love with practical strangers in elevators and jumping into swimming pools fully clothed, whispered a sly voice.

She shook her head to get rid of it.

Ajax looked at her during a break in the never-ending stream of people. 'Okay?'

She forced a smile. 'Fine.'

Then she felt Ajax tense beside her. A couple were approaching. Probably in their sixties. Handsome. Not unlike his parents. He greeted them with the same kind of dry air-kiss as he had his mother and then said, 'Erin, I'd like you to meet Sofia's parents—Mr and Mrs Karakis.'

Erin's insides plummeted. She shook their hands, and couldn't help blurting out, 'I'm so sorry for your loss. I can't imagine how devastating it has been for you.'

Sofia's mother looked at Erin as if she had two heads. As if she'd said something completely incomprehensible. Then they moved away again.

Erin felt bewildered. 'What just happened? Should I not have sympathised with them?'

Ajax was shaking his head. 'No—I mean, yes, of course. Because you are from the normal world, where people experience emotions and are compassionate. But in their world it was a loss, yes, but as you can see it didn't end their world.'

Ajax sounded a little bitter.

'You feel the loss more keenly than they do,' Erin observed. 'Probably for Sofia too.'

'I visit their graves,' Ajax confided. 'Mainly to see Theo, I'll admit, but he's buried with Sofia. There's never any evidence of anyone else visiting.'

'That's really sad.'

At that moment they were interrupted by someone else, and the endless round of introductions started again. At some point the sound of soft jazz music came over the lawn and Erin swayed on the spot. She'd always enjoyed dancing.

As another couple headed their way Ajax took her hand and said, 'Want to dance?'

Erin said gratefully, 'Yes, please—if it means we can avoid more meaningless conversations with people trying to impress you.'

But as soon as Ajax had taken her into his arms on the dance floor, where some other couples were moving in slow circles, she realised her mistake. She was pressed against Ajax, who was obviously taking full advantage of the situation.

She looked up at him and he smiled. It was wicked.

'You were the one who wanted to dance.'

Erin tried to put some distance between them, but it was impossible. So she gave in and let her body do exactly what it wanted: cleave itself to Ajax's like a magnet. The thin material of her dress was no barrier to his body, sheathed in a black tuxedo. She swore she could feel every taut muscle and sinew... And then, when he moved a certain way, one muscle in particular.

She glared at him and he shrugged. 'I can't help it. With other women I can control myself, but not with you.'

The fire in Erin sizzled, as much as she wished it wouldn't. He couldn't control himself around her...?

Almost accusingly, she hissed, 'You said this chemistry would fade.'

'That's been my experience with other women. But you have proved to be unique. It doesn't feel like it's fading to you, does it?'

She could feel the very tantalising evidence of his non-fading desire right now. She shook her head.

'So why deny yourself?' he whispered in her ear, his mouth almost close enough to touch her skin.

Erin tingled all over. Her mind was beginning to get blurry, but she forced herself to stay focused. 'Because, unlike you, I do have self-control.'

She smiled sweetly at him and saw his eyes flash.

This was a dangerous game they were playing, and she knew it. At that moment, though, she caught Andromeda's eye over Ajax's shoulder. She was dancing with her husband, and they couldn't have looked more stiff and unhappy.

She nodded her head slightly at Erin, acknowledging her, and Erin nodded back. But she shivered inwardly—not from desire, this time, but at the reminder of what lay ahead of her if she gave in to Ajax's version of a future for them. A sterile, sad life.

She looked away and forced ice into her veins.

'What's wrong?' Ajax asked.

Erin shook her head. 'Nothing—just someone walking over my grave.'

She somehow managed to get through the rest of the evening, staying as rigid as she could by Ajax's side. And then, mercifully, they were heading back to his parents' villa.

The helicopter landed at a far enough distance from the villa not to disturb Damia and Ashling, and they were driven to the house in two cars. Erin and Ajax in one, his parents in the other.

When they got out at the villa Andromeda was already there. She stopped Erin on the way in, when Ajax was already inside.

Andromeda looked at her and said, 'You're in love with him, aren't you? I saw you dancing. I saw the way you looked at him.'

Erin tried to suck in a breath, but she couldn't. She shook her head, desperately negating the tight feeling in her chest and the pounding of her blood at such an audacious suggestion. 'No, of course I'm not. I know what this is. We both do. It's not love.'

Andromeda smiled faintly, but it wasn't kind. It was sad. 'I'm sure he's told you what it was like for him and his brother. I'd hate for you to get hurt. You seem like a nice woman, Erin. You deserve more.'

Andromeda walked away, leaving Erin reeling, her words revolving sickeningly in her head.

'You're in love with him, aren't you?'

No. She wasn't. She couldn't be. To love a man like Ajax would be the worst form of self-harm. He'd already dumped her once. And while he was offering to spend his life with her, create a family, the offer wasn't born out of love. He might not dump her again, but he would gradually fade away—which would be worse than any kind of abandonment or outright rejection.

Even the prospect of loving Ajax and allowing him that much power to hurt her, as she'd only been hurt once before in her life—by her mother—made her feel dizzy.

'Erin? Are you okay?'

Ajax. When she least wanted to see him. He was at her side, holding her elbow. He looked angry.

'What did she say to you?'

'N-nothing, honestly. I'm just tired—and hungry, I think. We didn't really eat.'

Ajax took her hand in his before she could stop him, and it was easier to just leave it there. He led her into the kitchen, silent at this hour of the night apart from the humming fridge.

He said, 'Sit down,' and all but pushed her gently into a seat at the table.

Erin sat, and watched, bemused, as Ajax spent an inordinate amount of time opening and closing doors.

Eventually she said, 'What are you looking for?'

He looked at her. 'Eggs.'

She pointed to the pantry door. 'Try in there.'

He did, and said, 'Ah!' and came out with a tray of eggs, triumphant. Erin moved to stand up, but he put up a hand. 'No, stay there. I'm making you something to eat.'

'But you don't know how to cook.'

Ajax looked a little embarrassed, and Erin was gobsmacked to see him efficiently cracking eggs over a bowl.

Eventually he said, 'Since that night when you were in my apartment...'

The second night they'd been together, when they'd skipped dinner and gone into his kitchen at midnight, looking for food. Ajax hadn't had a clue where anything was, but he'd managed to find a chicken salad and some bread. Erin had teased him about his lack of culinary skills.

Ajax continued, 'Something you said stuck with me... about how could I be self-sufficient if I couldn't even boil an egg?'

Erin winced. Sometimes she was too straight. 'I'm sorry... I didn't mean it as an insult.'

He looked at her over the bowl, where he was now whisking the eggs like a professional. 'No, you did me a huge favour. I taught myself how to boil an egg and then I kept going. I make a mean omelette now. I can't say I've added too much to my repertoire, but I'm hoping to master a decent roast chicken at some point.'

'The easiest thing in the world,' said Erin, trying to ignore the way her insides felt as if they were melting and somer-saulting at the same time.

Ajax was now transferring the eggs to a warmed pan and adding in some things she couldn't see. But it smelled delicious. After a few minutes he came over and put a plate down in front of her. A perfectly fluffy omelette, garnished with fresh herbs and some bread.

She looked up at him, mouth agape. And then she shut it again. She was starving. She tasted the omelette and closed her eyes in appreciation.

Ajax poured wine into two glasses and put one down for her. He took another seat.

When she'd swallowed some more food and a sip of wine she said, 'Not hungry?'

His eyes were hooded and the gleam in them was wicked. He said, 'Oh, I am—but not for food.'

Erin refused to let him see how that affected her. Like a match to dry tinder. She was very conscious of her dress and the amount of skin she was showing. She forced herself to finish the omelette and eat some bread, even though her appetite had suddenly diminished.

She took another sip of wine and said, 'That was delicious, thank you. I should go up now…check on Ashling.'

'She's fine. I checked when I came in.'

Another tummy somersault. She ignored it. 'I'm still going to bed.'

She stood up, the silk folds of her dress falling to the floor. She must look ridiculous. Ajax didn't stand up. He sat in a louche sprawl in the chair, his bow tie undone, jacket gone. Stubble on his jaw.

He said, 'You know where I am, Erin.'

She refrained from saying anything and swept out of the kitchen with as much grace as she could muster, all but running to her bedroom as soon as she was out of his eyeline.

She got inside her room and kicked off her sandals, then went silently to the nursery. Her heart expanded when she saw Ashling asleep, lashes long on her cheeks. She pulled up the thin blanket and put her hand on her belly for a minute, feeling the rise and fall of her breath.

Once again she was struck by how protective she felt. She would never do anything to harm this child. In moments like this the betrayal of her mother was as acute as it had been almost twenty-five years ago. She would do anything to spare Ashling the same pain, and if that meant ensuring they kept Ajax at a distance then so be it.

The door to Damia's room was ajar. Erin took the spare baby monitor into her own room and changed into sleeping shorts and a singlet top, washed her face and got into bed.

But an hour later she was still lying there. Wide awake. Restless. Eventually she fell into a fitful sleep and a disturbing dream, in which she was at a party but was encased in ice and couldn't move. No one was looking at her. They couldn't see her. She was trying to grab their attention. And then Ajax was there, but not looking at her. He was with another woman. Erin was sobbing and calling out, begging for him to notice her—

And then she woke up, sitting straight up in bed, heart pounding, skin slick with perspiration. Still that awful icy cold lingered, reaching all the way into her heart.

She didn't think—she acted on instinct. She got out of bed and took the baby monitor with her. She left her room and walked down the corridor to Ajax's room, pushed open the door. He lay in a sprawl on the bed. Naked.

As she approached he woke up and came up on an elbow. His voice was rough. 'Erin…?'

She put down the baby monitor and lifted her arms, taking off the singlet top. She pulled down the shorts and climbed into his bed beside him. He looked stunned. She might have appreciated it more if she hadn't had the overwhelming lingering dread of that dream in her blood.

He touched her jaw. 'Am I dreaming?'

She shook her head. 'No, I'm real. Make love to me, Ajax.'

There was no triumph in his gaze, just pure desire as he pulled her over him and speared his hands in her hair, drawing her face down to his so he could kiss her. She revelled in feeling his body under hers, so strong and warm. His heart beat against hers. Her breasts were crushed to his chest. She opened her legs and he moved her subtly, so she was lined up with where his body was hardening.

There was practically no sound apart from their laboured breathing as he joined their bodies with one thrust. Erin sat back, putting her hands on his chest as she rode him, moving up and down. Ajax put his hands on her hips, holding her as he pumped into her, making her gasp out loud.

The orgasm broke over Erin almost before she had time to register it was coming. Ajax flipped them over, so he was on top, and just before he came he pulled free of Erin's embrace, so she felt the hot warmth of his climax on her belly.

After a few long moments of letting the world come back to its centre, Ajax got up and picked Erin up from the bed as if she weighed no more than a bag of sugar and took her into the shower. Under the hot spray he washed her, and himself, then wrapped them both in towels and took her back to bed, where she finally fell into a dreamless sleep.

When Erin stole out of the bed the next morning, she resolutely refused to look at why she'd gravitated to Ajax so desperately the previous night. Without even thinking about it. Following an instinct she hadn't been able to ignore. For her survival.

She was still wearing the robe he'd put on her after the shower, and she picked up her night clothes and left his room.

Back in her own room, after quickly checking Ashling, she had a shower and got dressed.

Ashling was just waking up, and Erin changed her and took her downstairs to give her some breakfast. She noticed that Ajax had washed the plate and pan from the previous night and left them drying on the sideboard. She almost wanted to curse him for being so…unexpected.

She took her and Ashling's breakfast out to the terrace and enjoyed the quiet before others emerged. She would put last night down to an urge to make the most of her chemistry with Ajax before it went away. He was right—why deny themselves? It was just sex.

But what about that dream?

Erin shut it down. The memory of how cold she'd felt was still vivid in the morning light. Of how she'd needed him.

Ashling was cranky, in spite of her good night's sleep, and Erin could see that her cheeks were red. She was teething.

After breakfast, Erin took Ashling down to the beach, to try and distract her, but she was soon working herself up into a state—she'd given her some medication, but it didn't seem to be working.

So Erin brought her back inside to try and find something else to alleviate the pain.

There was no sign of Ajax—which Erin was grateful for. She was sure he'd be mocking and arrogant after her spectacular capitulation last night.

Damia was on the terrace, and offered to take Ashling, but Erin said, 'No, you have the day off. You were working until late and we'll be out again this evening.'

Erin took the baby upstairs. Ashling's wails were now reverberating all through the villa.

To her surprise, Andromeda appeared, holding a teething ring. She said, 'It belonged to Theo. I kept it. Can I try?'

She held out her arms and Erin realised she meant to take Ashling.

Against her better instincts, Erin handed Ashling over, fully prepared for the little girl's wails to increase in crescendo, but to her shock the surprise of being in a stranger's arms silenced Ashling for a moment, and Andromeda put the teething ring against Ashling's lips. She latched on to it immediately, chewing down on it and holding it with both hands.

Andromeda was saying, 'There, there…that's not so bad, now, is it?'

Erin just gaped at her.

Andromeda looked at her a little sheepishly. 'I could never do this with Demetriou or Ajax. I wasn't encouraged to hold them.'

'I… I heard,' Erin said faintly.

Andromeda jiggled Ashling up and down a little and walked with her out to the terrace. Then the tiny hairs went up on the back of Erin's neck.

Ajax.

She turned around, saw he was looking past her to his mother. 'Is that…?'

Erin nodded. 'I know… I can't believe it either.'

Then Ajax looked at her. 'You left my bed again.'

Erin pushed aside the way he made her feel…confused and excited and scared all at once.

His expression was stark. He opened his mouth to speak again, but his mother came back with a now much more peaceful Ashling. She handed her to Erin and said, 'I'd like to see her sometimes, if that's possible… I mean, after this is over.'

'Of course,' Erin said, trying to hide her shock, 'you're her grandmother.'

The older woman touched the baby's cheek and then

looked at Ajax. With a suspicious brightness in her eyes she said, 'I'm sorry that I wasn't able to be there for you and your brother in a more meaningful way. I wanted to be... But...' She shook her head and left the small room quickly, before Ajax could respond.

He looked at Erin, stunned. 'Did you see that?'

Erin nodded. She felt a little sad. 'I think she's realising, since losing your brother and your nephew, that maybe she's been given a second chance. It's a good thing, Ajax.'

'If she means what she says,' he said tautly.

Erin appreciated the irony that Ajax now felt the same fears she had regarding him.

'Maybe you should go and talk to your mother. I'm going to try and put Ashling down for a nap, or else she'll be crabby for Damia later.'

Ajax said, 'Last night—'

She cut him off. 'It was just sex, Ajax. Nothing more. I agree—we need to let this run its course.'

He looked at her for a long moment and then said, 'This conversation isn't over.'

He left the nursery.

Hours later, Ajax waited for Erin in the hall. He felt restless and irritable. She'd managed to successfully avoid him all day—taking Ashling on an excursion to the village, according to Damia.

He would have gone after her, but his mother had waylaid him and said, 'Don't do what we did, Ajax, live half-lives. You deserve more, and you can have that with Erin. I've seen the way she looks at you...'

Ajax still couldn't understand what his mother meant. Erin only ever looked at him warily, or with barely concealed amusement. Like when he'd been exhibiting his pathetic range of culinary skills last night. Culinary skills inspired by her, even though he'd let her go.

Erin's voice came back to him. *'You dumped me.'* He winced. He had dumped her—unceremoniously. Because she'd got too close.

'I've seen the way she looks at you.'

Ajax shook his head at himself. His mother was obviously going through some sort of life crisis and was seeing things all over the place.

Erin wanted him at a distance, but she would kill him in the process if last night was anything to go by.

A question formed in his head. If Erin had got too close for comfort before, then where was she now? After all, he'd been prepared to make a lifetime commitment to her. Obviously both being aware that it would be based on companionability and chemistry. Nothing more.

'You deserve more.'

But he didn't want more. He didn't want to risk that awful devastation all over again. The loss of someone he—

He heard a sound and turned to see Erin at the top of the stairs. And in that moment—in a heartbeat—he knew that it was all too late.

He'd been fooling himself…living in denial. The one thing he'd promised would never happen again had crept up on him and happened before he could stop it, and he realised now that it had happened even before that second night with Erin.

It was the reason he hadn't slept with anyone else.

It was the reason it had taken him so long to go after her.

Because he'd *known*. Deep down.

Erin looked worried. 'Is the dress okay? It's too short, isn't it? Maybe it's meant to be evening-length, but you did say cocktail.'

Ajax barely took in the dress—it fell to mid-calf and it was strapless and figure-hugging. Not that he needed a reminder of Erin's figure. All he had to do was close his eyes and he was there, under her, as she slid on top of him.

'It's fine. You look amazing… We should go.'

She still looked a bit concerned, but she came down the stairs towards him and panic rose up, making his skin feel tight. He swallowed it down. When Erin got to him her scent tickled his nostrils. Fresh and light. Nothing complicated. Like her. Straight. When what he was feeling right now was anything but straight. It was a maelstrom.

She frowned. 'What is it? You're looking at me like I've done something wrong.'

She had—and she had no idea. She'd upended Ajax's world and it would never be the same again. She'd made a mockery of his notion that he could control everything. That he could protect himself.

But now was not the time or the place to spill his guts.

He lied through his teeth. 'Nothing is wrong. We should go.'

That evening's event was on yet another nearby island—an open-air art exhibition of some of the world's most famous modern artists. All of Ajax's family were there again, but there were other people too, and it was nice to have a sense of the normal world around her. People laughing and chatting.

Erin was delighted to see Leo and Angel Parnassus, and only too happy to let Angel spirit her away from Ajax temporarily. He was in a funny mood. She kept catching him looking at her as if she was someone he didn't know. Suspicious. Accusing.

But if it kept some sort of distance between them then she welcomed it. Because increasingly around him she felt as if she was losing sight of what was important. To keep herself and Ashling safe from harm. From betrayal. From being rejected. Dumped again.

So how does that explain how you gravitated into his bed like a wanton last night?

Erin ignored that and let Angel distract her. She was telling her how this whole social scene was a circuit, which happened every summer for members of Greek's high society, when they decamped from humid Athens to their various island boltholes and then spent a couple of months island-hopping on planes, helicopters or yachts.

It made Erin's mind boggle...the sheer wealth.

Leo and Ajax joined them, and Ajax put an arm around Erin's waist. She tried to stiffen against the inevitable urge to relax into him, but once again it was easier just to...*cleave.*

Ajax's parents hadn't come with them to this event. Andromeda had actually said that she would help Damia with Ashling. So when they got back to the villa that night it was just them, and a silent villa.

Wordlessly, Erin read Ajax's intent. He took her hand and waited for her to take off her shoes, then led her upstairs to her room. They both went in and checked on Ashling, who was asleep.

Erin was torn between wanting an excuse not to go where they were inevitably headed, and wanting to drag all of Ajax's clothes off him there and then.

He led her out, down to his room. He shut the door behind them and Erin stood with her back to it. He put his hands either side of her head and just looked at her.

Erin said, 'What is it? You've been glaring at me all evening.'

Ajax shook his head. He fingers traced her jaw, his touch gentle, belying the fierceness of his expression.

He said, 'You. You're killing me. I—'

Erin reached up and put her hands on his face, touching her mouth to his, cutting off his words, as if she knew he was going to say something she didn't want to hear.

She broke away after a long moment and said, 'No words. We don't need to talk.'

Ajax was mocking. 'I forgot…this is just sex.'

Erin nodded as she pushed Ajax's jacket off his shoulders to the floor, then tackled his bow tie and shirt. 'Yes, it's just sex.'

For the next couple of hours it *was* just sex—and Erin pushed away every internal voice or twinge of conscience and tried to convince herself of that.

CHAPTER ELEVEN

Two weeks later, Athens

AFTER ERIN HAD cleared a further absence from work—
unpaid—it was as if she and Ajax had entered into a tacit
agreement to stay in Greece and indulge this desire until it
burned out.

At night she would steal into his room, where they would
communicate with a primal ferocity that left her breathless
and desperate, wondering why their chemistry wasn't waning. The opposite, it felt like.

She was aware of Ajax looking at her more and more as if
he wanted to say something, but she would invariably make
an excuse to walk away or distract him. Instinctively she
knew she didn't want to hear what he might say.

But she felt as if a net was slowly closing around her. She
couldn't keep avoiding Ajax for ever. A decision would have
to be made. They had to return to New York and get on with
their lives. As it was, Erin's firm had been more than generous allowing her all this time off, but she couldn't take
advantage for much longer if she expected her job to still
be there for her.

And now there was a further potential complication in
the mix—one that Erin couldn't even bring herself to fully
contemplate. She'd looked at herself in the mirror that morning, after a sudden bout of vomiting, and a feeling of dread

coupled with absurd excitement had mixed in her gut—prompting another bout of sickness.

It mightn't be anything, assured an inner voice.

But this was exactly what had happened with Ashling—except she'd ignored it until the point where she hadn't been able to ignore it any longer.

Ashling handed Erin the toy she'd been playing with as they sat under the shade of one of the trees on the lawn in the gardens of Ajax's Athens villa.

'Thank you,' said Erin absently.

And then, as if manifested by her imagination, she looked up and saw Ajax walking across the lawn to them with a determined look on his face. Erin felt like running—and also too weary to run…as if she'd been running for a long time and wanted to stop.

He was dressed in jeans and a shirt—untucked, sleeves rolled up. He'd been working from home today. Ashling saw him and clapped her hands and stood up unsteadily. Ajax crouched down a few feet away and held out his arms, Ashling had no hesitation and ran straight into them, squealing with glee when he lifted her up high into the air, twirling her around.

Erin envied the simplicity of the relationship between them.

Ajax came over and kneeled down, putting Ashling back on the ground, where she pounced on her toys again. He looked at Erin. 'Can we talk?'

Panic flared. A sense of nausea gripped her at the memory of earlier that morning.

'I told Damia I'd help her with an English essay she has due—'

Ajax reached out and caught her hand gently, stopping her from standing.

She stopped and pulled it back.

He said, 'I'd prefer to talk elsewhere, but you keep running away from me every time I try to talk to you.'

'I was in your bed last night,' Erin said, almost accusingly—as if he was responsible for some witchcraft that got her to come to him like some kind of automaton.

Ajax snorted. 'As if that's where we'll get any talking done! Maybe in another ten years, when I don't want you as much as I—'

'We won't be together in ten years.' Erin cut him off, panic rising. The net was closing around her.

'Yes, we will, Erin Murphy. Because I love you, and I've been trying to tell you for days now, and you keep avoiding—'

But she was already on her feet, galvanised by a force deep inside that she couldn't fully understand. All she knew was that she had to leave…get away—*now*.

She started walking blindly up the garden. Ajax called from behind her. 'Dammit, Erin, would you just—? Where are you going?'

She turned around but kept walking backwards. Ajax was holding Ashling in his arms. She was looking confused, putting out her hand. Erin felt emotion rising, threatening to consume her.

'I'm sorry… I can't do this,' she got out, and she fled.

The driver had dropped Erin in the Plaka area of Athens. It was crowded with tourists and locals. She walked blindly for a long time, trying not to think of what Ajax had said.

'I love you.'

He didn't mean it. It was a platitude to get her to agree to stay with him…to create a life that would fall apart once he lost interest.

Erin recognised a doorway and stumbled to a halt. She went in and was greeted by a doorman, who pressed a button on the elevator for her. She stepped into the dark space, only then recognising it as the restaurant where Ajax had taken her on one of those first nights.

She wanted to turn around and get out, but it was too late. The elevator doors were opening again and a waiter was leading her to a quiet table. There weren't many people. It was between lunch and dinner time. The staff changeover was happening.

A glass of water and a glass of wine materialised in front of her—she didn't even remember ordering them. She took a big gulp of water, but ignored the wine.

'I love you.'

Erin shook her head. But then she thought of Ashling, her face confused, in Ajax's arms, her little hand held out.

A memory rose up, unbidden, of herself as a child, a toddler...crying and pleading, hanging on to her mother's skirt, her hands being prised away, her father lifting her up. And how it had felt to stretch out her hand towards her mother, watching her as she disappeared behind a closed door.

Even at that young age, Erin realised now, she'd believed that somehow *she'd* caused her to leave. Because she'd loved her mother too much and wanted her to stay. So she'd left.

Erin only realised she was crying when she looked up and saw Ajax standing there. He was immediately concerned, coming to her side.

'What is it? Is it really so bad if I love you?'

Erin pushed up out of the chair. She had to get away— *again*. She went towards the elevator, barely noticing that the restaurant was now empty.

The doors were open. She got in and stabbed at the buttons—any buttons—to shut the door and push Ajax back.

The doors started closing, but a hand stopped them and Ajax stepped in.

The doors closed. Erin backed away against a wall.

It finally rose up inside her—the truth of what she was feeling. But she couldn't articulate it.

She said, 'Please don't say it again.'

The elevator wasn't moving, but Erin was barely aware.

Ajax said, 'What? That I love you? Well, I do—and I'm going to keep saying it until you believe me.'

Erin shook her head. 'I don't want to believe you. Because if I believe you then you'll destroy me when you walk away. All this time I've been telling myself I'm worried for Ashling, but it's me. I'm scared for me. Because I can't go through it again. Watching my mother walk out broke something inside me.'

Ajax moved to come closer, but Erin put up a hand.

He stopped. 'You're not broken, Erin—far from it. Your mother abandoned you…that's a traumatic event that would scar anyone, let alone a small child.'

'I just walked away from my own daughter.'

Erin felt bile and shame. She'd literally repeated history.

Ajax shook his head. 'You couldn't walk away from your own child and you know it. This is very different.'

Erin's insides cramped. 'Is she okay?'

'She's fine—having dinner with Damia as we speak.'

Erin knew he was right. She would never be able to leave Ashling. She'd walked away from him, from his declaration.

Ajax said, 'It was my fault. I should have waited. But I've been growing impatient… We've wasted so much time… nearly two years… I want to spend the rest of my life with you, Erin. I want us to have so much more than what we've experienced in our lives.'

She shook her head, emotion rising. She had nothing to hide behind any more. 'I can't love you… I'm too scared of being hurt again.'

Ajax closed the distance between them and this time Erin couldn't stop him. He cupped her face in his hands and looked down at her with an expression she'd never seen before. Or maybe she had, and she'd told herself it wasn't what she thought it was. Feared it was.

Love. The thing she wanted. The thing she feared.

He said, 'It's too late. You already love me. And I love you. I think I've loved you from way back...that second night. That's why I let you go.'

Erin hiccupped. 'You mean dumped me.'

Ajax winced. 'You got too close. I could see myself becoming obsessed. I wasn't ready. But I didn't forget you. And I didn't want anyone else.'

Erin sniffed. 'You're just lucky that I was occupied having your daughter and that someone else didn't sweep me off my feet.'

Ajax went pale in the dim light of the small space. 'Don't even joke about that.'

A tiny, fledgling seed of hope was pushing out of the deep dark fear inside Erin. She said, 'I won't survive if you dump me again.'

Ajax shook his head, and now he looked fierce. 'Losing Theo almost destroyed me. I'd never known love could be like that and I wanted nothing to do with it ever again. But you brought me back to life. And Ashling. You made me want to believe again. To trust again. I'm not going anywhere. And neither are you. We are bound together for ever. I want a family with you. I want to shower our children with all the love and security we missed.'

Erin bit her lip and took Ajax's hand, bringing it to her belly, under her shirt. His eyes widened and she said, 'I don't know for sure, but if my symptoms are anything to go by I could already be pregnant again.'

Ajax's hand spread across Erin's belly. His voice was hoarse. 'Truly?'

She nodded, and felt any last doubts dissolving at the awe

on Ajax's face. 'That's why I panicked before and ran. I knew this, and I was afraid that if you didn't really mean what you said…if you were just saying it…then we'd be stuck together unhappily, like your parents and all those other people, for the rest of our lives.'

Ajax shook his head. He entwined his fingers with hers and said, 'Not possible. We're not them and we never will be.'

Then he got down on one knee, and Erin's eyes went wide. He kept her hand in his and said, 'Erin Murphy, will you please marry me, and have a family with me, and love me as I promise to love you, until death us do part?'

Love. The scariest thing of all. But without it she wouldn't survive.

Erin nodded and slid down on to her knees beside him, wrapping her arms around his neck. 'I love you, Ajax.' She was finally home.

Home.

When they emerged from the elevator some time later, a little dishevelled but giddy with happiness, Erin said, 'What is it about us and elevators?'

Ajax said, 'I don't know, but I'm going to make sure there's one in every one of our properties from now on.'

Erin laughed. 'Isn't that a little extravagant?'

Ajax picked up his fiancée, uncaring of who looked at them in the street, and said, 'Well, where else are we going to celebrate our anniversaries?'

'That's very true—but first can we go home to our baby?'

'Now, that…' Ajax kissed her '…we can do.'

EPILOGUE

Three years later

ERIN SMILED AT the scene before her. Chaos, in a word. But very happy chaos.

She was standing on the terrace of the villa in Athens. Where once there had been a pristine empty lawn stretching into the distance, with the majestic city of Athens in the background, now there was a bouncy castle, clowns, too many children to count, adults chatting and warding off minor accidents, tables groaning under the weight of food and drink, and at least two fluffy dogs alternately being pawed at by the children or hiding in the bushes for some respite.

Her father was on one side of the garden, discussing plants with the head gardener. He had a pointed party hat on his head, askew, making him look even more like a mad professor than he usually did.

Then Erin's eyes widened, and she put a hand to her mouth to try and hide a laugh of disbelief. Yes, that really was Ajax's impeccably cool and elegant mother, on the bouncy castle, being thrown hither and thither with any number of children. And she wasn't horrified—she was laughing. Shrieking with delight, in fact. And her sleek cap of grey hair was mussed up in a way that Erin would never have believed possible just a couple of years ago.

Andromeda had changed utterly. She was now a much beloved grandmother, making the most of all the love she'd missed out on with her own children. She'd divorced Ajax's father and since married the man she'd fallen in love with ten years ago. He was watching now from the sidelines, with an indulgent smile.

Erin's mother hadn't had such a radical change of heart, but she was making an effort and she and Erin had found some peace.

Erin had left her job at the firm—understandably, after falling pregnant again—and she'd since decided that she wanted to move into not-for-profit consultancy work. She had set up a firm that helped small businesses who couldn't afford the fees that the big law firms charged. They did a lot of work with charities and marginalised communities. It was unbelievably rewarding, and she loved it.

'*Yaya!* I'm coming!'

Ashling, four years old today, leapt up onto the bouncy castle and promptly upended her grandmother. To say she was fizzing with excitement was an understatement.

Agatha had come from the island to visit, and was currently holding a sleepy toddler in her arms. Teddy. Ajax and Erin had agreed that they would have loved to call him Theo, but it was just too close to the bone. And Theo had been Theo. So they'd settled on Teddy as a compromise. With his dark blond hair showing tints of red, he took after the Murphy side of the family. Except for the light eyes. They were as blue-green as his father's.

The tiny hairs on the back of Erin's neck stood up. She smiled before she even felt him. And then he slid his arms around her distended waist, his hands covering her sizeable bump.

Ajax kissed the side of Erin's neck and her blood hummed.

She put her hands over his. No sign of their chemistry waning. It only got stronger.

And soon they would welcome a new member into their family. It was the reason they were here in Athens and not on the island. She was due any day now. Baby number three…

Ajax moved to take her hand and she looked at him. They didn't speak. They didn't need to. They just smiled. The evidence of their love was all around them. It had broken the shackles of the past and brought them here, to this bright and shining place, where love was celebrated daily and where fear was no longer given room to breathe.

He led her down into the garden, and they were soon swallowed up in the joyous, loving mayhem.

* * * * *

PRINCE'S
FORGOTTEN
DIAMOND

EMMY GRAYSON

MILLS & BOON

To my readers,
you're all simply wonderful.

CHAPTER ONE

HE CAME TO with a gasp, the act of inhaling sending a hundred sharp knives stabbing into his chest. He uttered an oath and froze. Gradually the pain subsided. Each breath still burned like the devil, but at least he could sit up.

The room spun. He gritted his teeth and closed his eyes, waited, then slowly opened them again. The world slowed enough that he was able to evaluate his surroundings, from the plush rug laid atop gleaming mahogany floors to the glittering chandelier hanging above his head. Cautiously, he turned his head. He was sitting on a tufted leather couch. A marble fireplace dominated the wall to his left, the space above the mantel decorated with a painting of Westminster Abbey's Gothic towers. To the right lay a massive bed on a raised dais, the mattress draped in a luxurious midnight comforter and a mound of artfully arranged pillows.

A distant honk made him wince. Whatever he'd been through had left him not only with an aching chest but a monstrous headache. He slid his fingers through his hair, pausing when he located a lump at the base of his skull.

What the hell happened?

He stood and made his way to the bathroom. He turned on the faucet, cupped his hands to catch the blessedly cool water and splashed it over his skin.

He raised his head, his eyes flickering to the mirror,

then back again as confusion tugged at him. Confusion that quickly morphed into shock.

The face staring back at him was that of a stranger.

His hand came up, his fingertips tracing a long cut that ran from the slight hollow beneath his cheek down into the light beard following the lines of his jaw. The man in the glass mirrored his actions. Brown eyes stared back at him, fatigued and ringed by shadows.

Unfamiliar.

Who am I?

The question skittered through his mind, but encountered only silence. Silence and a gaping void that seemed to stretch on with no end in sight. No memories existed beyond this moment.

Dread pulled at him, fingers tugging, grasping at his consciousness. With a resolve that came to him as naturally as breathing, he stopped it. Panic had no place here.

He filled his lungs with a deep, cleansing breath before walking back into the bedroom. A quick search yielded no wallet or cell phone. The only luggage was a canvas duffel bag with leather straps. The clothes inside were simple yet well made, the tags featuring luxury labels he somehow recognized even though he couldn't even recall his own name. A thick white envelope, concealed in an interior side pocket, yielded nearly ten thousand euros. Whoever he was, it appeared he had money.

Or had taken it from someone who did.

Uncomfortable with the thought, his hand went back up to that cut, his fingers pressing against the wound. The sharp prick of pain centered him, pulled him back from the edge of diving too far into speculation that would get him nowhere.

A glance out the window revealed elegant buildings of brick and white stone stacked side by side. Some were storefronts, while others appeared to be office buildings. But they all carried the unmistakable mark of wealth. Taxis, red double-decker buses and pedestrians hurried to and fro beneath a darkening sky.

London.

He was in London. Something else flitted through his mind, but it darted away before he could grasp it.

One step at a time, he told himself. *See if anyone else is here.*

He moved away from the window to the double doors of the room. He listened for a full minute before carefully opening the door to a large, airy hallway with several expensive-looking paintings hung on the ivory walls between doors marked with room numbers.

A hotel then. Had he been attacked in the room? No, that didn't make sense. Surely if he had been attacked in here his assailant would have grabbed the duffel or at least searched it.

The headache returned with a vengeance. Twenty minutes later, after taking some pain medication he'd found in the bathroom and resting on the couch, he felt well enough to conduct another search of the room. He surveyed the lavish furnishings with a sharpened gaze. A flash of black caught his eye. On the floor underneath the couch lay an onyx business card. As he knelt, something shifted in his chest. He knew the card, knew the elegant cursive would have a delicate silver filigree style. Threads of apprehension and excitement drifted through him as his fingers closed around it.

The card was heavy, the edges rounded. On one side the card simply read *Smythe's*. On the other was a street address with a series of numbers in the bottom left corner. Someone had written *Saturday, 7:30* in silver ink in the right corner.

A sense of urgency suddenly took him. This card, and the appointment, were important. He glanced at his wrist, only to find the skin pale where a watch should have been. He picked up the phone by the bed.

"Good evening, thank you for calling The Bancroft, Anthony speaking."

He mentally noted the name of the hotel.

"Hello, Anthony. Could you please provide me with the date and time?"

"Certainly, sir. Today is April the fifth, and the time is almost seven in the evening."

"Is today Saturday?"

"Yes, sir."

He decided to take one last leap.

"Thank you, Anthony. My last question: what's the name listed for my room?"

A pause followed. "Sir?"

"Just clarifying what name the reservation was made under."

"Of course, sir. The name we have on file is John Adamos."

A Greek surname. One that didn't feel or sound familiar.

"Thank you."

He hung up the phone.

John Adamos.

He said the name out loud, repeated it several times. Each time it sounded as alien as when he'd first heard it.

His eyes moved back to the card. He had thirty minutes before the appointment time listed on the card. He could call the police or take himself to a hospital. But the hospital could take hours of examinations and scans. While he would need to see a doctor eventually, the medicine made his pain manageable for now. The police would interview him, possibly take a photo and circulate it to the media as they investigated what had happened to him. Something else that would take time.

He tapped the card against his other hand. This route, however, could give him answers within the hour.

He picked up the phone and dialed again.

"Good evening and thank you for—"

"Anthony, it's… John again." The name tasted foreign on his tongue.

"Yes, sir."

"Would you please have a taxi ready for me in ten minutes?"

Fifteen minutes later, John stood on the sidewalk that ran alongside a terrace of elegant town houses. The one listed on the card resembled the others in the row with its white brick, arched windows and elegant pillars guarding the main entrance. But unlike the glossy mahogany doors that graced the other homes, this one's door differed with its midnight black coloring. There was no sign, though, no indication that the house was anything but a residence. He ascended the stairs and pressed the doorbell. Scarcely two seconds passed before the door opened to reveal a man. A very, very tall man who looked as if he'd been stuffed into the black suit he wore and didn't look very happy about it.

"Good evening."

The man said nothing.

"I have an appointment."

One bushy eyebrow raised up toward the man's broad forehead. John pulled the card out of his pocket.

"I—"

The man's face underwent a startling transformation as John held the card up. A smile creased his face as his mountainous shoulders relaxed.

"My apologies, sir. Admittance is only allowed when the card is produced." He stood back and gestured for John to come in. "Welcome to Smythe's."

John hesitated a moment. A flicker of something teased

his mind: an image of a chandelier dripping in diamonds. A smoky, feminine voice.

Then it was gone.

He walked inside, careful to keep his face blank even as surprise filtered through him. The entry hall itself was stunning, with a wrought-iron railing curled intimately around a staircase that circled up, gleaming marble floors and paintings displayed on the wall. Not just any paintings, he realized, as information filled his mind. Renoir, Monet, Kahlo and Rembrandt, to name a few. If these were genuine, they would fetch millions at auction.

Yet of all the incredible things in the entry hall, it wasn't the art that froze him in place. It was the gleaming chandelier above his head.

Satisfaction shot through him and eased some of his tension. He had been here before.

"The elevator will take you up."

John turned to see the man, apparently a guard of some sort, gesturing toward a glass column in the center of the staircase. The guard pushed a button on the wall and a door in the column opened to reveal an elevator, the car made of the same black iron as the railing.

"Enjoy your visit."

The elevator ride was short and smooth. The door opened without a sound. John paused, his eyes sweeping and assessing everything that lay before him.

A short set of stairs led down to the tiled floor, the staircase flanked by marble pillars the same pale aqua as the walls. Mirrors trimmed in gold lined the room, making it feel twice as big. Glass cases stood every few feet along the perimeter of the room.

Jewelry cases, John realized as he descended the stairs. Every case contained artfully arranged jewelry, from loose stones to elegantly set necklaces, bracelets, earrings and rings sparkling with rubies, emeralds, sapphires and diamonds, even a crown.

"Hello, again."

The smoky voice from his memory slid over him, a voice designed to tempt and seduce. Yet, he noted as he turned, despite the inherent sexiness in the tones, he experienced nothing more than a casual flicker of interest.

A woman stood at the top of the stairs. A sleeveless black dress clung to her curves. Sleek ebony hair had been cut into a bob, the sharply cut fringe of bangs accentuating her striking cheekbones and large eyes.

"Welcome back, Mr. Adamos."

"Thank you."

She cocked her head to the side. A flirtatious smile flitted about her lips, but her eyes were shrewd.

"Is everything all right?"

He paused. Part of him wanted to dive straight into questioning. But a sixth sense urged him to proceed with caution, to test the waters and work up to his questions.

"Yes." He held up the card. "Saturday at seven thirty, yes?"

She stared at him for a long moment before descending the stairs. Each step was sensual, hips swaying, fingers lingering on the banister. Yet when she met his gaze, he saw a strong, calculating woman behind the theater. Whoever Miss Smythe was, she was certainly no fool.

"Champagne?"

"No, thank you."

She gestured toward a mahogany desk set against one wall, a floor-to-ceiling mirror behind it and a set of tufted leather chairs in front. He waited until she circled the desk and sat before he took his seat. She pulled a drawer out and, judging by the soft ticks, typed in a code. A click sounded, followed by the whooshing of a door swinging open. She reached down below, then set a black box on the desk between them.

"As promised."

John stared at the box. Then, slowly, he opened the lid.

The diamond glittered up at him from a bed of black silk. It was a diamond unlike any he'd ever seen. Black dots peppered the inside of the jewel, some pinpoints of color, others swirling out in tiny patterns that reminded him of a night sky. Tiny drops of pearls and aquamarine stones circled it, the entire arrangement set atop a silver band polished to a perfect shine.

Classic. Elegant. Romantic.

Flame. Red, silky flame spilling across his fingers. A laugh that made his body hard even as it made his chest light to hear it, to know he had made her smile. And then a name, whispered with such affection his chest tightened. "Julius..."

"It's stunning."

A genuine smile flashed on Miss Smythe's ruby-red lips, fleeting but proud.

"Thank you. I don't have many clients who request a salt-and-pepper diamond. It was a challenge I thoroughly enjoyed."

"Salt-and-pepper diamond?"

One perfectly sculpted eyebrow arched up.

"Yes. As we discussed at your last appointment."

"Remind me again."

She pulled the ring from the bed of silk and held it up. "Also known as galaxy or celestial diamonds, salt-and-pepper diamonds used to be seen as undesirable. Flawed. The black spots you see are bits of carbon or minerals that didn't crystallize during the formation of the diamond. But as the world evolves, they're starting to be appreciated for their uniqueness." She angled the ring so he could stare into the depths of the stone. "Unlike a traditional diamond that reflects light, a salt-and-pepper diamond pulls you in. Encourages a second look. The longer you look, the more you see."

He tried to reach out, to grasp a memory of the faceless red-haired woman. To summon an image of a woman he had apparently considered asking to be his wife.

An endless darkness thwarted his efforts. As if there was nothing beyond the past few hours. Suddenly angry, he tried harder, focused more, demanded his body release whatever it was concealing from him.

Searing pain shot through his head. His eyes scrunched shut as he suppressed a groan.

"Mr. Adamos?"

"A moment," he ground out.

Finally, the pain passed. When it did, he opened his eyes to see a bottle of water in front of him and Miss Smythe watching him.

"Once you're recovered, you have five minutes to tell me what's going on or leave."

He breathed in deeply, took a long drink of water and then sat back.

"A headache, Miss Smythe. Surely, you've heard of them."

Her eyes narrowed as she sat back.

"While I may interact with clients from a variety of backgrounds, if you're indulging in any illicit substance, I'll have you—"

"Strike that thought from your mind."

The authoritative command flowed naturally from his tongue. To her credit, Miss Smythe didn't flinch even as she gave him the tiniest of contrite nods.

"My apologies if I have offended you. But," she countered, leaning forward and crossing her arms so they gently pressed her breasts up, "you're still not telling me the truth."

"You're a beautiful woman, Miss Smythe. But it will take more than a little cleavage to have me reveal my secrets."

She let out a chuckle and leaned back into her chair.

"Worth a try." She sobered. "Mr. Adamos, to date our dealings have been nothing but professional. You paid on time, and in full. Your requests for the ring were obviously well-thought-out and detailed. But I have been in business long enough to know that something has changed since our last parting. Perhaps it is personal, and if so, I will drop the topic. But if it affects your purchase, or my company, I have a right to know."

He stared at her for a long moment. It would be taking a risk, an early one. Revealing his secret went against an instinct imprinted so deeply inside him he didn't question it. But he also recognized that, so far, this was the only link he had.

"I woke up an hour ago with no memory of who I am."

It gave him a small jolt of satisfaction to see her mouth drop open.

"Excuse me?"

"I woke up in a suite in The Bancroft an hour ago. I had a splitting headache and my chest felt like it was on fire. I have no memory of who I am, no wallet, no phone," he held up his left hand, "and no watch. All I could find, besides some very expensive luggage and an envelope full of euros, was your business card."

Her eyes darted between him and the ring box, now closed and pushed off to the side. "No memories at all? Not of your initial appointment five days ago?"

He waited a moment, let his eyes roam around the room. It felt familiar, but aside from the brief flashes he'd experienced outside when he'd first arrived, nothing else appeared.

"A flash here and there. Nothing substantial."

"Why not go to the police? The hospital?"

"Those routes will take time. When I confirmed today's date and time, I decided that coming here would offer me the quickest route to the question of who I am."

She tapped a manicured finger on the desk. Once, then once again, the sound echoing in the room. He maintained her gaze, accepting her assessment yet not backing down.

At last, she leaned back into her chair.

"The name you provided was John Adamos."

"A name I don't recognize."

She shrugged. "I wouldn't be surprised if it was a fake. Smythe's has been in business for generations. We thrive on exclusivity and mystery. Part of that includes not asking details of our clients. If they have a card, they get admitted. If they have money, we accept their order. Beyond that, we know very little about the people we work for."

He stood and began to pace. "When did I make the appointment?"

"Three weeks ago, when you submitted a request and the deposit."

"Deposit?"

"I require half, but you paid in full. One million euros."

He stared at her. "A million?"

"Yes." She shrugged a bare shoulder. "We're the best."

"And I said nothing about the woman this ring is for?"

Something wistful passed across Miss Smythe's face, so quickly John would have missed it if he hadn't been watching her carefully.

"No." She leaned forward. "But I've been in this showroom since I was a child. First watching my father, then learning, then leading. I know the difference between clients who want to impress someone, clients who are desperate, clients who are here simply for the thrill."

"The thrill?"

"Smythe's is by referral only to the world's elite. The art

you saw on the ground floor serves as an excuse for the people who come to our door should anyone ask questions. A private collection that only the most esteemed art lovers are granted access to." The same proud smile he'd glimpsed earlier returned. "Without the black card you had in your possession, probably given to you by a former client, you would have either been turned away by Henry or one of the other guards." She smirked. "It's incredible how many politicians, movie stars and royals will pay hundreds of thousands just so they can engage in a clandestine appointment and own a piece of jewelry from my shop."

His lips quirked. "Did I present as a spoiled bastard?"

The smirk faded. "No." Miss Smythe opened the box and gazed at the ring. This time there was no mistaking the sadness in her eyes. "No, whoever you purchased this for is a fortunate woman to have someone who cares about her so deeply. You declined champagne. You booked an hour and took great care in examining the jewels. Many come to me wanting the most expensive or exclusive. You wanted something that, as you told me, would be beautiful but unique, enigmatic." Another smile flashed, genuine and nostalgic. "This ring was one I greatly enjoyed working on."

That sense of urgency invaded once more.

"Is there anything else you can tell me?"

"You set your appointment for two weeks out. You came in last week, picked out this diamond," she said with a nod to the box, "and arranged to come back today to pick up the ring."

"And I left no contact information? No phone, no email?"

Her fingers danced across the screen of her computer.

"You left an address." She rattled off the numbers and name of a street. "It's on the island of Grenada in the Caribbean Sea, care of Esmerelda Clark."

Esmerelda. The name rushed through him. He knew the

name. Could see full lips turned up in a rare smile, green eyes dotted with gold and sparkling with laughter, red curls framing a freckled face.

"Do you know who she is?"

"No. As I mentioned, we honor our clients' wishes for privacy and do not conduct any background checks."

He steeled himself against the sudden frenetic energy that urged him to get up, to find Esmerelda Clark, to do *something*. He would find her. He had to find her. Surely, he wouldn't have put down the name of some random woman for such an important transaction. At the very least, she would probably have some answers about who he was.

But something innate told him that Esmerelda Clark wasn't just a resource. No, she was important. Perhaps even the woman he had planned to present this ring to.

"Will you write down the address for me?"

"Yes."

Miss Smythe jotted down the address on a piece of paper and handed it to him.

"I do have a request, Mr. Adamos."

"You've given me answers." He picked up the box. "And an invaluable ring. Name it and it's done."

Her lips tilted up.

"Call and tell me how the story ends."

CHAPTER TWO

TO ANYONE WALKING by on the white sands of Little Cove Beach, the woman lounging in the hammock was enjoying her vacation. Sun filtered through the palm trees and warmed her skin. A gentle breeze drifted in off the cerulean blue waves, carrying the crisp, salty scent of the Caribbean Sea. A glass of Grenadian rum punch sat within reach on the ground, droplets of condensation dripping lazily down onto the sand.

Esme Clark sighed. It was hard to enjoy her vacation when, just over a month ago, she'd been fired by her former boss and ex-lover. That her dismissal had been delivered so coldly by the man who just a week before had made love to her during a magical night in Paris had made it all the more humiliating.

Sex, she reminded herself grimly. *We had sex. That's it.*

For a moment, she'd actually imagined herself in love with her boss. She'd known nothing could come of it. He was a prince. The heir to the throne of a small island nation off the coast of Portugal that had done surprisingly well for itself in recent times. Despite the occasional sweet story in the news or the romance novels she liked to read in bed late at night, reality was far crueler. Princes did not marry their bodyguards.

But for the first time in her life, even knowing how it would have to end, she had thrown caution to the wind and succumbed to her own desires. Desires that had been haunting her for the past year ever since she'd been injured protecting Prince Julius during a parade. She'd tried to rise when he'd visited her in the hospital. He'd gently pushed her back, sat by her bedside and chatted with her, even gifted her a copy of one of her favorite books. He'd made her laugh. When she'd looked at him, she'd seen a spark in his eyes, an awareness of her as a woman.

For months, she'd resisted indulging in anything physical. Too bad the same couldn't be said for her emotions. Something had changed between them after that morning in the hospital. It had been small things at first, like him showing up at her physical therapy appointment to see how she was progressing. She had assured herself it was something he would have done for any one of his security detail who had suffered an injury in the line of duty. For all the whisperings of the prince's cold and transactional way of handling his role, he invested in his people.

Except it had been something more. She'd resisted the pull between them for more than a year, the heated glances, the deep curve of his smile when they were alone.

Until Paris. Until one night when she had finally given in. They'd slept together—to think of it in any other terms but that was to invite heartache—followed less than a week later by his summoning her to his office where he'd informed her that he would be looking for a fiancée at the direction of his father, the king. Icy fingers wrapped around her heart still as she remembered staring at him, trying to keep her mouth from dropping open. She'd known when she'd gone to bed with him that it would be a short-term affair at most. What she hadn't expected were the emotions that had stirred: jealousy, hurt, loss.

And then he'd added fury to the volatile churn of feelings

inside her chest by saying, in the coldest of voices, that given the circumstances it would be better if she was reassigned.

"It's over, Miss Clark. It has been since Paris."

Anger surged through her. She momentarily embraced it, savored the flash of fire in her veins. Anger was powerful. Anger yanked her away from the dark pit of sadness and self-pity.

And from desire. She kept it buried more often than not. But there were still moments, especially at night, when it would slide through her body, dipping into her dreams and stirring heated recollections of the way he'd slid her shirt from her shoulders, trailing his lips down the back of her neck and over the curve of her shoulder as his hands had cupped her breasts—

Stop. She'd mistaken seduction for tenderness, sex for lovemaking. Yes, Julius had been the best lover she'd been with. *So far,* she reminded herself firmly. *The best lover so far.* While she couldn't even begin to entertain the possibility of sex or a relationship right now, telling herself that she would move on helped.

That and the anger. The anger helped most of all.

Fortunately, she'd managed to harness some anger that day. It had kept the tears at bay and strengthened her voice as she'd simply bowed her head, replied "Yes, Your Highness," and savored the satisfying flare of shock in his eyes before she'd turned and walked out.

Instead of reporting to the Royal Security Office, where she would have had to face her coworkers and her father, the head of the royal family's security team, she had gone straight to her apartment in the wing reserved for palace employees. She'd packed up her few belongings, booked a ticket to Scotland and typed up a resignation letter in less than an hour. She'd hit send on the email as she'd arrived at the airport. Her father had called less than five minutes later, and had been calling almost every day since.

Once she would have been grateful for his attention. But it wasn't a personal interest in her. No, it was his concern for the effect her abrupt departure could have on his career that spurred his calls. Not her. Never her.

She'd sent every call to voice mail.

A sigh escaped her lips. She stared up through the fronds of the palm tree as the anger seeped out. Pain trickled in through the cracks in her heart, spreading and weighing her down until she felt so heavy she couldn't move.

Was there something fundamentally wrong with her? Was she destined to go her whole life being unwanted? Her mother had divorced her father and moved back to Scotland when Esme had been ten, then across the ocean to New York to follow a surgeon who had swept her off her feet when Esme was thirteen. Esme's father had been more focused on steadily climbing the ranks from palace gate guard to head of the entire royal family's security. Neither of them had cared much for being parents or the daughter they had created.

Their indifference had hardened her. She'd never allowed herself to be vulnerable again, including the few men she'd dated over the years, two of whom she'd allowed the intimacy of sharing her bed. None of them had been granted access to her heart.

Until Julius. Until he'd looked at her like he'd really seen her and slid past her defenses.

She sat up with a frustrated huff and maneuvered out of the hammock. Why on earth was she wasting time ruminating on the past and the people who had deserted her time and again? She was in Grenada, for God's sake, on the first vacation she'd ever taken. Yes, her heart was still broken. Yes, when she closed her eyes at night she still saw Julius's face, heard him whisper her name in the dark as he'd loved her body and brought her to heights of passion she had never imagined possible.

And yes, when she thought of how cold he'd looked when he'd told her she was being reassigned, how nonchalantly he'd delivered the news of his upcoming engagement, she felt as if someone had punched her in the stomach and left her gasping for breath.

But each day away from the most agonizing moment of her life was a step toward her future. The one good thing to come out of her and Julius's tryst was their walk through Paris hours before they'd finally given in to their shared desires. He'd mentioned seeing her at a café the day before, how relaxed she'd looked.

"I felt like I was seeing the real you for the first time."

"I don't even know who the real me is."

The honesty of her statement surprised them both. Sadness twisted in her chest. How awful to go twenty-six years of one's life and realize you had lived it in pursuit of things others wanted for you.

"Look at me."

She did, struck once more by her body's sensual response to him, a response made even more potent by the rare smile on his full lips. He looked at her with something more than just simple desire. Something that both seduced and frightened her.

"Perhaps there are parts of yourself yet to be revealed. But the Esmerelda Clark I know is an incredible woman."

She'd believed every word. Every single calculated, flowery bit of sycophancy he'd delivered with confident charm.

She swallowed past the lump in her throat and latched onto the positive that had come out of their exchange. She had lived so much of her life for others. Never for herself.

Boarding the plane and watching Rodina fade to a tiny emerald speck on the blue waters of the Atlantic had twisted her battered and bruised heart into a hard knot. She loved her country. The rolling hills offset by towering oak forests, the black sand beaches that gently faded into the ocean, and the towering mountains at the southern end of the country, always capped by snow, had been like living in a fairy tale. Yet the country had its practical side, too. They mirrored their neighbor to the east, Portugal, with their massive olive tree groves and wheat fields. Manufacturing had also steadily grown under the guidance of Julius's father.

She hadn't just loved her country. She'd been proud of it. It was why, when her father had pushed her to go through the academy to become a part of the royal's security team, she'd agreed. She hadn't quite known what to do with herself after graduating from university. And yes, part of her had hoped to please him. But she'd also been proud to serve Rodina, and proud of herself when she'd been assigned to Prince Julius Carvalho's security detail just six months after she'd graduated.

Julius's attempt at reassigning her had nearly killed her. He'd phrased it as a promotion, becoming the leader of his cousin Vera's security team instead of serving as a "simple guard" on his. But she'd seen the reassignment for what it was; an attempt to make a problem disappear. Vera was kind but served in more of a ceremonial role. The girl was young and preferred events like charity luncheons versus trips overseas to meet with leaders on economic issues. Leadership position or not, Esme's days would have been boring, lifeless. A punishment for allowing the one man she never should have fallen for into her heart.

Yet Julius's banishment had also set her free. For the first time in her life, she had no father pushing her to pursue the career he'd always envisioned for the son he'd never had. No mother whose distant elegance had caught Esme in the middle of trying to be the child her father had wanted while striving to be a cultured, well-behaved lady like her mother desired.

She missed Rodina. One day she would return. But she needed to figure out who she was first.

She stretched her arms up to the sky, then leaned down, picked up her cocktail and took a long, leisurely sip. The sweet, tart flavors of orange and pineapple juice mixed pleasantly with the rum. Waves lapped against the beach. The breeze stirred the fronds of the palm trees and created a shushing sound that teased the stress from her shoulders.

After another drink, she let the diaphanous robe she'd picked up at a beachside shop slip from her shoulders onto the sand and moved down the beach. The rum flowed warmly through her veins as she walked into the ocean. Hills covered in palm trees and orchids cradled the cove before sloping gently down into the water.

She had another three weeks in paradise. Living in the palace apartments reserved for staff and having no social life had left her with a comfortable savings account. She would enjoy her time here. And when that time was up, she would move on. She'd overcome rejection before. She would do so again.

With confidence and determination banishing the remnants of her pity party, she moved deeper until water splashed gently against her waist. She sank down, let the ocean close over her head and drifted for a moment in the shallows; blissfully alone, weightless. For the first time in a month, she felt at peace.

She released a breath, let herself sink lower. The swimming survival course had been her favorite part of academy training. It had been one of the rare times she'd let her mind stray and indulged in the fantasy of floating in the ocean on some faraway beach.

Her lips curved up in a smile even as her lungs started to

tighten. Perhaps she could get certified in scuba diving, or book a snorkeling excursion…

Awareness pricked the back of her neck as she heard a dim splash. Before she could surface, thick arms wrapped around her body and hauled her out of the water.

Panic pierced her for a brief moment. There was no backup, no button she could push, no phone number she could call.

All she had was herself.

Her training kicked in. She let her body go limp. The man swore as they pitched forward. His grip tightened for a moment, but as they hit the water his hold loosened. She pushed away from him and shot up. As soon as her feet hit the sand, she swiped the water from her eyes and spun. The man faced away from her and was getting to his feet. She lunged, wrapping one around his neck and grabbing the back of his head with her other hand as she pushed him down onto his knees.

Exhilaration pumped through her.

"Why did you attack me?"

"I thought you were drowning."

She froze.

No. It can't be.

Her hold loosened. He stood in one fluid motion, breaking her grip as he turned and wrapped his arms around her, pinning her arms to her sides.

She blinked rapidly, her mind trying to accept the reality of what she was seeing.

"Julius?"

He smiled down at her, and her damned body responded, flutters dancing in her belly as heat crept up her neck.

"Of all the welcomes I've imagined on my trip here, I can safely say that was not one of them."

CHAPTER THREE

His HANDSOMENESS HIT her hard, just like it had the first time she'd laid eyes on him at the academy. The broad forehead and sharp cheekbones, offset by full, sensual lips, were all familiar. But the thickness of his beard and the longer cut of his hair, now hanging in wet strands turned to dark gold, sharply contrasted with the brooding air the so-called "Ice Prince" had exuded back home.

She breathed in, an action she quickly regretted as her breasts pressed more fully against his chest. Between the barely-there coverage of her bikini top and his ocean-soaked T-shirt, she could feel the heat of his skin against hers, the hardened muscle. Memories stirred of the night they'd lain together in bed, naked bodies entwined, the intimacy of lying together almost as powerful as when they'd joined.

Stop! She had to get a grip. Yes, they'd had an incredible night together. But the relationship she'd created in her mind, one of mutual respect and a desire to support the country they both loved, one deepened by the knowledge that she might have been called on at any moment to surrender her life for his, had been nothing more than a fantasy.

"It was one night, Miss Clark," he said with such disdain she wanted to curl inside herself and hide from the shame his words birthed. *"But with my now impending marriage, it's best if you're reassigned elsewhere."*

Cold. Callous. Everything she'd heard whispered about him had been true.

Anger started to churn in her belly, rising up and twining through her veins with a fiery strength that eclipsed her heartache and humiliation.

"Why on earth would you think I was drowning?" she asked, keeping her voice neutral. "You know the survival course requires being submerged for at least two minutes."

His brow furrowed. One hand came up to push the hair out of his eyes. "I—"

She swept her arms up and broke his grasp. Planting both hands on his chest, she gave him a shove and was rewarded with the sight of the prince falling back into the ocean. She savored the sight of him tumbling beneath the waves before making a beeline for the beach.

The sound of Julius cursing behind her made her smile. She spared a glance over her shoulder and grinned when she saw the thunderous expression on his face.

"What the devil was that for?" he shouted.

She froze. The anger paused, then seethed, churned, burning into white-hot rage as she slowly turned to face him.

"You can't be serious."

He stared at her for a long moment, then looked down as he let out a frustrated sigh.

"Look, Miss Clark. Esme—"

"No." Her voice rang out over the waves. "You addressed me as 'Miss Clark' the day you fired me. You don't have permission to address me by my first name. Ever."

He scrubbed a hand over his face, then started walking out of the waves. She stood her ground and did her best to ignore the way his shirt molded to his muscled chest, the wet cloth revealing the dark golden hair that trailed down his stomach and disappeared beneath the waistband of his pants.

He stalked up onto the sand. With every step closer he

took, her heart upped its rhythm, until it was beating so fast it was a wonder she didn't pass out.

"Miss Clark, we have to talk."

Her traitorous heart leapt. She mentally snatched it, pushed her treacherous emotions away.

"If you're offering to hire me back, the answer is—"

"Would you just listen to me, damn it?"

Something in his tone slipped past her hurt. She waited a moment, two, then evaluated the man before her. The man who looked more like a tourist on vacation than a royal prince. The man who had easily lost ten pounds since she'd last seen him and now sported a cut on one cheek. The man who was looking at her with a touch of uncertainty in his amber eyes.

She'd cut off all ties to the palace when she'd left. Told the few acquaintances she had that she would be in touch soon with no real intention of actually following through. She'd also avoided the media, not wanting to see carefully curated photos of Julius with whatever princess or duchess or heiress his father had picked as the perfect wife.

Something had obviously happened since she'd left. Her heart pounded once, twice, her hands yearning to reach out and smooth the furrow between his brows. To wrap her arms around him just once more the way she had the morning after they'd made love. He'd been standing at the balcony doors, hands tucked in his pockets, shoulders rigid as if he'd already resumed carrying the weight of the world. She'd walked up behind him, laid one hand on his back. The muscles had tensed beneath her touch. Reality had told her to step back, give him space. The intimacy they'd shared last night and into the early hours of the morning encouraged otherwise. So she'd slowly slid her arms around his waist, laid her cheek against his shoulder blade. And when he'd finally released a breath, relaxing in her hold, accepting the strength she offered for whatever battle he was fighting, she'd tipped over the edge she'd avoided for so long.

An edge she found once again as he watched her, his eyes roaming over her face as if he'd never seen her before.

"It's over, Miss Clark."

Her chin rose, her spine straightening as she faced down her former lover.

"I'm done listening to you." She executed a formal bow. "Your Highness." And then she turned, swept up her robe and walked away, leaving a soaking wet prince alone on the beach.

John stared after Esme until she disappeared up the winding wood stairs that led from the beach up to the tiny cottage perched on a cliff. He turned away and swore.

That could have gone better.

He'd gone to the cottage as soon as his plane had landed. The taxi had zipped past elegant resorts shrouded behind massive shrubs, colorful homes and the turquoise waters of the Caribbean Sea.

He'd seen it, registered it. But his thoughts had been solely focused on finding the mysterious Esmerelda Clark.

Which is why when he'd knocked, then knocked harder still and finally peered in the windows, he hadn't been able to stop the string of curse words that had tumbled from his lips. To come so far and find the cottage empty had left him trembling with anger and a gnawing fear that the woman who might hold all the answers was gone.

He'd spied the stairs curling down from the back porch. Instinct had nudged him to walk down the winding staircase that descended down the cliff before leveling out into a narrow boardwalk across a stream, then several more steps down onto a yellow-white sandy beach.

And then he'd seen her. Standing on the sand in a bikini

that left little of her lithe, toned body to the imagination, hair spilling down her back in flaming red-gold curls. His anger and fear had evaporated in a moment. She was here. She was here and she was familiar in a way that he couldn't explain. He didn't know her middle name or what flowers she liked or what their relationship had been like before he'd ended up in London.

But he knew her. Knew her, craved her with not just his body but a need that surpassed the mere physical.

When she'd walked into the water, he'd held back, pulling himself back together piece by piece so that when he moved onto the beach, he wouldn't frighten her.

Except then she'd slipped beneath the waves and hadn't come back up.

He'd waited. But the seconds had stretched. He'd walked onto the beach, spied her red hair below the surface. When the seconds had turned into a minute and she hadn't moved, fear had propelled him into the water.

He rubbed his neck. The woman had a grip. And a grudge. The impressions that flirted with the edges of his broken mind had led him to the assumption that he and Esmerelda had been lovers. An assumption he thought confirmed by the brief flare of desire in her eyes when he'd held her nearly naked body close. A desire that had kindled an answering fire deep within him.

But she hadn't said anything about a romantic connection. No, she'd referenced working for him and tossed in that odd bow at the end. Had they been coworkers, or he'd been her boss, and tried to take the relationship from professional to intimate? Worse, had he crossed a line?

The headache returned with a vengeance and pounded at his temples. He'd obviously done something to taint whatever relationship they'd had. To make her walk away without a backward glance.

Ridiculous for the rejection of a woman he couldn't even remember to hurt. Yet hurt it did, a crackling pain beneath his skin coupled with an emptiness in his chest that rivaled the emptiness inside his head.

Enough.

He'd come this far, spent most of his money to find Esmerelda Clark. He would atone for whatever atrocities he'd committed in his murky past. But right now, he needed answers.

Five minutes later he stood outside the door of the cabin. He forced himself to not fling the door open and seek her out. As he raised his fist to knock, the door swung open. Esmerelda stood framed in the doorway, her eyes snapping green fire and her hair caught up in a loose bun at the nape of her neck. She'd pulled a blue T-shirt on but had yet to pull on shorts, leaving her long legs bare to his gaze.

"Did you get seawater in your ears?"

"Excuse me?"

"I said no."

She started to close the door. John flung up his arm and braced it against the door. Her eyes widened.

And then she got angry. She drew herself up to her full five-foot-five, her body tightening and shifting like a snake getting in position to strike.

She was glorious.

"If you are even contemplating forcing yourself in here, sir, I will break every bone in your body, starting with your—"

"I need your help."

She paused.

"Please," he added.

He knew the moment it worked because she slowly uncoiled, her body loosening, her stance relaxing a fraction as she regarded him with curiosity and suspicion.

"With what?"

He hesitated. Where to begin? He'd obviously done something to her in his previous life. Hurt her somehow.

Her eyes narrowed. She started to push the door shut. He had to plant himself to keep her sudden shove from knocking him off balance.

"I don't know who I am."

She stopped. Her eyes moved over his face.

His relief at sharing his predicament proved short-lived.

"Look, I can't help you." She glanced away, the first time she had done so, as if it made her uncomfortable to look at him. "I understand you're under a tremendous amount of pressure, not to mention the engagement—"

Disappointment speared his chest.

"We're not engaged?"

A stricken look passed over her face, pain flashing in her eyes as her lips parted in shock. He swallowed past the sudden thickness in his own throat.

"How can you even ask that?"

"Esme... Miss Clark," he amended as her lips thinned. "When I say I don't know who I am, I mean that literally."

Silence descended between them, thick and heavy. Dimly he heard the distant roar of the surf, the melancholy coo of a nearby bird, the thudding of his own heart. She stared at him, as if waiting for him to break character, to laugh and say it was all a joke.

"If this is some sort of scheme or manipulation—"

He reached down and grabbed her hand, ignoring her gasp and the electric awareness that surged up his arm. He leaned down and pressed her hand against the wound at the base of his skull. The initial touch made him bite back a hiss of pain. Her fingers tensed then gentled, tracing the swelling with a touch so soft it calmed some of the turmoil that had been churning inside him for the past twenty-four hours. As she leaned closer, he breathed in, smelling the salty scent of the sea clinging to her skin. Sea and something else... something floral and feminine that made him want to drag her against him and bury his face in her hair.

Mine.

The word shot through him, awoke something lodged deep in his chest. A possessiveness that felt right even as it unsettled him, to have such strong emotions for a woman he couldn't remember anything about.

"Turn around."

He kept his surprise at her sudden brusque demeanor hidden and followed her direction. Even though his mind resisted taking orders, took umbrage at being talked to like that, he forced himself to be vulnerable, to surrender something of himself.

"Crouch down, please. Sir," she added.

"You worked for me?" he asked as her fingers probed the wound once more, her touch now efficient.

"I did."

"What happened?"

"You fired me."

The words were said plainly, factually. It didn't mask the hurt lingering in her voice, the shade of embarrassment.

Before he could ask for details, she spoke.

"What's the last thing you remember?"

"Waking up in my hotel room yesterday afternoon."

"Blunt force trauma to the base of your skull." She walked around him and looked in his eyes. "Pupils appear normal. Any vomiting, dizziness?"

"No. Some nausea when I first awoke, but it disappeared quick enough."

"What did the doctor say?"

"Doctor?"

Her eyes widened before narrowing to tiny slits as she

planted her fists on her hips. The gesture made her look like an adorably pissed-off fairy.

"You did go to a hospital, didn't you?"

An ache started to build in his temples as he straightened to his full height. Instead of stepping back or showing any sign of hesitancy, she merely lifted her chin and met his gaze head-on.

Oh, yes. He liked this woman very much.

"A hospital would have taken time. I was given your name and address and came straight here?"

She frowned. "Got my name from who?"

He held up his hand.

"Before I answer any more questions, tell me…"

He paused. Physically steeled himself for whatever response he was about to receive.

"Who am I?"

One hand came up, her fingers rubbing at her forehead. She muttered under her breath in a language he knew—Portuguese—and then looked up at him.

"Sit down. Please," she added huffily when he arched a brow at her command. "I'll be right back."

He moved to the table and chairs set at the far end of the porch that ran the length of the cottage. The chair let out a protesting groan as he sat. Given the hints of rust poorly disguised by a thin layer of white paint, it was a miracle the chair had lasted as long as it had.

Esme appeared a moment later, clad in the wet shirt that clung to her body and a pair of shorts, two steaming mugs in her hands. She set one in front of him as she sat in the chair across from him.

"Spiced coffee."

Cinnamon and a touch of sweetness swirled on his tongue as he took a long drink. The hot liquid warmed his throat, gave himself something tangible to focus on.

"Thank you." He set his cup down. "John Adamos isn't my real name, is it?"

"Why do you ask?"

"It doesn't feel like my name. There's no recognition, no connection."

"No. It's not your real name." Her gaze flicked down to her own cup, then back up to his. A veil had dropped over her eyes. The woman in front of him was even more of a stranger than the one he had happened on down on the beach. Cool, collected.

Withdrawn.

"Your name is Julius Carvalho."

Something flickered inside him, a flame of recognition. Distant, but there.

"Julius," he repeated.

"Yes." She breathed in deeply. "Crown Prince Julius Adamos Carvalho."

Silence stretched between them once more. Laughter died in his throat when she didn't smile, didn't chuckle, simply watched him with that clinical gaze.

"Prince," he echoed.

"Yes. Heir to the throne of the island nation of Rodina."

CHAPTER FOUR

JULIUS HADN'T MOVED from the chair in over thirty minutes. For the first minute after her pronouncement, he'd simply sat, as if absorbing the enormity of what she'd shared. Then he'd asked questions, collecting information about his life as if he were preparing to study for an exam. Every now and then he would pause, breathe in deeply, then continue. It was the only sign that the conversation was taxing him.

The more he'd talked, the more she'd recognized that this wasn't a ruse. A realization that had opened the door to fear that curled around her heart and crawled up her throat. Fear at whatever horrid thing had happened to him in London and caused this.

He'd resisted contacting the palace, saying he needed time to process what she'd shared. It had taken nearly ten minutes to convince him to let her call her friend Burak, a fellow guard who had been promoted to the head of Julius's detail after she'd left, and see if she could ferret out any information. Burak had grudgingly admitted that Julius had taken a sabbatical.

"Only a select few know his exact location. He made the private security I hired at the airport and threatened to fire me if I didn't pull them."

"So you're just letting the heir to the throne wander around the world?" Esme asked incredulously.

"He checks in every forty-eight hours by cell."

The edge in Burak's voice had made her change topics. She liked Burak, counted him as one of a tiny group of friends. Even if she strongly disagreed with how Julius had been allowed to roam free, she knew firsthand how the man operated. If he had decided on something, the only person he would ever bow to would be his father. And even then, if he believed in it strongly enough, he would put up one hell of a fight. It had been one of the qualities that had made her admire him even as she wanted to wring his neck.

Just like now. From here she could see the bruise just below his hairline, red turning to a mottled purple. The ugly scarlet of the cut on his face. What had he gotten into that he would have sustained such injuries?

She turned away from the window, not wanting him to suddenly turn and see her watching him like a mother hen. She put the used coffee mugs in the sink, rinsed them out, focused on the cold splash of water on her fingers, the smoothness of the porcelain in her hands, the slight clunking in the pipes.

Focus on the tangible.

Julius's voice echoed in her head. He'd come into her hospital room shortly after the accident. She'd been rising up from the depths of a nightmare, one filled with the screams of people and a frightened horse as searing pain burned through her skin. He'd taken her hand, his fingers rubbing soothing circles on her skin, as he'd told her to focus on the things she saw in her room, the things she heard. A simple exercise, but one that had grounded her and given her time to collect herself.

Perhaps that had been the moment she'd started to slip from respect into love.

She placed the mugs in the drying rack. Her hands rested on the edge of the countertop, then curled around the edge, a death grip as she bowed her head and blew out a harsh breath.

Deus me ajude.

She still loved him. After everything that had happened, love still beat inside her for a man who had used and betrayed her.

This can't be love.

Infatuation? A fantasy? The longings of a woman who had been rejected her whole life?

She grabbed onto that last thought. Of course it was hard to let go. She and Julius had grown close over the past year. He'd been there for her during her recovery, the grueling hours of physical therapy. He'd also been the first man she'd gone to bed with in over two years. It was only natural that she would still have lingering emotions, that she would feel upset that someone she had respected and come to care about had been hurt to the point of forgetting his entire life.

Upset and torn. Should she tell him about what they'd shared in Paris? Reliving the humiliation of those last few moments in his office before she'd walked out, convinced she'd never see him again?

Except what would that accomplish, other than further complicating their current situation? It wasn't as if they'd dated or had anything beyond that one night.

Get it together, Esmerelda.

The heir to the throne was sitting on her porch with no memory of who he was or what had happened to him. Now was not the time to struggle with unrequited emotions. No, she needed to get him back home to Rodina and into the care of a qualified physician since the foolish man had taken the address from that London jeweler and used almost all his cash to pay for a seat on a cargo plane that hadn't bothered to ask for a passport. When he'd told her that lovely tidbit, she'd had a vivid and painful image of him strapped into the back of a hold crowded with boxes of contraband as a rickety plane spiraled into the ocean.

If she suppressed that horrifying vision and instead focused on the reality that the so-called "Ice Prince" of Rodina had flown on a cargo plane with a bag of cash with a million-euro ring secreted in the bottom, it was almost amusing.

The ring.

Just thinking about it sobered her instantly. She hadn't seen it yet. She had no wish to. Just the thought of it made her stomach roll.

"I can see the smoke coming out of your ears."

She froze, then silently swore. No one had snuck up on her in years. Slowly, she turned.

And realized that the house was far too tiny. How was it possible that a cottage that had seemed surprisingly roomy now seemed no bigger than a closet? He filled the space, all broad shoulders and lean muscle clad in the still-damp shirt and pants that, thankfully, had dried enough they no longer clung to his body.

"There's a lot to think about."

Thankfully her voice came out steadier than her chaotic stream of thoughts.

"Agreed." He glanced around the cottage, the casual gesture not masking the intensity in his eyes. "How did you find this place?"

"Vacation listing online."

Her jaw tightened as she followed his gaze. It wasn't the same caliber as the fancy Parisian hotel they'd made love in, or the sweeping glamor of the Rodinian seaside palace. Not even close, with the worn white wicker furniture and amateur photographs of Grenada on the faded blue walls.

But that had been part of its charm. It was clean, affordable and exactly the opposite of where she'd been living.

"Cozy."

"You mean cheap," she retorted.

Embarrassment crept up her neck as his gaze swung back to her, a slight smile tugging at one corner of his full lips. Lips she'd kissed, lips he'd used on her breasts, trailed over her stomach, then lower still to—

"Your blushes are telling."

"I don't blush." She moved to the living area and folded a blanket, needing something to do with her hands, to put distance between them. "I flush. There's a difference."

"Oh?"

"Blush implies roses, delicate pinks and beautiful women." She swallowed past the sudden lump in her throat. Beautiful women like her mother. Beautiful women like the future bride of Prince Julius Carvalho. "Flush is more accurate for someone like me."

"Someone like you?"

Surprised at the sudden hardening in his tone, she looked up to see him glowering at her.

"I turn red. Red underneath freckles, coupled with this hair, does not an attractive woman make."

"And who told you that?"

She laid the blanket on the sofa's sagging back and smoothed out the wrinkles. The sound of her mother's disappointed sigh when Esme had turned down yet another offer to have it professionally dyed to something "more suitable than that unfortunate mix of red and yellow," still sounded as piercing as it had the day her mother had said it.

On her thirteenth birthday.

"It doesn't matter." She'd told herself that so many times over the years until she'd almost believed it. "I don't know how we even got onto this ridiculous topic. We should be discussing what to do next with you and…all of this," she finished with a wave of her hand.

He inclined his head to her.

"Given you know more of…well, everything," he said with another faint smile, "I am at your mercy."

"All right." She sank down onto the arm of the sofa, details swirling through her mind. Her ability to analyze and create a plan was one of the few skills she felt truly confident in. That it was a part of her and not just something instilled on her by an aloof mother or a hard-nosed father.

"You should call the palace and let them know what happened to—"

"No."

Irritation trickled down her spine, but she kept it in check. She had conducted herself with the highest level of professionalism during her time as a guard.

Minus sleeping with the boss.

She silenced her conscience and returned his rigid expression with an impassive one of her own.

"I'm sorry, I must have misunderstood the part where you're at my mercy."

"If what you're telling me is true—"

"If?"

"You must admit, telling someone they're a prince and heir to a European nation is outlandish."

She cocked her head to one side and gave him a sweet smile.

"As outlandish as a prince showing up on the doorstep of the palace guard they fired from their service and claiming to have forgotten their entire life? Or perhaps as preposterous as said prince catching a cargo plane to—"

"Suficiente."

She didn't bother suppressing her smug smirk as he ran a frustrated hand through his hair.

He held up the prepaid cell phone he'd purchased at the airport.

"I found news stories to support what you told me."

Irritation flickered through her.

"I didn't lie."

"I know. Surely you can understand the need to see it with my own eyes, to catch up on…" He paused. "Well, my entire life. But," he added, stepping closer as he slid his hands into his pockets, "one thing was missing."

"What?"

"Any news on my engagement, the woman I'm dating, anything."

"Given that you hadn't dated anyone in over a year, I'm not surprised."

"Then I'm not engaged."

"Not yet. But you will be soon."

"To whom?"

"You didn't share with me. You may not have even known at the time who your fiancée was to be."

His lips parted. "How is that possible?"

"Because 'royal marriages are transactions for the betterment of the country.' A direct quote from both you and your father. I'm sure a list of recommended candidates was provided to you around the time or shortly after I left. You must have traveled to London to select a ring for her."

Jealousy coiled in her stomach, followed by shame. The woman chosen to be the future Queen of Rodina would have been someone she would have been proud to serve and protect. Up until she shirked everything she had vowed to uphold and slept with said woman's future husband.

He turned away, giving her a moment to blink back the hot sting of tears. He reached into the bag she'd brought inside while he'd ruminated on the porch after her incredible announcement and pulled out an obsidian-colored velvet box.

"You were listed as the primary contact for the ring. Why?"

She looked away from the box and out the window to the sea.

Focus on the future. Answer his questions. Get him help. Get him out of your life once and for all.

"It's standard practice to list a member of the security detail as the contact for any business a member of the royal family doesn't want the public knowing about."

"But you said you haven't worked for my security team for over a month."

"You must have made the appointment before you fired me."

"With an address in the Caribbean?"

That part stumped her. He'd most likely hired a detective, someone outside of the palace, to track her down. Why was anyone's guess.

And she didn't care. Couldn't care.

"Why did I fire you?"

It was too much. She'd lasted this long. But it was time for Julius to go. To return to his life and receive the care he needed from a doctor. To rejoin royal life and leave her behind.

"You'll either remember or someone else will inform you." She held out her phone. "You can use my cell to call in for your security check. Tell them what happened and they'll—"

"No."

Irritation flickered through her.

"I beg your pardon?"

"I just found out I'm a prince. A prince who is heir to the throne," he repeated, his voice dark and dangerous and hard. "What you just described sounds unappealing at best. My every move shadowed by a security team. An engagement to a woman selected like I'm shopping for produce at the damned market."

"What did you expect?" she snapped. "You're royalty. Real-life royalty. This isn't a fairy tale, Your Highness."

"Do you know what I expected, Esmerelda?"

She stifled the stirring deep in her belly at his use of her full name. The last time he'd said it, he'd moaned it against her lips as he'd slid inside her.

"I can only imagine, sir."

"I expected for you to be the woman I bought the ring for. That I would arrive here and find out I was a banker or a CEO, something mundane that would explain the massive amount of cash and the diamond." His eyes flashed as his fingers tightened around the box. "I thought this was for you, not some faceless woman chosen off of a list."

She tried to ignore the jab of the knife to her heart as he casually mentioned the possibility of having bought the ring for her. She'd known once they'd kissed, once she'd made the decision to finally share her body with him, that it couldn't last. That at most, it would never go beyond an affair. He was a prince. Princes married princesses, duchesses, politicians' daughters, other wealthy people who brought their own connections to the union. She'd known, and accepted, that there would be pain. To her, the year they'd spent together as prince and bodyguard, coming to know each other on a deeper level after her accident, followed by the most incredible night she'd ever spent with a man, had been worth the eventual heartache.

She just hadn't expected the end to come so soon, nor so viciously.

"It's not all glass slippers and champagne, sir. I'm sorry you had to find out this way, but I can't help you anymore. I'm sure a plane can be ready in an hour to take you home."

He stood, regarding her with an intensity that made her want to squirm. Would he suddenly remember? Would the memories come rushing back like they did in the movies, leaving her to experience his disgust and rejection all over again?

"I have impressions. Feelings. They're faint, almost as if a shadow has been wrapped around them."

He stepped closer. She stood her ground, willing herself not to retreat.

"But before I even heard your name, I remembered you." His hand came up, his fingers gliding across one of her wild curls. "When Miss Smythe named you as the contact, I knew that I knew you. That there's something important, something unfinished, with you."

Her heart cried out at the passion in his gaze. Her mind stifled the desire.

"Perhaps it's guilt for acting like a pompous jerk when you removed me from your detail."

His lips tightened.

"We were lovers."

"No."

The lie came quickly, uttered with such feeling she almost believed it herself. *Not a lie*, she reassured herself even as her conscience disagreed. He had never loved her. He'd had his fun, then chosen to distance himself so he and his reputation wouldn't be sullied by a one-night stand with his bodyguard.

"No?" His thick brows drew together. "I remember…"

She nearly caved at the confusion on his face. Nearly told him about the night in Paris.

"I have a reputation to uphold, Miss Clark. Your continued employment on my security team threatens that."

"We were not lovers, Your Highness. I was your bodyguard. We were friends. Or at least I thought we were." She looked away then, knowing she was stretching the truth. But she couldn't bear this again, to rehash the horrible things he'd said and relive the heartache only to have him rush off again as soon as he regained his memory. "Your father requested you marry. You reassigned me without even talking to me about it beforehand and delivered the news rather brutally."

"Why?" he demanded.

"You said it would look better. Your new team was all male." She let the implication hang between them as she tugged on her robe and belted it tightly at the waist. "I declined the reassignment, walked out of the palace and hopped on a plane. I was tired of letting people in my life guide my choices. I stopped briefly at the home my mother left me in Scotland to oversee my things getting moved in, then booked a flight to Grenada to figure out what I wanted for my life. And now you're here."

She faced him then, shoulders thrown back, holding his intense gaze.

And nearly crumpled as he flipped the lid open on the ring box.

CHAPTER FIVE

SHE HAD NEVER cared for diamonds. To her they had always seemed bland. But this diamond, flecked with black and surrounded by blue gems and tiny pearls, entranced her, drew her into its depths.

A sunbeam fell on the diamond and made it glint. The flash of light made her wince, breaking the spell.

"Your future fiancée is a fortunate woman. Whoever she ends up being, I'm sure she'll appreciate it."

"And it was not for you? You're certain of that?"

She waited a moment, suppressing her anguish, her bitterness. When she spoke, she hoped he wouldn't detect the depth of strangled emotion in her voice.

"I can assure you that you would have never proposed to someone like me."

"Someone like you," he echoed with a frown as he thankfully snapped the box shut and placed it back on the table. "The second time you've used that phrase."

She nodded toward the box.

"The woman who will wear your ring will fit the part. Beautiful, distinguished, most likely wealthy, and with a family pedigree that traces back centuries." She held up her hand, wiggling her fingers. "Not a former bodyguard who's never had a manicure and drinks rum cocktails on a beach on a tiny island."

"You sound far more interesting than my future fiancée."

She brushed aside the hurt. To this man with no memory, she probably sounded fascinating. To Prince Julius Carvalho, the heir to Rodina's throne, she was nothing. He'd made that perfectly clear.

He circled around the sofa. Instinct told her to run. Training kept her in place as he drew near, filling every corner of the room with his dominating presence.

"Thank you, Your Highness."

The use of his title didn't stop his advance. Whatever had happened to cause his amnesia had certainly not dulled his powerful presence, his ability to command attention as soon as he walked into a room. It rippled off him, drew her in like a moth to a flame.

Except she wouldn't get burned. Not this time. She would not survive it if she did.

Julius stopped in front of her, less than a foot away, although it could have been less than an inch with the heat swirling between them. Their eyes met and the temperature rose.

"Whoever made you think you're not beautiful or fascinating or worthy was a fool."

"My mother."

"A fool," Julius repeated. "When I came to, I had three memories. One was of a voice. Another was a chandelier." He leaned forward a fraction, golden-brown eyes glinting. "The third was of your hair."

Her heart stuttered.

"My hair?"

"Yes." He reached out and twirled an errant curl around his finger. "Like flames spilling over my hands."

Longing pierced her heart like an arrow. Her own memories of that night rising unbidden from the depths of her mind. The depths she'd pushed them to to try and forget. Memories of him raising himself up on his arms after he'd kissed her. Long, drugging kisses that made her limbs heavy. The look in his eyes when he'd trailed his fingers through her hair had stirred something deeper than lust. For one moment, as he'd stroked the tresses and murmured *"Tão bonito,"* she'd felt truly beautiful for the first time in her life.

Remembering was too much. Too painful. He'd made her believe something that could never be true.

"Why would I have that memory if there was nothing between us?"

She paused, fumbled for a plausible excuse. Another memory surfaced, a lifeline. Something she could distract him with.

"I was in the hospital a year ago. You visited me. I had a head wound and you brushed back my hair to look at the bandage."

When he'd leaned down, devastatingly handsome in a steel-blue suit over a white dress shirt, and smoothed back errant curls from the white bandage plastered to her forehead, something had shifted inside of her. Respect had segued into longing, loyalty into longing. She'd tamped it for months, convinced it was one-sided and simply a product of the intimacy of laying down one's life for another.

Until Paris.

Suspicion flickered across his face.

"You believe that's what I'm remembering? Nothing else?"

"I don't know." She shrugged, strove for nonchalance as she forced herself to step away from him. The sheer magnetism of him was making her breathless. She needed room to breathe, to remember why she couldn't be the person he turned to in this hour of need.

She moved back toward the small kitchenette and set about making herself a cup of tea. "I have no idea what's going on inside your head, Your Highness, what memories are fact and what are fiction."

"I see."

Silence reigned behind her. She willed herself to stay strong, to not be the first to give in. The rest of the world rose up to fill the void, from the creaking of the roof to the shooshing of the breeze that lifted the faded gauze curtains hanging over the window. Each sound grew louder than the last. Pressure built in her chest, heavy and constricting, until she could barely breathe past the tightness in her throat.

"You need to check in with Burak, your head of security."

There. That was professional. And it started the ball rolling on getting him out of her cottage.

"Otherwise the armada will sail across the ocean to find me?"

"What is it you fear?" She turned and frowned at him. "You flew on a cargo plane to find me, to get answers. The palace could provide you with everything you're seeking. That and resources to help you heal."

"When I came to find you, there was one person I was focused on tracking down. Not an entire country that, as you described, looks to my father and me for leadership."

A small wrinkle appeared between his brows as he blinked twice. Subtle, but she knew the signs of an impending headache. How many times had she sat in his office at the end of a long day as they had debriefed, seen the tells that so many people missed? How many times in the past few months had she grown bolder, moving to make tea or offer him an aspirin?

"I need time, Esmerelda. Time to wrap my head around the enormity of what you've shared." He gave in then, the quickest touch of fingers to his temple. "Time to reconcile what I feel versus what you've told me. I will not be rushed."

Hope flared, bright and brilliant, then winked out just as

quickly. It didn't matter if the desire that had brought them together was at the forefront of his mind. When he remembered, when he resumed his role back in Rodina, they would be right back where they had been five weeks ago. Hope was hopeless. It had no place here.

"When you do call Burak to check in, let him know you changed locations and that your wallet was stolen." She held out her hand for his phone, avoided touching his fingers as he passed it over. She plugged in Burak's number before she handed it back over. "They can have new identification, passport, credit cards and anything else you might need by tomorrow." She bit back a sigh. "You can stay here until they arrive."

She couldn't leave the heir to the Rodinian throne alone to fend for himself. The professional part of her knew that. Even if the personal part railed against it, instinctively knowing it wasn't a good idea.

The prince's eyes bored into hers.

"Are you sure?"

No.

"Yes. I'm not going to have your welfare on my conscience."

"Mercenary," he replied dryly. "But given that it benefits me, I won't argue." He glanced around the small cottage, the slightest lift to his brow. "Although I'm curious as to how two people will fit in such…intimate accommodations."

"There's a perfectly good couch in here. You can have the bed—"

"No."

Tension gripped her at his clipped tone.

"Excuse me?"

"I will not be taking your bed. Unless," he added with a quirk of his lips, "you're suggesting we share…"

Desire shot through her with such intensity she barely

had the opportunity to conceal it. The idea of crowding onto the queen mattress with Julius's six-foot-three body stirred memories of how their limbs had become entwined during their second round of lovemaking. Every time she'd moved, it had been to feel the slide of her naked skin against his. The intimacy of her breasts pressed against the curling hair on his chest, her thighs shifting against his, his hands cupping her rear and pulling her closer against him, had been almost as dizzying as when he'd slid inside her the first time.

"That would hardly be appropriate. Especially," she added as much for his benefit as her own, "given that you have a ring and possibly a fiancée out there somewhere."

His face darkened.

"I am not taking your bed."

"Then sleep on the floor next to it. I'm not enjoying the comforts of a bed while the prince takes the couch."

Even though she had initially pursued her career at the encouragement of her father, out of some ridiculous need for his approval, the job had become ingrained in her. Fed by her genuine love and loyalty for her country, the thought of letting the prince she had sworn to protect with her life sleep on the couch nearly made her choke.

He stepped toward her.

"I will toss you into that bed if I have to."

His words lit the sensual tension hanging in the room. Eyes wide, Esme watched in stupefied fascination as his own gaze darkened, then swept over her from head to toe. She'd swapped out her bikini bottom for shorts when she'd come inside, but she might as well have been naked given the way Julius's eyes burned.

"What gives you the right to give me orders?"

"I'm a prince, aren't I?" A dangerous smile curved across his face, one that made her swallow hard. "Isn't giving orders part of what I do?"

"Yes. But you're no longer my prince." Suddenly furious, with both him and herself, she strode past him, deliberately letting her shoulder knock into his chest as she headed for the door. He had lost the right to tell her what to do. She wouldn't let anyone do that anymore. Not her father and certainly not Julius.

"Do what you want, *Julius*. Although I recommend calling Burak." She paused in the doorway and gave him an ornery smile. "Unless you want to test just how quickly the palace can track you down and haul your royal butt back to Rodina whether you like it or not."

With that parting shot, she let the door slam behind her.

CHAPTER SIX

"YES, BURAK, I assure you all is well. Thank you."

Julius hung up and sat back in the porch chair, closing his eyes against the pain exploding in his head. His captain of security had been suspicious. But the code word Esmerelda had included when she'd inputted Burak's contact information into his new phone had reassured the man. Burak had been less than happy about Julius's sudden jaunt to Grenada and suspicious of Julius's story that his personal bag with his passport and wallet had been stolen. The one thing that had placated him was that Julius was on a much smaller island with far fewer people than England.

He'd liked Burak. The man had balanced respect with backbone, the soft melody of a Turkish accent lacing his firm voice. He'd also been incredibly efficient at organizing several of Julius's requests.

But there had been no sense of knowing, no connection to the man who had been a part of his security detail for over a year. Not like there had been with Esmerelda. They'd discussed details like getting him access to his finances and a new passport. It had been a productive conversation. But it had also prodded the always present headache, spreading from an obscure ache at the base of his skull to his temples where it pounded away with reckless abandon.

Further evidence that he needed time. Time to rest, recuperate, hopefully remember more before he assumed the role of heir to an entire country.

Although it wasn't just that. After Esmerelda's revelation, she'd disappeared inside, which had given him time to absorb the magnitude of what she'd shared. He'd read up on himself, scrolling through photo after photo of him in elegant suits looking pensive, cold, shrewd. The few pictures of him with any women were over eighteen months old. Plenty of articles had speculated on ambassadors he had spoken with at dinners, daughters of wealthy business leaders whose hands he had held onto "a moment longer than others."

But there had been nothing that had given insight into who he was as a man. No hobbies, no candid photos, not even a smile. The lack of information, and the absence of any defining personality, had stoked the disquiet that had first appeared when he'd looked in the mirror and not recognized the face staring back at him.

Time. He needed time. He had confirmed with Burak that he would be gone the remaining two weeks they had previously agreed to. Two weeks to rest, to perhaps regain his memory.

And to figure out the puzzle of Esmerelda Clark.

His mind turned back to that last moment before she'd fled the cottage. The snap of electricity between them, the tantalizing spread of color from the V-neck of her shirt up her neck, the wariness mixed with desire in her vivid green eyes…he'd been ensnared. Intoxicated.

And she'd run.

The desire to pursue, to catch and demand answers, had been strong. But from what little he'd learned of Esmerelda, patience would serve him better. Her flight, coupled with the sensual tension between them, had confirmed that there had been something more to their relationship than simple professionalism.

The next few weeks would give him the chance to heal, but also the opportunity to break down whatever barriers he'd erected between him and Esme in his previous life and uncover the truth.

What if she's telling the truth? That you were simply a cold, callous bastard?

Was he pursuing Esmerelda because she was the one thing he could remember? Had he created the memory of them, naked and wrapped around each other in a lovers' embrace,i because he had needed something, anything, to grasp onto? Or had an unrequited attraction surfaced from his trauma? Had it been one-sided on his part?

Uncomfortable thoughts. Yet none of them felt right. And whether they had been lovers or not, something terrible had happened between him and Esmerelda. Something that had severed his relationship with the woman who been his sworn protector.

His mind opened unexpectedly—just for a moment—but it was long enough. He saw Esmerelda's face, her freckles standing out starkly against pale skin as she stared at him, eyes shining bright with unshed tears. A memory, and a vivid one. Pain hit him in the chest, hard and ugly, along with a remembered determination that pushed him on to do what he had to do...

A wall rose up. He inwardly swore as the headache turned sharp, combining pressure with tiny hot pricks like a dagger held over an open flame being driven into his skull again and again. Were all his first memories going to be so painful?

Several minutes passed before the headache lessened enough for him to focus on other things. He glanced at his watch. It had been nearly an hour since Esmerelda had left. An hour that he had put to good use. But he didn't like how long she'd been gone. Yes, the woman could obviously take care of herself. But each passing moment was another moment she could be using to get away from Grenada, to disappear once again.

His chest tightened. Then loosened as he heard the creak of footsteps on the stairs. Esmerelda appeared at the top a moment later, her hair pulled into a loose bun on top of her head, errant curls slipping down to frame her face. A cloth bag hung over one shoulder.

"Groceries," she said as she caught his curious glance at the bag. "Not much, but enough to get us through today and tomorrow."

"Thank you."

She nodded, then moved quickly past him into the cottage. He waited a moment, assembled his thoughts, reviewed his strategy, then followed her inside.

"I got in touch with Burak. He wasn't happy about my supposed change in itinerary, but he's made arrangements for me."

"Good."

He watched as she pulled out a knife and cutting board and started chopping up fruit.

"One of the arrangements is a residence here on the island. Larger than this one."

Much larger.

The knife blade slowed in its downward arc and became stuck in the papaya Esme had been slicing.

"You're leaving then?"

"I am."

She looked up, blinked rapidly, then nodded as her breath whooshed out.

"Good. That's good."

"I'd like you to come with me."

A frown appeared.

"I'm not going back to Rodina."

"Neither am I. Not for at least two weeks. I'm staying here on Grenada."

Her lips parted.

"You're what?"

"I'm staying. And I'd like for you to stay with me."

"Perhaps I didn't make it clear." She set the knife down carefully, as if she was trying to resist the temptation to stab him with it. "I want nothing more to do with you. I am sorry about your accident, but you expressed that you had no interest in working with me anymore."

"And now I'm saying otherwise."

"You can't just change your mind like that!" She went from simmering frustration to full-blown anger in seconds. "I've moved on. If you haven't noticed, I left the country I was born and raised in and decided to travel halfway around the world thinking that I might just have a slight amount of time to get myself together before tackling the next phase of my life, only to have the man who fired me from his team chase me halfway across the world and show up on my private beach that I paid good money for. Do you think you can just waltz in here and take over my life once more? Do you truly think that after you…"

She paused then, as if trying to get her words right before she spoke. He made note of it, filed it away for later.

"After you reassigned me without talking to me at all, just dropped this bombshell on me with no warning, you assigned me to a role that I had expressed that I was not interested in in the slightest, that I would just give in to your demands?"

"I did think that having amnesia might make a difference."

"Well, it doesn't," she fired back. "I'm getting on with my life. You should do the same."

"I'll ensure you have a reference for future employers.

I will also pay you one hundred thousand euros for you to serve as my bodyguard."

Her eyebrows climbed up to her hairline.

"That's nearly a year's salary."

"I'm interrupting your vacation. And after firing you. Paying you an outrageous sum seems like the least I could do."

He smiled, a slow, sensual smile designed to tempt. And tempt it did. Not that it would make a difference."

Her eyes narrowed. "Is that all I'm expected to do? Or would there be other duties as assigned?"

"Such as?"

"Sharing your bed."

Fury ripped through him.

"That's not what I would be purchasing, Miss Clark."

She blinked at the chill in his voice, then surprised him as a chilly yet satisfied smile slowly tilted her lips up.

"You might have lost your memory, Your Highness, but you're still in there. Just as cold and bastardly as ever."

With that, she turned to leave. He went after her, his long strides eating up the distance between them. He caught her elbow and turned her around.

"Then I'll try a different tactic."

She yanked her arm away.

"There's nothing you can say that will make me—"

"Please."

She stared at him, stunned.

"What?"

"Please, Miss Clark. Maybe by the time I return to Rodina, my memory will have returned. But if it doesn't, then I will be stepping into a role that literally impacts people's lives. I will do far better if I have time to recover, and recover with the presence of someone who feels familiar to me. Someone who knows me, better than I know myself."

She was bending. He saw it in the way she bit down on her lips, crossed her arms over her chest as if to ward him off even as her defenses began to crumble.

"Why can't Burak fly over—?"

"I don't know him."

She frowned.

"You don't remember me either—"

"You're the only person in my life, or rather my former life, with whom I feel any recognition. With you, I feel calm. My recovery will go better if I were to have someone near that I'm comfortable with. It might even help speed up the process of me regaining my memory."

She stared at him, evaluating. Could she see that he had another agenda in mind? Yes, everything he was saying was true. But he also wanted to find out what had happened between them, to get to know the woman who stood before him. To understand the attraction that flared in her eyes every time she was near him. To understand why he was so sure that what had happened between them had been life-changing. To understand his reaction to Esme Clark, the way she made his blood heat.

Her breath came out in a rush, followed by a softly muttered curse.

"And what if you don't recover your memory?"

"No matter what does, or does not, happen, I will return to my role within the palace." He paused, watching her. "You told me the one thing you know for certain is that you love your country. If you love it so much, help me."

Her head snapped up.

"Don't you dare use that to manipulate me."

"I'm only trying to manipulate you a little." At her raised brow, he held up his hands. "Okay, I'm trying to manipulate quite a bit. But there's truth in what I have to say, too. You love your country. And right now, your country needs you.

The family you once served needs you. That it will give me a chance to right the wrong I did to you is a bonus I probably don't deserve."

She stared at him for so long he wondered if she would say no.

And then she sighed. Triumph surged inside him.

"I don't like this."

"Don't like what?"

"I don't like the uncertainty, giving up the time I planned for myself." She tugged at the band holding up her hair, reddish gold curls tumbling down over her shoulders in a riotous cascade that made the seductive memory flare once more. "I lived for years with someone else making choices for me, arranging my life to suit their desires and wants. I'm not going back down that road again. Not just when I've broken free."

He regally inclined his head to her.

"I will not ask anything of you beyond these two weeks."

She arched a brow.

"Unless you change your mind and want something else," she said knowingly.

His eyes glinted again, but this time with humor.

"It depends on what I want and how badly I want it."

CHAPTER SEVEN

THE SUN ROSE over the eastern waters of the Caribbean Sea. Waves rose, turned golden by the sunlight, before splashing back down into blue-and-white foam. A seagull cawed in the distance. Manicured green lawns raced down to the private beach of fluffy white sand, the yard dotted here and there with a soaring palm tree or a well-tended bed of bright blooms.

Idyllic. Perfect. And Esme wasn't enjoying a single moment.

A yawn escaped her as she snuggled deeper into the robe she'd found in the bathroom. Luxurious and cozy, it warded off the early morning chill. Within an hour, she knew the temperatures would climb steadily and drive vacationers into the ocean waters or the nearest pool.

But for now, with a gentle breeze bringing just a touch of coolness off the water, it was soothing.

She needed soothing after the night she'd had. Once she'd said yes to the devil and agreed to accompany him for two weeks to his "new residence," she'd packed her tiny suitcase and walked with him down to the beach. A dinghy had been waiting and carried them out to an impressive two-story catamaran with big white sails that had ballooned out under the captain's expert skill and taken them south to Prickly Bay and the exclusive Lance aux Epines community.

It wasn't like she hadn't been exposed to wealth and luxury in her year on Julius's security team. But when her eyes were roving over crowds of people assessing for threats, when she was mentally evaluating potential exits in case of various hazards or disasters, she hadn't done much ogling.

Julius hadn't said much on the boat. In fact, he had been nothing but a gentleman since she had agreed to accompany him. All sensuality had disappeared, replaced by a man who was certainly friendlier and softer than Prince Julius Carvalho, but far removed from the man whose eyes had burned with desire as for one heart-pounding moment she thought he'd kiss her.

But he hadn't. Once she said yes, it was as if he pulled back whatever he felt, or thought he felt for her, and was striving to show her he could behave himself. Would not ask more of her than he already had. And wasn't that what she wanted? That she found herself missing the tension, the spark of desire, had only made her cranky and short with him. A pity, because the sail down the coast to Prickly Bay had been peaceful, the crew professional, and the views unparalleled.

And when the boat had pulled up to the private dock of the Dove Villa, it had been almost like a fairy tale. Cinderella's coach, or in this case sailboat, pulling up to the palace.

The villa was beautiful. No, not just beautiful. Stunning. An architectural wonder. Gleaming ivory walls offset by white pillars guarded the two-story front door. Yet instead of appearing so expensive she was afraid to step inside, the red tiled roof had added a touch of relaxation to the otherwise austere exterior. Inside met outside with the sliding walls of glass that could be rolled into recesses in the wall and open the massive rooms to blue sky and ocean breezes.

Julius had reached out a hand to help her off the catamaran onto the dock. She'd walked off herself, regretting the petulant move when he'd simply turned away and walked up the path to the villa. A butler, Aroldo, had met them and given them a tour.

The furniture was understated, a mix of whites and blues, yet of obviously high quality. More white pillars held up soaring ceilings and made room for large fans that rotated silently as they kept the villa pleasantly cool during the hot afternoons. Tiles faded to a soft red dominated the main rooms, while weathered gray hardwood added both elegance and relaxation to the bedrooms.

Julius had thanked Aroldo and asked him to show Esme to her room before bowing his head to her.

"Perhaps I'll see you at dinner."

But she hadn't. She hadn't seen him all evening. Restless, she'd unpacked, then re-sorted how she'd hung up her meager clothes. She'd prowled online job listings, waiting for something to click, to feel right.

Waiting for a knock at the door. She'd waited in vain.

She'd tried to focus on the beauty of her room. A large bed stood in the center, thick white pillows arranged perfectly against a light gray headboard. Opposite the bed sat a couch, this one covered in the same gray material as the headboard, with a large window just above the back that overlooked the expansive grounds. To her left lay the bathroom, with a freestanding white marble tub in front of a wall covered in mosaic tiles of emerald and scarlet red arranged into a tropical flower against a brilliant blue sky. To her right, the entire wall was comprised of glass, including two massive doors that opened onto a private terrace with steps descending to the infinity pool.

The rooms balanced elegance with relaxation, quality with comfort. Yet the location and the investments in furnishings, from the lamp stands fashioned of gold to the crystal vase overflowing with red roses, made it clearly known that this was the kind of place only the wealthiest could afford.

But even the loveliness of her surroundings could only soothe for so long. Growing edginess had driven her into the kitchen shortly after sundown. A bowl of *pelau* had been left for her in the fridge with heating instructions, along with a note from Aroldo inviting her to help herself to anything in the kitchen and to call if she needed something. The chicken and rice dish, made heartier with a mix of carrots, celery, beans, red peppers and a dash of brown sugar, had assuaged her physical hunger.

Yet still she felt hollow. Empty.

It wasn't just Julius, although he certainly played a significant role. She had questioned her decision to follow him so quickly, how a simple "please" had led to her changing her mind, and her plans, for the next two weeks. All for a man who had broken her heart.

Part of it, she was coming to realize, was because in some twisted way, Julius had tossed her a lifeline. Two more weeks of something else to focus on other than what she was going to do with the rest of her life. How she was going to shape it just the way she wanted, without outside pressure. Without bending to the whims of someone else.

"Good morning."

Her lips firmed into a frown even as her heartbeat quickened at the sound of his voice. The second time in less than twenty-four hours the man had snuck up on her.

"Good morning, Your Highness."

Tension rolled off him as he sat in the lounge chair next to hers.

"Please call me Julius."

"Saying 'please' isn't going to get you everything you want." She glanced at him then, her chest tightening as the sun added golden highlights to his dark blond hair. "I spent a year referring to you as 'Your Highness,' 'sir,' et cetera. Hard to break that habit."

"It's odd," he mused, staring out over the ocean, "but when you use those titles, it makes me feel…distant. Almost tired."

Surprised, she glanced at him fully. He wore a white shirt unbuttoned at the collar with the sleeves rolled up, dark blue pants and… She blinked. Barefoot. The Crown Prince of Rodina was barefoot. Julius almost never went anywhere without a tie. He certainly never went barefoot.

Except for Paris.

She pushed the thought away.

"You carried a great deal on your shoulders."

"Did I?"

"Yes. You sit on multiple committees, including finance and transportation. You were also involved in military operations and, your personal cause, education."

"Given how little you seem to think of me as a man, I'm surprised by the respect in your voice."

She shrugged.

"Great leaders can be very different behind closed doors."

Silence followed. She forced herself to lean back in her chair, to focus on the crystal-clear waters of the pool, the ocean just beyond.

"Tell me why my reassignment of you hurt so much. Please," he added with the hint of a smile as she arched one brow.

The obvious answer, that she had fallen in love with and slept with her boss, wouldn't do. Yet as she turned his question over in her mind, she analyzed it in a way she hadn't before.

"I was embarrassed." Truth added a rawness to her voice that made her clear her throat. "My father is the head of palace security. He lives for his work. Always has. I had considered going to the States for graduate studies after I got my degree. Something around law or political science. He suggested I go through the academy." Over two decades of pain rose up and wrapped around her heart like a vise. "It was the first time he had shown interest in what I did. So I did what he suggested. I was out in six months, completed another three months of advanced training at the commandant's recommendation. Assigned to general palace security for six months when I graduated, and then your detail the following year."

"Your father must have been proud."

She shrugged to mask the hurt. "As much as he was capable of being. Still, I grasped onto the crumbs of his approval like it was a lifeline. And…" She could feel the blush rising up her throat, that damned telltale hotness that made her feel transparent, vulnerable. "Others were more impressed. Each compliment, each commendation, made me feel whole for the first time in my life. When I was promoted to your detail a few months before my twenty-fifth birthday, for the first time in my life my father said 'well done.'"

"I took that away from you."

A warm hand settled on top of hers. Startled, she turned to look at him. She'd glimpsed occasional flickers of kindness in Julius. But the understanding on this man's face, so familiar yet so different, from the compassion in his gaze to the regret that pulled at the corners of his mouth, touched her in a way she wasn't ready for.

"Yes." She pulled her hand back. Did she imagine the hurt that flashed in his eyes before he settled back in his chair? "That's what it felt like. I didn't have any warning."

"I'm sorry."

She gave him a small, sad smile. "How can you be sorry for something you don't even remember?"

He looked out over the ocean, a small frown forming between his brows.

"I do remember it. Some of it at least."

Panic skittered down her spine.

"Oh?"

"Your face. You looked heartbroken." He looked back at her then. "And I put that there. That pain in your eyes. After you swore to protect me with your life."

Guilt settled on her shoulders, heavy and clawing. She didn't want to tell him, didn't know if it was the right thing to tell him so soon after the onset of his amnesia.

"I was angry. And hurt. But it was within your right to reassign me."

"Not if it made you hurt, Esmerelda."

The way her name rolled off his tongue made a shiver pass over her skin. Not ready to confront the desire that still lingered in her veins.

"I appreciate the apology, sir. I will get over it."

"I suspect you're a woman who rises to the occasion or surpasses it more often than not. But tell me," he said, leaning forward, filling up her vision and her senses with his closeness, "how often do you make that journey alone?"

His voice filled her, winding through her and warming her blood.

Her phone dinged. Grateful for the reprieve from diving any deeper into her past, she pulled it out of the pocket of her robe. She muttered a curse as she read the text.

"Something wrong?"

"I emailed a friend at Scotland Yard to ask about any reports of muggings or assaults near the hotel you were staying at." She sighed. "Nothing."

"The doctor said it looked like a blow from a blunt object."

She frowned. "When did you see a doctor?"

"A doctor from one of the resorts in St. George's came by last night." Julius's fingers wandered to the back of his neck, crept up to rest lightly on the wound. "No evidence of any lingering concussion, although I do have an appointment this afternoon for some scans."

"And the memory loss?"

Julius's lips thinned. "Hopefully temporary. The head wound is unfortunate, but other than the loss of consciousness and initial nausea when I woke up, there's no evidence I'm still suffering from a concussion."

Confused, Esme propped her chin on her hand.

"So what does that mean?"

"Most likely dissociative retrograde amnesia."

"Pardon?"

"It means I saw something scary and disassociated from the event by forgetting everything about my previous life."

The words came out as a growl. Esme felt herself slip back into her old role, the one of peacemaker, of guard and protector.

"You're angry at yourself."

"Extremely."

"Because you feel weak."

"Aren't I?" he snapped. "Apparently I saw something frightening and instead of facing it, I retreated into my worthless mind."

"Your mind's not worthless, Julius."

Her use of his first name did what it was intended. His shoulders relaxed, his frown lessening as he blew out a harsh breath.

"It is disconcerting to think I ran from danger. Even more so when I hear how I treated my employees." His laugh was short and humorless. "I shudder to think of the ruler I was. What kind of ruler I will become."

The guilt gnawed deeper, making her sick.

"Julius—"

"No more." He suddenly looked tired, the shadows beneath his eyes darker and more pronounced. "I am in need of a walk."

He stood and moved to the edge of the terrace. She pulled the lapels of her robe closer, seeking comfort in the plush material. She needed to talk to the doctor who had treated him, find out if telling him the truth would be better or worse for his recovery. Because keeping the secret of their time together was feeling more and more selfish. Yes, he'd hurt her. But he also hadn't outright fired her. He had also made it clear in Paris that what they would have would be temporary.

She'd been the one to go and fall in love. To think they might have more than just one night. She knew he would have to marry someone suitable. The he was meant for someone else.

"Esmerelda?"

She blinked and focused on him.

"Sorry. What did you say?"

"Would you like to join me?"

"Oh. I don't want to interrupt—"

"I would prefer the company of someone else than just my own," he said with a sardonic smile.

"Of course, sir."

"Julius."

He said it softly, but the single word was threaded with steel. She hesitated. It would be a submission. Surrender.

Part of her argued it was the best thing she could do given everything he'd been through. The still aching part of her soul fired back that after he'd cut her loose in such a cold manner, had taken away the career she had told him had been so important to her, he didn't deserve any capitulation.

But when she silenced those voices, focused on her heart, she found that the answer was simple.

"Thank you… Julius."

Triumph flashed in his whiskey-brown eyes. Suddenly afraid that she had given up something valuable, she fumbled for an excuse to go inside, to flee to the safety of her luxurious room.

Warm fingers curled around hers. Her heart stopped, then slammed into overdrive. Her feet moved of their own accord, following Julius as he gently but firmly pulled her down the deck to the stairs.

Minutes later, they arrived at the beach, hands still entwined. Every time she started to pull away, his fingers tightened just enough that to pull away would have been obvious.

Worst of all, she didn't want to. Even during their all-too-brief romantic interlude, they had never held hands. It made her feel young, cherished, protected.

"Oh!"

The exclamation escaped her lips before she could stop it. Up ahead, hanging from the tops of two massive palm trees, was a wooden swing.

"Do you like to swing?"

"I'm not sure."

She felt Julius's gaze on her, felt it burn through her.

"How can you not be sure? I have amnesia, and even I feel comforted by the sight of a swing."

"I never had a playset growing up," she admitted. "Beautiful toys, things to keep myself company. But nothing like a swing or a slide. My mother didn't like getting her hands dirty and preferred the label on the toy versus the functionality. My father worked too much to be concerned with trivial matters."

"Trivial matters?" Julius repeated. Disdain dripped from his voice. "How is raising a child trivial?"

"I was not intended. My mother and father were dating. I came along. They never even married. They lived together for years, although my mother made frequent long trips back to Scotland and England. My father just wasn't interested in children. My mother preferred a more exciting life. Having a small child hindered that."

It hurt less to talk about now. She had never once been wanted. Not until her surprisingly successful career in security. Not until she had, for one brief moment, been wanted by a man without condition, simply because he desired her. And it had been because of that she had had the courage to walk away from everything. Because of the knowledge that it was possible, even if that man's dismissal of her had been the most painful thing she'd ever had to go through.

"Where is your mother now?"

"America. She met a doctor when I was thirteen, had a whirlwind courtship and now spends her days lunching and sunning by a pool."

"And your father didn't care?"

"I believe he shrugged and said he hoped she was happy. He doesn't care about much other than his job."

A long pause ensued, broken up only by the surf cascading onto the white sandy beach.

"I'm not certain of many things these days," Julius finally said, "but I'm certain I would not like your parents."

She stifled the retort that came automatically to mind. For too long she had defended her parents and their lackadaisical attempts at serving in the roles of mother and father. Had wanted to believe that they cared more than they did.

"I don't much like them myself. I love them," she added thoughtfully, "as I imagine many children love the caretakers they know. They don't know anything else, or any better."

Another beat of silence ensued.

"What is my relationship like? With my father?"

His voice sounded strong, steady. Yet underneath she heard the current of uncertainty, the slight twist of doubt.

"On the outside, amiable. Mutual respect, partnering on

various political and legal matters." She turned to face him then, wanting him to see the truth. "In private, he loves you very much, as you do him. The pressure you've placed on yourself to succeed comes primarily from within." She hesitated. "I'm not sure from where. We didn't have the kind of relationship where you would have shared what drove you. But your father believes in you. He knows you will be a good leader."

Julius regarded her for a long moment before taking her other hand in his and squeezing them both.

"Obrigado." He cast a glance at the swing, then back at her. "You should get on."

She chuckled. "I don't think many twenty-six-year-olds swing."

He stepped closer, both hands still wrapped around hers. Her breath caught in her chest as she tilted her chin up to look at him.

"You wanted to figure out what you wanted from your life." He nodded toward the swing. "Seems like a simple step. Does Esmerelda Clark like to swing or not? Find out."

When he phrased it like that, it did seem extraordinarily simple. She stepped back, missing the touch of his hands even as she hated that she missed it. She turned away and slipped onto the swing. The wood was warm from the sun. The ropes were made of thick twine, scratchy against her palms. She dug her toes into the sand and prepared to push off.

The swing gave a tug. Startled, she looked up to see Julius's hands wrapped around the ropes.

"Hold on."

His words whispered over her. He pulled back, then let go. A moment later she flew out over the water, blue beneath her and above. Startled by the sensation of flying, of weightlessness as she reached the pinnacle, she threw back her head and laughed.

She didn't how long Julius pushed her on the swing. Probably only a minute or two, but it felt like one of those blissful moments in time that stretched forever, where the rest of the world faded away and left nothing but contented pleasure.

She glanced back over her shoulder with a grin. And nearly fell off as Julius suddenly stopped the swing.

"What—"

He circled around, his hands still on the ropes, caging her between his body and the swing. The morning heat changed, crackling with sensual tension as she looked up at him. The whiskey brown had turned almost golden as he gazed down at her.

"You've smiled at me like that before."

Her throat constricted.

"What?"

"You smiled at me like that before," he repeated. His eyes took on a faraway look as his mind tried to grasp the past. "In... Paris. We were in Paris. There was a café and flowers. I said something to you, and you laughed and smiled at me."

"Okay."

She tried to stand up, but he held his ground. She sat back down, unwilling to put her body against his, not with this electricity humming between them.

"I don't know if you realize this, but people do smile and laugh at each other. Even princes and their bodyguards."

"This was different," he insisted. He leaned down until she could see the dark flecks in his eyes, could smell the rich scent of cedar rolling off his skin. "I saw it in your eyes. You felt something for me. Tell me what it was, Esme."

Her fingers tightened around the ropes. She couldn't lie. She had already stretched and twisted the truth enough, justified her insistence that they were not lovers. But what could she say now? This Julius, the softer, protective, yet no less commanding man who had emerged from whatever atrocity had occurred in London, could entice her back into his arms. Into his bed. He would insist the few idealistic memories he had of her meant they were to be together. And damn it, with how raw her still hurting heart was, she didn't know if she would have the strength to resist.

Only for him to go back to Rodina and assume his responsibilities. To marry another woman, to have children with her.

Or worse…for him to remember. To remember and look at her once more like she was nothing more than a woman he had had one night with and no more.

"I don't think your memories can be considered reliable given what's happened, sir."

The words had their intended effect, as did her formal address. He released the ropes and stepped back. She surged to her feet and hurried up the beach toward the path, not caring if she looked guilty or not.

"Esmerelda."

Oh, how she wanted to keep running. But wasn't that what she had been doing for over a month? Running away, running toward something, even if she didn't know what that something was?

She forced herself to stop, to turn and face him. He stood on the beach, shoulders thrown back, the wind ruffling his hair. Even from this distance, she could see the regality on his chiseled features, feel his confusion and anger.

"I will find out the truth," he shouted, his face hard and unyielding. "That's a promise."

CHAPTER EIGHT

JULIUS AWOKE WITH the memory of funeral music pulsing through his veins, as if he'd been hollowed out by grief. The image of a woman with hair as blond as his, her kind face covered in makeup to make her look in death as she had in life, was seared into his brain.

Throwing back the covers, he stood and strode to the glass doors overlooking the ocean. His chest rose and fell as he tried to get a handle on his racing heart, his erratic breathing. Hard to do when the grief he'd felt at his mother's funeral over twenty years ago flooded him as fresh as if he'd watched her coffin lowered into the ground yesterday.

He pressed his forehead to the glass. The coolness soothed the hot sweat on his brow, grounded him in the moment.

Elizabeth.

Her name came to him, a whisper in his mind that pulled up memories of warm hugs, a soothing voice tinged with a British accent, and the scent of violets. Each remembrance, of a kiss to his forehead after falling into the cold waves at some nameless beach, of sitting on a couch under a blanket watching some black-and-white movie, was both a godsend and a stab to his heart.

Gradually, the memories receded, leaving behind a different type of emptiness. He had wanted this, had craved a connection to his past. But remembering his mother, the things he had loved about her, made the knowledge that she was gone and had been gone for years even more painful. Like having a cherished treasure dangled before one's eyes only to have it yanked away moments later.

One deep breath, then another. Slowly, he accepted his grief, the newfound memories. Perhaps tomorrow, or the day after, he would revisit them, honor his mother as best he could.

But now, with the wound of loss so fresh, he needed to pause. The reopening of his grief had brought with it a faint memory of why he had withdrawn from the world, become the cold, hard man he'd witnessed in the photographs, heard about from Esme's account of his reassigning her. It wasn't a complete picture, more like a puzzle with important pieces still missing. But he had the gist of what had happened.

He'd been hurt. As people tend to do when they're in pain, he'd withdrawn. Unlike others, who had healed and gradually rejoined the world, he was beginning to suspect he'd burrowed himself deep into a hole of apathy.

A suspicion that made loathing churn in his stomach. If the doctor was right, he'd run from something in London. Even though he knew there was more to his and Esme's story than what she was sharing, he didn't doubt her grief, her humiliation, when she told him about his firing her from his detail. He wanted to remember. But, he wondered as he pulled the glass doors apart and stepped out onto the terrace, did he truly?

A sigh escaped him as he moved to the railing. Was this to be his life for the foreseeable future? Wanting his memories to return, yet being on guard as to when they would appear and how emotional they would be?

Remembering Esmerelda's face when he'd delivered the news of her reassignment had been a punch to the gut. Yet seeing her smile so vividly, the emotion in her eyes, had warmed him.

Until she had sworn that he had misinterpreted the memory, just as he had his first recollection of her.

He didn't believe her. Not about their personal history. It was an odd sensation, to entrust one's life to someone knowing they were concealing something. But despite her perfidy, he still felt as soothed by her presence as he did fired up by the passion swirling like a tornado between them, still experienced the thrill of a connection rooted somewhere in his murky past whenever she was near.

Although since their short sojourn onto the beach, he hadn't talked with her in over two days. When he'd gone to the hospital for his scans, she'd sat upfront with the driver, stayed quiet in a corner as machines had whirred about his head. Nothing of concern had been noted. The doctor had reiterated his initial instructions.

"Rest. Relax. I'm confident your memories will come back."

They'd returned to the villa and Esmerelda had promptly disappeared. The evening staff had drifted in just after five and prepared dinner. The butler, Aroldo, had mentioned that Esmerelda had dined in her room, then gone out for a walk around the grounds. The same had happened yesterday. He'd spotted her here and there, eyes scanning the landscape, occasionally walking the perimeter of the grounds when he ventured outside.

Doing her job, yes. But she didn't have to ignore him.

Her evasion grated, as did how much it bothered him.

He would not allow her to do the same tonight. Tonight he would take the tray himself if necessary—

"Good morning."

Soft, delicate, with a tinge of huskiness that brushed over his skin. Esme stood just outside the doors to her room, her curls pulled up into a ponytail, leaving her freckled face bare to his hungry gaze.

"Good morning."

She smiled, the gesture doing little to belie the wariness lurking in her eyes, as if she were afraid he might pounce.

"I was going…" Her voice trailed off. "Would you…?"

"Have you always been this eloquent?"

Red tinged her cheeks at his teasing tone. Whoever had told her that nonsense about flushing or whatever term it was had been a fool. The woman was a beautiful blend of colors: tan skin beneath coffee freckles, emerald-green eyes, red hair threaded with gold.

"I'm going to take one of the boats out." The faint pride in her voice had him suppressing a smile. "Would you like to join me?"

"Two days ago you could barely stand to be in my company." He cocked his head to one side. "Now you're proposing a boat ride?"

"I'm going out. You're welcome to join me or not."

She turned away and started for the stairs. His esteem rose, as did the intrigue surrounding this enigmatic woman. She had a backbone. He liked that about her.

"I'll be down in five."

She glanced over her shoulder, nodded once to shown she'd heard him and then continued on. He watched as she moved down the path until she disappeared around a corner. Whatever her motives were in inviting him out onto the ocean, it would give him time to get to know her better since she'd kept him at a distance the past forty-eight hours.

Four minutes later he strode onto the dock. A sleek, spacious speedboat greeted him. Portholes indicated a cabin belowdeck. Esme, seated at the helm, glanced up, her eyes hidden behind large sunglasses.

"Where are we headed?"

"The ocean."

"Did you always keep important details to yourself?"

he asked as he climbed aboard and sank down onto a plush leather seat kept cool by an overhead canopy.

"Need to know, sir."

"Call me Julius."

"No thank you, sir." She tossed a saucy smile over her shoulder. "It's protocol, and I am your bodyguard."

"Yet you were something more."

Seated behind her, he couldn't miss the tensing of her shoulders beneath the white T-shirt, the tightening of her fingers around the steering wheel.

"Could we keep the past behind us? Just for an hour?"

She looked over her shoulder, her eyes hidden. But he could hear the vulnerability in her voice, the rawness that hinted at the depth of her pain. Pain that kept her from sharing the truth with him.

Suddenly angry with himself, regretting whatever he'd done to cause that pain, he nodded. She turned away and, gradually, her shoulders dropped, her body relaxing.

She guided them out of the bay with an easy confidence he admired. Even though a part of him wanted to grab the wheel, to take the helm and drive the boat across the waves, he knew he was in good hands.

An odd sensation, he reflected, as his gaze drifted over a sailboat cruising by. He felt that he was not the kind of man who handed over control easily. Based on what little he had remembered thus far, coupled with the minute details he'd gleaned from Esmerelda, Burak and the media, he seemed regimented, regulated almost to an extreme.

Was his ability to trust now, to place himself in the hands of someone he barely remembered, because he had no history to stop him from doing so? Or was it because of the woman at the wheel taking them further out onto the open ocean? This strong woman who had never been pushed on a swing and whose shocked laughter had stirred not just his desire but his heart?

Probably, he mused as he slid on his own pair of sunglasses as the sun glinted off the waves, a mixture of the two.

He shoved away his thoughts, leaned back into the seat and enjoyed the ride.

What was I thinking?

Esme glanced at a small mirror positioned on the dashboard that provided some protection from the ocean spray. Julius sat on the seat, arms draped casually along the back, his long legs stretched out. Wind ruffled his dark blond hair. Sunglasses now obscured his eyes so she couldn't tell if he was sleeping or watching the passing sea. In black swimming trunks and a gray T-shirt, he looked like any other beachgoer in the Caribbean.

Not at all like the disciplined prince she'd protected for over a year.

Over the past hour they'd barely exchanged five words. He'd appeared content to lay back and rest. That he trusted her and didn't pester her with questions had unnerved her as much as it had touched her. Julius had placed his trust in her before in a professional capacity. But then he'd had an entire dossier on her, not to mention security clearances, reviews of the very small number of men she'd dated and several extensive interviews that had felt more like inquisitions.

Now, he had a handful of memories and thirty-five years of emptiness. Yet still he trusted her.

Even though you're lying to him.

She pushed that uncomfortable thought away. Not only was she evading his questions, all created by her initial distortion of the truth, but she had lied to him this morning, too. She'd awoken just after sunrise and gone out onto the deck. It had been impossible to miss the sounds of someone clutched in the throes of a nightmare coming from the open window to his room. She'd had to force herself not to go to him, especially when she'd heard him gasp a word that had brought tears to her eyes.

"*Mãe.*"

He'd been dreaming of his mother. He'd only been fourteen when Her Majesty the Queen had passed away. Esme had been five. All she could remember of the event was dressing in black and standing next to her mother as vehicle after vehicle had passed by in a funeral procession, the people around her weeping and tossing flowers onto the street. The first four months she'd been a part of his detail, he hadn't said a word about his mother. But after the parade incident and her ending up in the hospital, he'd mentioned her occasionally. Little things, like commenting that his mother would have found an ambassador at a dinner in Lisbon amusing or that she would have liked a painting at the Louvre. She had thought those confidences an indicator that they had grown closer after the accident.

Reading too much into something simple, she told herself. *Desperate for anything anyone would give you.*

The past was the past. She'd made choices she had to live with. For now, she had followed the instinct of inviting Julius out onto the water and distracting him from whatever nightmare he'd lived through last night.

"Am I seeing things?"

She grinned.

"What do you see?"

"An umbrella sticking up out of the middle of the ocean."

"Welcome to Mopion."

The tiny speck of land rose out of the water, white sand topped with a wood-and-thatch umbrella. Esme anchored the boat just off the reef. After a short ride in the dinghy that skimmed over colorful coral and fish, Julius hopped out and hauled the boat onto the sand.

"Beautiful." He glanced around with a slight smile. "Although after walking the length of it in less than thirty seconds, I'm not sure what else there is to do."

"Swim. Snorkel. Relax. There's a cooler for when we get back on the boat, too."

She smoothed her hands over the white swim shirt she wore as protection against the blazing sun. It provided some security. But her decision to wear bikini bottoms was now inspiring doubt. She felt naked, vulnerable, with so much skin on display.

"Take a look at this."

Julius wasn't ogling or even sneaking covert glances at her. No, he was examining the pole of the umbrella. Telling herself she was relieved instead of disappointed, she moved up the sand.

"Initials," she said with a small smile. "There's so many."

Some were simple letters, others with hearts, stars and even a few Cupid's arrows.

"Looks like a popular place." Julius looked around. "Although not today. There's hardly a boat in sight."

"Hurricane season."

"So naturally you came here."

She shrugged as she stood and moved back toward the water.

"Affordable, and Grenada is far enough south that it rarely gets hit. Plus," she said as she tossed a smile over her shoulder and stretched out her arms, doing a spin in the sand, "I get to enjoy places like this all to myself."

Julius moved suddenly, stopping her midtwirl by placing his hands on her waist. She grabbed onto his shoulders to steady herself. His touch made her suck in a breath before she could summon her defenses.

"Why did you invite me today?"

She hesitated. The old Julius would have been apathetic at best, and coldly furious at worst, to know someone had witnessed a moment of vulnerability. How would the new Julius handle it?

"I heard you this morning. Dreaming." She tilted her head to the side as she watched him: the surprise that flickered in his eyes, the thinning of his lips. "Or perhaps remembering."

Slowly, he released her. A chill raked over her skin despite the sun burning overhead as she took a step back.

"Remembering."

Surprised, she watched him as he walked a few feet away and stared out over the ocean.

"I remembered my mother. Elizabeth. I remembered her death. Her funeral. A couple moments from my childhood."

What more was there to say? She had heard the grief in that one uttered word this morning. It had been strange to hear the depth of emotion in the voice of a man who so often seemed intractable. The brief flutter of panic she felt at hearing that he was remembering disappeared almost as quickly as it had come, her concern overriding her fear.

"She was by all accounts an incredible queen. She volunteered a lot. Engaged with the people."

"That sounds...familiar. Like her." He blew out a harsh breath. "I want to remember more."

What could she say to that? What would it be like to have one's entire life, the people they cared about, erased in a matter of seconds?

"I'm sorry."

He shrugged, his back to her.

"The doctor said any returning memories were a good sign."

"A good sign for your long-term health, yes. Doesn't mean you have to like what you remember."

He let out a low laugh.

"No, I suppose it doesn't."

She gave in to instinct, went to him as she had once before. This time, however, instead of stiffening beneath her touch the way he had the morning after their night together in Paris, he leaned into her touch.

Her heart pounded against her ribs, almost painfully. Her defenses wavered.

Dangerous. Too dangerous, a voice frantically whispered in her head.

Accepting her touch, opening himself to her. It all led to dangerous places where emotion crept through the cracks and weakened her resolve to keep her heart intact.

"Let's swim."

He turned. Her hand fell away, only for his to come up and brush strands of hair from her face.

"Thank you, Esmerelda."

Before she could come up with a response, he dropped his hand and moved away.

Oh, yes. She was in trouble.

Time flew as they slipped into the crystal-clear water and swam in lazy circles around the island. Aroldo had thoughtfully packed snorkel masks and fins, allowing them to strike out over the coral and spot schools of fish along with the occasional stingray resting on the sandy bottom. She kept a watchful eye out for passing boats and tourists lurking with cameras. But none appeared, leaving them cocooned in a rare moment of solitude.

By the time they climbed back into the dinghy and struck out for the boat, nearly two hours had passed. She was exhausted, the kind of exhaustion that accompanied a bone-deep contentment. Seeing the same state of relaxation on Julius's face, the sadness no longer in his eyes, made it even better.

Not, she realized with a slight smile as she climbed back on the boat and did another quick scan of the ocean, because she felt like she had to or because it had been the right thing to do. No, she'd done it because she had wanted to.

She disappeared belowdeck and changed into a white sundress. As she climbed back up to the deck, she pressed a button Aroldo had showed her that dropped the back sides of the boat down into an enlarged terrace. Julius, still in his swim trunks and with his muscled chest on display, set the cooler down on a countertop just behind the cockpit.

"Did you pack this?" he asked as he opened the cooler and glanced inside.

"No, Aroldo did."

Julius's smile flashed, quick and uninhibited. It stole her breath.

"That makes more sense."

He laid out containers of ripe strawberries, glistening mango and thick slices of cheese, along with shrimp, crab and several sauces. Esme's eyebrows climbed as he pulled out a bottle of champagne.

"It's barely noon."

"And you're on vacation."

"I'm working. Technically," she added with a touch of sass as he frowned, "I shouldn't even be drinking at all."

He poured two glasses and handed one to her.

"Your boss sounds terrible."

She laughed and accepted the glass. The sweet flavor of peach hit her tongue as bubbles danced down her throat.

"The old prince would never have drunk champagne, let alone had a drink before five."

A hint of darkness raced across his face.

"All the more reason to do it."

CHAPTER NINE

THEY PILED FOOD on their plates and moved to the stern of the boat. Julius sat on one of the leather lounges while she stretched out on a towel, one leg dangling over the side.

"What do you like to do in your spare time?"

She paused in the middle of popping a piece of rosemary-and-ginger chocolate into her mouth.

"Do?"

"You're obviously adept at handling a boat. And swimming. Do you spend all your time on the water?"

The chocolate turned bitter in her mouth. She tried to cover up her unease by taking a long drink of champagne.

"A decent bit," she finally said. "That and reading. Although I didn't get much time to myself when I worked for the palace."

"For me."

He lounged on the leather seat, his sunglasses back on, his body relaxed. Yet she knew better, knew what lurked beneath the surface. Not a relaxed wealthy vacationer, but a predator, a lion waiting to pounce.

"Yes."

"I find it curious that the woman I just spent the past two hours with has completely disappeared." He leaned forward. "As soon as I ask about you, you become tense."

"I don't like talking about myself."

"Why not?"

Whether it was the champagne or the sun or just the sudden fatigue of presenting a face to the world, she opted for the truth.

"Because I don't know that much about myself."

She could feel his surprise.

"How so?"

"I've always done what was expected. What others wanted." She pushed a strawberry around her plate, the fruit leaving a red smear of juice in its wake. "When I was five, that was wearing clothes I didn't like to please my mother. When I was thirteen, it was crying alone in my room when my mother moved away because my father didn't like tears."

"And when you joined the academy?"

She looked up then, faced him head-on.

"I wanted my father to be proud of me. I wanted...something. Any kind of connection." Her whole body grew tight, confusion spiraling through as questions she'd asked herself over and over again the past few weeks rose to the surface. "I went after a career I doubt I would have pursued had it not been for a childish wish."

"I imagine many others do the same."

Disappointment sliced through her. He didn't understand. She got up and set her plate on the counter, pulled on her dress as she walked back to the terrace and dropped onto her towel. She turned her gaze to the ocean, to the islands covered in lush green and sweeping mountains that dotted the blue waves.

"I'm sure they do," she finally said. "I love Rodina. I told myself when I first registered that loving my country would make up for picking a career that was my father's dream and not mine."

"Was it?"

"I don't know." She pulled her legs to her chest, rested her chin on her knees. "Even though I was good at it, I was never sure if it was something I wanted for myself or just because I was finally…"

She grasped for a word, a phrase, something that would give voice to the tumultuous storm that had been raging inside her for years, only recently brought to the surface when the one thing she'd been good at, the one thing she'd been recognized for, had been taken away.

All because she'd dared to grasp the one thing she had wanted, truly wanted just for herself, in her whole life.

The boat rocked beneath her. Shyness and embarrassment overtook her. She kept her eyes trained resolutely on the horizon, refusing to look at him. She'd been humiliated enough already.

The heat from his body as he sat next to her seeped through the thin material of her dress.

"I finally felt seen," she whispered.

He wrapped an arm around her shoulders. She stiffened, then surrendered to temptation and let her head relax against him.

"When I played upon your sense of duty and loyalty back in the cottage, you agreed almost immediately."

"You always were good at using people's emotions."

She said it without malice, but could still feel his body tense.

"I sound like a bastard."

"You could be." A sigh escaped her as she leaned deeper into his warmth. Utterly shameless.

Just one minute. One more minute and then I'll move.

"Then why did you keep working for me?"

"Because there was more to you than that. I didn't always agree with your methods, but I never doubted your intentions. You fought for the people. For the country."

Oh, how that had mesmerized her. To see someone who others viewed as cold, intractable, and yet come to see how deeply they cared. Unlike her mother, a vapid creature with no interests other than herself, and her father, addicted to his role but not the people he served, Julius's convictions had ensnared her, deepened her commitment to her role, to her country, to *him*.

"Wasn't there an abbot or some other religious figure who said the road to hell was paved with good intentions?"

His voice rumbled against her cheek.

"You are a good ruler, Julius. You and your father made me proud to be Rodinian."

He froze. Then his arm tightened and pulled her closer, enveloping her in that intoxicating cedar against the backdrop of sea air.

"How did I ever deserve you as my protector, Esmerelda?"

She lifted her head, turned to look at him. Her breath caught in her chest as she realized just how close their lips were. Her eyes moved from his mouth to his gaze. Need burned hot, making deep brown flare into amber. One hand came up, fingers grazing her jaw before they tangled in her hair and pulled her closer, stopping just shy of her mouth.

His lips parted. A whimper escaped, almost pleading, as need built in her, coiling her body tighter and tighter until she could barely resist it.

But she wouldn't be the first to yield. Not this time.

He murmured her name once more.

And then he kissed her.

Oh, dear heaven.

No slow, teasing kiss that had brought their bodies together in the Paris suite. This kiss claimed, conquered, branded. His lips moved over hers, confident and yet with a frantic edge that made her heart beat out of control as fire suffused her body.

He crushed her against his body. Delirious desire shot through her veins. She straddled his lap, her fingers sliding into his hair as she returned his kiss, pouring over a month's worth of longing and heartache into their embrace.

His tongue teased the seam of her mouth. Her lips parted and he plundered. With each stroke, energy pulsed through her. One hand stayed on her back and kept her anchored against him. The other quested upward, fingertips leaving a searing trail as they delved into her curls and pulled her head back. She arched against him, a protesting whimper escaping as he moved his mouth from hers. The whimper turned into a moan of satisfaction as he kissed the line of her jaw, down her neck, then lower still until his lips grazed the swells of her breasts.

"Julius…"

His hand moved from her back to her shoulder to the ties of her dress straps. She felt the material give as he pulled—

This is wrong.

The thought slammed into her. She wanted him. Dear God, how she wanted him. But they couldn't do this, couldn't make love, with so much unknown between them. With her lies hanging over them. And for all she knew Julius was engaged to another woman, or soon to be.

She started to say his name again, to tell him to wait while she gathered her thoughts. The sound of a boat horn cut across the water. Julius's head snapped up.

Relief mingled with disappointment as Esme scrambled to her feet and hastily tightened the straps on her dress.

"Looks like a yacht." She moved to the front where leather seats ringed the bow of the boat. "Still a half mile away. But they're heading in our direction. Just trying to give us a heads-up."

She waved in case anyone was watching through the binoculars, then turned.

Julius stood on the stern, his hands curled into fists at his sides. He stared at her with a hunger that made her feel like the most beautiful woman on earth even as it nearly frightened her with its intensity.

Had she wanted to be seen before? Because when he looked at her like this, as if he could see to the very depths of her soul and all the good and bad things inside her mind, it was both wonderful and terrifying.

"Esmerelda…"

She waited, apprehension chasing away the lingering traces of desire.

"I'm sorry."

Of all the things she had expected to hear, an apology was at the bottom of the list.

"Excuse me?"

"What happened here was wrong."

Bile rose in her throat, thick and bitter. She'd thought the same thing, but hearing it come out of Julius's mouth made her sick to her stomach. He didn't want her. He'd taken one taste and wanted no more. Nothing had changed. Nothing ever changed.

No. She was stronger. She was no longer depending on others for her own salvation. She wouldn't run, wouldn't crumble.

Her chin rose.

"I agree, sir."

He swore and started forward.

"That's not what I meant."

"It never is."

She moved, keeping one of the leather lounges between them. He stopped, his eyes narrowed to dangerous slits.

"Damn it, Esmerelda, listen to me—"

"That yacht is approaching quickly." She slipped back into her professional role, her voice void of emotion. "They may or may not have binoculars. They most certainly have phones or other recording devices onboard. If we want to ensure your anonymity, we need to go now."

Within a minute they were back on the water. She urged the boat's speed up as fast as she dared, wanting to get back to the villa, to put as much distance between herself and the island where she'd nearly made the second biggest mistake of her life.

Despite the wind rushing by, her focus shifting between the water and the navigation system, she knew the moment he moved to the seat behind hers.

"You misunderstood me."

"I didn't."

A string of colorful Portuguese curses sounded behind her.

"That's certainly new," she said, raising her voice to be heard over the wind. "I don't recall hearing you swear like a sailor."

"One has a right to swear when someone is refusing to listen."

A quick glance confirmed there were no boats anywhere nearby. She killed the engine, waiting until the boat slowed and began to drift with the current, keeping her gaze forward.

"I told you before when you first came to me that I was done listening to you." To her horror, tears pricked the backs of her eyes. "I gave in once. I'm not doing so again."

"I meant that nearly making love to you on the back of a boat in the middle of the Caribbean was wrong." She felt him just behind her, felt his tension and energy rippling off his body. "That giving in to our physical attraction was wrong when we haven't sorted out everything that happened between us before my accident."

The explanation made sense. Indeed, as her embarrassment cooled, it all sounded terribly rational. Which made her response seem all the more outlandish.

All the more dangerous. She'd submitted again, had allowed herself to be carried away by emotion. But all she was doing was digging her grave deeper. And what about Julius? If she did give in, what would happen when he did remember? Would this softer side of him disappear? Or would he keep aspects of the man she saw now, a man who loathed the thought of being married off to a woman he hadn't chosen for himself? A man who could potentially be hurt by an affair, too?

Suddenly overwhelmed by everything that had happened the past few days—Julius's unexpected arrival, his amnesia, their kiss—all hit at once and stripped away what few tatters remained of her pride.

"It's better to keep things unknown."

"Better for who, Esmerelda?"

She heard the accusation in his voice, the censure. She brushed it all aside as she grabbed the key still in the ignition.

"For both of us, Your Highness."

CHAPTER TEN

THE THIN THREAD of navy that clung to the horizon spread slowly upward, drenching the Caribbean Sea in darkness as day turned to night. Soft shades of pink and lavender decorated the sky above the villa. It reminded Julius of a painting he'd once seen at a museum in London, a decorated warship being pulled out to sea to be scrapped. A beautiful sunset that had deepened the sensation of loss, the passing of an era as an elegant ship past its prime was sent to a shipyard to be broken into pieces.

Another impression, a flash in time, of him standing before the painting, the gallery around him quiet as he'd stared, trying to reconcile his commitment to duty with an ache that hollowed out his chest and left him painfully empty.

A feeling he'd experienced once more when he'd heard the raw grief in Esmerelda's voice. When she had severed the connection between them. A connection that went beyond mere desire. A connection he had felt ever since he'd woken up to this new life.

Stars winked into existence overhead. They'd arrived back around one. Esmerelda had tied off the boat and walked back to the villa without a single glance in his direction. He'd debated following her, demanding answers, kissing her senseless and feeling her come alive beneath his touch again.

But he'd kept his distance, doing his damnedest to respect the boundaries she'd erected.

For now.

Had she simply been running from him again, he would have pursued. He was done with the subterfuge, the deception, what he suspected at this point were outright lies.

Yet he had kissed her as if his life had depended on it, had nearly stripped her bare and driven himself into her on the back of a boat where anyone could have seen them. That he had so nearly lost complete and total control had been unnerving to say the least. It had also struck at something deep inside, something innate that had risen from the dark and pulled him back.

His head dropped back against the back of his chair. It was odd to look at a vase and know that it was most likely a Waterford. To thank Aroldo in French without even thinking about translation when he'd come back to the villa. There were parts of himself that came naturally, logical aspects that were so ingrained not even a traumatic injury could wrench them away.

Yet what he suspected was one of the most critical moments of his life, a defining event involving a woman who had tried to help him today out of simple kindness, evaded him.

"...better to keep things unknown..."

Something pulled at his memory, a loose thread that dangled just out of reach. The more he tried to grasp it, to form an image of what had happened, the more his head started to pound.

He let out a growl as he exploded out of his chair. It was time for answers.

His suite included an alcove with bay windows that overlooked the bay and the faintest glimpse of the lighthouse. A pale gray desk with a slate-colored top stood in front of the windows, a laptop in the center.

So far, his searches had been restricted to himself, reading articles about suspected romances, goodwill trips to other countries and even archived stories dating back all the way to his birth. He'd also read up on his parents and Rodina.

The one person he hadn't searched had been Esmerelda. He'd wanted answers about her past, about who she was and who she had been to him, to come from her.

But that wasn't to be.

He typed in her name and "security guard Rodina." The first result, a video link, made him frown: *Bodyguard saves island prince from runaway horse.*

His chest tightened with dread. He clicked. It was from a little over a year ago, a parade through Rodina's capital. The video panned over floats from local schools, companies, the military. His father rode by in a sleek car, commentary from the video host noting the vehicle had been manufactured in one of Rodina's factories.

Then he saw himself, an odd sensation to watch as he walked behind the car, occasionally waving to the crowd with only the hint of a smile on his face. A stark contrast to the elegant yet friendlier waves of his father.

Esmerelda and a man he now recognized as Burak had walked just behind him. Both wore black suits with white shirts. Esmerelda's eyes roved, taking everything in, assessing. In the few seconds he watched her, he saw immediately why she had been so good at her job. She never stopped looking, alert as she soaked in details. He once again cursed her parents for eroding all sense of personal confidence.

Off-camera, someone shrieked. His heartbeat accelerated. Esmerelda's head whipped around. She didn't waste a second as she turned and ran toward Julius. A horse bounded onto screen, its rider frantically clinging to the reins even as he started to slide off.

Esmerelda was safe. Julius knew she was, had seen her with his own eyes just hours ago. That didn't stop his heart from pounding as he watched the horse rear up, watched Esmerelda push him out of the way just as the hooves came down on her back. She collapsed onto the road, rolling just as the horse reared up and came down again on her chest.

The camera zoomed in, capturing both Julius and Burak rushing to her side, before the feed cut off.

He slammed the lid of the computer shut and scrubbed his hands down his face.

It provided another piece of the puzzle, another clue as to what had happened between them. He couldn't remember, couldn't hear the sounds of the crowd, the scream of the horse, the shouts of terrified onlookers. But something told him his life had changed after that moment when Esmerelda had unflinchingly flung herself into harm's way to save his life.

Thinking about it now, he wanted nothing more than to storm her room and pull her into his arms. Touch her, reassure himself that she truly was all right.

To hell with it.

Esme jumped as a loud knock sounded on her door.

"Esmerelda. Open up."

Her eyes fluttered shut. She lay on her bed, curled up with a yellowed copy of her favorite Jane Austen novel. The familiar words had brought comfort while the scent of well-loved pages had soothed her errant emotions after the incredible events of the morning.

Reading had also provided a distraction from the way her lips still burned from his kiss. The way her body still tingled in places it shouldn't after she'd nearly let him undress her on the deck of a boat in the middle of the sea.

"It's open."

The door swung open. He stalked into the room, his steps almost silent. Yet the energy he brought into the room, the sheer power that filled up every corner, made her breath catch. It took every ounce of willpower to stay where she was propped up with a mound of pillows at her back.

"When were you going to tell me?"

Her fingers tightened on the pages. Her hour of reckoning had come.

"Julius—"

He moved to the edge of the bed, his large frame looming over her.

"You put yourself in harm's way, Esmerelda."

Her mind screeched to a halt.

"Wait…what are we talking about?"

"I saw the video." He turned away and began to pace her room like a restless wild animal prowling about a cage. "You pushed me out of the way."

The parade. She stifled a groan. The event had gotten some minor attention on the international circuit.

"I was doing my job."

"By putting yourself in danger?"

His voice vibrated with anger and pricked her own temper.

"I believe the definition of a bodyguard involves something akin to that, yes. More of a focus on serve and protect, but protect does imply—"

"Parar."

He stopped in front of her window, hands on his hips, his shoulders rising and falling with his ragged breathing. Her ire cooled as she recognized that this was not a man chastising her for doing her job.

She laid her book down and slid off the bed. She walked up behind him. Slowly, she laid a hand on his back, felt the tension bleed away at her touch.

"I'm all right."

He turned then, grabbed her hand and held it in his.

"The horse came down on your chest."

"Yes."

"Show me."

She knew what he meant, hesitated only a moment before pulling aside the neckline of her shirt. His eyes zeroed in on the half-moon scar just below her collarbone.

"I watched the video." His fingers came up, rested on the white marking. The intimacy of it, of him touching such a vulnerable part of her, stole her breath. "You didn't hesitate."

"I couldn't."

He whirled away from her.

"Do you always give yourself away so lightly, Miss Clark?"

Fury climbed up her spine, radiated throughout her body.

"It was my choice and don't you dare question it."

"Choice," he spat out as he turned back to her. "Except just this morning you told me you followed this path to please your father. You sacrificed your own body to shield me. And why? For duty? For a man who apparently cared for nothing but his job?"

"It's not just a job," she snapped back. "You told me countless times you and your father were the crown. There was no Julius without the title. It wasn't a matter of pride or ego, it simply was. You took your responsibilities and duties seriously, not because it brought you esteem or satisfied some selfish pleasure, but because you knew you could do it and do it well. There were times I saw how tired you were, how you wanted to step back, but you always moved forward."

"Moved forward at the expense of building relationships with others. I've read countless articles," he said at her confused look, "scoured TV and magazine interviews. Did you know I rarely talk about my mother? Don't even mention her. I can remember her, how much she loved me, and yet all I talked about was elections, construction projects, deficit spending. Even in that video of you..." He paused, looked down and sucked in a breath. "My father is king. He smiled at people, waved. I looked hard. Cold."

Her heart broke then, but in an altogether different way from when Julius had dismissed her. This time the fractures were for the man standing in front of her, a man torn between past and present, between the duty he had forgotten and the man he was without the burden of the crown.

"You could be, yes."

"Why?"

She shook her head.

"I don't know. I tried asking a few times after the accident."

"Why then?"

She hesitated. This was what came from telling lies. One lie led to another, forced her to pause and think about what she was going to say.

Or you could just tell him now.

She looked up at him, at the tension furrowing his brow, at the pain and anger and fear lurking in his eyes.

No. Telling him now would be unburdening herself to get the weight of her own mistakes off her shoulders. Selfish. Adding to his conflict.

"We became closer after the accident." She would stick to the truth as much as possible. "You visited me in the hospital. You brought me a book. After that you started talking to me more, asking my opinion about legislation or something similar from a citizen's perspective."

"You said before we became friends."

"We did." She smiled sadly. "It was a very nice time in my life. I made friends at the academy."

"Like Burak?"

"Yes," she answered truthfully, despising the little flare of satisfaction at the jealousy in his voice. "Him and a few others. But after all the training, the last thing we wanted to do at the end of the day was talk more politics. Grabbing a drink at a pub, going sailing, watching movies. When I talked, you listened. You told me..."

Her tongue suddenly felt thick, her eyes hot.

"Told you what?" he prompted softly.

"You told me I made you a better leader."

It had been two weeks before Paris. How many times over that year had she caught him looking at her, wondered if he felt something more? As many times as she'd dismissed her thoughts as foolish, the naïve emotions of a love-starved young woman with a handsome, dynamic man for a boss.

But that day, after he'd asked her opinion on an email he'd drafted to an ambassador regarding a recent disagreement they'd engaged in and she'd made suggestions to soften his tone, to offer an olive branch and maintain the relationship, he'd looked at her and smiled just enough to make his whiskey eyes crinkle at the corners.

"You make me a better leader, Clark. Thank you."

When she'd stuttered out *"You're welcome,"* his gaze had lingered, drifted down her body before returning to his computer.

And she'd known. Known the building attraction, the sensual tension she thought she'd imagined so many times, was not one-sided.

"And then I fired you."

Oh, God.

She closed her eyes. The way he'd done it had been awful. But the reason...oh, the further time moved away from that hideous day, the more she recognized that the reason itself was not wrong. If the roles were reversed, she wouldn't want a woman who had slept with her husband guarding him, being around them constantly. She could be angry, furious with him over how he'd done it.

But the reason made all the difference.

She opened her mouth to tell him, to let him know that there had been more than simple vanity or a royal's capriciousness behind his decision. He glanced over her shoulder and, before she could say a word, moved past her. For a moment, she thought he was going to leave. When his footsteps paused, she turned to see him standing next to her bed. Her chest tightened as he picked up her book off the bed, a dark green splash against the white feather comforter.

"Was it this book?"

"Yes."

He turned it over, his fingers lingering over the worn leather cover, the silver embossing on the spine.

"I remember it. I remember picking it up and thinking of you."

Her pulse thudded, slow beats that echoed in her ears.

"Oh."

He set the book down on the bed and came back to her. His fingers brushed the material of her shirt to the side again, his eyes burning as he stared down at the scar.

"I never told you why I handled my duty from a distance? Placed a wall between me and my people, between me and everyone."

She shook her head.

"Whenever I tried to ask, you would change the subject or simply not answer."

His fingers drifted lower. His palm flattened against her chest, just above her breast, where her heart beat. A breath escaped him, as if he had needed to convince himself that she was still there, still alive.

"I'm sorry, Esmerelda."

She gave in to temptation and reached up, framing his face with her hands.

"No. Don't apologize. I'm the one who should—"

"Don't you dare." He caught her in his arms, his hands settling on her back and pulling her against him. "You pushed me out of harm's way."

"Yes, but that's not it. I—"

The words caught in her throat as he crushed his mouth to hers. This time she didn't hesitate. She moaned against his lips, her hands gripping his hair and pulling him closer. He swung her into his arms and carried her to the bed. Their mouths were still fused together as he lowered her to the soft surface, then covered her with his body. She arched against him, legs moving restlessly, nipples hardening as he continued to kiss her with reckless abandon. He pushed his hips against hers and she felt the hard length of his arousal against her core. She cried out.

"Esmerelda."

Her name came out on a guttural groan as he buried one hand in her hair, the other slipping up her side beneath her shirt, trailing over her stomach, before settling on her bare breast.

"Oh, Deus..." He lifted his head, stared down at her with eyes burning.

She blushed.

He grabbed the material of her shirt and pulled it up. Cool air kissed her breasts before his mouth descended, hot and wet, making her bow up off the bed as he sucked a nipple into his mouth and laved it with his tongue.

"Julius!"

He moved to the other, repeated the same tantalizing, delicious act of torture on her other breast. When she pulled at his shirt, he sat up and yanked it off before lowering himself back down. His bare chest pressed against her breasts. The intimacy of his skin naked against hers, the sheer heat of his body, sent a bold, erotic thrill through her. She reached up, her hands framing his face as she pulled his head down and pressed her lips to his.

More. God, she wanted more. Rational thought tried to break through, to remind her what she had been about to tell him. She needed to tell him before things went any further.

And then he pulled back. He stared at her, his chest rising and falling with heavy, ragged breaths. Embarrassment started to creep in.

"Julius—"

He rolled off the bed and stalked over to the window, hung his head and let out another harsh breath.

"I lost control. I'm sorry."

"Don't…" She fumbled, trying to come up with the right words. "Julius, I kissed you back—"

"I never should have come to your room in this state." He swore as he turned, his face shrouded in shadow. "I'm coming to understand I'm the sort of man who held himself back. Who kept things inside." He raked his hand through his hair. "And I lost control. Just like that."

He took one step forward, out of the shadows and into the golden glow of a lamp. Shock robbed her of speech as their eyes met. Desire burned, just as it had on the boat. But so did something else. Something she heard in his voice, felt in the way he'd touched her. Something that went deeper than simple lust.

Julius was coming to know himself once more. The past was merging with the present. Except this time, he still wanted her.

And I want him.

Before she could wrap her mind around what she'd been fighting the past few days, could accept that the man standing before her felt something similar to what she did, Julius moved past her toward the door.

"Wait!"

"Tomorrow, Esmerelda. We'll talk tomorrow."

The edge to his voice reminded her of the crown prince,

authoritative and unyielding, his accent more pronounced. He was hurting, perhaps just as confused as she was.

She let him go.

The click of the door closing echoed in her room. Slowly, she sank into the embrace of her pillows. One hand drifted up, her fingers trailing over her swollen lips.

The last five minutes had been enlightening on multiple fronts. The question that had plagued her since he'd first appeared on the beach, however, remained the same.

What was she going to do?

CHAPTER ELEVEN

WAVES LAPPED GENTLY against the beach. Julius's bare feet sank into the wet sand, the ground cushioning his steps as the warm water swirled around his ankles before receding back into the ocean.

He needed this moment of peace before he went back to the villa. Needed the physical distance from the woman within its walls.

The memory of Esmerelda's body beneath his, her strong curves pressed against him, her passionate response as he'd tasted her body, made him hard almost instantly. Yet beneath the pulsing hunger ran a deep thread of guilt. While he couldn't remember his history with Esmerelda, he knew enough to know he'd hurt her deeply. The memory of her looking at him, her face stricken with hurt, as he'd determinedly pushed on with whatever he felt he'd had to say, haunted him. Yet twice yesterday he'd kissed her. Once where anyone passing by could have seen. Once in the privacy of her room where he'd pushed the boundaries even further.

Esmerelda had said they'd never been lovers. But something else had existed between them. An unacted-upon mutual attraction? Perhaps a plan to become something more, but he'd cut it short because of the engagement?

It was past time he and Esmerelda had a talk. He needed to know what had happened between them, needed to apologize for what other transgressions he had committed, before he could hopefully receive her forgiveness. Before they could move forward.

He reached into the pocket of his pants and pulled out the black box, flipping the lid open as he held it up. The diamond glowed, the freckles inside illuminated by the silver glow of moonlight.

The first time he'd held the ring, he'd thought of her. The idea of putting it on another woman's hand had him snapping the box shut and shoving it back into his pocket. Had he found some way for him and Esmerelda to be together? Was that a scenario she had ever entertained? Everything she'd said so far had suggested she hadn't wanted to be fired. But what about something more?

He followed the winding path back to the villa, his steps lit by sconces casting golden light onto the stepping-stones. The past kept them apart, as did their positions. He was the crown prince. She was his bodyguard. How could they explore their attraction if they never stepped away from their roles?

"Good evening, sir."

Julius looked up to see Aroldo on the terrace.

"Good evening." He nodded at the night sky. "A little late for you, isn't it?"

"Yes, sir. Doing my final rounds and then I'll be on my way. I will be gone tomorrow, so Michael will be attending to you and Miss Clark."

"Anything planned for your day off?"

Aroldo chuckled. "Hardly a vacation day. My daughter Hanna owns a rum distillery." Pride rang in his voice as he smiled. "She's hosting a masquerade gala tomorrow night to raise funds for our annual Spicemas carnival."

"A gala?"

"A bit fancier than many are used to. But Hanna is…

strategic," Aroldo said. "Those not used to such affairs will enjoy themselves. Those who are will enjoy the food, the festivities, and hopefully donate."

An idea popped into his head.

"Is this gala open to anyone willing to make a donation?"

Aroldo's eyes narrowed. When he saw that Julius was serious, a conspiring twinkle appeared in his eye as he bowed his head.

"But of course, sir."

Satisfaction wound through him. A night to get away from the villa, to shed the titles of prince and bodyguard and simply exist as a man and woman, could only help. Not only could it lower the walls his past behavior and the difference in their stations had erected, but it would give Esmerelda a chance to indulge, to savor the moments she had so often been deprived of.

"Tell me where to send the money and it will be done within twenty-four hours. Esmerelda and I will be attending, although we'll be taking advantage of the masquerade to not reveal our identities to any of the guests."

"Of course, sir." The butler sounded faintly affronted that Julius would even suggest his betraying a guest's confidence. "I won't even tell my daughters." He looked down at Julius's bare feet. "I can procure you a suit and mask. I don't believe Miss Clark brought any evening wear."

Damn. Of course she hadn't. She thought she was going to be spending her days on a beach, not guarding her exboss or attending black-tie events.

He glanced down at his watch.

"It should be almost dawn in Paris. I'll have a special order arriving at the airport tomorrow in the early afternoon."

"It will be delivered the moment it arrives." Aroldo paused. "If I might, sir, my other daughter Joana is a seamstress. She has some creations that are suitable for the gala and that I believe would be to Miss Clark's liking."

"Anything you recommend."

Aroldo beamed.

"It will be done, sir."

As the butler hurried off, Julius smiled. He had no doubt that Esmerelda's first answer to his plan would be no, followed by a series of logical reasons as to why it wasn't a good idea. He formulated a list of responses as he entered the villa. The lights had been left on low, creating a golden glow that made the large space feel cozy and comforting. He turned the lights off as he walked down the hall. The moon shone bright through the skylights and lit his way.

He paused in front of Esmerelda's door. Temptation took hold of him, urged his steps closer. The memory of her—the taste of her skin, the music of her sharp cry as he'd kissed her breasts, the heat of her touch—filled him. He raised a hand to knock.

And stopped. If he knocked, if they picked up where they had left off, his physical desires would be satisfied. He had no doubt they would spend all night, if not most of the morning, enjoying each other's bodies. Exploring, savoring, delighting.

But the deeper yearning would still be there, the void in his memories rivaling the emptiness in his heart. He didn't just want Esmerelda in his bed.

He wanted her, all of her.

Slowly, he lowered his hand. Then he turned and walked down the hall, the thud of his footsteps mirroring the heavy beat of his heart.

Tomorrow.

He opened the door to his own room. A soft click sounded behind him. He looked over his shoulder.

All that greeted him was an empty hallway and Esmerelda's closed door glowing silver in the moonlight.

Esme sat at the kitchen island, her hands wrapped around a steaming cup of tea. Every sound, from the creak of a floorboard to the caw of a seagull, made her glance over her shoulder.

Where is he?

She'd laid on her bed for what felt like hours after Julius had left. One minute she'd decided to race after him, only to talk herself down the next. When she'd finally decided to find him, to tell him everything and lay bare not only their history but her desires, his room had been empty.

Both frustrated and relieved, she'd gone back to her room and sank into a hot tub. Not half an hour later she'd heard Julius and Aroldo on the terrace. She'd gone to fetch her robe, had been pulling it on when she'd heard his footsteps in the hall. Heard the pause outside her door.

Coward.

Her moment of bravery had evaporated beneath the twin weights of exhaustion and fear. She'd wanted him to knock, to open the door, to make the first move. To give her proof that she wasn't imagining things. To give her a much-needed dose of bravery to voice her wants.

And then he'd moved on. She'd opened her door just a crack, watched him move down the hall, before softly closing her door and sinking onto her bed once more.

Yet sleep had evaded her.

I want him.

So simple, yet so complicated. This time there was no underlying need for validation, none of the sycophancy that had overshadowed their first encounter. Then, there had been a sense of gratitude, that a man like him would deign to kiss a woman like her.

Unattractive. Unwanted. Unlovable.

Funny how one moment could wake someone up. Wake them up to the cold, hard truth that sometimes other people weren't right, they were simply awful. People like her parents, who had been so caught up in themselves and their own wants and desires that they hadn't bothered with their own child. People like the man Julius had been before, who had dismissed her so cruelly.

The seconds after she'd walked out of Julius's office had yanked her from that dark place where she thought she had to work more, do more, be more to be enough for others, and thrust her into the reality that whether she knew herself or not, she was enough.

A realization she had worked to accept over the past few weeks, along with exploring what she wanted instead of living her life for someone else.

And what she wanted, right now, was Julius.

In the span of a heartbeat, it had all fallen into place. She wanted Julius, wanted this complex man who had flown halfway around the world to seek her out. The desire she felt now didn't hinge on a need to be loved by someone else. It existed simply because she wanted it.

It was thrilling. Terrifying. It was still fated to end the way it had the first time; with them parting ways. But this time, it was on her terms.

As the shadows from the moonlight had shifted across the silk covers, she planned. She would tell him everything. She would lay bare their past, tell him her wishes now and place the choice at his feet. To have one last affair before he returned to Rodina and she continued on with her new life. Or to part ways now with the memories, both good and bad, of who they had been and what they had shared.

After I give him a piece of my mind about wandering off.

She'd slept until nearly ten in the morning and awoken

to an empty villa. Panic had sent her running from room to room. The housecleaning crew had already been through, leaving behind fresh vases of flowers and polished floors in their wake.

But still no Julius.

What kind of bodyguard overslept and let her charge wander out of her sight?

She'd called Julius. He'd sent her to voicemail. She'd texted him. He'd told her Aroldo's son-in-law, a police officer, had a day off and was accompanying him on an errand in town.

It hadn't been until Aroldo had arrived to prepare lunch and confirmed not only that his son-in-law was with Julius but also a well-trained officer who was being generously compensated for his time that she had managed to let herself breathe.

Julius had texted around noon, telling her that was she was off-duty and the best thing she could do was relax.

She hated it. But unless she could somehow trace his phone and call for a ride, she wouldn't be able to track him down.

So she'd had lunch on the terrace, explored the villa's library. She'd even spent an hour lying by the pool with a book, forcing herself to try and relax as she waited for him.

It hadn't worked.

Now, with four o'clock fast approaching, she hadn't seen him all day.

Frustrated, she blew on her mug, watched steam curl up from the pink-tinted rose tea. Then stiffened as she heard footsteps coming down the hall. Her heart careened into her throat, butterflies flapping madly inside her chest as she sucked in a calming breath.

You can do this.

She turned just as Julius walked into the kitchen.

"Hello."

She bit back a flash of irritation at his casual greeting, strove for the same level of calm he exuded.

"Next time, I need to know where you're going and who you'll be with."

He stayed by the door, hands tucked into his pockets, his eyes moving up and down her body. Heat seared her fingertips as her hand tightened around the mug.

"Yes, Mom."

She narrowed her eyes.

"Your safety is not a joke."

His expression sobered.

"That was thoughtless. I'm sorry. I'm not used to the security and protocol. But Aroldo's son-in-law was both an excellent guard and guide."

"And generously compensated," she added dryly.

"That, too," he added with a grin that made her heart clench.

Now. Tell him now.

"I—"

"Would you like to go to a masquerade with me tonight?"

Her lips parted. Of all the things she'd anticipated him saying, an invitation to a masquerade hadn't even made the list. "What?"

"A masquerade."

"But…where?"

"Aroldo's daughter Hanna operates a rum distillery near Grand Anse Beach. She's hosting a gala to raise funds for the island's annual Spicemas carnival in August. Aroldo compared it to the carnivals celebrated in late winter in countries like Brazil and the States."

"Oh." Mentally she started running through her checklist. "It's a little soon, but if I could get a copy of the floor plan, I could evaluate—"

He stepped closer, a slight smile lifting the corners of his mouth.

"Not as my bodyguard, Esmerelda. As my date."

Her mind slammed to a halt.

"Your date?"

Strange that the thought of going on a date frightened her more than going to bed with him. A date demanded more than a joining of bodies, more than a simple affair. It involved emotions and expectations. Was she prepared for something like this? Or would it cause old wounds to open, to lose the grip she had on her newfound confidence?

Before she could grasp onto a rational thought and think things through, he closed the distance between them, stopping inches away from her chair. His hand came up, his fingers gliding over her cheek, smoothing back a stray curl.

"We've been at odds since we met. Or at least since I first met you," he said with a small smirk. "Neither of us are denying the attraction between us. An attraction I suspect has been there for a long time."

She didn't deny, didn't look away. Not this time.

"But there's always something in the way. The past. Our roles." He leaned down, his eyes heating as his hand slid into her hair. "Tonight, we're just going to be us."

Her chest rose and fell as she breathed deeply, tried to force herself to think past the desire humming inside her.

"And after tonight?"

God, she sounded wanton. Breathless. Husky.

"After tonight, the choice is yours."

She hesitated. "I believe that tonight it will actually become your choice."

A frown furrowed his brow. "Oh?"

"I want to talk…to tell you what happened between us. Before I left."

His face cleared. "I would like that, too."

"We could talk now—"

"One night, Esmerelda." He moved, brushed his lips across hers in a kiss so light it might have been the graze of butterfly wings. "One night of enjoyment, of just being two people on a date. Just us." Another kiss had her rising up to deepen the kiss, only to be thwarted when he released her and stepped back. "Then we'll talk."

"Okay." She released a pent-up breath and nodded. "Okay. I'd like that." She glanced down at her T-shirt and shorts. "I've got a sundress or two that might work. Maybe Aroldo could recommend a store that has a shawl..." Her voice trailed off as she looked up to see Julius's smug expression. "What?"

"I got you something."

She followed him down the hall to her room, anticipation building despite her best efforts to keep calm. It had been ages since she'd received anything more than a card wishing her a happy birthday.

He opened the door and stepped back. With a curious glance at him, she crossed the threshold.

And stepped into a dream.

Beautiful dresses were draped over the bed, hanging from the chandelier, laid out over a chair. Dresses in colors her mother had always warned her off from because it would be "too much" with her hair, her freckles. Gowns bedecked with jewels, garments fashioned from silk, dresses with yards of tulle that made her think of a princess from her favorite childhood fairy tale.

She had never cared much for clothes as a child. Barefoot had been her preferred shoe, shirts and pants she could get dirty her favored clothing. Her mother had foisted pretty dresses on her with warnings to sit still. For the longest time, Esme had associated quality clothing with being bored. By the time she had graduated college and started showing an interest in wearing something other than casual wear, she had been entering the academy, where her options had been limited to the three uniforms they wore during training, followed by black suits with white shirts once she'd landed her job.

Right now, though, as her fingers reached out and brushed over satin the color of a spring morning sky, she realized she liked pretty dresses very much.

"Julius…they're lovely."

He moved behind her, his hands settling on her shoulders. Her eyes grew hot as she looked down at her feet.

"But?"

"They're not…me." She swallowed hard and forced out a chuckle. "I can run two miles in just over thirteen minutes and ranked first in marksmanship. Can you really picture me in one of these?"

"In and out."

A shiver danced down her spine at the heated promise in his words.

"Julius…"

"Tonight isn't just about us, Esmerelda." He leaned down, his breath warm on her ear. "It's about you getting a chance to breathe. To enjoy yourself the way you had planned to before I crashed your beach."

"You mean before I trounced you?"

Her words died on a breathy moan as he nipped her earlobe.

"Minx." Before she could respond, he moved to the dresses laid out on the bed. "I had a dozen flown in from Paris this afternoon, although a few were made here on Grenada." He reached for a blue gown. "This one was made by Aroldo's other daughter Joana." He grinned at her. "Are you really prepared to tell Aroldo you didn't even try it on?"

A sense of breathlessness overtook her as Julius held up

the gown. The bodice, fashioned from satin, featured a V-neck cut that flirted with the edges of propriety. Pale blue blended into midnight at the waist, a tumble of color that reminded Esme of day turning to night. It swept down into frothy folds of chiffon. Some of the material had been attached to the straps at the back and hung down to form cuffs fashioned out of the same dark blue and threaded with silver.

"It's stunning."

She glanced at herself in the mirror. At her toned arms and smaller bust, her mass of curls and freckles upon freckles.

But then she remembered the swing on the beach. When Julius had looked down at her and smiled and asked if she liked to swing or not.

Find out.

Did she like wearing beautiful dresses? Yes, she still preferred being outside, being in the water or by the ocean. She loved walking in the sand, through the terraced vineyards in the fall and feeling the grass brush against her bare feet like velvet before the weather turned too cold.

Yet a part of her that was slowly coming to life wanted a touch of luxury, to feel confident in something other than her job. To feel beautiful.

She released a pent-up breath.

"I'll try it on." She let out a soft laugh. "I almost feel like Cinderella getting ready for a ball."

"Does that make me the fairy godmother?"

"I'll buy you a magic wand," Esme promised with a smile as she accepted the dress. "But it may not even fit."

"One way to find out." He caught her elbow, kissed her on the forehead so sweetly it made her throat tighten. "I'll leave you to make your selection. Meet me at eight in the main room."

She waited until the door closed behind him before she sagged.

Can I do this?

Yes, she wanted to tell him everything, to have no more secrets between them. Yes, she wanted to be with him again, to make love one last time.

And yes, she wanted tonight.

She shucked off her clothes and pulled the dress on, the luxurious blend of satin and chiffon whispering over her skin. She could feel the pull of temptation. Not just to wear an elegant gown, to play at being a princess for an evening, but to have a night with Julius in public. Yes, they'd be wearing masks. But it would be the first, and last, time she could simply enjoy being with him in front of others, without keeping her face schooled into a polite mask, mentally evaluating her actions and trying to keep her focus on Julius the job, not Julius the man.

She pulled up the zipper, although it only came up to her waist. Aside from the wide straps and the swaths of fabric that billowed beneath her arms, her back was bare.

She turned. And gasped.

The woman staring back at her from the mirror was someone she'd never seen before. The blue brought out the red gold of her hair, enhanced it. Instead of patterns and designs clashing with her freckles, the simple color scheme had her appreciating her speckled skin.

For the second time in her life, she felt beautiful. The first time had been when Julius had laid her back on his bed and gazed at her naked body. He hadn't said a word, but the appreciation blazing in his eyes had spoken volumes.

This time, however, as she grabbed the skirt and swished back and forth like a little girl, she felt beautiful all by herself.

Isn't there something magical in that?

CHAPTER TWELVE

JULIUS GLANCED AT his watch. Just after seven and the sun had already set. The drive from the villa to St. George's would take some time, although from what Aroldo had said, the festivities would continue well into the night.

There was no reason to rush. No specific event to get to. But every passing minute increased the tension tightening his neck, the unease in his gut.

What if she decided not to go? This afternoon she had seemed…at peace. A touch of playfulness that had stirred his blood, a hint of shyness that had made him want to gather her close and protect her.

Except what if he was pulling her close only to push her away? To hurt her once more?

He moved to the edge of the villa's grand hall. The missing pieces of his past were slowly falling into place. Along with the answers, though, came the realization that while he had been committed to his role as a leader, he had been a lonely and personally unhappy man. One who eschewed personal connections, buried himself in work. His mother's passing had buried him until he could barely breathe. Evading the ache, burying the sadness, had been his only answer. Avoiding grief from what had been, grief from what could be.

Never thinking about what the opposite of grief could be.

Never allowing himself the indulgence of hope. Would the man he'd been, the one who kept his mind focused and his heart hard, accept the changes he was making now?

You saw me that day...

When she had uttered those words last night, the pain in her voice had nearly undone him. He'd hurt her so deeply she'd fled the country she loved. She'd told him they hadn't been lovers. But they had been something more than prince and bodyguard. Tonight, he would have answers.

He leaned against a pillar and stared out over the dark sky. How would this night end? Would she be able to let go at the gala, to see him as the man instead of the royal heir? Would he be able to accept what she had to tell him?

And perhaps the weightiest question of all, the one that hurtled him toward yet another unknown: where would it all lead?

"Hello."

The tension in his neck eased. He turned and froze.

Framed between two white pillars, she looked stunning. She'd left her hair unbound and flowing, wild curls tumbling over her shoulders. The dress clung to her breasts, followed the curve of her waist and then flared out into volumes of skirt. When she moved, the fabric parted to reveal a long, slender leg.

"Deus me ajude."

She smiled at him, a smile that caught him both for its beauty and its confidence. It was a smile he hadn't seen on her before. It lit up her face, her eyes crinkling with a pure happiness that attracted him both body and soul.

"Thank you. Julius."

Her use of his name heated his blood. He waited until she was just in front of him. He held out his hand, noted her slight hesitation before she placed her hand in his. He pulled her against him, watched as her lips parted, nearly gave in.

But he simply leaned down and brushed a kiss against her cheek. Surprise and disappointment flashed across her face before she could conceal them.

"You're welcome."

A car whisked them away to the distillery, perched on a low cliff near the white powdery sands of Grand Anse Beach. Golden light poured from the massive windows as men and women dressed in everything from glamorous evening wear to more festive costumes walked up a cobblestone pathway. Terra-cotta flowerpots lined the walkway, filled with magenta-colored bougainvillea and tall stems dripping with white amaryllis blooms.

The car stopped in front of the walkway. Julius slipped on his plain black mask and turned to Esmerelda. He held out his hand.

"Ready?"

She slipped on her mask, pale blue and trimmed with pearls, then accepted his hand. His fingers closed over hers.

"Ready."

The interior was stunning, with dark glistening floors, pale walls, and café lights draped across the ceiling. The distillery itself was on display behind giant windows that allowed guests in the event space to witness the process of manufacturing rum. Waiters in crisp white shirts and linen pants carried around silver trays with bubbling flutes of champagne, rock glasses filled with rum and a variety of cocktails. White tables carried bowls of Barbados and Caribbean lilies in vivid shades of pink and orange. A band sat on a raised dais at the far end of the room. Banjos, guitars and steelpans backed up the deep voice of the lead singer as his melodious voice drifted over the crowd against an upbeat song.

"The singer is Aroldo's nephew," Julius said in Esmerelda's ear as he led her toward one of the buffet tables. "His calypso band will compete in the Spicemas festival." He nodded to a tall round display. Small bowls were artfully arranged with flickering candles in between, each filled with spices, from the vivid yellow of turmeric to the tiny clusters of cloves. "The name is a nod to Grenada's spice production."

She glanced around the crowd. He could practically hear the gears turning in her mind.

"There's a lot of people here."

He nodded toward a man standing near the door. "Aroldo booked several private guards for the evening."

A reluctant smile appeared beneath her mask. "Am I that predictable?"

"Yes." He leaned down, unable to resist a taste of her lips. "Enjoy, Esmerelda. Something tells me you deserve indulgence."

They accepted glasses of champagne and found a seat in the corner. The music transitioned into reggae as more guests streamed into the building. A woman with Aroldo's dark blue eyes circulated among the tables, inviting people to tour the distillery.

"Would you like to go?"

Julius glanced at Esmerelda, saw her glance shift to the machinery behind the glass.

"No. But," he added as she started to sit back in her chair, "you should go. You're here as a guest, not a bodyguard."

Her lips, painted a sparkling caramel, turned down at the corners.

"It feels...wrong."

"But it's not."

The air changed between them, became charged with suppressed feelings: desire, vulnerability, passion.

A tall, willowy woman approached the table. Her hair, black and thick, had been wound into an intricate braid atop her head. The scarlet hues of her dress made her dark brown skin glow. She smiled at them.

"I'm Hanna, the owner of the distillery. You must be the mystery guests my father invited."

"Perhaps," Julius replied with a slight smile.

"Welcome. I appreciate you supporting our island." Hanna nodded to Esmerelda's dress. "I'd recognize my sister's handiwork anywhere."

Esmerelda laughed softly. "Touché. It's stunning. She could sell anywhere in the world she wanted to."

"I hope one day she will get the confidence to do so." She gestured to a small crowd gathering by the door that led into the distillery. "Would you like to join us for a private tour?"

"She'd love to," Julius answered before Esmerelda could decline. He felt her irritation, her sideways glance. But she rose and followed Hanna. A quick survey of nearby tables revealed more than one set of male eyes on her departing form.

His jaw tightened. Hard to be caught between the pride and happiness at seeing her feel as beautiful as she looked to him while wanting to lock her away where no other man could ogle her.

He stood and walked back to the spice display. Other small round tables in varying heights carried similar exhibits, from elaborate masquerade masks from the Spicemas carnival to pictures of the devastation a hurricane had wrought less than twenty years ago.

As he read, learned of the struggles faced by the island nation, the slim threads of responsibility that had been emerging with every recovering memory strengthened. As he saw the crowds of people sitting outside homes reduced to nothing but rubble, read of the challenges still faced by such loss, the threads knitted themselves together into something he recognized in the look he'd glimpsed on his own face as he'd read news articles, social media posts and blogs.

Duty. Obligation. Allegiance.

The sheer weight of it pressed on him, warred with how he felt about Esmerelda. Before his memories had started to return, before his present self had begun to merge with his past, she had been his focus.

But now…now he felt the pull, felt what the role of prince meant. Had he fought this battle before? Had he been a coward and simply given up? Or worse, had his former self discovered something he hadn't yet? That in order to carry on leading a country, he had to give up the one thing he wanted?

Fingers threaded through his. The pressure that had begun to build in his head eased as he looked down at their joined hands.

"Aroldo told me there are still struggles. He said a hurricane took out almost all of the buildings on the island. That was twenty years ago." She nodded toward the nutmeg seeds resting in the bowl. "One tree can take up to ten years to be fruitful."

"Generations lost in hours." He shook his head slightly. "It makes my current plight seem inconsequential."

She gave his hand a gentle squeeze. "But they haven't given up."

"No." He nodded at one photo that showed dozens of sailboats piled together like an angry child had scooped them up from the ocean and dumped them on top of one another. "It hits different. Seeing where the country is now, the work they've done, the work that still needs to be done."

"You're questioning yourself."

"Yes."

She leaned in. That floral scent that had been taunting him since the day he'd pulled her from the water wrapped around him. Orchids, perhaps, or some other exotic flower, touched with hints of vanilla and ebony. Sexy yet sweet. A scent that teased at one of the memories that had grown clearer but still lurked just beneath the surface of his consciousness.

"That makes you a good leader, Julius."

A satisfying warmth spread throughout his body. Not once had Esmerelda ever voiced anything but support for him as a leader, even as he doubted and questioned. That she continued to maintain her belief in his abilities, despite whatever had happened between them, touched him.

He brought her hand up and brushed his lips across her knuckles as the offbeat rhythms of reggae transitioned into a sultry, dark jazz.

"Dance with me."

Her eyes widened behind her mask.

"I can't."

"Can't or won't?"

That telltale flush crept up from the bodice of her dress, spread over her décolletage and moved up her neck.

"What if someone recognizes you?"

"Now you're making excuses." He leaned down, his lips a breath away from her ear. "You want to dance with me, Esmerelda. So do it."

He heard the catch of her breath. Savored the soft exhale.

"All right."

He led her out onto the dance floor. He laid one hand on her waist and cradled her fingers in the other. The music sank beneath his skin. He pulled her closer, rested his cheek on her silky curls, cherished the feel of her in his arms. They drifted in and out of the other couples. The world blissfully faded away, leaving just the two of them in each other's embrace.

"Esmerelda…"

She relaxed against him, her trust meaning more than he could express.

"Yes?"

Her voice, low and gravelly, heated his blood. An invitation rose to his lips, to ask her to stay with him tonight. One hand glided up her back to draw her closer. His fingers brushed a raised scar on her back. He'd forgotten last night that the horse had first kicked her in the back when she'd shoved him out of the way. His throat tightened. He started to say something, to thank her, to chastise her, he wasn't sure.

But the words disappeared as he heard a horse's frightened whinny echo in his head, screams, wince as he felt the sharp scrape of gravel on his hands.

And the swift, stark fear.

He saw it then, a memory as real as his surroundings. Esmerelda's face twisted in pain, her eyes seeking out his face as he knelt beside her. The tiny smile of relief before her eyes rolled up and her head lolled to the side. He remembered the ride to the hospital, insisting on riding with her in the back of the ambulance. Pacing inside a private waiting room for hours before finally being allowed into her hospital room. Walking in and seeing her so pale beneath the freckles, her attempt to salute. Something inside him had come to life, as if it had been straining for years against the chains he'd bound around it and finally broken free.

Behind that memory, another rose.

He lifted red curls off her back, felt his throat tighten at the sight of the half-moon scar on her shoulder blade. For the first time in years, he surrendered to his emotions and pressed a soft kiss to the scar. The one she had sustained for him...

Julius reared back.

"Julius? What is it?"

So strange, how the different memories came back. Some felt like whiplash, whereas others trickled in.

This memory, the night he had raised a hand to her face, had cradled her as she'd leaned into his touch and accepted what he had offered, simply appeared, there all along waiting for him to open his mind to what he had shared with this woman.

This woman who, when he had asked if they had been lovers, had looked him in the eye and told him no.

Heat drained from his body, replaced by a chill that filled his chest.

"You lied."

CHAPTER THIRTEEN

THE MUSIC STOPPED. A loud bang sounded from the direction of the beach, followed a moment later by an explosion of red, green and yellow sparks visible through the glass panels in the ceiling. Gasps and excited exclamations circled through the room. Guests moved en masse toward the doors that led out onto a large stone terrace overlooking the sea.

The world around them moved. But Julius and Esme stood frozen in place, until they were the only two left in the room.

Only through sheer will did Esme manage to control her breathing and keep it from coming out in short, frantic gasps. Only through resurrecting the walls she'd built to shield herself against her parents' constant disappointment did she manage not to cave at the naked hurt in his eyes.

"Julius—"

"Not here."

He walked around and stalked across the room. She followed, her chin raised, shoulders thrown back. Yes, she had some mistakes to answer for. But damn it, she would not let him paint her as the villain of their story.

He waited until they were in the limo and the partition was raised before he spoke.

"You lied."

His voice was calm, cool. Yet beneath it she heard something that broke her heart. Hurt. She'd been so frightened those first few days of being hurt again, of reliving her own pain, that she hadn't bothered to think through the repercussions of what her lie would do.

"Yes."

"I asked you if we had been lovers. You said you had been my bodyguard and a friend."

"We had sex. We were not lovers."

He turned his head to look at her then, his face impassive.

"Is that how you excused it? With semantics?"

Tired of hiding, she tugged at the ties on her mask and pulled it off. "I knew what we had would never go beyond an affair, accepted it. But I at least thought you cared." She kept her voice steady. "I told you how important my job was, how it had become the only thing in my life that I was proud of. You took that from me without a discussion, without any courtesy for what I wanted. My parents did that. You did that. It hurt almost as much as how you dismissed me after what we'd just shared." She sucked in a deep breath. "I told myself that because love was never a part of what we had that we weren't lovers. But it was just an excuse. I lied. I'm sorry."

He stared at her for so long she wondered if he'd even heard her. Then he turned his head and looked out his window into the night.

"As am I, Esmerelda, for hurting you."

The villa came into view, a jewel bathed in golden light against the backdrop of a Caribbean night.

Julius pressed the intercom button. "Stop here, please."

The car stopped halfway up the winding drive.

"The car can take you back to the villa. I need a moment."

Julius got out and walked down toward the beach. Esme waited for all of three seconds, then got out and followed.

He stopped on the beach, one hand in his pocket, his mask hanging from the other by its ribbons. Lightning lit up the horizon in the distance, briefly highlighting where sky met sea. Then it disappeared and everything turned to midnight once more.

"I wanted to talk this afternoon." She stopped next to him. "To tell you everything."

Thunder rumbled, low and deep, rolling across the waves and up over the beach. The inner child in her who had curled up in her bed beneath a blanket to hide urged her to run back to the villa. The warrior she'd become anchored her feet in the sand and stood tall.

"You did. I'm not angry with you. I was, initially." He glanced down at her. "I'm mostly angry at myself. I knew there was something more between us."

She swallowed hard. "There was. We cared about each other, especially after my accident. At least…" She hesitated, then blazed forward. "I thought we did. I thought there was some affection between us."

"I still don't remember most of that year yet. Or my firing you. I just remember that night in Paris."

Her lips twisted. "Of course. The sex was good."

"More than good." His voice deepened, came out almost on a growl. "You know that as well as I do. It was incredible."

"It was. I like you, Julius. I admired you before, respected you. That was enough to get me into your bed. But the man you've been these past few days, it's like the man you were always meant to be. The compassion and kindness I saw glimpses of when I worked for you just seem like a part of you. The prince you were would have attended the masquerade and donated money, considering it an investment in the community and a good public relations move. The man you are now took the time to listen to stories like Aroldo's."

He turned to face her then.

"What are you saying?"

Her hands came up to rest on his jaw, framing his face as she raised up.

"I want you, Julius. Whether it's just tonight or the rest of your time here, I want to be with you."

"And after?" He gripped her shoulders. "What happens when I return to Rodina?"

Fear fluttered to life. She pushed it away.

"Don't think about after." Her words were nearly swallowed up by a sudden howl of wind that ripped at her skirts. "For tonight, let's do what you said. Just be us." She leaned up, brushed her lips over his. "Be with me."

Thunder clapped as the wind strengthened, ushering in the scent of rain mixed with the salt of the churning sea.

Then he leaned down and kissed her.

CHAPTER FOURTEEN

DOUBTS FLED AS Julius plundered her mouth. His lips sought as he explored her, tasted her. She moaned, her lips opening to him. He took everything she offered and demanded more. One hand cupped the back of her head, urged her closer.

Raindrops fell, the coolness a stark contrast to the heat inside her.

"As romantic as this is," Julius said with a carefree grin that made her breath catch, "I think a change of scenery is in order."

He swept her up into his arms and started up the stairs. The rain fell harder, drenching them both. She leaned back, tilted her head and laughed. When she looked back at Julius, he was staring at her as if he'd never seen her before.

"What?"

"That's the first time I've heard you laugh. Truly laugh." His hold on her tightened as he walked into his room through the terrace door. He set her on her feet, keeping his hands on her waist as he pulled her flush against him. "You're stunning when you laugh."

She kissed him, pouring all of her love and passion into it as she ran her hands up his back. He responded in kind, his primitive growl thrilling her as lightning lit up the room. He kept her cradled in his arms as he stood and crossed to the bed. He set her down gently, grabbing her hands in his and lifting her up to her knees.

"Don't move."

She watched him as he advanced, the lightning casting shadows over his masculine face that made him seem even darker, more dangerous. Before, in Paris, it had been sweet and soft, romantic, yet at times distant, as if Julius had been holding a part of himself back.

Here, now, she saw everything. More thrilling, and more terrifying, he let her, showing her his hunger, his desire.

His fingers slid under the hem of her blouse. Up and over her head, leaving her clad only in a strapless bra. His hands slid up her naked waist, around her back. The material fell away. Suddenly shy, she resisted the urge to cover herself.

"Beautiful." Julius stared down at her as if he couldn't believe she was real. "So beautiful, Esme."

One arm wrapped around her waist. A moan escaped her lips as he bent his head and sucked the tender tip of her breast into his mouth.

"Julius!"

His tongue flicked over the sensitive peak before he placed soft kisses on her breast before moving to the other. The strength of his arm wrapped around her anchored her as the sensations of pleasure spread from where his mouth made love to her body, filling her with a liquid warmth that made her limbs heavy even as it made her chest feel light.

Emboldened by his touch, she placed her hands on his chest and pushed back.

"My turn."

Fire flashed in his eyes. Slowly, he sat on the edge of the bed next to her. She undid the buttons on his shirt one at a time, her breath catching as she unveiled his muscular chest. At last, she pushed the shirt off his shoulders and placed her lips to the skin over his heart.

She rose up once more on her knees, looped her arms around his neck and pressed her body against his. The dark curling hair on his chest rubbed against her breasts, the coarse contrast sending an erotic shudder through her body. She bowed her head and kissed the pulse beating at the base of his throat.

Before she could continue her exploration, he shifted, rolling and pinning her to the bed.

"Not fair!" she cried out with a laugh that turned into a groan as he licked one breast.

"You can play more next time."

He moved down her body, trailing kisses down her stomach as his hands made quick work of her skirt and underwear.

"Next time?" she finally managed to say as his hands gripped her thighs.

"Next time," he repeated firmly. "You have memories of us, memories of a night in Paris. I have nothing but a few flashes of dreams. And now," he said with a wicked smile that made her feel like the devil himself had caught her in his grasp, "I want to make those dreams a reality."

He lowered his head. Her hands fisted in the sheets as he kissed the insides of her thighs, gently nipped her flesh. When he placed his mouth on her, she bowed up off the bed into his caress, a sharp cry escaping her lips. He pressed her back down and held her firm as he licked, kissed and sucked, at times gentle and sweet, other times with a passionate finesse that left her breathless and restless.

Suddenly, she felt her body shift. Tiny bits of electricity began to build inside her body, pulsing as one as they rushed to the center of her body.

"Julius," she gasped, "Julius, I'm… I'm going to…"

She shattered. Pleasure careened through her body, spiraling out and lighting every nerve on fire before leaving her weak and trembling.

Dimly, she felt the bed shift beneath her. She opened her eyes to see Julius removing his pants. She watched, unashamed, as he straightened and stood completely naked before her. He'd lost weight, yes, but he was still as she remembered. Broad shoulders narrowing down to a tapered waist, a chest and arms kept muscled by rowing, horseback riding and sparring.

Her cheeks grew warm as her gaze trailed down to his hips and his hard length. Heat suffused her body as he reached down and wrapped his hands around himself.

"You do this to me, Esme."

Feminine satisfaction curled through her.

"Should I apologize?"

His lips quirked up as he stalked closer to the bed.

"No."

He reached into the drawer of the bedside table. After he was sheathed in a condom, he moved back onto the bed. He gently pushed her back into the pillows. She lay there, waiting, watching his gaze roam over her. The longer he looked, eyes pausing on freckles here and freckles there, the more some of her desire started to slip away, replaced by the ugly tuggings of self-consciousness.

"Beautiful."

He covered her body with his, tangling his hands in her hair and kissing her hard once more. With the evidence of how much he wanted pressed against her hips, her doubts receded, replaced by embers that grew into flames.

Flames that licked at her skin as he slowly slid inside her body.

"Julius!"

"You feel so good, Esme." He buried his face in her hair, inhaling her as if he would die without her. "So good."

Their bodies found a rhythm, moving against each other, climbing higher, soaring toward the highest peak until she crested once more. He followed a moment later on a groan, shuddering against her.

After, he rolled to the side but kept his arms around her waist, pulling her closer until her back was flush against his chest.

"Don't go."

She closed her eyes for a moment. He'd said almost the same words before in Paris. Her heart clenched at the reminder that, no matter what this was between them, it would never result in a happily-ever-after.

So say yes now.

"I'm not going anywhere."

Not yet.

CHAPTER FIFTEEN

JULIUS SAT IN a lounge chair by the window, the curved back cradling him as he watched the storm stir the sea into crashing waves, the peaks made jagged by wind that ripped across the ocean.

It was glorious in its fury. Lightning forked across the sky. For a moment, the Atlantic was lit by a brilliant white light that would have delighted even the most curmudgeonly of individuals.

Julius noted the beauty. The uniqueness of the landscape.

And found it wanting compared to Esmerelda.

She slept a few feet away on her stomach with the sheet pulled just up to her waist. His eyes slid over her bare back, the toss of curls that partially obscured her face, her arms clutched around a pillow.

He raised his glass to his lips, sipped the rich whiskey and savored the slight burn down his throat. She had asked for nothing more than tonight. How many men in his position would have been thrilled at a night of pleasure with no strings attached?

Yet a hard stone had settled in his stomach at the thought of only one evening, perhaps a few if he took her up on her offer of continuing their affair until he left Grenada. He didn't want this to be the end. There had been something there between them from the beginning of this whole adventure. Something that had made her, and only her, stay in his memory. The more he talked to her, spent time with her, the more he couldn't begin to fathom how his former self had let her walk out of his life.

His eyes drifted toward the wall safe hidden behind a painting of one of Grenada's waterfalls. Every time he thought of the ring, he thought of Esmerelda. He'd bought it for her.

But had he? What if he had wanted to, was experiencing the desires he'd silenced in order to fulfill his duty to his people?

He sighed and let his head drop back onto the chair. He'd reviewed the laws of Rodina, along with the marriages of the past five generations of royals dating back to the mid-eighteen-hundreds. The heir apparent had always been bound by expectations and the best interests of the country.

All his speculation brought him, repeatedly, back to the one truth he didn't want to face. He had not found a way to strike a balance between his duty to his country and his feelings for Esmerelda.

Another bolt of lightning dove down toward the churning sea. Thunder followed less than a second later, roaring as if to let the whole world know of its immense power. It rumbled across Julius's skin, a not unpleasant feeling, and slowly he let his eyes drift shut.

The dream came to him, vivid and detailed.

Esmerelda naked beneath him, her body dotted with freckles. He kissed them, each one that he could, thrilling at the throaty sound of her laugh.

"There's too many for you to kiss them all."

"I don't mind trying." He kissed one on the curve of her hip, savored the hitch in her breath as his lips trailed to the fiery red curls between her legs. "Besides, we have all night. And as you like to point out, I'm very thorough."

Her laugh turned to a moan, her fingers threading through his hair as he made love to her with his lips.

"Julius..."

His heart twisted in his chest. He'd been denying it for months, telling himself he was mistaking appreciation for something more.

But as he moved up her body and covered her with his own, he knew it wasn't indebtedness or gratitude. No, he—

"Julius?"

She sat on the ottoman opposite him. Possessiveness gripped him at the sight of her in his dress shirt, her long legs shown off to perfection. The glimpse of freckled thigh that nearly made him groan out loud.

"I'm sorry to wake you."

"It's all right." He held up his glass. "Care to join me?"

Her eyes flickered to the whiskey.

"Yes."

Surprised, he tilted his head to one side. When he reached out for her hand, she placed her fingers in his grasp without hesitation.

"Is everything all right?"

The storm nearly drowned out the sound of her soft sigh.

"Yes. Just…restless."

He held out his own glass. She took a sip, her eyes drifting shut as she made a noise of appreciation he felt all the way to his groin.

"What's wrong?"

Thunder clapped once more. She stood, rubbing her hands on her bare thighs as she moved over to the decanter.

"Do you mind?"

He stood and crossed to her.

"No. But seeing as you're my guest," he said with a soft kiss on her lips, "I'll get it."

He poured her a glass, watched her fingers tighten as

she accepted it and took a healthy sip before moving back to the ottoman.

"Is it the storm?"

She waited a moment, then slowly nodded. "I used to be scared of them. Now they don't bother me if I'm awake. But if they wake me up, it takes a while to get back to sleep."

"What did you do to get over your fear?"

She stared down into her glass. "I just…did."

He frowned. "What about your parents?"

"My mother was usually out at some function or another. My father told me to be brave."

Anger surged through him.

"That's it?"

"That's it."

He set his glass down on the table next to his chair and held out his hand.

"Come here."

She stared at his hand. For once her emotions were transparent and vivid. Fatigue, weariness, embarrassment.

But what made his pulse pound and his heartbeat quicken was the naked longing in her eyes.

Slowly, she set her own glass down and stood. He held his breath, waited until she was right in front of him, before he clasped her hand in his and gently tugged her down onto his lap. She curled into him, her face falling against his neck as he wrapped his arms around her and let his breath rush out as his body shuddered.

Home.

The thought appeared unbidden. The word inspired no memories, no recollections of a house or a castle or some other place. But he knew its meaning, knew in that moment that home would be wherever this woman was, so long as she was by his side.

"You're safe."

She leaned back slightly, her lips just a breath away from his. "I know. I'm with you."

The trust she placed in him, her surrender, rendered him speechless. He cupped the back of her head, kissed her with a gentleness that seemed to surprise both of them. His other hand drifted down, tugging at the buttons of the shirt she wore. Revealing her freckled beauty inch by inch until the shirt whispered to the floor.

Before he could move, she stood. Pushed him back into his chair and knelt before him.

"Esmerelda—"

She placed a finger over his lips. "I want this, Julius."

His protests died as her fingers slid beneath the waistband of his silk pants. She unveiled his hard length, her hands teasing, her smile confident and glorious as she lowered her head and took him in her mouth. He groaned, his hands sliding into her hair as she ran her tongue over him, kissed him, brought him to the edge of control.

Her throaty chuckle nearly undid him. She moved, rising above him like a flame-haired siren as she straddled his lap and guided him inside her wet heat. Her body closed around him as she placed her hands on his chest and started to move. His hands closed over her waist, guided her as she rode him.

Lightning flashed. Thunder crashed. They both soared over the peak, her cries of pleasure mingling with his groan as she collapsed against him.

Julius awoke to sun streaming in through the windows and an empty bed. Unease sent a jolt of energy through him. He'd fallen asleep with Esmerelda in his arms, her face relaxed and content. Had she awoken and, satisfied with their one night, left? Or had she had second thoughts?

One way to find out.

He tossed back the covers and stood. He was in the process of pulling on a pair of shorts when the door to his room opened.

"Good morning."

Esmerelda walked into the room carrying two cups of coffee. With another sundress on, this one the color of bright lemons, her hair falling wild and untamed about her face, she looked relaxed. More herself, he realized with a satisfied smile as his apprehension slipped away. He accepted a mug and took a deep sip.

"I wondered where you were," he said. He leaned down and kissed her, satisfaction curling through him when she didn't pull away.

"I'm used to rising early," she said with a small smile. "Back in Rodina I had to get up at five a.m. in order to be ready for the day."

"Was that the time I set?"

"It was."

He grimaced. "Bastard."

She reached over and laid a hand on top of his.

"You owe it to your past self to give him a break. No, he wasn't the warmest and fuzziest of princes," she said with a small smile, "but he ruled and did very well for the people of Rodina."

"So you've said."

She stared down into her coffee mug, her sudden silence cluing him in that something was on her mind.

"What are you thinking?"

"One of the times I prompted you to take a break, you told me you couldn't. That there was work to be done. I said the work would still be there in five minutes." She looked at him then, sadness making the green of her eyes all the more vivid. "You said it would, but you might not be. That life was short and you had a duty to do your job while you could."

"My mother."

Just thinking of Elizabeth made his pulse pound in his throat.

"I believe so." Her hand settled on his once more.

They sat. Sadness permeated the air, but it wasn't unpleasant. It was healing, revisiting the memories he had reclaimed, finally allowing himself the chance to grieve as he suspected he never had.

"A conclusion I came to myself a couple days ago. I chose duty over grief. Logic over emotion."

"Understandable."

"For a time. But then it became comfortable. Easy." He squeezed her fingers. "I retreated into my indifference. It was cowardly."

"Cowardly." She echoed his word with a slight smile. "I was cowardly, too."

"How so?"

"I was very good at being a bodyguard. I'm active, I kept in good shape. I genuinely love Rodina, so serving in a role that helped me serve my country was appealing. But it also allowed me to put off examining my life. Figuring out what I wanted to do for me." She scoffed. "Isn't it awful that sometimes staying in the rhythm of past mistakes is easier than trying something new that could make you happier?"

"I did the same."

She looked at him then, her gaze thoughtful.

"Yes, you did."

A different type of intimacy settled between them. For the first time since he'd arrived, he felt as though they were seeing each other, truly, in all their beauty and faults. And still they sat side by side, content.

"Join me on the balcony."

She smiled and accepted his hand up. He kept his fingers wrapped around hers as they walked onto the terrace and settled at a bistro table by the edge. Aside from the glistening drops still clinging to the trees, there was no evidence of the storm that had battered the island the night before.

"What would you like for breakfast?" he asked.

"I've already had some fruit."

"Fruit is not breakfast," he replied. "You're on an island where you can have anything you want."

She glanced down, her cheeks turning red.

"That's one of the things I love."

Her head shot up, her eyes widening.

"What?"

"I can always tell your emotions by the color of your skin. For example, right now with that beautiful bright red and your cheeks like apples, I know you're embarrassed."

"Stuff it," she replied, her cheeks growing even redder.

"I also know," he added, his voice deepening, "that whenever you look like a rose, you're thinking about everything that we did last night."

A smile tugged at her lips.

"It is one of the curses of being a redhead."

"Not a curse." He paused. "It was one of the ways that I knew that there was more to our past relationship than what you were telling me."

He had mostly reconciled what had happened, the way she had manipulated the truth. But it lingered in the back of his mind. A conversation unfinished.

She glanced out over the ocean.

"I am sorry for that," she said softly. "It was never my intention to lie to you. It just…"

Her voice trailed off. Regret hit him as he remembered the pain in her voice when he'd first arrived. Her shock and pain.

"I'm sorry, Esmerelda. Unfortunately, that's all I know how to say now. I wish I could remember why. Could remember what I said."

Esme sighed.

"It was painful yes. But it was more how you did it, which we've already been over." She looked back down at her coffee. "I was embarrassed, too. I thought we had a little more time together. I thought that our affair was more than just a one-night stand. Not that I expected anything to come of it," she added quickly. "I always accepted that we were from different worlds. That you would have to eventually move on as I would. I just didn't expect for that to happen less than a week after we…" The rosiness returned to her cheeks. "After Paris."

"Why do you think it did? Truly."

"Your father is doing well for his age. But he's nearing seventy. He's been vocal about wanting to step down before he's seventy-five, perhaps sooner, and pass you the crown."

Julius's hand tightened around his cup. He could barely wrap his head around being a prince. Now he might be a king in less than five years?

"Hence his encouraging me to get engaged."

"I believe so." She sighed. "I wouldn't want my husband's former lover still around. It was an understandable move."

Jealousy seized him at the mention of her phantom spouse. The thought of any other man touching her the way he had, saying vows to cherish and protect, having a family with her, made him want to hurl his mug at the wall.

"No, it wasn't."

"But—"

"No buts, Esmerelda. I treated you horribly after everything you did for me. Not just saving my life, but serving me selflessly for over a year." She opened her mouth, probably to utter another protest. "Don't let my slightly better treatment of you than how your parents treated you eclipse the fact that I handled things the wrong way."

Her lips parted as her eyes widened. She sat back in her chair, eyes blinking rapidly.

"Well," she finally said, "that was profound."

"And accurate."

"To a point." She held up a hand to silence his own protest. "One bad deed does not deserve another. I could have simply put you off instead of lying." She glanced out toward the sea, her expression turning pensive. "But it did help. I don't think I would have ever left if you hadn't given me a reason to."

"Do you think staying in Rodina would have held you back?"

"I'd like to think not. But I was always living my life for someone else. The love my parents offered me was conditional on doing what they wanted for me. What they thought was best." Her chest rose and fell on a soft sigh. "I didn't realize how much I needed to make a choice for myself until I was on that plane flying away." She turned back, her smile glowing. "I've already grown so much these past few weeks. Imagine what could happen next. I could be anyone I wanted to be. Not something someone else wants for me."

His chest twisted into a hard knot. The right thing to do was be happy for her, be glad that she had found purpose amidst pain. Yet as he looked at her, the confident tilt of her chin, the slight smile on her lips, all he felt was something dark and desolate, a hollowness that rivaled the emptiness in his mind.

He stood, set both their mugs on the table, and pulled her to her feet, indulging in a long kiss that seeped into his veins and banished the heaviness that had settled on his shoulders.

"What were you thinking you wanted for breakfast that made you blush?"

"Oysters."

He arched a brow. "Is that meant to be foreplay?"

She laughed. "No, I've just always associated oysters with vacations and indulgence."

"Did I eat them?"

"I don't know. I was paying more attention to the crowds and possible assassins instead of watching what you had on your plate."

He lightly swatted her on the rear for her impudent answer before swinging her into his arms, enjoying her gasp of surprise before he set her back in her chair.

"Well, I don't know if I enjoy them or not, but I'll try them."

He texted Aroldo. Fifteen minutes the butler brought out a silver tray laden with eggs Benedict, fresh fruit, a variety of cheeses and in the middle of the tray a silver bowl with raw oysters on ice.

Aroldo glanced between the two of them, a small smile on his face as he set the table.

"Enjoy, Your Highness…miss."

He bowed his head and disappeared back into the villa. Esmerelda made a soft noise that sounded like a strangled laugh.

"Do you think he knows?"

"Yes."

"Oh, God." Her hands flew up and covered her face.

"He's seen far worse than some rumpled sheets, believe me."

"I know, but he seems so…fatherly. It's like getting caught naked."

"If you're suggesting we go back in and make love again, I'm all for it."

Her laugh trickled over him. "And ruin all of Aroldo's hard work?"

They dined on the eggs and fruit. Julius nearly choked on the first oyster he tried.

"It's slimy."

Esmerelda dipped hers in the small container filled with

cocktail sauce and popped it into her mouth, her eyes drifting shut as she moaned.

"They're delicious."

"Slimy," Julius repeated.

"More for me, then."

He watched, amused and grateful to see her like this. Relaxed, joyful. Even though so much of his identity remained wrapped up tightly in his mind, even though their future together remained up in the air, he felt happy for the first time in his limited memory.

They spent the rest of the morning on the terrace by the pool, alternatively lounging in the chairs and swimming in the warm waters. A shower after lunch led to him wrapping her water-slicked legs around his waist and driving himself into her, her back pressed against the tiles, her mouth fused to his. The afternoon included a ride in a Jeep and a hike to a waterfall, where Esmerelda terrified and aroused him by jumping off a cliff into one of the pools. When he chastised her, she splashed him, resulting in a battle that ended with them laying on a stretch of sand behind the falls, kissing and running their hands over each other until they worked themselves into a frantic frenzy. They'd barely made it back to the villa before he'd carried her to his room and made love to her again.

Dinner was salad and a Grenadian stew, discreetly left under a tray on the terrace table with a note from Aroldo stating that he would return in the morning. They lingered over the wine, talked, savored each other's company and then savored one another's bodies once more as the sky darkened. They fell asleep once again wrapped in each other's arms.

It was around midnight when Julius awoke and remembered.

CHAPTER SIXTEEN

THE DIAMOND GLEAMED beneath the rosy light of dawn sweeping across the sea and up onto the terrace. Miss Smythe's words came back to him as he stared at the ring.

"The longer you look, the more you see."

It had always been for her. He remembered now, sitting in the elegant opulence of Smythe's, dismissing twenty-carat diamonds and pure red rubies.

And then he'd seen it. The salt-and-pepper diamond. The inclusions scattered inside had reminded him of her freckles, of how he'd kissed her in Paris and made her laugh.

The longer he'd looked at Esmerelda, the more he'd seen. She'd gone from being a highly rated graduate and an effective bodyguard to a flesh-and-blood woman he couldn't get out of his mind.

Her courage had humbled him. Her dedication had intrigued him. And the shy smile she'd shot him in the hospital after her accident when he'd given her something so simple—a book he'd somehow recalled her mentioning a week before the accident—had shot past years of defenses and grabbed hold of his cold heart.

He'd denied it at first. Chalked it up to an emotional reaction to her saving his life. But her actions had created an intimacy neither of them had expected. Instead of just issuing orders, they'd talked. He'd come to respect her opinions on Rodina, even if he didn't always agree with them, found himself looking forward to seeing her each day.

Then they'd gone to Paris. They'd traveled together before. But Paris had been the first time they'd had hours of nothing: no meetings, no press conferences or fundraising events. He'd stepped out of the hotel, away from the bodyguard on shift just to have a minute to breathe. Then he'd seen her at the café, head tipped back, curls tumbling down her back and freedom in her eyes as she'd soaked up her surroundings. It was as if the thin veil he'd purposefully pulled down between them had been ripped away. The feelings he'd barely kept at arm's length over the year had risen, overwhelming his resolve.

The longer I looked, the more I saw.

He reached out, laid a finger on one of the pearls circling the diamond. That night had been one of incredible pleasure. But it had also solidified the connection he'd felt growing between them. When she'd come to him the morning after on the balcony, her touch smoothing away some of his inner turmoil, he'd known that what he felt for Esmerelda had been much more than casual lust.

When his father had come to him on his return from Paris and brought up the need for an engagement, it had been a reprieve. He did well with orders, with facts and lists. But feelings, emotions…those hadn't factored into his life for years. As he'd made the arrangements for Esmerelda's reassignment, he'd kept himself numb, resolute against the occasional flicker of conscience or the annoying tug of his heart.

And then she'd left.

The ache came as swiftly as the sunlight spreading across the sea. It had taken him days to acknowledge he missed Esmerelda, and several more before he made his decision. He'd told himself that Esmerelda was a good choice. Her loyalty to the throne, her dedication to the country, her vast knowledge of politics and government, were not the traditional assets of wealth, land and power brought by previous brides and grooms. But Rodina's economy was stable and strong. The entire island had been a part of Rodina for generations. And he and his father had both made significant headway in international forums.

All justifications he'd presented to his father a week after Esmerelda had left. Justifications his father had swept aside with one simple question.

"Do you want to marry her?"

Julius hesitated. He had never made a decision, let alone one so crucial, with emotions playing a pivotal role.

"Yes."

Francisco smiled. "Then what are you doing here? Go find her."

So he'd done it. He'd jumped in headfirst, digging the black card he'd been presented with by a reclusive billionaire out of his desk and flying to London while a private detective from England had tracked Esmerelda down and provided her address in Grenada.

And now he was here, with his memories intact and Esmerelda sleeping in the room behind him. Anticipation filled him. When she awoke, he would tell her everything. Then he would present the ring to her properly. They could be engaged for as long as she wanted, have whatever sort of wedding she desired.

So long as she was by his side, nothing else mattered.

Esme awoke to rays of morning sun warming her face. The bed was empty, but a glance at the clock revealed it was after eight o'clock. Julius had always been an early riser.

So had she, she thought with a satisfied smile as she stretched. Until she indulged in a passionate affair with a lover who knew her body better than she did and spent hours worshipping it.

"You're awake."

Julius walked in. He smiled and leaned down to kiss her. She sat up and raised her face to him. "Good morning."

"Good morning."

She frowned, trying to pinpoint his mood. There was an energy to his movements, bordering on uncontrolled, that seemed off. Yet there was also a touch of formalness in his face and tone that reminded her of the old Julius. A distance that couldn't be bridged, not even by the intimacy of the bedroom.

"I remembered."

She froze. "Remembered?"

"Everything."

She sat for a moment, waiting. But when he didn't look at her in disgust, when he still smiled at her, she smiled back, throwing back the covers to go to him.

"I'm happy for you, Julius."

She hugged him. He wrapped his arms around her, his hands a comforting warmth on her bare back.

"Wait…does that mean you remember what happened in London?"

He nodded, the light in his eyes dimming a fraction. "I was on my way back to the hotel. I heard a scuffle coming from an alley. Two men fighting. I went to break it up. One ran off. The other turned on me and pointed a gun at my face."

Her entire body tightened.

"What?"

"He fired."

Fear clogged her throat.

"Julius…"

"Obviously something went wrong." His lips twisted into

a slight smile. "The gun jammed. I lunged for him and we got into a fistfight. I remember pain," he said, touching the back of his neck, "and stumbling into the parking garage hotel. There was a private elevator entrance down there for the penthouse. The doors closed and that's all I remember."

"He must have mugged you."

"I called Scotland Yard. They're running searches on my credit cards to see if any have been used recently, and they're pulling CCTV footage from the area. I remembered everything about the week after we spent the night together in Paris. I remember our conversation when I told you that you were being reassigned."

Trepidation slithered up her spine. She had grown so much in just a few days. Could she handle what he had to tell her? Hear him, accept it and move on?

"Julius—"

"I was intentionally cruel."

She leaned back. "Why?"

"I wanted to make you hate me. I thought it would make it easier for you to move on. It wasn't right," he added. "I made a choice for you that wasn't mine to make."

Her eyes grew hot.

"Thank you, Julius."

"It feels like…" He looked at some distant point over her head. "Like I've been put back together. Like all the pieces are there."

She forced a smile onto her face, trying to focus on his relief instead of her own selfish worry that in regaining his memory he'd lost a bit of the man he'd discovered here on the island.

"I remembered the ring, too."

Her stomach dropped. She'd known this was going to happen. Once again, it had come too soon. But she would handle it better this time.

"I see." She planted her hands on his chest and tried to push him back, but he held her fast. "I'm not comfortable standing here naked while you tell me about the ring you purchased for another—"

"I bought it for you, Esmerelda."

For a moment she couldn't breathe, could only stare up at him as the words repeated over and over in her head.

"What?"

"After you left, all I could think of was you. Just the thought of sharing dinner, let alone my life, was impossible."

He reached over and grabbed the black box off a side table. Her heart surged into her throat as he opened the box to reveal the ring nestled inside.

"Esmerelda, would you be my queen?"

Her hand flew to her throat. Never in her wildest dreams had she ever thought she and Julius could be together. Could have a life together. It almost seemed too good to be true.

Something tugged at her, a thread of reality pulling at the beautiful tapestry of dreams Julius had woven around them.

"Julius, I… I don't know what to say."

He frowned.

"Say yes. We can have as long of an engagement as you want. Whatever kind of wedding you want. And then we can be together. Rule together."

She stepped away, and this time he didn't stop her. She grabbed her robe off the floor and pulled it tight around her. When she turned back, he was watching her with a hooded gaze, his fingers clenched around the ring box.

She pushed her curls out of her face.

"Julius…it's very sudden."

"We've known each other over a year."

"Yes, in a professional capacity."

He ran a hand through his hair. "Would you prefer we date? Go public with a relationship first—"

"No."

Frustrated with herself, with him for springing this on her so suddenly after the roller coaster they'd ridden over the past week, she wrapped her arms around her middle and moved to the windows. She heard him move behind her, felt his presence at her back.

"What's going on, Esmerelda?"

"Why me, Julius?"

"What?"

She turned then, hated seeing the frustration and confusion on his face.

"Why do you want to marry me? Why, after dismissing me, did you change your mind?"

He reached up and cupped her face. She leaned into his touch, the same way she had in Paris, her heart teetering on the edge of hope and anguish.

"Because I realized you were the right choice. We work well together. We both love Rodina. We can do more for the people as a team than any of the women my father had listed. And he agreed. He supported my choice. But this was my plan for us."

Each sentence he uttered was a death knell to hope. How cruel was life to dangle such an incredible week in front of her, to tease her with intimacy and tenderness and newfound confidence, only to rip it away once more?

"I'm an asset in my own way, then."

He frowned. "It's not just that, Esmerelda. We care about each other. Genuinely care," he added, his emphasis on *genuine* making her nauseous.

"I need more than that, Julius."

His lips parted. But nothing was said.

Her heart gave one last, painful gasp. Then a shield dropped down, the same shield she'd used to utter her words of resignation and walk out of his office all those weeks ago.

"I see."

"Damn it, Esmerelda, I just regained my memory. I'm shirking generations of tradition because I want you as my wife."

"You didn't even ask me what I wanted." She stepped back. "If becoming your queen was what I wanted. You just assumed I'd jump at the chance. You planned everything without asking what I wanted."

"I told you, we can do the engagement and the wedding—"

"What about after?" she asked, repeating his words from the night when they'd stood on the storm-tossed beach. "After the pretty pictures and the walk down the aisle?"

"My father would abdicate one year after our marriage. I would become king and you would be queen."

"Would I be like your cousin? Like Vera? Going to luncheons and sitting on charity boards?"

"My mother did." His voice cooled even as anger leapt into his eyes. "She served Rodina. Her work was no less important."

"And from what I remember your father saying, she loved it. She was good at it because she loved it. But for me…" Her voice trailed off as she sought to put her chaotic thoughts into words, to explain what she was feeling. "What about economic forums? The trade summit we attended? Would I just be an ornament or actually serve the people?"

His frown deepened. "My mother was no mere ornament. The queen is a figurehead. A leader who serves the people, too."

She stood frozen in place. Part of her, the part that had never stopped loving him, urged her to accept the ring. To be with the man she had fallen for. But the woman she'd become, the woman she was growing into, hesitated. She had just broken free of the expectations of others. She knew people like Julius's mother, like Vera, were needed.

Did it make her selfish, then, that she wanted something different?

Excluding the details of the role, was accepting his ring, especially one tied to duty with no room for love, just going back to an old pattern? Saying yes with the hope that someone might one day love her in return, even as she lived out her days as an ornament instead of an equal partner?

His lips thinned. "I take it marrying me is not what you want then."

She threw her hands up in the air. "I don't know, Julius! I've always tried to live for others' expectations. To be dismissed one week and then proposed to the next, because I'm valuable…" She nearly choked on the last word. "I know public appearances are important. Charities are critical. But to have that be my life…my only life…"

"It's more than that." Thunder moved across his face, darkened his eyes as a vein pulsed in his throat. "I thought you would understand duty."

"I do. But… I want more than just duty, Julius. You know the kind of woman I am, how much I read and research and stay involved with what's going on with our country. Whether or not I'm queen, the woman who is by your side deserves to have a choice in how she serves."

"Being a royal rarely provides choices."

"But there is more than one way to rule," she insisted. "You taught me that, showed me that every time you and father disagreed on something. Why can't a queen do more than be a public figurehead?"

"I'm not saying she couldn't."

"Except you have it all planned out." Her heartbeat in her throat so hard it nearly made her choke. "Planned it without talking to me, without thinking about who I am, what I might want, what I could give back."

He stared at her, his amber eyes glittering. "I have let down my guard with you more than I have anyone else."

"I know."

She reached up to lay her hand on his jaw. He pulled back, a fraction of an inch, but it could have been a mile for how much distance it put between them. Hurt, she snatched her hand back and crossed her arms over her chest, the thin silk of her robe cold against her breasts.

"When I get married, I want it to be because I love someone and he loves me. I want it to be a partnership. Not a loveless transaction where I have little to no say. Where the rest of my life is already laid out for me."

The snap of the ring box closing echoed in the room.

"If there is even the barest hint of that being a possibility, then your answer was the right one."

Ice dripped from every word. The brutal prince was back in full force, his eyes hard as flint, his face carved from granite.

For one moment, she contemplated telling him what she needed. What she wanted. What could be if she could have just a little time to think, to process.

And then fear raised its ugly head once more, fear and years of pain, of disappointment.

She ignored him and walked back toward the bed. She plucked her sundress off the ground, the sunshine yellow a brutal contrast to how dark she felt inside. She slid out of the robe and pulled her dress on. When she turned back, Julius was watching her, his face cold, one hand wrapped around the ring box.

Silence reigned between them. Both of them so angry. So hurt. Neither willing to yield.

She left the room without saying a word. She didn't know what else there was left to say. In less than five minutes her one suitcase was packed, the dress stuffed inside in favor of a T-shirt and shorts, her hair pulled back into a bun. She moved to the window and gazed out over the terrace, the beach, the view of the ocean, for the last time.

Her phone felt heavy in her hand as she dialed.

"Esme." Burak's voice boomed over the line. "How are—?"

"His Highness is in Grenada. Dove Villa off Prickly Bay."

Silence followed.

"Burak?"

"What—"

"His Highness was attacked in London. He tracked me down to Grenada and hired me to be his temporary body-guard while he healed."

Burak's expletive echoed from thousands of miles away, followed by a series of rapid-fire questions.

"You'll have to ask him."

She hung up, swallowed the guilt that she had just betrayed him and walked out with suitcase in hand. He stood in his doorway, dressed in nothing but lounge pants that hung low on his hips.

"I do owe you thanks," she said quietly as she neared him.

"You owe me nothing."

"But I do. If you hadn't reassigned me, I don't how long I would have drifted along in a state of complacency." She smiled sadly. "It was the shock I needed to realize something needed to change in my life."

He looked down at her suitcase.

"You're running away again."

She bristled.

And you're not stopping me. Again.

Then she stifled her anger. Anger had gotten her into this mess in the first place. Had she kept her cool when he'd arrived on Grenada, she would have made the call far sooner.

"I'm making a choice."

He stared at her, chest rising and falling, but he kept his hands clenched by his sides. The ring box had disappeared.

"I'm…" A ringing cut him off. He pulled his phone out of his pocket and glanced at the screen. His face hardened as his head snapped up.

"You called the palace."

She raised her chin. "It's what I should have done in the first place."

Was it pain that flashed in his eyes? Or had she mistaken anger for hurt? Regardless, she had done her duty, and severed any connections remaining between them.

It was like walking through a fog, she thought, as she moved toward the end of the hall, one that made the world around her seem blurred. Elements of familiar pain wove through the ache pulsing in her bones.

She paused where the hallway, turned and looked back.

"You'll make a wonderful king."

Framed in the doorway to his room, with the ocean rising and falling beyond the window, his dark blond hair brushed back from his forehead and shoulders thrown back despite the weight that rested on them, he looked every inch the heir apparent.

She executed a formal bow.

"Your Highness."

And then she was gone.

CHAPTER SEVENTEEN

JULIUS TUGGED ON the rope attached to the mainsail—*mainsheet, not rope*, he silently corrected himself—and savored the thrill as the sail pressed out. The boat picked up speed, curving around the northern tip of Rodina. The palace stood tall and proud nearly two hundred feet above his head, perched on a cliff that overlooked the Atlantic Ocean to the north and the west, and the distant, hazy coastline of Portugal to the east.

It had been nearly three weeks since he'd been back. Three weeks since Esmerelda had left. His fury, the gut-wrenching sensation of betrayal that she had called the palace had been short-lived.

There had been nothing left for him on Grenada. Nothing but memories of a fleeting time that he suspected was the happiest he had been in a long time.

Perhaps the happiest he would ever be.

He'd returned Burak's call after Esmerelda had walked out, assuming the mantle of leader as if it had never slipped away. Within an hour he'd been on a private jet flying across the Caribbean Sea, despite his head of security's insolent insistence that he wait for a team to come get him and ensure he was fit to fly after his attack.

His new head of security had greeted him at the airport. A tall bear of a man, Burak was intelligent, shrewd and relentless. He'd asked numerous questions, ranging from the hotel Julius had stayed at in London to the doctor he'd seen on Grenada. Questions Julius had answered concisely as he'd reviewed schedules, proposed legislation and news stories, catching up on the pieces of his life he'd missed out on the past week.

The only thing he deflected on was his and Esmerelda's relationship. When Burak had prodded, Julius had speared him with an icy gaze and said, "If you want to keep your job, you will never, ever suggest that Miss Clark behaved in a manner unbecoming her position."

Judging by his narrowed eyes and tight mouth, Burak hadn't liked his answer. But he'd accepted it with a grudging nod before moving on to other questions.

The only other person who had been told the full truth of what had transpired was his father. When the plane had landed, Julius had requested an immediate audience with his father. Francisco had greeted him at the palace, his hug sparking both affection and guilt. Once they'd been secure in the privacy of Francisco's study, he'd asked after Esmerelda and if she had accepted his ring.

Julius had hesitated. Francisco had leaned forward, lacing his fingers together as if to stop himself from reaching out to his only child.

"What's on your mind, son?"

He told his father everything, from waking up in his hotel room to Esmerelda's departure and everything in between. Francisco had listened. It wasn't until Julius reached the end that he had finally spoken.

"That's rough."

The simple summation had made Julius laugh and broken the tension. His father hadn't pushed, hadn't berated or lectured him. He'd simply asked if there was anything he could do and, when Julius had responded in the negative, said he was always available if Julius needed to talk.

Before Julius had left, his father had circled the desk and enveloped him in a tight hug that spoke louder than any words could say. The sheen in Francisco's eyes, the slight fear of what might have happened in that London alleyway, went unsaid but not unrecognized.

The quiet support, the subtle demonstrations of love, struck him anew. After his mother's death, he had shunned all emotional connection. His eyes had always been fixed on the future, never the present or the past. Tasks, lists, always having a goal to work toward, had kept him focused. Kept his heart safe, even from his own father, who had done nothing but offer him quiet yet steady love and support.

Until her.

Every time he thought of how she had bowed to him, hurt once more by his cruel words yet still so proud before she had walked out of his life once again, his chest tightened until he could barely breathe. Nights were the hardest, especially reaching as he woke and having his fingers brush cool, empty sheets instead of Esme's warmth.

He maintained a façade throughout his days as he eased into his duties, professional yet with a touch of the humanness he'd discovered in his weeks on the island. More smiles, the occasional joke. It was amusing, and gratifying, to see people exchange wide-eyed glances as they wondered what had happened to finally make Prince Julius's cold exterior thaw.

The beach appeared, the black sand a sharp contrast to Grenada's powdery white shores. He angled the boat toward the dock and winced as the hull hit harder than he'd intended. But, he reminded himself as he tied off the boat and stepped onto the dock, he had made vast improvements. It had shocked a number of people when Prince Julius, renowned for doing nothing but working, eating and sleeping, had booked private sailing lessons.

He'd wanted to do something, anything outside of his role as prince. Being on the water, feeling the familiar rise and fall of the waves, smelling the salt air, had been a comfort he hadn't even realized he'd needed until he'd first boarded with his instructor. He'd dedicated an hour every night to practicing.

When he'd taken the boat out for his first solo trip around the north end of Rodina two days ago, he'd nearly called her. Had wanted to share it with her.

But he hadn't. She had left. He had offered more of himself to her than he had to anyone since his mother had passed. Had finally risked it all and made a decision based on his heart.

It hadn't been enough.

You know that's not all of it.

He closed his eyes and breathed in the scent of the ocean. The heat of the sun seeped into his skin, bringing memories of a tiny island in the Atlantic up from the depths. He opened his eyes and started up the stone steps carved into the cliff. He reached the towering gate at the top of the stairs and punched in the security code. Heat from the sun warmed his back. The gate creaked as he pushed it open, clanged as he shut it. He focused on the sound of his feet on the pavestones, the gentle swishing as an afternoon breeze stirred the flower-tipped stalks of lavender that lined the walkway.

The past invaded. He couldn't stop the image of her stricken expression when he'd told her his reasons for why she would make the perfect queen. As the feeling of being rejected had faded, reality had sunk in, cold and vicious. He had done what so many had done to her in the past, especially her parents; he had reduced her from a dynamic, interesting woman to a list of qualifications. Had taken her comments about being an ornament as a personal slight against his mother and all the good she had done instead of hearing Esmerelda's words.

In the moment, when Esmerelda had looked at him and asked for more, he'd felt the pain of rejection like a knife to the heart. The pieces of himself he had shared hadn't been enough for her. The risk he'd taken deemed inadequate.

But then he remembered her face. Her own sense of rejection. His inability to voice the true depths of his feelings for her.

It had been reasonable for him to withdraw after his mother had been yanked from him so quickly, here one moment alive and happy, then gone in a matter of weeks. Yet, he grudgingly admitted as he walked into the palace gardens, it had also become an excuse over the years. It was easier to stay aloof, to never feel the gut-wrenching grief that had nearly consumed him when his mother had passed.

Until now. Until a different kind of grief shadowed his every step, haunted his waking hours, plagued his dreams. The grief of having held someone he deeply cared about and letting her slip away not once, but twice.

"You look terrible."

Julius looked up as his father walked into the garden.

"Recovering from a traumatic head injury is a good excuse for not looking my best."

"Hmm." Francisco glanced down at a stalk of lavender. "I rarely come here. It's a nice spot, though."

"It is."

Francisco moved to a spot in the wall with a wrought-iron fence instead of the exquisitely painted tiles that covered the garden walls. Beyond the fence the ground rushed out in an explosion of green before sloping sharply down toward another beach. The waves rose and fell in gentle swells, the water rising up onto the dark sand before receding back into the ocean.

Julius joined his father at the fence and stared out. Hard to believe that a week ago he had been on the other side of this ocean struggling with the idea of his identity revolving around a title.

"I can feel you thinking too hard."

Francisco scoffed. "No such thing. But," he added with a slight smile, "if I were thinking, it might be to ask what thoughts you have toward moving forward."

A stone settled in the pit of Julius's stomach.

"Let me know if you have any suitable candidates in mind."

"Are you sure?"

"Yes."

The word rolled off Julius's tongue, but with a distinct lack of conviction. Once he had believed the sentiment of finding the best wife to suit Rodina's advancement with his entire being. It had been easier to see a future marriage and even a family as for the better of the country rather than an investment he would make on his own.

But now, the thought of kissing another woman, sliding the ring onto her finger, sharing children with her, made him feel empty, like someone had hollowed out his chest and left nothing behind except sorrow.

"What of Esmerelda?"

Julius's head snapped up.

"I don't want to talk about her."

Francisco ignored his son's icy tone.

"Do you realize that you coming to ask my permission to propose to Esmerelda is the first thing you've asked of me since your mother passed? It's always been the job, what's best for the country, best for the people. Another reason why you'll be a good king. But," Francisco added as Julius started to interrupt, "how good can a king be if he works himself to the bone and becomes too tired, too worn down, to be a good leader?"

Julius grimaced.

"You sound like her."

"I've spent a lot of time thinking this past year. A lot," Francisco repeated as he once again looked out over the sea. "I've also watched you. I noticed long ago how you were around Miss Clark. It was as if your edges had been smoothed out."

Slowly, Julius reached into his pocket. His fingers wrapped around the jeweler's box. How many times had he pulled it out over the past few days, holding it up to the light, running his fingers over the diamond, the aquamarine gems, the tiny pearls. Miss Smythe had answered his numerous questions during their initial consultation, helped him pick the gems and stones: aquamarine for the happiness she'd brought to his life. Pearl for the wisdom she had shared with him as they'd talked of Rodina.

And the diamond, speckled. Flawed, like Esmerelda saw herself. Yet to him, beautiful beyond measure.

The longer you look, the more you see.

"She is an incredible woman." Francisco tilted his head to one side. "Did you tell her you loved her?"

The edges of the ring box cut into his palms as he gripped it tighter. Did he love her? He cared about her, yes. But as he turned his father's question over in his mind, certainty flooded his veins. His feelings for Esmerelda went far deeper than affection. He desired her, craved her presence, missed her saucy smile and joyful laugh. Yet he trusted her, too, not just with his life but his heart. That she cared just as deeply about Rodina as he did was another bond that he had at first categorized as making her an ideal queen, not recognizing that it bound them together, too.

"I told her I cared about her."

Francisco threw back his head and laughed. Julius frowned at him.

"Helpful, Pai. Very helpful."

Francisco's laughter quieted as a nostalgic smile tugged at his lips.

"I wish I had had more time with your mother. So many things I wish we had done. We weren't in love when we got engaged," he said. "I did it for duty. But when we did fall in love…" His voice trailed off as his gaze turned distant.

Julius smiled slightly. "She told me."

"One thing I never regretted, though, once I realized how I felt, was telling her every day how I felt about her."

Francisco left, leaving Julius alone once more in the garden.

He pulled the box out of his pocket and opened it. The ring glinted in the sunlight. The longer he stared at it, the more a fool he felt. Yes, Esmerelda had the potential to be a queen Rodina deserved. But she was also the only woman he wanted. The only woman he had ever loved. She deserved to hear that, to hear that he wanted her by his side because of who she was, not because of what she had to offer. That he wouldn't just shove her into a box of his own making but give her the power to lead her own life.

She deserved the choice to accept him, or reject him, but with a full picture of what he was offering. He didn't like the latter possibility, despised the nervousness at giving up his power and surrendering to his emotions.

But, he thought with renewed determination as he tucked the ring back into his pocket, if anyone was worth the risk of opening up his heart to, it was Esmerelda.

His phone dinged. He pulled it out of his pocket, read the email that had just landed in his inbox.

And smiled.

CHAPTER EIGHTEEN

"Miss Clark?"

Esme stood and smiled at the young man who gave her a friendly smile as he walked out of a boardroom.

"Yes," she replied as she shook his hand.

"Welcome to Executive Security."

She stepped inside and blinked at the jaw-dropping view of New York City's Brooklyn Bridge and the East River flowing beneath it.

Two other people, a man and a woman, sat at the table. They both gave her pleasant smiles as she sat in the offered chair.

"We've spoken to your former employer."

Her smile froze on her face.

"Yes?"

"Exemplary," the woman said. "They were sorry to lose you."

Relief made her so weak she had to resist the urge to sink back into the plush office chair.

"It was hard to leave."

"Why did you?" the man who'd greeted her asked.

"I've lived in Rodina my whole life. I needed a change of scenery. And my mother lives here."

Not that it had impacted her decision in the slightest. She'd reached out to let her mother know she was in town, her first time in the States in nearly ten years. Her mother, predictably, had been on a cruise in the Bahamas and rushed to get off the phone and back to her husband.

Instead of making her feel sorry for herself, it had been cathartic in a way. Her mother would always be the way she was. Her focus on herself, her inability to enjoy motherhood, hadn't been Esme's fault. Neither was her father's inability to see her as anything more than her accomplishments.

Something Julius's blunt assessment had helped her realize.

She swallowed hard. Julius cropped up far too often in her thoughts. She shoved him away and tried to focus on the people in front of her. But doubt kept plaguing her.

Did she even want another bodyguard position? Would that make her happy? She'd originally gone into the profession to make her father happy, but now…

They asked her a few questions, but she could tell it was mostly to tick the boxes. Whoever they'd spoken to in Rodina, coupled with the fact that she had been on a security detail for an actual prince, had impressed them. She'd built up the kind of reputation that made her the perfect candidate for any security job.

"Last question," the woman asked. "Where do you see yourself in five years?"

Esme froze.

"I'm…" She offered up a slight smile, one that hopefully would pacify. "I'm not sure. Leaving Rodina was a big step for me."

"Of course." The woman returned her smile with a kind one of her own. "How about what you want out of your life? What do you want out of your career? What's important to you?"

Julius.

The sudden surety of her unspoken answer floored her.

She wanted Julius. Loved him. Had had the chance to be with him and had shunned it out of fear of losing her new-found independence, of being shoved into yet another box and smothered with someone else's expectations.

When he'd proposed, she had been so focused on how he'd had everything planned out, a plan he hadn't bothered to ask her about, that she had let pain overtake her, keep her from telling him her own feelings and what she needed. What would allow her to accept his proposal.

And Rodina…being a queen, leading a country, might not be her first choice of a job. It would come with scrutiny, long hours and rules. So many rules. But she had been so afraid of accepting the role in the form Julius had presented it to her that she hadn't stopped to think about what she could do. What she would do if given the chance to be a leader.

She hadn't stopped to talk to Julius, to ask him, to challenge him. She'd been so afraid of what his answer might have been that she had chosen to run instead of standing and fighting for herself, for them and what they could be.

"Miss Clark?"

Esme blinked. Three faces were regarding her with mixtures of concern and confusion.

"I'm sorry." She stood and smoothed her hands over the bottom of her suit jacket. "I don't think this role is for me. I thought I needed something else in my life. But it turns out I was wrong. Thank you for your time. I'm sorry to have wasted it."

And with that she turned and walked out.

Her foot tapped an impatient rhythm as the elevator descended. She needed to do something, find a way to meet with Julius and tell him everything. Would he accept a phone call? A text message?

No. That was the coward's way out. This was the kind

of conversation that required them to be face-to-face. She pulled out her phone. Her fingers flew over the screen as she typed out an email request for a meeting at His Highness's earliest convenience.

Then, before she could lose her nerve, she hit "send."

Forty-eight hours later, Esme stared at the key in her hand as she stood in front of the hotel elevator. The number embedded in the platinum card stared back at her, taunted her.

Room 333. The penthouse suite where she and Julius had spent the night together.

Did Fate just have it out for her?

No, she thought as she rubbed at her temple. It was only natural that the suite be rented out to royalty, politicians and other important guests. With its location at the top of The Martinique, it was not only well protected but offered exquisite views of Paris and the Eiffel Tower.

A sigh escaped her. When she had received the email requesting her presence in Paris to meet with the king less than an hour after she'd emailed Julius, her stomach had dropped to somewhere in the vicinity of her feet. Did the king want to question her? Grill her as to why she had spent a week in Grenada with his son? Or perhaps he had found out about her affair with Julius. She no longer worked for the royal security team, so no risk of getting fired. But he could still make life very difficult for her.

Worse was the possibility that Julius had forwarded her email to his father and asked him to intervene. Her email had been formal, simply asking for a meeting. She should have gone through the proper channels, but she hadn't been able to bring herself to email the public relations office or his secretary. Burak hadn't called or texted since she'd called him to let him know where Julius was. Her father had also been strangely silent, his incessant phone calls dropping off.

The possibility that someone had uncovered her week with Julius had dogged her steps the past two days, from the soaring steel towers of New York City to the sprawling *arrondissements* of Paris.

She stepped inside and held up the key card. The elevator rose, carrying her closer and closer to the mysterious meeting with King Francisco. She had met the king on a few occasions. He had even come to her hospital room to thank her when she had been recovering from the parade accident. A skilled but kind, compassionate leader.

Would he show her kindness now? Or savagery as he protected his son and the reputation of the crown?

The elevator dinged. The doors slid open again. She tamped down her nervousness and stepped inside.

The suite was exactly the same. Warm wood floors gleaming under the golden rays of the setting sun. Ivory-colored furniture offset by red and blue pillows that added color to the elegant surroundings. A fireplace trimmed in white, the hearth filled with a vase of flowers for the summer season instead of burning logs.

And beyond the sitting room, glass doors thrown open to the balcony and the Eiffel Tower standing proudly over Paris.

She'd stood in that doorway, just out of sight, with Julius at her back. He'd slid her shirt up and over her head, placing heated, sensual kisses on her neck as he'd undone the clasp on her bra and then reached out around to fill his hands—

"Your Highness?" she called out, partially to stop the flow of memories and partially because she realized, with a quick glance, that the suite was empty.

No one answered.

Frowning, she pulled up the email on her phone and re-read it. Labeled with the royal family's official seal at the top, the email was brief. It requested her presence on the twelfth of June at seven o'clock in the penthouse suite of The Martinique in Paris for a meeting with His Majesty the King.

"I prefer this meeting to Grenada."

Esme's head snapped up. She stared as Julius walked out of the door that led to the bedroom. His dress shirt showcased the breadth of his shoulders. He'd rolled the sleeves up to his elbows, the white material stark against his tan skin. Her eyes traveled up, over his chest and up his neck to his heartbreakingly familiar brown eyes.

"You...where is..."

"I think I need to mark this on the calendar, too. The first time Esmerelda Clark stuttered."

She heard the teasing in his voice and resisted. She squared her shoulders and drew herself up, shoving away all of her emotions.

"Your Highness. My apologies for intruding. I received an email—"

"May I see it?"

She stifled her irritation at being interrupted and handed over her phone, taking care to ensure her fingers didn't brush his. His eyes moved over the words.

"Ah, yes. I think there's a typo."

"A typo?"

"Yes, it shouldn't have said 'His Majesty the King.' It should have read 'His Royal Highness the Crown Prince.'" He looked up, a wicked gleam in his eyes. "Oops."

Confused, unsure of what to expect, overwhelmed by the memories surrounding her, she took a step back. Julius's arm shot out, his hand grabbing her elbow. Words of protest died on her lips as he yanked her against him before sliding one arm across her back and another beneath her knees. With a small shriek, she found herself lifted into the arms of Crown Prince Julius Carvalho.

"Put me down."

"Not until you promise not to run away."

She groaned and closed her eyes, trying desperately to ignore how good it felt to be cradled by him once more.

"I don't understand."

She felt him lean in closer, felt the heat of his body. A moment later his forehead touched hers and she drew in a shuddering breath. That such a simple touch could affect her so much frightened her.

"Esmerelda. Look at me."

She slowly opened her eyes but kept her gaze fixed over his shoulder on the Eiffel Tower.

"I can't look at you, Julius. Not yet. I know I requested a meeting, but I thought I would have time to prepare myself."

"Fine. Then just listen."

Perhaps it was worse not to look at him. Because not looking at him aroused her other senses, made her more aware of the rumble of his voice in his chest, the cords of muscle in his arms as he gripped her close.

He walked with her to the glass doors. She started to protest as he walked onto the balcony, then stopped as he sat down on a lounge, still cradling her like she was a precious jewel.

"You were right."

"Of course I was."

She felt his smile.

"I hurt you."

She started, but kept her gaze averted. Her heart thudded in her chest. This had been part of the risk she had accepted when she'd sent that email. Telling him what she needed, sharing her own feelings, could still result in heartbreak. But at least she would have given it her all, tried to advocate for herself instead of simply submitting or running away.

"Yes. You did." She let out a breath. "Although I imagine I did my fair share of hurting."

"Yes." He pressed his cheek against her hair, a shuddering sigh whispering over her face. "I took away your choice. Again."

Her eyes grew hot.

"Yes. But I—"

"Let me apologize, Esmerelda. Then you can have your turn to grovel."

She faced him then, lightly punched his shoulder. "Who said I'm going to grovel?"

"Call it intuition." His smile disappeared as his eyes darkened with regret. "I wanted you so badly, Esmerelda. I knew I could make it work, so I did. I thought you wanted me, too."

"I—"

He kissed her then, a smoldering kiss she felt all the way to her toes.

"Whether you did or not, I assumed. I made plans for you. I've been leading for so long I did what I always do. Make plans, execute them. When you didn't jump at the chance to wear the ring, I took it as you rejecting what I had offered. A monumental offer, given my predilection of avoiding emotion. But," he said as he kissed the tip of her nose, "I was still holding back. I told myself I was risking enough. Giving enough."

She swallowed hard. "It wasn't fair of me to push for so much so soon. That doesn't mean," she said quickly as he opened his mouth to interject, "I don't deserve it. But you did offer me a great deal, Julius, and I let my own past get the better of me instead of giving it some time or having a conversation. I tried to be independent instead of listening to my own heart. I asked questions, but I didn't tell you what I needed from you, what I could bring to throne." She lowered her head. "You were right. I did run away."

"Perhaps if I had told you…"

His voice trailed off. His arms tightened around her as

he stood and carried her to the railing. The Eiffel Tower came to life as he set her on her feet, light glittering across the iron structure.

"I love you." He lowered his forehead to hers. "I've loved you for so long."

Happiness spread through her, swirling through her chest and filling her body until she felt as if she could float. He cradled her face with such tenderness she couldn't hold back a tear from escaping.

He swiped away the tear with a finger. "I suspect I've made you cry far too many tears in our time together."

"Yes." She reached up and let her hand settle on his cheek. "But love often involves tears. And I do love you, Julius."

A harsh breath escaped him.

"Just like I didn't know what I had done to deserve such loyalty from a young woman, I don't know how I deserve your love."

"It was nothing you had to earn, Julius. I gave it freely because of who you are." She swallowed past the thickness in her throat. "I should have told you in Grenada. Should have told you what I needed from you, what I wanted. But I was too afraid. I accused you of not talking to me, and then I did the exact same thing. You offered me so much then, and I was so wrapped up in my own pain I could only see my own fears and not what you had overcome to even make that proposal." She bit down on her lower lip, looked away. "I'm sorry."

He grasped her chin in his fingers and tilted her face up so he could look her in the eye.

"I told you that day in the hospital that I was humbled to be the recipient of such loyalty. Today," he whispered softly as he leaned in, "I am humbled to be loved by such an incredible woman. One who gives despite having so much withheld. One who can look at herself and what she needs to change, who wants to grow beyond her boundaries or the restrictions others place on her. One who I love deeply and who I can only hope will one day forgive me for holding myself back."

The words drifted around her, beautiful words that made hope and longing surge in her chest so fiercely in that moment she felt like she could fly.

Except reality held her back. He might love her now. But what did that mean? A tragic parting like the princess and the newspaper reporter in the old black-and-white movie she had watched on repeat in the late hours of the night, where they had admitted their love for one another and shared a bittersweet kiss before the princess had returned to her royal life?

"Julius, I… I appreciate you sharing how you feel."

One eyebrow shot up.

"'Appreciate' is not exactly the kind of sentiment a man wants to hear after he's just professed love to a woman."

"How about 'I love you, Julius'?"

He nodded once, then suddenly released her.

"One moment."

He disappeared. Flustered, she stepped away and moved to the balcony. She smoothed the skirt of her dress, focused on the lights of the Tower. Contentment settled over her, along with a peace that steadied her racing heart and brought a smile to her lips. For once, she was exactly where she wanted to be. He loved her. She loved him. She wanted to be with him. Whatever came next would come in its own time.

Footsteps sounded behind her. One deep breath, then another. She turned, ready to face him.

Her heart nearly burst as her mind registered that Julius was no longer standing but kneeling before her. In his hand lay the black jewelry box, the lid open and the speckled diamond gleaming with the rosy lights of a Parisian sunset.

"I'm not just asking you to become my wife, Esmerelda. What I'm asking is so much more, and it may be too much." Love burned in his eyes as he took her hand in his. "Just as you were ready to move forward, to be your own person, I'm asking you to become a servant of the people of Rodina. A servant to the country and all that entails. It has its merits, yes, but it also has hardships. Being under constant scrutiny, having your every choice questioned."

"You're not exactly selling this proposal," she said with a soft laugh. "And I'm nervous, Julius. I don't know how to be a queen."

"I am, too. But you are not only the woman I want. You're the queen Rodina deserves." His grip tightened on hers. "You love Rodina. You're intelligent. You care. Those traits mean more than anything anyone else could have brought to an arranged marriage. I believe that wholeheartedly. Which means I need to let go, to let you carve out your own path when it comes to your role if you choose to accept it."

Her eyes widened at the magnitude of what he was saying. That he would give up control, trust her to make her own choices as she helped him lead the country he loved, meant more than any ring ever could have.

The last weight hanging from her heart loosened, then fell away.

"Julius…"

"Maybe that's not enough," he continued. "But I can't live with knowing I had the chance to ask you to be my wife, to be the woman I want by my side, and didn't. I would rather move on knowing I took the risk, told you how much I love you, and you said no than go the rest of my life wondering what could have been."

The seeds of hope that had been steadily growing burst inside her chest. Her smile grew until it nearly hurt, she was smiling so hard.

"Tell me that's a yes, Esmerelda."

She nodded, barely able to choke out a "yes." He slid the ring onto her finger then stood, sweeping her into his arms and pulling her flush against him as he leaned down and sealed their engagement with a sensual, possessive kiss. She flung her arms around his neck and kissed him back, laughing against his lips as he picked her up and spun her around in a circle.

"It fits," she said, holding up her hand as he set her back on her feet. The diamond glittered, the tiny little black flecks dancing mischievously within the crystalline depths. The pearls gleamed, an innocent touch of beauty, while the aquamarine stones sparkled in the sun.

"It was always for you." He caught her chin in his hand, brought his lips to hers once more and kissed her until she clung to him. "I went to London to purchase a ring. I had a detective track you to Grenada, intended to follow you apologize and propose to you. Show you, not just tell you." He grasped her hand in his and raised it to his mouth. "This ring was designed for you, Esmerelda. Pearls for the wisdom and grace you carry, aquamarine for hope and happiness, and a salt-and-pepper diamond. Imperfectly beautiful, with flaws that make it stronger. And," he added with a kiss to her nose, "because it reminded me of your freckles. Your beautiful freckles."

She did cry then, tears coursing down her cheeks as he held her. What greater gift could she have asked for than a man who loved her, truly loved her and all her imperfections?

"I love you, Julius."

"And I love you, Esmerelda." He grasped her shoulders, held her back. "You're sure?"

"Yes. I know it won't be easy. It will take some getting used to. But I'm sure."

He watched her, eyes darting over her face as if looking for a sign that this was too good to be true.

"And this is what you want?"

"Yes." She stepped closer then, bringing her hands up to frame his face. "I emailed you from New York. I interviewed for a job there and they asked me what I wanted from my life. All I could think of was you. I almost told you back in Grenada that I wanted to be with you, but I was terrified that if I told you I wanted your love, it would be too much."

"Marrying you, becoming a queen, doesn't mean I still can't be myself. I get to combine one of my greatest passions with a new career. And," she added as she raised up on her toes, "I get to marry the man I love."

He crushed her to him.

"My queen," he murmured into her hair, "and tomorrow the whole world will know it."

"Tomorrow?"

"An engagement announcement, if you're willing. I want the world to know you're mine."

His possessive tone thrilled her, sent little sparks dancing through her veins.

"I'm more than willing."

"Good." He leaned, pressed his lips to her forehead. "Tonight, however," he murmured as he kissed her cheek, the tip of her nose, "I want you all to myself."

She took his hand, led him back into the bedroom as the lights of the Tower sparkled behind them. She laid on the bed, her breath catching in her chest as he lay next to her and pulled her body against his. As he lowered his mouth to hers, she smiled.

"There's nowhere else I'd rather be."

EPILOGUE

One year later

ESME STARED AT her reflection in the tri-mirror.

"Joana," she breathed as she smoothed her hands over the silk skirt, "this is beautiful."

The bodice of her wedding dress, fashioned from the most exquisite lace, featured a sweetheart neckline with a touch of sexiness. The fitted waist flared into a stunning skirt that swept down to the floor and pooled behind her. Swaths of lace flowed from her shoulders down her back like fairy wings.

"You make it beautiful, Your Highness."

Esme glanced over her shoulder at Joana and her sister, Hanna. The two had been flown in a week earlier to partake in the festivities leading up to the royal wedding, as well as to serve as two of Esme's bridesmaids. The three had grown close over the past year, with Joana officially named as the preferred designer of Princess Esmerelda.

Even though she wouldn't officially receive her title until after the wedding ceremony was complete, the press had jumped on her future moniker and run with it. The engagement announcement for a prince and his bodyguard had entranced the public. A news outlet had rediscovered the video of Esme pushing Julius out of harm's way during the parade.

Rodina had been catapulted into the international spotlight as the media swooned over the "storybook romance." Leaked details from London about Julius's brush with a mugger, who had eventually been caught using his credit card, had added intrigue to their love story.

A love that had taken them back to Grenada less than two months after they'd left, where they'd joined Aroldo and his family for Spicemas. Amongst the parades, dancing and celebrations, their friendship with Aroldo, Hanna and Joana had been solidified.

A whistle cut through the room.

"You look incredible," Burak said as he walked into the room. He winked at her. "Your Highness."

"Not quite yet," she replied with a laugh directed at her "man of honor." Burak had taken one look at her and Julius together and promptly forgiven her duplicity. He'd been amused by her request that he be in her wedding party, although it was a duty he had also taken seriously.

The delicate melody of a violin trickled in. Esme's breath caught.

"Is it time?"

Joana nodded, her eyes bright.

"Are you ready?"

She'd been ready ever since Julius had slipped the ring on her finger.

She accepted her bouquet of lilies from Hanna and moved to the door. A moment later her father appeared, his silver hair combed back from his forehead. His eyes widened.

"Esmerelda…"

Her breath caught at the naked emotion in his eyes. When she'd returned to Rodina, her father had at first been coldly angry with her for deserting. Even learning that she was engaged to a prince hadn't softened him.

But then one day she'd caught him staring at her during a formal dinner. The next day he'd called on her in the royal apartment that had been set aside for her as the fiancée of the crown prince.

"You looked happy," he'd said, his voice rough. "I don't think I ever saw you happy before."

"I wasn't."

He'd nodded. "I'm sorry."

It had been a new beginning for them, one that had evolved and strengthened over the past year. Her relationship with her mother was still distant. Aside from her mother's initial excitement over shopping for a wedding dress, eclipsed fairly quickly by Esme's insistence on using Joana as her designer, her mother had played her usual role and stayed in New York, only flying in last night to attend the ceremony.

A part of Esme would always long for something more. But then she would look around at the people she had in her life: Julius. His father, a man she still struggled to call "Francisco" or "Father" instead of His Majesty. Aroldo, Hanna and Joana. Her own father. Burak. Even the mysterious and talented Miss Smythe was in attendance for the wedding.

And she had purpose. Julius had encouraged her to carve out her own role in the palace, one that would both support Rodina but also bring her happiness. She'd accompanied Julius to an international energy summit and debated legislation on healthcare with members of Parliament. But she'd also stepped back from her fear of being shoved into a box and tried some of the community activities Julius's cousin Vera engaged in. She'd come to enjoy serving on the board for the library, and collaborated with several local authors and a publisher to host an international literary festival the following year. Whether it would succeed in drawing in guests from Europe and beyond like she hoped remained to be seen.

But she was trying. She was doing something with her life. She was truly, deeply blessed.

The music swelled. Her father held out his arm.

"Are you ready?"

"Yes."

They moved into the hall and stopped outside the massive wooden doors leading into the palace chapel. A moment later the doors were flung open, revealing an aisle strewn with red rose petals. Burak escorted Joana and Hanna down the aisle.

And then she saw him. Julius stood at the altar, incredibly handsome in a black tuxedo. When their eyes met, he smiled. She smiled back, her heart nearly bursting with love. A collective sigh moved through the room, although she barely heard it.

They moved down the aisle. At last, she stood in front of Julius. He shook her father's hand as she passed off her bouquet, then led her up the stairs to the altar.

"You're beautiful, Esmerelda." He raised her hand to his lips, kissed her knuckles.

"It's not quite the time to kiss the bride," the priest said with an indulgent smile, much to the amusement of the guests.

Esme barely heard the words spoken as he grasped her hands, his eyes bright with love. When he said "I do" in a clear, ringing voice, she couldn't stop the tears that spilled down her cheeks.

"I now pronounce you man and wife. Now you may kiss the bride."

Julius pulled her close, resting his forehead against hers for one blissful second, and then pressed his lips to hers.

"You were wrong," he whispered against her mouth.

"How so?"

"I'd say this is as close to a fairy tale as it gets."

* * * * *

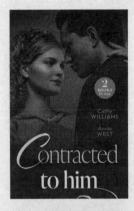
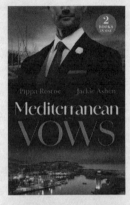

COMING SOON!

MILLS & BOON®

Coming next month

MY ONE-NIGHT HEIR
Natalie Anderson

'You stunned me into silence.' His expression softens. 'I was trying to stay in control. I couldn't do this there.'

'This?'

The brush of his lips is balmy, teasing. His tenderness takes me by surprise as does the moment he takes to lean back and search my eyes. I realize he's seeking my consent.

I can hardly think. 'This is...'

'What I've wanted to do all night.' His gleaming gaze bores into me—intense and unwavering. 'You're why my pulse is racing.'

I just topple right into his arms. He scoops me close and then his mouth is there again—on mine. And I melt.

It turns out that kissing is the best ever way to neutralise panic. The best way to stay in the moment, to not give a damn about anything else in life—not even imminent death. Kissing is the best ever thing full stop.

Continue reading
MY ONE-NIGHT HEIR
Natalie Anderson

Available next month
millsandboon.co.uk

afterglow BOOKS

Afterglow Books are trend-led, trope-filled books with diverse, authentic and relatable characters and a wide array of voices and representations.

Experience real world trials and tribulations, all the tropes you could possibly want (think small-town settings, fake relationships, grumpy vs sunshine, enemies to lovers).

All with a generous dose of spice in every story!

OUT NOW

Two stories published every month.
To discover more visit:
Afterglowbooks.co.uk

LET'S TALK

Romance

For exclusive extracts, competitions and special offers, find us online:

- **f** MillsandBoon
- **X** @MillsandBoon
- **◉** @MillsandBoonUK
- **♪** @MillsandBoonUK

Get in touch on 01413 063 232

For all the latest titles coming soon, visit
millsandboon.co.uk/nextmonth

MILLS & BOON

THE HEART OF ROMANCE

A ROMANCE FOR EVERY READER

MODERN
Prepare to be swept off your feet by sophisticated, sexy and seductive heroes, in some of the world's most glamourous and romantic locations, where power and passion collide.

HISTORICAL
Escape with historical heroes from time gone by. Whether you passion is for wicked Regency Rakes, muscled Vikings or rugge Highlanders, awaken the romance of the past.

MEDICAL
Set your pulse racing with dedicated, delectable doctors in the high-pressure world of medicine, where emotions run high and passion, comfort and love are the best medicine.

True Love
Celebrate true love with tender stories of heartfelt romance, from the rush of falling in love to the joy a new baby can bring and a focus on the emotional heart of a relationship.

HEROES
The excitement of a gripping thriller, with intense romance at its heart. Resourceful, true-to-life women and strong, fearless men face danger and desire - a killer combination!

From showing up to glowing up, these characters are on the path to leading their best lives and finding romance along the way – with plenty of sizzling spice!

To see which titles are coming soon, please visit

millsandboon.co.uk/nextmonth

GET YOUR ROMANCE FIX!

Get the latest romance news,
exclusive author interviews, story
extracts and much more!

blog.millsandboon.co.uk